12

P9-DNV-808

Free Public Library of Monroe Township
713 Marsha Ave.
Williamstown, NJ 08094

Monroe Township Public Library

3 4201 10169012 U

THE POLITICS OF BARBECUE

THE POLITICS OF BARBECUE

A NOVEL BY BLAKE FONTENAY

JOHN F. BLAIR PUBLISHER
Winston-Salem, North Carolina

Published by
JOHN F. BLAIR
PUBLISHER
1406 Plaza Drive
Winston-Salem, North Carolina 27103
www.blairpub.com

Copyright © 2012 by Blake Fontenay
All rights reserved, including the right to reproduce this book or
portions thereof in any form whatsoever.
For information address
John F. Blair, Publisher, Subsidiary Rights Department,
1406 Plaza Drive, Winston-Salem, North Carolina 27103.

COVER IMAGES:
Beale Street image courtesy of Tetra Images/Getty Images
Neon pig image © Can Stock Photo Inc./robgotgoodshot

Library of Congress Cataloging-in-Publication Data

Fontenay, Blake.
  The politics of barbecue / by Blake Fontenay.
     p.   cm.
  ISBN 978-0-89587-585-3 (alk. paper) — ISBN 978-0-89587-586-0 (ebook) 1. Mayors—Fiction. 2. Arson—Fiction. 3. Political corruption—Tennessee—Memphis—Fiction. 4. Satire. I. Title.
  PS3606.O59P65 2012
  813'.6—dc23
                        2012001565

10 9 8 7 6 5 4 3 2 1

Design by Melissa Clark James and Debra Long Hampton

Free Public Library of Monroe Township
713 Marsha Ave.
Williamstown, NJ 08094

To Ma, who gave me every opportunity to succeed in life, and Buck, whose prolific career as an author deluded me into thinking it would be easy to get a book published

THE POLITICS OF BARBECUE

Prologue

Nothing, he decided, was more mind-numbing than waiting for a vagrant to do something. Vagrants didn't do anything quickly, with the possible exception of those who begged for money on the Main Street Mall on weekdays.

Some of them could move with astonishing quickness to cut off the angles of escape for hapless tourists or office workers on their way to lunch. The best vagrants could backpedal like cornerbacks in football even as they made their lame pitches for spare change. "Can you help me, mister? I need to catch a bus to Chicago," they'd say as they reacted to the jukes of their prey.

But not this particular vagrant. He moved as though he never had anywhere he needed to be—ever again. He had been lying in a vacant lot across the street with several other vagrants before deciding to take a piss. He'd made it into the alley and relieved himself, all right, but then he appeared to get confused about how to return to his sleeping spot. Excessive amounts of Thunderbird tended to have that effect on a person.

The vagrant slowly shuffled in one direction, then retraced his steps and shuffled the opposite way. This went on for five minutes, then ten, then fifteen. The man in the shadows watching him feared the vagrant might collapse in the alley beside tonight's target, which would ruin the mission.

Finally, perhaps attracted by the streetlight, the vagrant wandered back across the street and collapsed into the tall grass littered with empty Bud Ice cans and Wild Irish Rose bottles. The lot was mostly quiet after that, save for some snoring and muttering and a fart or two.

None of the vagrants was sober enough to hear or see the man moving past them into the alley.

Truth was, even people much more alert would have had trouble spotting him. He was dressed in black from head to toe. And he moved with the practiced stealth of someone who'd been on other covert missions like this one, taking care not to clink against each other the two black spray-painted metal cans he was carrying. Once in the alley, he was practically invisible.

Carefully, he made his way to the target—a ramshackle house with white paint peeling from its wooden siding. The man gently set down the cans long enough to open a window. Then he set the cans on the floor inside before carefully slipping over the window sill himself.

Somewhere a block or two away, a dog barked. Otherwise, all was quiet. The man went about his work quickly, scouting to make sure all the rooms were unoccupied.

Which took very little time. The house was tiny—small living room and dining room in front, two small bedrooms and a kitchen in back, bathroom roughly in the middle.

It was like many houses he'd visited recently in South Memphis, with leaky roofs that left huge water spots along the walls, plumbing long ago stripped of its copper pipes, piles of trash and vagrant excrement everywhere.

The man didn't need any more reasons to hurry, yet the disgusting odor inside the house gave him one anyway. He expertly sprinkled the liquid from the cans throughout the house, making sure every square inch of floor space was covered. And the walls, too. A few splashes on each would guarantee the success of his mission.

When he was done, he slipped out the back door, carrying one of the cans with him.

He took a bottle from the right pocket of his fatigue pants, then filled it halfway with the last of the liquid from the can. He gently set down the can, careful not to make any noise. Then he pulled a bandanna out of his left pocket and stuffed it into the bottle.

The lighter came last. He pulled that out of his left pocket, then lit and threw the Molotov cocktail in one fluid motion. He was halfway down the alley before the first flames flickered inside the house.

He was nearly to his car when the flames erupted, billowing from the house's windows and doors with a loud rush. Suddenly, dogs were barking up and down the street. And within the houses, he could hear stirring as sleepy residents tried to figure out what was going on. As he reached his car, he paused for a second, just long enough to admire the charred remains of one of his previous missions.

Despite the valiant efforts of the Memphis Fire Department,

that house had been a total loss, burned to its foundation. And tonight's target would be, too.

The man cranked the engine and eased away slowly into the night, humming a happy tune.

Chapter 1

Joe Miller was bored out of his mind. Which wasn't unusual. After all, he worked in public relations, in a job that had an excitement quotient only slightly higher than that of the fast-food industry. Joe's job was to churn out press releases for his clients, who were, in Joe's considered opinion, a bunch of dweebs. Joe had spent most of last week generating press releases about the grand opening of a new pawnshop, one in a chain of about a thousand scattered across the Deep South.

Cash on the Barrelhead was the name of the chain, headquartered in Birmingham. It was Joe's job to make it seem as if the opening of the twelfth location in the Memphis area was every bit as exciting as the opening of the eleventh, which he had written about only six months ago. Cash on the Barrelhead was expanding its reach to a run-down strip shopping center along Stateline Road in Southaven, Mississippi, just south of Memphis.

Joe tried his best to make Cash on the Barrelhead's incursion into Mississippi sound like a big deal. "The March on the Magnolia State," he tentatively titled the release, hoping he would come up with something else. Joe tried for a while to think of a better alliteration to use but eventually quit. As if anyone in the media really gave a rip about another pawnshop opening anyway.

But that's what paid the bills. As a youngster, Joe had dreamed of working as a newspaperman. But by the time he got to college, he'd heard enough horror stories about the future of journalism that he decided to switch his major. Newspapers were dying, everyone told him. He should pick a profession that would make him some money. So Joe chose PR.

It was liberating, in a way. The courses weren't hard, and the girls were amazingly beautiful. PR was a major that definitely attracted the honeys.

Joe's five years in college, stretched out because of his practice of taking only twelve credit hours per semester, were pure heaven. He breezed through Middle Tennessee State University with a 3.25 average despite spending most of his weekends in Blue Your Mind, a college bar that incorporated the school colors into its name. He met at least a dozen of his future wives while drinking at that hole-in-the-wall bar, located about a half-block off the Murfreesboro city square.

After college, Joe had moved back to Memphis and gotten a job with the Riker-Elmore-Slaughter PR firm. It wasn't a dream job by any stretch. Joe told himself it was only temporary. And that's what he was saying eight years later as he banged out press releases for mind-numbingly boring businesses like pawnshops.

Joe was still laboring over the first sentence of his press release about the opening of the Stateline Road Cash on the Barrelhead when the phone rang. It was his boss.

"Joe Miller here," Joe said into the phone.

"Joe, it's me. Your boss. I've got a new assignment for you."

"Sounds exciting," Joe told Mike Riker, lead partner at Riker-Elmore-Slaughter, with all the enthusiasm he could muster. Mike's assignments were usually tedious, but whatever it was couldn't be worse than what he had been doing before the phone rang. So Joe braced himself for an assignment that would almost certainly be anything but exciting.

"Joe, I need you to take a meeting with the mayor," Mike said. *Take a meeting.* He made it sound like such a thrill. Like meeting Mayor Pigg would be a big deal.

"Yes, sir," Joe said. "Glad to do it, sir." Joe had been told long ago that feigned enthusiasm could take him far in his career. It hadn't worked so far.

"Mayor Pigg's upset about something," Mike said, "and I need you to calm him down. Before you go over there, I want you to meet with Cal Cameron, and he'll fill you in on what's going on. He's on his way over right now."

Calvin Cameron was the head of the Memphis Tourist Information Bureau. Although the bureau was a quasi-governmental agency funded by hotel tax revenues, it relied on Riker-Elmore-Slaughter for much of its public relations work. Joe had worked with Cameron before, unfortunately. Cameron was the nervous type, always worried that things wouldn't go as smoothly as they should. Joe was laid-back, which made his dealings with Cameron rather strained.

Joe headed down to the lobby. Cameron arrived within five minutes. He was a tall, painfully thin man with a long nose, whitish lips, pale blue eyes, and a receding hairline. His mousy brown hair was streaked with gray around the temples. He wore a dark blue suit and a crisply pressed white shirt with a gray silk tie. Joe shuddered at the thought that he might end up looking that way in ten years. Or even five. This job was turning him into an old man before his time.

Cameron wasn't able to tell Joe much as they rode the trolley from Joe's office in a restored 1920s building overlooking Court Square to Memphis City Hall. All Cameron knew was that the mayor was upset about something. And that something was tourist-related. So Cameron was looking for moral support.

Memphis City Hall was one of those buildings that, when it was constructed in the early 1960s, had probably been considered on the cutting edge of architectural design. It had not aged well over the last forty-plus years, though. Joe thought it looked like a giant Rubik's Cube painted in Wite-Out. And Joe was barely old enough to remember Rubik's Cubes and Wite-Out.

The mayor's office took up the entire seventh floor of city hall and offered spectacular views of the Mississippi River and downtown. For most of the building's history, the mayor's office had been on the second floor. That office had no windows at all but was much more accessible to the public, just a short flight of stairs up from the main lobby entrance. The mayor's predecessor had seen the need for more impressive digs. Which undoubtedly suited the office's current occupant just fine. He got the benefit of the nicer office without dealing with any of the political fallout his predecessor had endured.

The receptionist waved Cameron and Joe through to the mayor's conference room, where they waited in an uncomfortably long silence until the mayor entered.

Pete Pigg had become mayor of Memphis through one of the quirks of local politics. In the late 1970s and early 1980s, black candidates had run for mayor three separate times. In each case, the field included several white candidates. And each time, because no candidate won a majority of the votes in the general election, a runoff was held. Each runoff pitted a black candidate against a white candidate. And because whites still made up the majority of the city's residents, the white candidate invariably won the runoff election.

Finally, by 1990, local black activists had enough. They filed a lawsuit alleging that the city's election system unfairly diluted black voting strength in violation of federal voting rights laws. And a judge agreed with them, ruling in 1991 that runoff elections would no longer be allowed in city elections.

The payoff was immediate, as the city elected its first black mayor that same year. That mayor went on to set a city record for longevity in office, winning reelection four times. But the lawsuit that had helped him win was outdated almost as soon as it took effect. The city's demographics had shifted to the point where blacks actually made up a majority of the population. By the mayor's fifth term, that majority had grown to around 65 percent of the electorate.

No one saw that as much of a problem until the city's first black mayor stepped down. Since he had dominated local politics for the better part of two decades, a major power vacuum developed when he finally decided to retire.

 Candidates—twenty-three in all—came out of the woodwork to run. Five members of the Memphis City Council. Four members of the Shelby County Commission. Two state senators. Two former police chiefs. A congressman. The sheriff. The register of deeds. And an assortment of political novices including a computer consultant, a midlevel manager at FedEx, a minister, a dentist, a well-known blues singer, an unemployed house painter, and Pete Pigg.

Pigg, whose real name was Peter Applewhite, had plenty of name recognition. He was the owner of a Beale Street barbecue restaurant, the Pigg Pen. The restaurant was popular with tourists and locals alike. And why not? The ribs were great, the waitresses (whom Pigg called his "Pigglettes") were beautiful, and customers got a kick out of tossing their gnawed-on pork bones from their tables into three-foot-high metal buckets strategically placed around the restaurant.

A colorful character in his own right, Pigg had made a name for himself back in the 1970s when he dared to take on the "Peanuts" cartoon syndicate's lawyers, who complained that the restaurant's name too closely resembled that of the Pig-Pen character. Pigg had prevailed in court, then celebrated his victory by wearing a Charlie Brown shirt and giving deep discounts on his most popular menu items. "Eating for Peanuts," Pigg had called the promotion.

Pigg hit his stride during the mayoral election. Rather than dressing up in a suit, Pigg had made most of his campaign appearances wearing his trademark quilt-patched overalls. His TV commercials were goofy but memorable, peppered with corny slogans like "Nobody knows how to cut pork like Mr. Pigg" and "Mr. Pigg is smokin.'"

His opponents ignored him, but in a field crowded with blowhard politicians, he emerged among disenchanted voters as a perfect protest candidate. He won 17 percent of the vote on Election Day, allowing him to edge out the city council chairman and the blues singer, who each had 15 percent. With no runoff election, Pigg became the city's chief elected official. At his victory party that night, he proudly told several television stations, with a straight face, that he was "happier than a Pigg in mud."

But the man who appeared before Joe Miller and Calvin Cameron was anything but happy. Pete Pigg marched into the conference room with a scowl on his face and a copy of the *Wall Street Journal* tucked under his arm.

Mayor Pigg was only five-foot-six, with the kind of physique a man gets from working around barbecue his entire life. He was completely bald and had beady brown eyes and a ruddy complexion that could have been the product of sunburn, excessive alcohol consumption, or both. Being elected mayor hadn't influenced Pigg's sense of fashion. He was wearing a pair of quilt-patched overalls that looked just like the ones from the campaign trail. In fact, based on the odor that followed Hizzoner into the room, Joe was convinced they actually were the same overalls.

"Cal, we've got a big problem here," the mayor said without acknowledging Joe's presence. He tossed the *Wall Street Journal* on the conference table in front of where Cameron sat. "Did you see this?"

"Um, see what, Mr. Mayor?" Cameron said cautiously.

"Not much of a reader, huh, Cal?" Pigg said, a trace of froth appearing in one corner of his mouth. "Check out that story on the front of the Marketplace section. The one about the Lucky 7 Casino Company quietly buyin' up every paddle-wheel riverboat along the lower Mississippi."

Cameron stammered, clearly intimidated by the mayor and afraid of saying the wrong thing.

Wuss, Joe thought.

"Well, Cal, if you had read that story, you might know that Lucky 7 plans to use all of those boats to shuttle tourists back and forth to their casinos along the river between St. Louis and New Orleans," Pigg said. "And you might also know that their plans don't include stops in any of the major cities along the way. They want all those rubes from the Midwest to the Delta to hang onto their money until they get delivered dockside to a Lucky 7 Casino. Which means that casino thirty minutes down the road from us in Tunica, Mississippi, is goin' to take away even more money that should by all rights be spent in Memphis!"

"Well, yes, that is a setback," Cameron said, trying to gather himself. "But—"

"A setback?" Pigg said. "A setback? This is a damned disaster! Look, I knew what I was gettin' into when I ran for mayor. The schools in this town are a mess, and crime's out of control. We can't raise taxes fast enough to make up for all the people movin' to the suburbs. And lately, the local rag and the TV stations have been going nuts about that 'serial arsonist' burnin' up houses in some of our finest slums. But tourism, that's the one thing we've always had goin' for us."

Pigg paused for effect, and also to pull a piece of floss from his pocket and extricate a shred of pork stuck between his teeth. He showed his visitors the courtesy of turning his head away from them before he spit the offending hunk of meat onto the mayoral carpet.

"We've always been able to get the tourists," Pigg continued. "They come to see Graceland. They come to get drunk on Beale Street. They come to see those stupid ducks at The Peabody hotel. Or whatever. The point is, no matter how messed up the rest of this city is, tourists still find plenty of reasons to come."

"So what's the problem?" Joe said. If he was going to sit through this, he at least wanted to feel like someone knew he was here.

"The problem, Mr. I-Don't-Know-Your-Name-and-Don't-Really-Care, is that tourism isn't a business that stands still. Places fall in and out of fashion. One day, you're the number-one-ranked destination in *Suitcase* magazine, the next you're road kill for Seattle or Santa Fe or Wilmington–freakin'–North Carolina. We need sumpin new. Sumpin big."

"What do you have in mind, sir?" Cameron said. Having the mayor temporarily redirect his anger toward Joe had helped him regain his composure.

"In a word, barbecue," Pigg said. "When people think of Memphis, they think of barbecue. And I'm not just talkin' about my place either. This town is crawlin' with great barbecue joints."

"Like Carnivore Charlie's?" Joe added helpfully, knowing full well that Pete Pigg hated Carnivore Charlie's and its proprietor worse than he hated light beer and sober women.

"Yeah, smart ass, even Carnivore Charlie's," Pigg said. "And every May, we're the host of the World Championship Barbecue Cooking Contest, which is the preeminent barbecue competition in all the world."

"Or at least this side of Kansas City," Joe said. For some reason, he felt like pushing his luck today.

"Cal, I don't know why you brought this boy with you, but you need to teach him to shut up and listen," Pigg said. "What we need in this town is a Barbecue Hall of Fame."

"A hall of fame?" Cameron said. "What kind of exhibits would you have in a hall of fame about barbecue?"

"Use your imagination, pencil neck!" Pigg said. "We could have exhibits tracin' the history of outdoor cookin' dating all the way back to the days when the cavemen did it. We could dig up the first meat smoker ever built. Or a replica, at least. We could have photos and information about all the past champions of the

World Championship Barbecue Cooking Contest. A food court where people can sample the goods. A gift shop with all kinds of barbecue sauces and dry rub mixes. Barbecue aprons. Spatulas. T-shirts. Key chains with little piggies on them. Hell, we can have a guy dressed up in a pig costume being chased around the place by a guy in a chef's outfit. You guys have got to start thinkin' big!"

"That sounds like the way to go, all right," Joe said. "Of course, if you really want to make a good impression on the people of Memphis, it might be better to fix problems with crime or schools or some of that other stuff you mentioned."

Pigg snorted. "Boy, how long have you lived in Memphis?"

It was a question native Memphians often asked of people. If the answer was anything less than "All my life," the person was considered just another outsider who didn't know nothin'.

"Except for the time I spent in college, I've lived here all my life," Joe said.

"College boy, eh?" Pigg said. "And I suppose the University of Memphis wasn't good enough for you. Well, let me tell you sumpin, college boy. You must have spent your whole life with your nose buried in books. Because if you knew anythin' about Memphis, you'd know you can't fix problems like that. Some things about Memphis just are. And always will be. But I'll tell you a secret, college boy. You've got to do sumpin to take people's minds off all those problems. And I'm telling you that this Barbecue Hall of Fame is that sumpin."

"That sounds great, Mr. Mayor," Cameron said. The last thing he needed was for this upstart flunky from the PR firm stirring up trouble. "A Barbecue Hall of Fame sounds like a fine idea. What do you need us to do?"

"What I need you to do, Cal, is take this boy of yours and go figure out a way to sell this idea to the public," Pigg said. "Remember when we were tryin' to get the NBA team years ago? We were tryin' to get a crappy team from Vancouver that had never lost less than sixty games in a season. But the business community ran a big PR campaign—what did they call it, 'NBA Now'?—and got all the yokels whipped up and actin' like we were gettin' the Lakers or sumpin. So go out and launch a PR campaign for this. Don't call it 'Barbecue Now.' But sumpin like that."

"How about 'Barbecue Never'?" Joe said, just before Cameron grabbed him by the arm and dragged him from his seat.

"That sounds great, Mr. Mayor," Cameron said. "We'll get to work on it right away. We'll be back in touch soon."

Joe worked hard to suppress a laugh as he allowed Calvin Cameron to nearly push him out of the conference room. Joe knew Cameron would give him a lecture on the trolley ride back to the office.

It was worth it, though. At least this little excursion to the mayor's office had taken his mind off that stupid pawnshop press release.

Chapter 2

"Ooh! So you met the mayor!"

Scott Paulk said that to Joe with all the fake enthusiasm he could muster. Scott was the last person who would be impressed by meeting the mayor. Joe knew that even before he told Scott about his day.

Scott and Joe had been buddies for years, dating back to their days at Middle Tennessee State. And Scott had never been impressed with politicians. Or any establishment figures, really. Joe was the same way, at least to some extent, which was probably why they had become such good friends. Of course, after their years of hard partying in college, it was Joe who broke down and got a real job first. Ever since then, Scott had ragged Joe about being a sellout.

"Yeah, yeah, I saw the mayor," Joe said. "You have, too. Lots of times."

"Oh, but that was different," Scott said. "I met him before he was actually mayor."

"Met him?" Joe said. "You practically lived at the Pigg Pen."

Scott shrugged as he wolfed down another bite of his catfish po' boy. "Yeah, I've spent some time there. But I've spent time at just about every place on Beale Street."

That was true enough. Although Scott occasionally did work as a handyman, his steady gig was as an Elvis "tribute artist" performing for tourists on Beale. Joe had to admit that Scott looked the part, particularly with his makeup and his hair slicked back. Scott was tall and blue-eyed and had an athletic build—athletic for a guy who spent so much of his free time drinking, at least. Scott could also sing a little bit, even though Joe would never admit that to his friend.

Besides working on Beale Street, Scott actually lived there, too, in a loft apartment over one of the storefronts. In fact, his was the only apartment on Beale Street. Most people would find the relentless noise in the heart of the city's entertainment district a bit much. But Scott wasn't like most people, in that he still partied the same way he had in college. So living on a street where the bars didn't shut down before four in the morning wasn't an issue for him.

"So what's the big deal?" Joe said. "You've seen Pete Pigg on Beale Street. I've seen him in his office. Same difference."

"No, it's not," Scott said. "I've been to the Pigg Pen to do my thing—drink beer, eat barbecue, and hit on the Pigglettes. But you met the Honorable Pete Pigg because you have to do his bidding. You're like a bureaucrat now. A functionary. What's happened to you since college? You used to be a man who'd never back down to a bottle of Jose Cuervo. Now, you're a whiny little bitch who's scared of a fat bald man."

"Scared? Scared?" Joe knew Scott was just pulling his chain, but it was working. "You should have heard the way I talked to him, man. Cal Cameron was all 'Yes, sir, no, sir.' I was cracking on his stupid idea. This city's got a million problems, and he thinks he can use barbecue sauce as a salve to patch them up."

Scott nearly spit out the gulp of Coors Light he had just taken. "A salve on the city's wounds? Man, you really took some of those lit classes in college seriously, didn't you? You're a regular poet. A pansified, press-release-writing poet."

"Nice alliteration. Maybe you studied more than you let on, too," Joe shot back.

"At least I left Murfreesboro with my balls intact," Scott said.

"What's that crap on your face?" Joe was eager to change the subject anyway, but the black smudge on Scott's right cheek was in fact a bit distracting.

"Oh, that's just eyeliner from my Elvis costume," Scott said, pawing at his face and making the smudge more prominent in the process. "I had a late evening last night and fell asleep before I got a chance to jump in the shower."

"Well, why don't you go to the bathroom and clean up before the game?" Joe said. "We may be in Midtown, but this isn't a gay bar."

In point of fact, they were at Heck's, one of their favorite hangouts. Although just a ten-minute drive from downtown, Heck's was far removed from the tourist scene where Scott earned his living. Locals knew about the place, of course, but no one ever got around to letting tourists in on the secret.

From the outside, Heck's looked like one of those old-fashioned drugstores from the 1950s, with a red-and-white-striped awning, red-brick walls, and large plate-glass windows on either side of the front door. It looked so much like a drugstore because that's what it had been. The inside had spectacular wood-finished walls, partially covered with five-foot-high dry erase boards. Roy Heck, the proprietor, had put up the boards after years of fighting a losing battle against drunks who liked to carve their initials (and unsavory messages) into his woodwork. After putting up the boards, Heck kept the bar well stocked with different-colored Sharpie markers and encouraged doodlers to knock themselves out.

Joe and Scott liked the place just fine, even though they spent most of their time outside in the back parking lot, which was converted into a Wiffle ball field late at night and on weekends.

"Okay, I'll be right back," Scott said, finishing his po' boy and downing the last of his beer before heading to the bathroom.

"Put on some lip gloss and even out your foundation while you're in there," Joe called after him. He glanced at Scott's plate and spotted a couple of fried pickles his friend had missed. Joe shoveled them into his mouth. If Scott was going to give him crap about the meeting with Mayor Pigg, he would a least pay a toll.

"Ready to get whupped, loser?" a voice behind him asked.

Joe turned slowly, still chewing a mouthful of pickles and grease, to study the hippie hovering over his table. The guy was lanky and tall, probably about six-foot-two, with stringy blond hair that went halfway to his waist. He had tattoos all over his arms, his neck, and God knew where else.

"What's up, Broad?" Joe said, not particularly caring if he spat a little food as he did so.

"That's Brad, you slow-swinging sissy!" the hippie replied. "And all I need to know is how many times you want me to strike you out in tonight's game."

Brad was part of the Wiffle ball team Joe and Scott's team

Free Public Library of Monroe Township
713 Marsha Ave.
Williamstown, NJ 08094

was scheduled to play that night. Brad and his teammates, who were equally scraggly guys, were known around the Wiffle ball yard as the Detroit Tokers. And the name seemed apt, given their lifestyle, although it was debatable whether or not any of them had actually set foot in Detroit or anywhere outside the South.

"Strike me out?" Joe said. "About the only thing you'll be striking is a match as you fire up another bud, bud."

"You know you can't hit my riser pitch—never could, never will," Brad replied.

"Riser pitch? Is that what you're calling it now? I thought that was your reefer pitch. If anyone swings and misses, it's only because they're too busy sniffing that funny odor that's on the ball after you handle it."

Brad threw back his head and laughed. "We'll see you outside, Josephine," he said as he headed out the back door.

Game time was in ten minutes—time enough for Joe and Scott to have one more beer.

Scott was back at the table a minute or two later, carrying two Styrofoam cups. Roy Heck had long ago outlawed glass bottles at Wiffle ball games because they invariably led to too much broken glass in his parking lot.

"Thanks for grabbing me a beer," Joe said.

"What are you talking about?" Scott said. "Both of these are mine. I get tired of running back and forth to the bar between innings."

"Thanks, pal. I'll grab one for myself on the way out," Joe said. They stood and walked to the bar.

"Now, what were we talking about?" Scott said as Joe put in his order.

"You were breaking my balls about having a real job."

"Oh, yeah, about that," Scott said, pausing to take a long pull on the beer in his left hand. "What I was going to tell you about the mayor is, watch your back."

"Watch my back? I thought you loved the guy. You used to stay at his place all night, singing karaoke and leering at the hotties with him."

"Yeah, Joe, I know I did. But there are bar friends, and then there are friend friends. And Pete Pigg is not your friend friend. People think he's a goofball, but you don't get to sit in the big chair at city hall unless you're a ruthless dude."

"Oh, come on," Joe said. "I know you hate politicians, but you can't lump Pete Pigg, the Baron of Barbecue, into that category."

"I can and I do," Scott said. "There are no innocents in the political arena. He didn't end up where he is by accident."

Joe sensed this wasn't a point worth arguing. Not with Mr. Anti-Establishment himself. "Duly noted," Joe said, again sensing a need to change the subject. "Want to get out there and take some batting practice before the game?"

"Let's do it," Scott said, pushing open the door to a parking lot filled with guys milling around with cups of beer and yellow plastic Wiffle bats in their hands. "Hey, guys, guess what? Joe here is servicing the mayor!"

Joe sighed as he followed his "friend friend" out the door. With an intro like that, he knew he was in for a long night of heckling.

Chapter 3

Mayor Pete Pigg was well into his fourth martini of a two-martini lunch.

Well, so what? Nothing in the city charter prohibited drinking on the job. At least Pigg assumed so. He hadn't actually read it all the way through yet. That was one thing about his new job that he disliked: so much boring reading.

He stared at his half-empty glass and signaled for the waiter to bring him another drink. He was in The Olive Pit, a martini bar on Second Street, halfway between The Peabody hotel and Beale Street.

While less well known to tourists, Second Street was on a par with the legendary Beale Street in terms of quality restaurants and bars. The Olive Pit was sandwiched between Ochin Horosho, a Russian restaurant, and Go Catfish! which specialized in beer-battered fried fish. As a fellow restaurateur, Pigg had to admire both of those places for their marketing gimmickry. Ochin Horosho's advertised special was "Roast Peabody Duck," an irreverent nod to The Peabody's famed duck mascots. And Go Catfish! was known for having the cooks parade past the tables after orders were taken, encouraging patrons to pour some of their own beer into the frying batter. Which of course meant those patrons had to buy more beer. Which was pure genius, to Mayor Pigg's way of thinking.

But The Olive Pit was Mayor Pigg's favorite spot for entertaining business contacts, particularly since, more often than not, they would pick up the tab. Being mayor did have a few perks, after all.

The mayor's cell phone rang. His ring tone was the first few bars of "Walking in Memphis." He had changed it after becoming mayor as a way to show his loyal constituents how much civic pride he had. It seemed so much more mayoral than his old "Why Don't We Get Drunk and Screw" ring tone.

"'Lo?" he said into the phone.

"Mayor, it's Cedric." Cedric was his manager at the Pigg Pen.

"Yeah, Cedric, what's up?" Cedric was reasonably competent and didn't steal from the cash register, two traits that were hard to find in a manager.

"Well, sir, we've got a slight problem." Just the words Mayor Pigg didn't want to hear.

"Oh, yeah? What now?"

"It's Carnivore Charlie's, sir." It usually was.

"What about them?"

"They've got a new promotion going."

"They usually do," Pigg said. "What's the big deal?"

"Well, this one's different. It's, uh, making fun of you, sir."

"What? How?"

"They call it the Tax Relief Special. They'll take $4.04 off any tab of $30 or more."

"Why $4.04?" Mayor Pigg wasn't following.

"Uh, sir, that's the city's property tax rate—$4.04 per $100 of assessed property value."

"The tax rate? How can they blame me for that? I've been mayor only a few months. I haven't even had a chance to raise taxes yet."

"I know, sir. It's very unfair. But it seems to be drawing some extra people over there."

Pigg swore under his breath. "Okay, thanks, Cedric," he said before he clicked off the phone. Carnivore Charlie's was going to drive him to drink. So to speak.

Pigg's fifth martini had just arrived when his lunch date walked in the door. Her name was Dawn Funderburke, but since she had become famous, she was known simply as Dawn.

She had grown up in Collierville, a well-to-do suburb east of Memphis. Although she had won beauty contests since she was twelve, her big break came when she went on a reality show called *Ham It Up* at age sixteen. *Ham It Up* was a competition in which aspiring actors were called upon to do skits with only thirty minutes of prep time.

Dawn had won the competition during the show's first season, then parlayed that into a movie career. She started off fairly small, with an independent film done by a Memphis-based director, but then graduated to commercial Hollywood films. She was mostly typecast as a not-too-bright sexpot. Not exactly Academy Award material, but the work made her a nice living. She was even rumored to be up for consideration as the love interest in the next James Bond movie.

Even after becoming famous, she kept a home in Memphis, in the trendy Mud Island neighborhood downtown. She did her best to avoid celebrity treatment, using her many interviews to urge locals to treat her as "just Dawn." To keep autograph hounds at bay, she encouraged fans who spotted her out on the town to respect her privacy but to e-mail her website with their contact information and the time and place where they had seen her. Four times a year, she hosted "Dinner with Dawn," during which the fans who had reported Dawn sightings in the last three months met with her at a location not disclosed to the public and got not only autographs but also free food and some precious face time with the budding star.

It didn't always work. A few overzealous fans and paparazzi didn't want to play by the rules. However, there seemed to be fewer aggressive types since a YouTube video surfaced of Dawn kneeing a would-be groper in the groin during an after-party at the Cannes film festival. That sort of thing never happened back home, since giving Dawn her space was a matter of civic pride for local residents—sort of like not complaining about the humidity until it hit 95 percent.

Additionally, Dawn managed to win points with her neighbors by her deep involvement in hometown civic affairs, which was why she had agreed to meet with the mayor.

Although only five-foot-two, she was a stunning blond beauty with dark brown eyes and a killer figure. Heads turned as she made her way to the toady-looking man at a table near the back. More than a few patrons began pecking away at their smartphones.

"Good to see you, Miss Dawn," the mayor said, stumbling as he rose to greet her.

"Good to see you, Mr. Mayor."

"Please, sweetie, call me Pete. And might I just say you're lookin' mighty fine today. In fact, you look so good you could get a train to take a dirt road."

Dawn had heard that one only about a hundred times. A Southern expression that should have died a quiet death decades ago.

"So what can I get you to drink, Miss Dawn?"

"Please, call me Dawn. And it's a bit early in the day for me to be drinking."

"It's after eleven, isn't it?"

"Well, yes. But I have a meeting with my business manager later today. Does this place serve coffee?"

"I don't think so. Not unless it's got a coupla fingers of vodka in it."

"I think I'll pass, Mr. Mayor, er, Pete. So why did you want to meet with me today?"

"Well, little darlin', I'm workin' on a project I'd like your help with. I'm going to bring the World Barbecue Hall of Fame right here to Memphis, Tennessee. And I need to get some of this town's movers and shakers behind me."

"Well, Mr. Mayor, I don't know much about barbecue, except how to eat it. I don't really know what I—"

"Listen, it's not really that complicated," Pigg said, pausing to take another generous swig of his martini. He let out a low burp, forgetting for a second that he was trying to make a good impression on a pretty lady. "I just need some people to stand out front with me, to attend press conferences, tell reporters what a great project it's goin' to be, and such like that."

"Is it going to be a great project?"

"Honey, that's one thing you can count on. This is gonna be the biggest thing this town's ever seen."

"Well, I'd like some time to think about it."

"What's to think about, baby? This town's built on barbecue. And having a museum—no, having the Smithsonian of barbecue—is just what we need. And you're the perfect spokeswoman. All you have to do is smile and look pretty. And I know you can do that."

Men are all the same, Dawn thought. "Yes, well, I would need to talk with my manager and have my lawyers go over any paperwork."

"Look, there's no paperwork. If you love your city, and I think you do, then you need to get behind this. I'll never ask you to do anythin' you don't wanna do. And if I do, you just quit and walk away, no questions asked. Whaddaya say?"

"Okay, I'll give it a try," Dawn said with a sigh. "For the sake of the city."

"Great. I'll be callin' you soon about our first press conference. And I'm gonna give you my card. It's got my cell number on the back."

Dawn waited for Pigg's next comment with an uncomfortable sense of anticipation. She knew all too well what the Honorable Pete Pigg, mayor of Memphis, was going to say next.

"Feel free to call me, day or night," Pigg said, licking his lips lasciviously. "Anytime."

Dawn took the card reluctantly. Since becoming famous, she'd been approached by all kinds of people with all kinds of propositions, business and otherwise. As a result, she had a good instinct for sniffing out sketchy deals.

And as innocent as Mayor Pigg made this project sound, she had a gnawing feeling that something about it wasn't right.

Chapter 4

Before he became mayor, Pete Pigg always thought he'd en-joy press conferences. What wasn't to like? Being the center of attention, having people hang on every word you said, getting your actions gloriously chronicled in the newspapers and on TV.

The only trouble was that the reality was nothing like that. At least it hadn't been during his first months as mayor. On the campaign trail, Pete Pigg had grown used to being portrayed as a laughable and lovable distraction from the serious candidates in the race. After winning the election, though, journalists had abruptly stopped treating him as comic relief. As a novelty act, he'd worn out his shelf life.

On the two previous occasions when he called press confer-ences, his jokes had all bombed. When he had been asked tough questions during the campaign, he usually got himself out of trouble by saying, "Now, don't you go barbecuein' the Pigg," or something of similar wit. These days, nothing. No laughter. Just more questions. And more questions after that.

But Mayor Pigg was determined to work this particular press conference to his advantage. The World Barbecue Hall of Fame was going to buy him back some political capital.

"Thank y'all for comin' here today," he intoned from the podium set up in the Hall of Mayors, a large, open room off the main lobby of city hall. Joe Miller, Calvin Cameron, Dawn, and a phalanx of mayoral bodyguards stood behind him. A gaggle of reporters was directly in front. Farther back from the podium was the cadre of city hall employees and assorted flunkies he'd ordered to attend the press conference for no other reason than to provide moral support. He knew he could count on them to cheer at the appropriate times and boo when the reporters' questions got too rough. If they didn't, Mayor Pigg would send them back to their old jobs washing dishes at the Pigg Pen.

"This is a historic day in the city of Memphis," Mayor Pigg continued. "Memphis is called 'the City of Good Abode.' And for generations of tourists, it has been just that."

Pigg had to admit that Cal's boy, who wrote the speech, had a way with words. If only somebody could do something about the kid's attitude.

"But today I'm announcin' plans for a tourist attraction that will one day be bigger than Graceland," the mayor continued. "Bigger than Beale Street. Bigger than Sun Studio, Soulsville, and the Memphis Zoo. I'm pleased to announce that Memphis will be the site for the World Barbecue Hall of Fame, an attraction that's certain to bring hundreds of thousands of new visitors to our community every year. While they're here, they'll pump millions of dollars into our economy. And they will continue the revitalization of the north end of downtown. Because the site for this wonderful attraction will be the northwest corner of Auction

Avenue and Front Street, next to The Pyramid."

Mayor Pigg paused, the cue for his entourage to burst into applause. As it did, Joe Miller recoiled. He hadn't written anything about a proposed site for this boondoggle. Out of the corner of his eye, Joe caught the look of shock on Calvin Cameron's face, too. Mayor Pigg had obviously inserted that part on his own. Why hadn't he mentioned the Barbecue Hall of Fame's location before?

"Also with me today, to show support for this stupendous attraction, is a woman you all know well—Dawn, the world-famous movie actress who has brought the bright lights of Hollywood back to her hometown. Would you like to say a few words, Miss Dawn?"

"Thank you, Mayor Pigg," the starlet said as she stepped to the microphone, which again drew applause from the city hall flunkies. Actually, Joe would have applauded, too, if he weren't trying so hard to look professional. The woman, whom Joe had never before seen in person, was quite a looker.

"I just want to tell the people of Memphis that this is going to be a great project for our city. As Mayor Pigg said, it'll bring tourists, jobs, and money into our community. And I'm going to do everything I can to support this project."

"Thank you, Dawn," the mayor said, reclaiming his spot at the microphone. "And now, I'll be happy to take a few questions. Let's start with you, right down there in front." He pointed to a veteran female TV reporter.

"So, Mr. Mayor, exactly who will qualify to be inducted into this Barbecue Hall of Fame?" she asked.

"Yeah," one of her younger male TV colleagues interjected, "people or pigs?"

That remark brought titters from the reporters in the front half of the room, while the peanut gallery reacted with confused murmuring. Was it okay to laugh at that joke? Sometimes, it was hard to tell whether reporters were insulting the mayor or just trying to prompt more of his homespun humor.

"The answer to that would be people who barbecue pigs," the mayor said as smoothly as he could. "But I think we'll have room for plenty of both."

"And will the Pigg Pen be supplying the barbecue sold at the concession stands at this museum?" That question came from Alvin Allen, the city hall beat reporter for the Memphis daily, *The Avalanche*.

The murmur in the back of the room grew louder. That certainly wasn't an attempt to be funny. The reporter was brazenly questioning the boss's motives. How dare he?

"I'm sure we'll open up that contract, and every contract for goods and services on this project, to a fair and unbiased biddin' process," Mayor Pigg said, his voice tightening. "This will distribute economic wealth throughout our community."

"Speaking of distribution," said a young woman with spiky red hair and a nose ring, "when will Dawn's next movie be in theaters?"

"We're not here to talk about Dawn's movie career," the mayor said. Pigg recognized her as a snarky blogger who pounded his job performance in many of her posts. How did she get press credentials for city hall?

"Dawn, is it true you're dating Jude Law?" the young woman persisted.

Simone something—that was her name. Her blog was called "Simone Says." *Real clever*, the mayor thought.

"I don't really know Jude," Dawn said, stepping back to the microphone. "But if he were here, I would tell him what a great project we're about to launch in Memphis, Tennessee."

Joe was impressed by her smooth attempt to steer the conversation back to the subject at hand.

"Mayor, could you answer a few questions about the Ghetto Blazer?" asked one of the male TV reporters.

They were a dime a dozen, always looking to move on to bigger TV markets. Mayor Pigg couldn't remember if he had seen the guy before. "The Ghetto what?" he asked.

"The Ghetto Blazer," the reporter answered. "That's what we're calling the arsonist who's responsible, by our count, for twenty-three separate house fires in North Memphis, South Memphis, and Orange Mound over the last two months. Surely, your police have some leads. Unless they were too busy arranging security for this press conference, that is."

"*Boo! Boo!*" The mayor's entourage wasn't going to sit quietly for any more of this.

"I think we've had enough questions for one day," Mayor Pigg growled.

"Mr. Mayor, have you heard the rumor that Nick Nelson, the owner of Carnivore Charlie's, is planning to run against you in the next election?" another reporter shouted over the booing.

"That's it, we're done here!" the mayor shouted, angrily snapping off the microphone switch.

Mayor Pigg pushed his way through the crowd of reporters, heading toward the elevator that would take him back to the refuge of his office. The reporters fell in behind him, continuing to shout questions. The police bodyguards did what they could to keep the reporters away from their boss. Like the mayor's previous attempts at press conferences, this one had quickly devolved into a feeding frenzy.

The mayor's flunkies broke away to return to their offices. And Calvin Cameron headed straight toward the front door, not saying a word to Joe. That left Joe and Dawn standing there in the quickly emptying room, alone except for the portraits of the city's former mayors.

"Well, that didn't go as well as it could have," Joe said.

"No, it didn't," Dawn said. "I'm sorry, but I didn't catch your name."

"I'm Joe Miller." Joe would have liked to say something clever to impress the magnificent beauty standing next to him. But for a change, he was at a loss for words.

"Do you work for the mayor?" Dawn asked.

"God no," Joe said reflexively. "I mean, I sort of do. I work for a PR firm here in town, and the mayor asked us to help publicize this project."

"Looks like you have your work cut out for you," Dawn replied.

The more she talked, the more Joe thought that maybe she wasn't as ditzy as she was portrayed in the media. So the gossip rags had her pegged wrong. *Big shocker there*, Joe thought.

"I guess I do," Joe said. "And you, too."

Dawn laughed, which made Joe's heart rate quicken. "I suppose you're right. I have to admit I had some reservations about this, even before what just happened."

"So why did you sign up?" Joe said. "I mean, I'm getting paid, and I really don't have a lot of choice. But you're Dawn. You're rich and famous. You don't have to get involved with something like this if you don't want to."

"I know, I know," Dawn said, giggling at Joe's flattery. "But believe it or not, I wanted to do this because I thought it would be good for our city."

Joe had no reply to that. He'd spent years perfecting his too-cool-to-care persona. Dawn's apparent altruism was foreign to his way of thinking.

"Well, I guess I'd better get back to the office," Joe said. "I'm sure Mr. Cameron is going to raise hell with my boss as soon as he pulls himself back together."

"And I need to meet with my agent," Dawn said. "He wasn't crazy about me agreeing to commit to this without talking to him first anyway."

"Well, maybe I'll see you around sometime," Joe said, feeling like he was back in high school.

"I'm sure you will," Dawn said with a smile.

"You will? I mean, I will?"

"Yes," Dawn said. "I promised the mayor I would do some TV spots about the Barbecue Hall of Fame. So I guess I'll be working with you on those, right?"

Joe hadn't heard anything about the TV spots. Another detail Mayor Pigg had neglected to share with him. But if it meant more opportunities to spend time with Dawn, Joe wasn't going to complain.

Chapter 5

Mayor Pigg barely made it back to his office and settled into his chair before Waldo Jefferson barged in.

Jefferson, chairman of the Memphis City Council, was big, black, and, at the moment, angry, which was more than enough to get Pigg's attention.

Jefferson stood six-foot-four and weighed over 250 pounds and had an Afro and muttonchop sideburns. Someone had told him that Afros were back in style and that growing one would make him look younger. It hadn't, particularly since his hair was gray in spots, creating a polka-dot effect. His hairdo was all the more striking because it clashed so severely with the immaculately cut Brooks Brothers suits he always wore.

"Pigg!" Jefferson fairly screamed. "Just what the hell are you tryin' to pull?"

First, Pigg had to put up with those media jackals, and now this. Jefferson was leaning over the mayor's desk with his hands on his hips. Pigg, who sat with his right leg draped across the desk, was too intimidated to move. Since Jefferson was one of the candidates Pigg had beaten to win the mayor's job, relations between the two hadn't been great the last few months.

"What's the problem, Waldo?" Pigg said, trying to sound calm.

"What's the problem? What's the problem? The problem is that I was listening to your press conference over the office intercom."

Pigg made a mental note to himself: the intercom, used to broadcast council meetings and news conferences, was one more thing he'd have to watch out for around city hall.

"You've got a problem with me holdin' a press conference, Waldo?" Pigg said. "If I knew you were interested, I would have invited you. Shoot, you could have stood up there at the podium with Dawn and me. I don't know if you've met her, but she's a very pretty lady."

"You think I wanted to stand up there with you and some Tootsie Roll and listen to you answer a bunch of dumb questions?" Jefferson said.

"Then what do you want, Waldo?" The mayor's foot was falling asleep, poised as it was at an awkward angle on the desk, but he was still too tense to move it.

"I want to be in the loop. You think you can just waltz downstairs and announce a project like that without the help of the city council? That site you picked, across the street from The Pyramid, do you even know what kind of land use it's zoned for?"

"No," Pigg admitted. "Do you?"

"No," Jefferson shot back. "But you can bet it isn't zoned for no World Barbecue Hall of Fame. And if you think you're gonna get that zoning without my help, then you've lost your damn mind. Nobody gets seven votes on the Memphis City Council without talking to Waldo Jefferson."

Finally, Pigg got it. The city council chairman was beginning to speak a language he understood. The language of the political shakedown.

"So now we're talkin', Waldo," Pigg said. "What do you want?"

"What do I want?" Jefferson said. "I want a piece of whatever you want, Mr. Mayor. Because I know you wouldn't be doing this if you weren't working some kind of angle."

"You don't believe I'm doin' this to educate the world about the wonders of barbecue?" Pigg asked. He was starting to regain his composure. This kind of negotiating he could handle. After all, it was why he had wanted to become mayor in the first place.

"No, I don't," Jefferson said. "I may not run a restaurant like you do, but I know most people would rather eat barbecue than talk about it or look at stupid exhibits about it."

"I feel you," Pigg said. It didn't sound quite right, but he'd heard Cedric use that expression. Maybe saying it would help Mayor Pigg build rapport with Waldo Jefferson. Or at least keep him from getting his ass kicked. "I think we can probably help each other out. If you can help me get the city council's support on the zonin' and any other issues that come up, then I think I can guarantee you get more than your share of those economic benefits I was talkin' about downstairs."

"Exactly what kind of economic benefits are we talking about here?"

Pigg smiled and dropped his foot to the floor with an awkward clunk. If he had doubts before, he now knew how to handle Waldo Jefferson. His first months on the job had been filled with conversations like this one.

"Well," the mayor said, "perhaps you or a family member might be involved in some type of business that could lend its skills and expertise to this project. I don't know, maybe some consultin' work. A project of this size is bound to require the use of several consultants."

"Well, Mr. Mayor, now that you mention it, maybe I do have a situation like that. See, my brother-in-law has this public relations business. But he's been having trouble getting clients."

"You know, Mr. Council Chairman, I know 'zactly what that's like. It's so hard for a young man to get started in business these days. But I think this project presents a unique partnership opportunity for your brother-in-law. See, the Memphis Tourist Information Bureau has retained the services of one of the larger PR firms in town to assist with the project. Now, I would imagine that as a small businessman, your brother-in-law could benefit greatly by partnerin' with this other firm on the project."

"I'm sure he could," Jefferson said, leaning back and smiling for the first time.

"Well, hell, consider this a done deal," Pigg said. "We'll sign your brother-in-law on as . . . What's his name, by the way?"

"Rupert. Rupert Graham."

"Yes, we'll sign Mr. Graham as a partner with this other firm . . . Oh, hell, I can't even think of the name of the firm Cal Cameron hired. But we'll sign Mr. Graham on at a rate of, oh, I don't know, does five thousand dollars a month sound fair to you?"

"Well, five thousand a month might take care of Rupert, but what about a finder's fee? You know, for the guy who found him the job."

"Oh, right," Mayor Pigg said. "Well, ten thousand a month to Mr. Graham's firm sounds like a nice round number. I'm sure you and he can work out any, uh, payroll division issues that might arise."

"Payroll division issues—now, I like the way you put that," Jefferson said with a chuckle. "So where's this money going to come from?"

"Well, since the city council approves the budget for the mayor and his administrative staff, I think it would be helpful if we just added that $120,000 to next year's budget for media relations. Do you think you could help me with sumpin like that, Mr. Council Chairman?"

"I believe I could, I believe I could," Jefferson said. "Now, does Rupert need to go meet with anyone from this other firm? Discuss strategy and all that bull? You know, to make it look right."

"Nah, I don't think that'll be necessary," Pigg said, even daring to wink at the man who had menaced him a few minutes earlier. "I'm gonna be keepin' Cal's boys busy with real work. Just give me a company name and an address where we need to send the checks."

Chapter 6

Augustine Eldridge knew he had a short window to get his work done.

He and his film crew were in the Mud Island River Museum in late afternoon, preparing to shoot a scene in his latest project. Eldridge had picked this particular time of day, this particular time of week, and this particular time of year because the chances of encountering other visitors were almost nonexistent.

The river museum had been a sensation when it opened in the late 1980s as part of the Mud Island River Park. Mud Island was actually a peninsula jutting into the Mississippi River near the north end of downtown Memphis. The park, on the southern tip of the peninsula, included the river museum, an outdoor amphitheater, and a mile-long scaled-down replica of the Mississippi itself.

The museum had been fairly popular before its novelty wore off. It had many impressive exhibits chronicling the history of early American life along the river, including a full-sized replica of a steamboat on one of the lower floors.

It was in that steamboat that Eldridge planned to shoot a scene for his new porno film, *Memphis in Lay*. The title was, of course, a takeoff on Memphis in May, the city's month-long festival of music, barbecue, and more music.

The movie was going to be Eldridge's irreverent tribute to his adopted hometown. Eldridge had moved to Memphis after growing tired of being just one of the many pornographic film producers in California's San Fernando Valley. He expected to make a fresh start in Memphis, where he fully expected to win over the yokels with his flamboyance and charm.

It hadn't exactly played out that way. Although Memphis had, at different points in its history, been a town with an anything-goes attitude toward the sex trade, Eldridge arrived during an era when the pendulum had swung back in favor of the prudes. Most of the city's strip clubs had been shut down a few years ago. The local business community had made it clear to Eldridge that he and his kind weren't welcome. Which only increased his determination to transform Memphis into the porn capital of the eastern United States.

His concept for *Memphis in Lay* was brilliant in its simplicity. Eldridge was going to shoot the explicit scenes with recognizable Memphis landmarks in the background. Beale Street, of course. And outside the gates of Graceland. In front of the storied Sun Studio. And today, on the paddleboat replica inside the Mud Island River Museum.

His actors were two guys and a girl, all of whom had been working at a downtown nightclub the night before. That was one thing about the San Fernando Valley scene that Eldridge never liked—having to deal with actors who took themselves too seriously. Every one of them thought they were just a juicy porno role away from landing a spot in a Hollywood feature film. Not these Memphis kids, though. Eldridge was surprised at how many of them were willing to do porn simply for a good paycheck. Of course, the guys also did it for recreation.

These three were typical college kids. The boys looked a bit scruffy, but that was okay. The girl had dark red hair and a giant set of boobs. And no matter how well or poorly these three "performed" together, Eldridge bet her looks alone would be enough to sell movies.

While lookouts took up positions along the museum's corridors to make sure no one other than the film crew wandered in, the actors disrobed and the cameramen and sound equipment operators geared up for action.

That's when Eldridge's cell phone chirped, startling him. For the briefest instant, he thought the museum must have installed some sort of nudity detection system.

"Eldridge!" Eldridge barked into the phone.

"Boss, it's me," said Pedro Suarez, Eldridge's business manager. A Mexican national, Suarez had, through a mixture of grit and ruthlessness, made a decent living running several nightclubs in East L.A. Eldridge met him while scouting one of Suarez's clubs for talent. Suarez had started out strictly as a talent broker. But he had such good business instincts that Eldridge brought him along when he moved east.

"Yeah, what's up, Pedro?" Eldridge said with some irritation. "We're about to start a shoot. And who knows how much time we're working with here, you know what I mean?"

The girl cooed in the background as the boys began to caress her. They apparently couldn't wait to get started. *These kids today have no patience,* Eldridge thought.

"Yeah, yeah, I know, boss, I know," Suarez said. "But I thought you'd want to hear about this press conference the mayor just held."

"Why would I care about something like that, Pedro?"

"I didn't see it myself, but I got a call after it was over from Alvin Allen, a reporter for *The Avalanche.*"

"A reporter? Why on earth would you talk to a reporter?" Eldridge was starting to get mad. His actors were improvising on the set rather than waiting to take direction. In retrospect, plying the boys with Viagra on the way to the shoot looked like a mistake.

"I asked the reporter the same thing: why would I talk to him?" Suarez said. "But he told me the mayor's got this crazy plan to build something called a World Barbecue Hall of Fame."

"World Barbecue Hall of Fame, huh?" Eldridge thought he saw where Suarez was heading with this. "That does sound like a good location to shoot. But wait a minute, this thing isn't built yet? How long will it take to throw together something like that? We're on a tight production schedule."

Overhearing the word *tight,* one of the boys whispered something in the girl's ear, which caused her to laugh uncontrollably. Eldridge scowled and walked a few paces away to get out of earshot. If these kids started going at it, he hoped his crew had the presence of mind to get it on video.

"No, boss, it's not built yet. But the mayor has picked out a site," Suarez said.

"Look, Pedro. This means exactly what to me?"

"Well, Allen told me that the mayor said he wants to build at the intersection of Front Street and Auction Avenue. The northwest corner of Front and Auction. Allen was hoping to get in touch with the owner."

"The northwest corner of Front and Auction?" Eldridge said. Now, he really did see where Suarez was heading.

"Yeah, boss. You know who might hold the title to that property?"

"You know, I think I do," Eldridge said. "Funny that the mayor would make an announcement like that without talking to us first, isn't it?"

"Yeah, it is," Suarez said. "But that's not exactly bad news, is it?"

The actors were making all sorts of amorous noises as they began foreplay on the deck next to the paddle wheel. Eldridge really wanted to shoot them near the bow, with the ship's name in the background, but he was too preoccupied at the moment to notice.

"So, Pedro, what are you thinking?"

"I'm thinking, boss, that if the mayor went public with the name of the proposed location without talking to the owners, he must want that property bad. Real bad."

Eldridge smiled as he snapped the phone closed, not bothering to say goodbye. When this day had started, Eldridge felt lucky. He and his crew had managed to get their videocams and microphones past the bored ticket taker at the river museum without attracting suspicion, which was lucky enough. And the coast appeared to still be clear as his actors began their work, which was also lucky.

But this latest bit of news was the luckiest break of all. The city of Memphis apparently wanted to buy one of his investment properties—and not even one of the better ones. Augustine Eldridge had a feeling his wallet was about to get a lot fatter at the expense of the city's taxpayers.

Chapter 7

Joe Miller pushed off in his canoe from the boat ramp next to the Wolf River Harbor Coast Guard Station.

He lived only about five minutes from the boat ramp by car, so he often took his canoe out on the harbor when he wanted to clear his thoughts.

The harbor was a three-and-a-half-mile stretch of water separating Mud Island from the rest of downtown Memphis. At one time, before the Wolf River had been rerouted by engineers, it actually did cut off Mud Island from the mainland. Now, though, the Wolf River emptied into the Mississippi on the north side of a land bridge that connected Mud Island to the rest of Memphis, making the name *Mud Island* something of a misnomer. The harbor stopped on the other side of that same land bridge, as if waiting for a chance to reconnect with the river that bore its name. The south end of the harbor merged into the Mississippi.

Joe was starting his trip about midway along the length of the harbor. If he chose to go south, he would get a spectacular view of downtown Memphis to the east and the Mud Island River Park to the west. And if he went north, he would see some of the tony waterfront homes along Mud Island and the stark industrial development on the harbor's eastern shore, finally giving way to an oasis of trees, swamp grass, and relative tranquility at the northern end of the harbor.

Joe headed north. While it was sometimes fun to watch and hear the hustle and bustle of the city from the water—the cars whizzing along Riverside Avenue, the horse-drawn carriages clopping down Front Street, the trolleys giving tourists views of both the best and worst downtown had to offer—Joe had a different agenda this particular day.

He had a woman on his mind. And he hoped this trip would help him clear out some of the cobwebs. Joe wasn't used to developing crushes on girls. Most of the attractive ones he met in bars, he approached right away. If they were interested in him, then great. If not, he just moved on to the next potential target. He never got emotionally invested either way.

But Dawn was something different altogether. It wasn't just that she was famous. Okay, maybe that was part of the attraction. Maybe a large part. But Joe knew there was more to it than that. When he talked to her after that disastrous press conference, he had sensed some chemistry.

Or was that just wishful thinking? His friend Scott was convinced that every woman he encountered was immediately attracted to him. Joe's outlook was more realistic. It was entirely possible, Joe knew, that Dawn had a well-practiced public persona that required her to be nice to everyone in her official capacity—particularly people who happened to be working for the mayor. Or maybe that wasn't even her public persona. Maybe her parents had just raised her to be polite. Not all celebrities were total head cases, were they?

Even so, Joe had sensed something more. Whether it was her body language or the easy way they had carried on conversation, Joe felt he had a shot at arguably the city's biggest sex symbol.

There was debate that Dawn held claim to that title, of course. Some yahoos believed the woman who did the TV commercials for Steve-O's Sporting Goods was actually the city's sexiest woman. The Steve-O's girl certainly did look good in spandex. However, Joe knew full well that Steve-O's was a national chain and that the woman was just a paid spokesmodel. Joe's guess was that she had never set foot in Memphis.

Dawn, on the other hand, was the real deal. Born and raised in Memphis. Or Collierville, which was close enough. And from the way she acted at that press conference, she really cared about her hometown. Which made Joe care about it, too. Not that he hadn't cared before. He'd just never thought about applying that caring to any kind of meaningful action.

Now, he would be working side by side with Dawn on an important project that could brighten the city's future. It could help Memphis recover from the blow of losing those riverboats to Tunica. It could bring tourists besides the ones who were drawn to Graceland, Beale Street, and the other music-related attractions. And it could put millions of dollars into the local economy. . . .

Joe stopped himself. His thoughts were taking him into unfamiliar territory. Being Mr. Been-There-Done-That had always been his stock in trade. Nothing got him too excited. And yet here he was, thinking about this barbecue museum the same way he imagined Calvin Cameron did.

Joe couldn't help himself. He liked Dawn, he was willing to admit that. And she liked this project, for whatever reason. So, by extension, he wanted to like the project and help it succeed. And in the process, he naturally hoped to launch a romance with the next Bond girl. He was, after all, a man of modest wants.

At the same time, Joe knew he couldn't use his usual barroom strategy of walking up to her and asking for her phone number. If she said no, well, that would sting a lot more than being turned down by one of the waitresses at Heck's. That's why Joe needed this time in the canoe. He had to come up with a plan.

Joe propelled his canoe through the harbor. It was easier to think on the water, that was for sure. Not like at the office, with phones ringing and bosses asking stupid questions or trying to look over his shoulder while he surfed the Internet.

God, he loved it out here, even if the Wolf River Harbor was just an inlet from the Mississippi, even if it carried the stench left by the polluted runoff from every town along the river's watershed between here and Minnesota. This was his refuge. And a bad day on the water still beat a good day at the office every time.

But what to do about Dawn? Should he suggest meeting with her to talk about publicity for the Barbecue Hall of Fame project? Lunch, perhaps? Or could that be misinterpreted as too professional? For a change, Joe wanted to seem serious. But at the same time, he didn't want Dawn to get the impression he was interested in her only for that reason. But what if she was interested in him only for that reason?

The whole situation was enough to keep Joe's head spinning. He was so lost in his thoughts that he approached the northern end of the harbor before he realized it.

He hadn't even noticed the stately homes sitting high on the west bank, or the three massive loading docks on the east bank. That part of the Wolf River Harbor offered one of the sharpest contrasts in a city of sharp contrasts. The homes were among the most expensive and exclusive in the city, the first part of downtown to become thoroughly and completely gentrified. But the loading docks, just a few hundred yards away, were still part of the city's gritty industrial district, places where gravel and other materials were loaded on barges for trips up and down the Mississippi.

This far north, however, the shore of the harbor remained in a semi-natural state, dense stands of trees blocking the view of any man-made structures on either bank. It wasn't unusual to see ducks or herons along the shore. And so long as no ski boats were roaring around, the northern end of the harbor was tranquil.

Joe never quite got the ski-boat thing. It wasn't unusual to see the boats in the harbor during summer, but Joe wondered how many of the people out skiing were aware that the city's North Sewage Treatment Plant emptied into the Mississippi just north of the Wolf River. Which meant the harbor, even at its northern end, collected the seepage of human waste produced by a city of 660,000. Joe didn't understand why people would willingly water-ski in what amounted to a giant toilet bowl—but hey, to each his own.

In any case, no ski boats were on the water this day. No one was around to spoil Joe's daydreaming. He reflected on the good and bad of his previous relationships with women. Could anything he had learned help him here? Nothing sprang to mind. Joe realized that mistakes were difficult to see until he had already made them.

After sitting in the canoe for what seemed an interminable

time, Joe finally got frustrated. Looking at his surroundings, he was struck again by an old houseboat sitting on the eastern bank. It had been there as long as Joe had been canoeing the harbor. In fact, judging by the boat's condition, Joe assumed it had probably been abandoned for at least twenty years.

Who has the money to just leave a boat behind? Joe thought. Sure, a couple of rusting barges were along the shore farther south. But Joe assumed those were owned by businesses. After they outlived their usefulness, it was probably cost effective to just let them sit there and deteriorate away to nothing—even if it added to the visual blight.

But a houseboat? That was different. Didn't the owner want to resell the thing to get some of his money back? Was it such a wreck that no one wanted to buy it? Joe had seen that houseboat dozens of times and had always avoided it because it looked so ratty. But now he was dying to get a closer look.

He paddled the canoe as near to it as he could. The water in the harbor was relatively low, so the houseboat was completely on dry land. Joe reached out to grab a corner of it to anchor his canoe. He was sitting low in the water and had to look up to see the deck.

And as he did so, he saw a pair of arms pointing a crossbow down in his direction.

"Howdy, stranger," a voice from above said. "Permission to come aboard denied."

Chapter 8

Joe's mind raced. Who was this nut with the crossbow? And was he really prepared to use it?

Joe couldn't afford to take chances. He reached with his right hand under the gunwale of his canoe. Using double-stick tape and Velcro, he had attached a small can of Mace there.

If he ever needed to use the Mace, Joe had always thought it would be on one of his trips up the Wolf River, not in the harbor. Although the Wolf River cut through the heart of Memphis, it was surrounded by heavily wooded bottom land not even the most determined developer could hope to penetrate. The lack of development made the bottom land a popular spot for fishing, four-wheeling, and all manner of criminal activity.

Joe kept the Mace on hand because he knew there was always a chance he would paddle around a bend just in time to witness gang members disposing of one of their rivals. Mace probably wasn't the best weapon for that type of situation, Joe realized. He kept it hidden on the canoe just so he wouldn't feel completely empty-handed.

Now, facing an armed assailant, he realized what a silly choice Mace was. Joe had never liked guns, but a gun would have been better in this situation. Much better. Even so, Joe wasn't going to get impaled by a medieval weapon without putting up a fight.

Moving as fluidly as he could, Joe whipped out the Mace and aimed it at the bearded, weathered face of the man standing over him on the deck of the old houseboat.

"Oh, you have got to be joking," the man said, barely stifling a laugh.

"I don't think so," Joe said, hoping his voice didn't waver too much.

"So, let's think this through," the grizzled madman said. "You spray me, I shoot you. I wash out my eyes and get better, you end up feeding the catfish."

"Well, that's one possibility," Joe admitted. "But you know, it's not easy to hit a moving target with a crossbow bolt. And by comparison, it's not hard to hit someone with a cloud of spray. Now, since that looks like a Barnett crossbow, chances are something's going to go wrong with it the first time you fire it. The string will fray, the bow will splinter, whatever. Barnett is British. It's a lot like a Jaguar, MG, Triumph, or any other British-made sports car in that it looks good but doesn't work so well. And even if the crossbow doesn't break, you'll have a hard time reloading it with your eyes full of Mace."

"Well, I'm not so sure I agree that's a likely scenario," the man said. "But I have to admit, I like your spunk. And you seem to know a little something about crossbows."

"I had a Barnett crossbow when I was in high school," Joe said, starting to think for the first time that he might be able to escape this encounter without being run through with a sharpened steel rod. "I used to love using it for target practice. Once, after I wrecked my '72 Chevelle and had to replace the doors, I put one of the old doors out in a field to see if the crossbow could shoot through it."

"I bet I know how that turned out," the man said. "At thirty feet or less, that crossbow put another hole or two in the Chevelle."

"It did."

"Isn't it dumb the way people in the movies always hide behind car doors in shootouts?" the man said, seeming to forget that he and Joe still had weapons aimed at each other. "If a Barnett crossbow can shoot through one of those hulking car doors from the seventies, no way a door on one of these modern tin cans would be any protection against a bullet. At least, I wouldn't want to bet my life it would."

"So, do you think maybe we can put our weapons down?" Joe ventured. "I didn't mean to cause you any harm. I've just been out here canoeing many times and seen this old houseboat. I always wanted to check it out."

"Yeah, I think I've seen you out here before," the man said, lowering the crossbow. "I wasn't really planning to shoot you. I just like my privacy, so I use the crossbow to scare people away. Usually."

"Do you live on this boat?" Joe asked, dropping the Mace toward his lap.

"I do," the man said. "I know it doesn't look like much, but I don't need much. You want to come aboard and have a look around?"

Joe figured if the crazy hillbilly was going to kill him, he would have done it already. What the heck? "Sure. By the way, my name's Joe Miller."

Joe tossed the man a rope tied to the bow of his canoe. The man caught the line and tied it off against one of the houseboat's rusty railings.

"Pleased to meet you, Joe," the man said as he helped Joe scramble onto the deck.

"So, do you have a name?" Joe asked after waiting a few seconds for the man to offer one.

The man smirked, for some reason thinking that was funny. "My name's Barry," he said. "Just call me Backwater Barry. Let me give you the nickel tour of this old boat, which I call Florence. And no, I never dated or knocked up or was related in any way to a woman named Florence. That name just came to me one day."

From up close, Joe could see that Backwater Barry wasn't much older than he was. Maybe ten years at the most. Of course, Backwater Barry had the full-on scruffy beard and matted hair of a homeless person, but his eyes were bright blue, not bloodshot as Joe would have expected.

And there was something about him. Backwater Barry didn't carry himself the way most homeless people did. Joe couldn't quite put his finger on it, but his new friend looked different somehow. Familiar, even, although that didn't fit because Joe wasn't acquainted with anyone in the homeless community in Memphis.

As promised, Backwater Barry gave Joe a quick tour of the houseboat's interior. It wasn't much to look at. The cabin was furnished with only a small metal card table, a lantern, and three metal lawn chairs that appeared as rusty as the railing on the boat's deck. Backwater Barry apparently slept on a ratty-looking mattress laid out in a corner of the galley. Plastic plates, silverware, and pots and pans were piled in the sink. And looking oddly out of place was a shiny new filing cabinet against the wall opposite the stairs leading up to the deck.

Backwater Barry reached into a weathered cooler on the floor and pulled out two Miller Lites. "Like a beer?" he asked Joe.

"Definitely," Joe said. The beer was actually quite cold. Looking down, Joe noticed the cooler was well stocked with ice. "Hey, man, do you mind if I ask you a question?"

"I don't mind if you ask," Backwater Barry said. "But I may or may not be able to give you an answer."

"Fair enough," Joe said. "I'm wondering how you managed to get ice out here. I mean, this boat doesn't look like it's rigged with a generator. And for that matter, where'd you get the beer? Not that I'm ungrateful or anything."

Backwater Barry laughed. "Hey, I like to rough it, but I'm not a complete savage. Some of the kids who fish along the east bank come to see me. I get them to buy me a few groceries and ice from a sundry store a few blocks from here."

"And you pay them to do that?" Joe asked cautiously. He didn't know a delicate way to ask what he wanted to ask.

"Hell, yeah, I've got to pay them," Backwater Barry said. "But truth be told, there are only a couple of 'em I trust. With some of those kids, if you give 'em twenty bucks, you'll never see 'em again. Which, I have to admit, isn't always a bad thing."

"And, um, this money you have . . ."

"Let's put it this way," Backwater Barry said. "I have a reliable source of income."

"And that would be?"

Backwater Barry's expression turned serious for the first time since he aimed his crossbow at Joe's face. "Let's talk about something else," he said after an awkward pause. "Do you like to fish?

I do. I know, I know, the fish in the harbor aren't fit to eat. But I love the sport of it. And it saves me a little money on groceries when they're hitting."

Joe thought fishing was one of the most boring pastimes mankind had ever invented, but he also sensed this was an opportunity to turn the conversation in a direction that would be more comfortable for both of them. So he asked Backwater Barry a few questions about bait and fishing techniques just to pass the time.

As they started their second beers, Backwater Barry shifted the conversation back to Joe. "So, Joe, what do you do for a living, as folks like to say?"

"Well," Joe said, pausing to take a strong pull on his beer, "I'm in public relations."

"Public relations?" Backwater Barry laughed. "Oh, man. I should just give you the rest of the beers in that cooler and let you drown your sorrows."

Suddenly, if not for the first time, Joe was ashamed of his profession. But it was strange to feel insecure while talking to a bum.

"Yeah, yeah, I know," Joe said. "I'm a complete sellout."

"Well, maybe not complete," Backwater Barry said. "I guess it depends on who your clients are. Who do you work for?"

"One of the big firms downtown," Joe said, doubting Backwater Barry would recognize the name if he mentioned it.

"Yeah, okay, but who does your firm represent?"

"Right now, we're working on a project for the mayor," Joe said. "He wants to build a Barbecue Hall of Fame on some land just north of Auction Avenue. A couple of miles down on the east side of the harbor."

"Oh, I know where that is," Backwater Barry said. "That's interesting to hear."

"Are you a big fan of barbecue?"

"I usually don't turn it down," Backwater Barry admitted. "But that's not what I meant. For years, nothing much has happened on the east side of the harbor. Just a bunch of old gravel-crushing operations and such. The kind of businesses that decide they need to modernize their facilities every hundred years or so."

Backwater Barry really was different. Joe didn't think most homeless people spent time studying the business practices of companies on the industrial waterfront. For that matter, he didn't think many homeless people used words like *modernize* either.

"Yeah, the east side looks pretty decrepit," Joe said. "At least I've always thought so while I've been out here canoeing. Particularly compared to all the upscale housing on the west side. But what's strange about that?"

"Well, before all those houses started shooting up on Mud Island in the mid- to late eighties, surveyors were crawling all over the place on the west bank. Now, I'm seeing the same thing on the east side of the harbor, from this area at the north end all the way down to that property at Auction Avenue."

"Really?"

"Really," Backwater Barry said. "Since I'm on the harbor all the time, not much happens around here that I don't know about. But what's funny is that the surveyors don't work for any of those companies with docking facilities along the waterfront. At least I don't think they do."

"Why not?" Joe was definitely more interested in hearing about this than talking about fishing.

"Well, they were all casually dressed, not in uniforms or anything," Backwater Barry said. "And they were trying to be low-key about what they were doing. They were always looking around to see if anyone was watching. They couldn't see me on the houseboat, of course, but I saw them well enough. They would work one small area along the bank, disappear for a day or two, then work another area farther down. I watched 'em for a couple of weeks, and they must have covered about three miles of waterfront."

"So? Anything suspicious about that?" Joe asked.

"Well, a couple of things," Backwater Barry said. "For one, if they were working for a gravel operation, they wouldn't have needed to survey the whole waterfront. Those places are all independently owned. Nobody owns that whole chunk of land. Also, if this was just a routine expansion of one of those businesses, I'm guessing *The Avalanche* would have written about it by now. Has it?"

"No," Joe said. "Maybe it doesn't know, though."

"Maybe somebody doesn't want the media to know," Backwater Barry said. "And one other thing makes me suspicious, particularly since you told me about the Barbecue Hall of Fame."

"What's that?" Joe said. "I don't see a connection between Mayor Pigg's project and some surveying work on these industrial properties."

"I wouldn't either," Backwater Barry said, taking a last pull on his beer and tossing it into a corner of the galley covered with crumpled cans. "But one day, I saw two guys from a surveying crew getting into their truck after they were done taking measurements. And that truck had a City of Memphis logo on it."

Chapter 9

J oe closed his eyes, allowing the smells and sounds of Beale
Street to fill his senses. The restaurant next door was cooking
red beans and rice. The one two doors down was grilling cheeseburgers. And of course, the place directly across the street was
doing barbecue—barbecue pork nachos, as best Joe could tell.

The music was spilling into the street, too. The piano player
in one of the bars was doing a pretty fair impression of Jerry Lee
Lewis. The singer in another place was belting out the chorus of
"Mustang Sally." And a young reggae band was butchering Bob
Marley in the outdoor amphitheater on the corner. All those
sounds blended with the din of tourists laughing and talking as
they strolled the cobblestone street.

Joe breathed deeply and took a sip of his double-Stoli screw-
driver. He opened his eyes and took in the scene. The crowds
were beginning to pick up as midnight approached. Up and down

Beale, the glare of neon juke-joint signs illuminated a hundred mini-dramas playing out. Members of a bachelorette party cutting loose. Frat boys trying to score phone numbers from every woman they passed. Day-trippers from Arkansas and Mississippi taking in the wonders of big-city life.

And of course, there was Joe's friend Scott, doing his usual thing. He was dressed in his Elvis outfit, complete with hideous makeup. Joe couldn't imagine anyone with self-respect putting on a getup like that to go to work.

Scott was a few yards away, working through the last couple verses of "Suspicious Minds" for three pretty young women from Amsterdam. When the song ended, they wanted to pose for photos with Elvis—or at least the closest they could get more than thirty years after his death. All three planted long, sloppy kisses on Scott before taking their yard-long frozen margaritas and heading down the street in the general direction of Carnivore Charlie's.

Okay, maybe Joe was looking at Scott's situation all wrong. For a guy with no career ambition, Scott Paulk had stumbled into a pretty sweet gig with this Elvis business.

After pausing to wave and watch approvingly as his friends from Holland disappeared into the crowd, Scott walked to the outdoor tiki bar Joe was leaning against.

"Now, give this story to me again," Scott said. "You went on a canoe trip, where you ran into a homeless dude who calls himself Backwater Barry and nearly kills you with a medieval weapon. And then this guy, who lives on a wrecked boat at the end of the harbor, tells you he thinks the mayor might be part of some sinister conspiracy. And you believe him?"

"As a matter of fact, smart ass, I do," Joe replied. He wished he'd waited to tell Scott the story when neither of them had been drinking. But those opportunities were few and far between.

"And exactly how many of those did you have before you went on this canoe trip?" Scott said, gesturing to Joe's drink.

"None," Joe shot back. "You know I couldn't make something like that up. I'm not that creative."

"No, I'll be the first to admit that," Scott said. "But it all sounds a little crazy, bro."

"Yeah, maybe a little," Joe admitted. "But is it really that far-fetched? Weren't you just warning me the other day about how I need to watch my back around Mayor Pigg?"

"That's not what I meant," Scott said. "Pete Pigg can be a sneaky son of a bitch, particularly if you've got something he wants. But the guy grills barbecue for a living. And now he probably shakes down developers and city contractors. But why would he be interested in the east side of the Wolf River Harbor? That's not exactly a garden spot, you know. It's been a hard-core industrial area for as long as I can remember. Heck, it's been hard-core industrial since the real Elvis was alive."

"I know, I know. But I happen to believe this guy."

"And why is that?"

"Well, for one thing, I can't see anything he'd possibly gain from making up a story like that."

"Shoot," Scott said, gesturing for the bartender to bring him a drink. "He's a crazy old man who lives in a swamp next to a stinky old harbor. He probably doesn't have a whole lot of entertainment options. Yanking your chain was probably the highlight of his week."

"Why would anyone make up a story about something like that?" Joe asked.

"Why not? You told him you're working for the mayor, right? Maybe he just wanted to get a rise out of you. To see your eyes bug out if he told you something wild about the big man. Probably made him feel important."

"No, I don't think so. This guy wasn't your run-of-the-mill wino. There was something different about him."

"Yeah, your average wino doesn't run around shoving crossbows into people's faces. Although they'd probably make more money panhandling if they did."

At that point, a young guy wearing an Arkansas State University T-shirt interrupted their conversation. He was maybe twenty, with shaggy blond hair parted to cover his entire forehead right down to the eyebrows. It was obvious from his breath and his bloodshot eyes that he had been sampling the best of what Beale Street had to offer.

"'Scuse me, Elvis," the kid said to Scott, not even acknowledging Joe's presence. "My friends and I were hopin' you could do us a favor."

"What can Elvis do for you, brotha?" Scott said, slipping into his character voice.

"Well, see, the deal is, we've got a fraternity pledge with us," the kid said, nodding toward his friends standing a few yards away. One of them was a skinny kid dressed in drag who didn't look old enough to be out of high school. "We need you to sing 'Love Me Tender' to him while we film it on our camcorder. Then we gotta post it on YouTube."

"Elvis may not be in a 'Love Me Tender' mood," Scott said, looking at the pledge, who appeared to be adjusting his brassiere.

"Oh, you gotta do it, man," the frat boy said. "I'll give you ten bucks. Or twenty, if you kiss him when it's over."

Joe could tell by the look on Scott's face what was about to happen.

"Well, you know," Scott said in his Elvis voice, "I appreciate that you fellas from Jonesboro, Arkansas, have come all the way to Memphis to learn about the King. But you gotta learn more about the music of the Mid-South before I give you a personal performance. Have you ever heard of Robert Johnson?"

"Robert Johnson, sure," the frat boy said. "I've seen him on that old show *Miami Vice*."

"Not quite, young fella, not quite," Scott said. "I'm gonna give you one more chance. A bonus round, if you will. Does the name Son House mean anything to you?"

"Whose house?" the frat boy asked.

"That's it," Scott said, a trace of anger creeping into his voice. "Hit the road, partner."

The frat boy blinked but said nothing, trying to process what the faux Elvis had said.

"You heard me," Scott said. "Get lost, loser."

The message finally made its way to the frat boy's brain. "Go to hell, jackass," he said as he turned back toward his friends. "You and your gay lover."

So he had seen Joe standing there after all. Scott and Joe watched for a few seconds as the Arkansas State kids made their way unsteadily down Beale Street.

"Now," Scott said, using his normal voice again, "what is it we were talking about?"

"Backwater Barry," Joe said. "And I know what you'll say about this, but I'm not so sure he's really a wino."

"Now, I'm starting to worry about you," Scott said with a laugh. "Maybe you're the wino. How many of those things have you had?"

"Not enough to dull the pain of a conversation with you," Joe said. "I don't see why you're having such a hard time believing this."

"Well, break it down, Joe. The guy says he saw a city logo on a truck? How far away was the truck parked? If he's slinking around on a houseboat, I doubt he could see all the way to the top of the ridge. And how would he know that logo was the city seal? I mean, even if he's Super Wino, probably eight out of ten Memphibians don't know what the city seal looks like."

"The correct term is Memphians," Joe said. "And eight out of ten Memphians probably don't know that Pete Pigg is their city's mayor."

"I'm still having trouble coming to grips with that myself," Scott said. "But even if you think this guy is reliable, I don't know how he could have seen what he said he saw and know what he claims to know."

"So what do you want to do, Scott, play Twenty Questions with him?"

"As a matter of fact, I would," Scott replied. "Do you think we could get out there to see him without him shooting one or both of us with a crossbow bolt?"

"Maybe," Joe said. "But I don't see the point. Last I checked, you don't care about politics. So why do you care what the mayor is or isn't up to?"

"Oh, I don't know," Scott said. "Maybe I care because I spent a bunch of time in his saloon and I'd like to know what he's branching into these days. Or maybe I just want to go out there and see this guy for myself so I'll know you weren't jerking my chain with a crazy story."

"Look, if you want to go, we'll go," Joe said.

"Excellent," Scott said, pausing to sip the mint julep the

bartender had finally brought him. "You've been bugging me for years to get out in that canoe. So this'll give us a reason to do it."

And with that, Scott sized up the crowd ambling up and down Beale Street. His eyes fixated on a fat couple wearing sandals, cargo shorts, T-shirts, and floppy sun hats. Tourists. Maybe big-tipping tourists. His target audience.

Scott knocked back most of his drink, then set the glass on the bar and moved toward the tourists, humming the first few bars of "All Shook Up" to get their attention.

Joe watched him go. Although he'd known Scott for years, he never could quite figure him out.

Chapter 10

Mayor Pete Pigg was having a bad week.

From the calls Pigg was getting about the Barbecue Hall of Fame project, it was obvious that city council chairman Waldo Jefferson had been bragging to his sleazy buddies about their little arrangement. And that meant Mayor Pigg had been forced to cut deals with more politicians when he should have been spending his time figuring out how he could maximize his own self-interest.

He had promised to campaign for one city councilman who was expecting a tough reelection battle against a feisty preacher whose Sunday sermons drew decent ratings on a local TV channel. He had agreed to offer his political backing for a thousand-home subdivision in the Cordova neighborhood that was officially under wraps but soon would be introduced by a developer who also happened to be chairman of the city's planning commission.

He'd signed off on travel expenses for another planning commissioner who desperately wanted to learn more about a new type of water-resistant asphalt that was being discussed, conveniently enough, at a ten-day seminar in arid Las Vegas. And he'd agreed to give another councilman's idiot niece a job answering phones at the Memphis Light, Gas and Water customer service center.

Actually, maybe the idiot niece might work out okay. She wasn't bad looking and appeared to be the sort who wouldn't mind sleeping with the city's top elected official if that's what it took to get ahead in her career. Even with that small consolation, Pigg was so tired of working the phones that his blood pressure spiked when he heard his "Walking in Memphis" ring tone for the twelfth time that morning.

"'Lo!" Pigg barked into the phone.

"Boss, it's Cedric," the Pigg Pen manager said.

"Yeah?" Pigg was irritated. And since Cedric worked for him, he didn't have to conceal his irritation the way he so often did as mayor. No need to play diplomat with the hired help.

"Boss, I got more bad news," Cedric said hesitantly. Those were words he absolutely hated saying to Pigg.

"Kinda figured that," Pigg said. "I've got a whole big city to run, but I know you've always got issues over there at the restaurant. So what drama are we dealing with now? Did someone forget to clean out the bone buckets and a twelve-foot-high pile of chewed-up pork ribs collapsed onto some tourist? Is one of the Pigglettes trying to hold back our cut of her tip money? Are you sleeping with one of the Pigglettes and now you've got an STD that's going to require you to miss work? Please don't tell me it's that."

"No, boss, no," Cedric said. "It's just that Carnivore Charlie's has another new promotion. And it's a good one."

"Aw, Cedric, why do you waste my time with this stuff?" The mayor was close to hanging up so he could finish working through his payola checklist for the Barbecue Hall of Fame. "How good can it be, really?"

"Well, pretty good, sir. You know his waitresses, the Beefeaters? The girls he hired when the district attorney closed down the strip clubs? Well, he's got them all wearing these really low-cut outfits."

"Cedric..."

"No, no, not like the ones they've been wearing," Cedric continued. "I mean, some of them were wearing more when they were pole-dancing than they are now while they're screwing up drink orders. But it's not just that. Your friend, the owner—"

"Don't say his name, Cedric," Pigg growled.

"Well, anyway, his new promotion is having the Beefeaters go around to every table after customers finish eating. And they take some wet naps and personally wash the male customers' fingers, right there at the table. The female customers, too, if they act like they're into that sort of thing. They call it 'taking care of the juices,' or something like that."

Pigg groaned. He had to admit that his chief business rival, Nick Nelson, knew his stuff. "So what's the damage?" he asked.

"Well, sir, they started about a week ago, and our business has been off 40 percent since then," Cedric said.

"Forty percent!" Pigg tried to spring from his chair and nearly fell to the floor. "And this started a week ago? Why didn't you tell me sooner?"

"Well, you know we had a guy spying for us, pretending to be a customer," Cedric said. "He used to hang out over there, then come to our place and tell us what was what in exchange for a few free drinks. After Carnivore Charlie's started that wet nap promotion, the guy stopped coming to our place. We sent one of our dishwashers to check it out, and our guy—our ex-guy—was sitting there with a stupid expression while some Asian hottie scrubbed his hands. And I wouldn't be surprised if he hadn't even eaten anything sticky."

"Okay, okay, enough," Pigg said. "I don't have time to deal with this now, Cedric. Maybe we can come up with sumpin, like havin' the Pigglettes tuck customers' napkins in when they sit down."

"That's a good idea," Cedric said. "You wanna give that a try?"

"Well, maybe," Pigg said. "You know how our customers are. Most are the type who go to the barbershop hopin' the girl who cuts their hair will lean in too close and brush 'em with her udders—pervs, in other words. So I think this would fly. I've just got to figure out if any of the Pigglettes would file a sexual harassment lawsuit if we asked 'em to do the napkin-tucking thing. Like that Kati girl."

"Actually, Kati quit and went to work for Carnivore Charlie's yesterday."

Pigg growled under his breath. "Okay, maybe Kristi, then. The point is, I can't be makin' decisions like this while I'm rushed. And believe it or not, Cedric, I wasn't doin' my nails when you called." He clicked off the phone in disgust.

Pigg jumped when the intercom buzzed a few seconds later. "What now?" he bellowed into the speaker.

"A man is here to see you, sir," the disembodied voice of his secretary replied. "Bobby Shotwell Jr. He says he's with the Union of Trade Unions."

Pigg groaned and reached into his desk drawer for a bottle of Pepto-Bismol.

"Sir? Sir?"

"Yeah, yeah, send him in," Pigg said with a loud sigh.

Bobby Shotwell Jr. burst through the door less than five seconds later. He was a young man with big dimples and sandy brown hair, maybe twenty-five or thirty at most, boyishly handsome and strikingly dressed in a metallic blue suit made of some kind of material that shimmered under the office's fluorescent lights.

"Mayor Pigg! How good to see you this fine day!" Shotwell said, thrusting his hand forward.

Shotwell's daddy had been big in local political circles, serving as Shelby County's sheriff for many years. Bobby Shotwell Sr. had long since retired, allegedly with a fat wad of bribe money, and his son fancied himself the heir to the old man's political clout—for no reason people around Memphis could figure out. As far as anyone knew, Bobby Shotwell Jr. had never held a real job of any kind. But he always showed up whenever a major government contract was in the works, playing the angles for any stray consulting money that might be floating around.

"Help you, Mr. Shotwell?" Pigg said, ignoring the outstretched hand.

"Mayor Pigg, as you may know, the Union of Trade Unions Local 317 has retained my services as a government liaison."

"Izzat so?"

"Indeed it is," Shotwell said. "And my client has asked me to share its concerns about the Barbecue Hall of Fame."

"Concerns?" Pigg said. "And what would those be?"

"Well, sir, as you know, the Union of Trade Unions is an umbrella organization for all the construction unions in the area—the carpenters' union, the plumbers' union, the pipe fitters union—"

"Yeah, let's skip this part," Pigg said. "I know what the Union of Trade Unions is. As you might remember, I've been runnin' a restaurant and bar in this town since before you were born. And I think I know why you're here. So let's just get to the point, okay?"

"The point?" Shotwell said. "Well, here it is. The Union of Trade Unions has heard that the city of Memphis might be thinking about using non-union labor on this Barbecue Hall of Fame to save money. My client thinks that would be a bad idea."

"Your client thinks savin' the taxpayers of Memphis some money is a bad idea?"

"Well, now, Mayor Pigg," Shotwell said, "my father was a public servant in this town for many years, so I think I understand how well public servants take care of the taxpayers' money."

Shotwell actually paused to wink. It was almost too much for Pigg. This little weasel really thought he was a player.

"Anyway, Mr. Mayor," Shotwell continued, "you know there are other concerns besides getting a project done at the lowest possible cost. Like quality. Non-union workers don't give you that guarantee of quality. Do you think tourists are going to be able to enjoy barbecue exhibits if they're in a building with a leaky roof or an air-conditioning system that doesn't work properly? We had eleven days with high temperatures of one hundred or above last summer. To guarantee quality, you need properly certified union workers. And to guarantee you'll have those workers, you need a project labor agreement. So I've taken the liberty of preparing one for you."

With a flourish, Shotwell pulled a folded document from his suit-jacket pocket and placed it on the mayor's desk. He stood expectantly as Mayor Pigg glanced down at the paper. Pigg's expression was about the same as if Shotwell had presented him a pile of dog droppings.

"Project labor agreement, huh?" Pigg said. "Boy, you gotta be kiddin' me. You really think I'm signin' that?"

"Well, I expect you'll want your city attorney to look it over first, but yes, I do, Mr. Mayor." Shotwell was working hard to keep his voice calm and level.

"And let's suppose I don't," Pigg said. "What would you say about that?"

"Well, Mr. Mayor, I'd say you might be taking my client's political clout too lightly. The Union of Trade Unions has over three thousand members in the Mid-South. And most of them are what you might call politically active. Now, Mr. Mayor, those folks would be good people to have on your side when it comes time for your reelection. They could carry signs for you, knock on doors, raise money . . . or not. And even if you don't think you need the Union of Trade Unions to get another term, some of the city council members might not be quite so sure of themselves. And that means, God forbid, that they might hold up approval for the Barbecue Hall of Fame. Which I don't want to happen, and I know you don't want to happen."

Shotwell finished his speech with just a trace of a smug smile. He'd delivered his prepared lines perfectly. And he knew enough about politicians to figure he had the upper hand.

Pigg glanced at him, then snorted. "Let me tell you sumpin, boy. When you come into this office, you're playin' in the big leagues. And when you're in the big leagues, you don't want to go to the plate without a bat in your hands, if you catch my drift."

"Actually, Mr. Mayor, I'm not sure I do," Shotwell said, his smile fading.

"Well, let me 'splain it to you then," Pigg said. "I'm not the least bit worried about you, Mr. Bobby Shotwell Jr., nor am I worried about the Union of Trade Unions Local 317 or the Memphis

City Council. This project is gonna get built without any damned project labor agreement, and it's gonna be the biggest thing to hit this area since the Mississippi River first rolled through three thousand years ago."

"Well, Mr. Mayor, you're certainly a confident man."

"That I am. And I'll tell you another thing I'm confident about. You're a shakedown artist, Mr. Shotwell, and I don't like shakedown artists. 'Specially not ones breathin' up the air in my office. So get the hell outta here. And don't try to make trouble for me, or I'll see to it that you won't work as a 'government liaison' anywhere else in this town."

Eyes bulging and sweat trickling down his forehead, Shotwell beat a hasty retreat.

Before the door could swing closed behind Bobby Shotwell Jr., a young Hispanic man stepped into the mayor's office. He was short, perhaps five-foot-eight, with a broad but handsome face and slicked-back hair. He wore a gold bracelet around his left wrist and a gold chain around his neck. He was dressed in black designer jeans and a pink silk shirt unbuttoned halfway to his navel. Across his chest was a large tattoo of a naked woman diving downward above the inscription, "Dive Into the Pleasure Zone."

"Help you?" Pigg said as he watched the young man take a seat opposite him.

"Maybe," the man said, his voice carrying no trace of the accent Pigg expected. "My name is Pedro Suarez. I've come to talk to you about your Barbecue Hall of Fame."

"Well, I appreciate your initiative, boy, but we're probably a few months from actually startin' construction. Maybe we can get you on with one of the work crews then."

"I'm not interested in a construction job," Pedro Suarez said.

By now, Pigg's nostrils were filled with the overpowering scent of his visitor's cologne.

"You're not?" Pigg said. "You're a Messican, aren't ya?"

"Mexican-American, actually," Suarez said coolly. "And this may come as a surprise, but we don't all work in construction, Mayor Pigg."

"So what are ya here for, then? I don't have time to spend jaw-bonin' with somebody who didn't make an appointment."

"I have a feeling you'll be interested in what I have to say," Suarez said. "I'm the business manager for Augustine Eldridge."

"So?" That name sounded vaguely familiar, although Pigg couldn't quite place it.

"Mr. Eldridge owns some property that I believe you have expressed an interest in. On the northwest corner of Auction and Front, directly across from The Pyramid."

"Oh," Pigg said. It took a moment for the information to sink in.

"And I should inform you that Mr. Eldridge already has plans for that particular piece of property. As you may know, he's a film-maker who recently moved here from California. And he's interested in converting that building into a movie studio."

Pigg snorted. "Gus Eldridge? The pornographer Gus Eldridge?"

"He prefers the term *adult filmmaker*, actually," Suarez said.

"I think you ought to know, Mr. Suarez, that a lot of folks around this town aren't real crazy about your boss movin' here. Me, I don't care one way or the other about you people makin' your dirty little movies. But you're in what they call the buckle of the Bible Belt. And if you and your boss cause problems, nobody's gonna shed any tears if I have to run you out of here."

"I would hardly describe restoring and putting a historic

downtown building back into use as causing problems. I'd think you would be grateful that Mr. Augustine wants to invest capital in Memphis."

"Okay, lissen up, smart ass," Pigg said. "There's no way you could fix up that old buildin', even if I was gonna let you. It hasn't been used in years. A good strong wind would knock it over. You'd have to spend millions."

"Well, regardless of what people in the Bible Belt might think about our profession, it is lucrative. Money is not going to be a problem."

"Well, then, let me tell you that not havin' the mayor on your side is gonna be a big problem. You think you can get that dump rezoned without my help?"

"Actually, we've done quite a bit of research, and a movie studio would be allowed under the existing commercial zoning. We're well within our rights to develop that property."

"Rights? You're tellin' me about rights? I don't know if you read the letterin' on my office door when you came in, but I'm the mayor of the city of Memphis. If I want that property—and I do—I can use eminent domain to claim it. You ever hear 'bout eminent domain down in Tijuana, Mr. Suarez?"

"I'm actually from Rosarito. It's farther down the coast. But to answer your question, Mr. Eldridge and I are familiar with the concept. In order to use the power of eminent domain to seize property, you first have to convince a judge that the government needs the land for some legitimate public purpose. And under Tennessee law, it's doubtful any judge is going to see a barbecue museum as fulfilling such a purpose."

"You don't know much about judges around here, boy. When properly motivated, some of 'em have been known to come up with creative interpretations of the law, if you know what I mean."

"I do know what you mean. And Mr. Eldridge is capable of providing that kind of motivation, too, if necessary. And even if he loses, he can appeal to a higher court. Mr. Eldridge's lawyers are resourceful. They can keep a case tied up for years."

"Listen, you miserable beaner, you don't want a fight with me."

"No, Mayor Pigg, we don't. So Mr. Eldridge has come up with a solution that's mutually beneficial to his interests and yours."

"And what would that be?"

"He will sell you the property. For ten million dollars."

"*Ten million dollars?*" Pigg's blood pressure was so high that he felt his head really might explode. "*Ten million dollars?* There's no way that land is worth anywhere near that much."

"Real estate is worth what somebody is willing to pay for it. And my guess is that since you want to build this Barbecue Hall of Fame and have access to taxpayer money, you'll find it in your heart to meet our price. Thank you for your time, and have a pleasant day, Mr. Mayor."

With that, Pedro Suarez stood and padded out of the mayor's office.

Pigg sat there fuming a few seconds. He started to reach for his Pepto, then had a better idea. He pulled a pint bottle of Jack Daniel's out of his desk drawer and took a long pull.

Again the intercom buzzed, causing him to jump. Again.

"What now?" Mayor Pigg said.

"A gentleman is on the line for you, sir," his secretary replied. "A gentleman from Chicago. He said you'd be expecting his call."

Pigg took another pull of Jack and smiled. Maybe this week wasn't going to be so bad after all.

Chapter 11

The Ghetto Blazer wasn't sure he liked his new nickname.

It was beyond his control, of course. In his line of work, leaving a note suggesting a better nickname would be patently stupid. Which the Ghetto Blazer was not.

After one of the TV journalists came up with the nickname, other TV and print reporters quickly latched onto it. One station, shedding any pretense of political correctness, had even created a logo it used while reporting his exploits. The logo depicted an angry-looking man in stereotypical ghetto attire—baggy pants, a sleeveless T-shirt, and a bandanna—running with a trail of flames filling the background behind him.

The Ghetto Blazer had to admit that the logo looked kind of cool. But the name—ugh! The Ghetto Blazer? It sounded like a tricked-out version of a Chevy SUV. Or maybe some sort of fashion item. Like a member's jacket for gang-bangers.

The Ghetto Blazer smiled at the mental image. But only for a moment. Then his expression turned serious again as he focused on the task at hand. He had to stay sharp because with each of his missions, his work was becoming more risky.

The first few fires hadn't attracted much attention from the police. After all, who cared if a few ramshackle houses in the city's poorest neighborhoods went up in flames? He even varied the neighborhoods enough that the fire department's arson investigators didn't pick up a pattern until he'd struck half a dozen times.

But now, his work was drawing media attention. The TV crews, always on the lookout for dramatic footage, often led their morning newscasts with his handiwork. Which pleased the cops none too much. And made them that much more vigilant.

Plus, this was a more difficult job than usual. Not just one house, but a row of five run-down bungalows set close enough together for the Ghetto Blazer to get them all in the same night. If he was careful.

He preferred to enter his targets through side windows, which decreased his chance of being spotted. Usually, he headed out the rear door after his work was done, more in the interest of haste than anything else. The idea of scrambling out a window while fire exploded all around him never seemed like a great idea to the Ghetto Blazer.

There was also the issue of the fuel containers. He'd been using two cans for each job, but with five houses to burn, he'd need more than that.

After taking a couple of deep breaths, he crept down the alley as stealthily as he could with four fuel cans in his latex-gloved hands. He was using plastic cans now, which had the benefit of being less noisy.

He had started with metal cans for a reason. While he didn't want police or fire investigators to know who he was, it was important that they know the fires were intentionally set. A couple of charred gas cans generally removed any doubt about that.

In arson cases, insurance companies usually started their internal investigations suspecting the property owners. Which suited the Ghetto Blazer just fine—anything he could do to make life harder for those slumlords.

At this point, though, given the Ghetto Blazer's previous missions, his work couldn't be regarded as anything but arson, so leaving metal cans behind was pointless. As long as the arson investigations were done quickly, that would reduce the bureaucratic red tape concerning the properties. Or at least the Ghetto Blazer hoped it would.

He crept in the window of the middle house first. He'd watched all of the places for days, as he always did before making his move. For a while, a crackhead had been holed up in the middle house, but he hadn't shown up the past three nights. The Ghetto Blazer suspected he'd done something to get himself locked up at the Shelby County Jail. But being the careful arsonist he was, the Ghetto Blazer wanted to scope out that house first just in case.

It was empty. He quickly went about his work there, spreading enough fuel to guarantee the house would be a total loss no matter how quickly firefighters arrived. Partial damage wouldn't do.

The Ghetto Blazer repeated the process at each of the other four houses. Then he returned to the alley to retrieve the fifth can of fuel he'd brought, the one he needed to light the Molotov cocktails, which he then set into a plastic crate.

He glanced around the alley one last time and took several deep breaths. He'd have to be extra careful this time.

Drawing out a Molotov cocktail and igniting it with his lighter, he expertly tossed it through the window of the first house.

Without stopping to inspect his work, he jogged down the alley, milk crate in tow. He stopped long enough to toss another cocktail through a window of the second house, then continued toward the next.

By the time he reached the third house, the flames were starting to glow through the windows of the first two. No time to waste now.

He reached the fourth house and made another throw. Like the others, it sailed through the open window before landing on the floor in an explosion of fire and broken glass. Four for four.

His heart pounded as he reached the fifth house. By now, tongues of flame were licking through the open window of the first house. Any time now, the commotion in the surrounding neighborhood would begin.

As the Ghetto Blazer reached for the final Molotov cocktail, his heart sank. It had tipped on its side, spilling fuel all over the inside of the crate. He had no time to make another cocktail. And without one, the mission wouldn't be a complete success.

Fighting his temptation to run away with the job 80 percent done, the Ghetto Blazer improvised. He sprinted toward the final house holding the crate away from his body, hoping to avoid any fuel that might slosh over the sides.

At the edge of the window, he stuck his lighter into the crate and flicked the metal wheel. As the spark caught and fire began to fill the crate, the Ghetto Blazer quickly tossed it inside.

Then he ran with all his might as the roaring sound of fire mixed with the confused jumble of noises coming from the occupied homes across the street.

Chapter 12

It was, if nothing else, a fine day for paddling.

Joe mentioned that to his friend Scott a couple of times as they made their way toward Backwater Barry's houseboat. Joe had been trying for years to convince Scott to go canoeing with him. But Scott had put him off and put him off. Then, suddenly, Scott was interested in an excursion to meet this homeless guy.

In fact, that night on Beale Street, Scott had practically insisted on meeting Backwater Barry. Only now that they were actually on their way to see him, Scott seemed disinterested and even listless.

"Are you okay?" Joe said as they made their way north in the Wolf River Harbor.

"Yeah, man," Scott said. "Why wouldn't I be?"

"You're awful quiet this morning," Joe said.

"Well, you said the key word right there: it's morning. And in case you've forgotten, I work nights."

"Oh, I hadn't forgotten that, Hound Dog. But you're not your usual talkative self today. If you're not up for this, just say the word and we'll turn back."

Joe was halfway hoping Scott would say yes. If Scott was acting this weird, Joe wasn't exactly thrilled about taking him to see a guy with a loaded crossbow. If Scott showed his usual attitude, he and Joe might end up wearing crossbow bolts home as souvenirs.

"Oh, I'm all in," Scott said. "After the way you described this guy, there's no way I'm gonna miss out on meeting him."

"As long as you're sure."

"I'm sure."

"Hey, Scott, let me ask you something. You're not just going with me so you can mess with this guy, are you? Because I know you've got kind of a weird sense of humor. And while I've come to appreciate your strangeness over the years—many years, actually—I can pretty much tell you this guy won't. And the dude has a crossbow. You may not think he'll use it, but I've met him, so I think I know better than you do."

"Are you finished, Joe?" Scott said.

"Just tell me you're not going to do that."

"I'm not gonna do that. I just want to meet him. He sounds like an interesting guy. And you know how much I love interesting life experiences."

"I do, I really do. I just don't want to wind up like the sheriff of Nottingham at the end of some Robin Hood movie, okay?"

"Understood. Thanks for the lecture on personal behavior. Now, please shut up and let me row my end of this boat in peace."

So Joe did. And within a few minutes, they were within sight of Backwater Barry's houseboat.

Backwater Barry wasn't in view as Joe steered the canoe close. Then again, he hadn't been in view last time. Joe could only hope

Backwater Barry would recognize him. Preferably before he started shooting.

"Yo, Barry, it's Joe Miller," Joe called. "Do you remember me?"

"Of course I remember," Backwater Barry said as he popped out the cabin door. Joe was relieved because he appeared to be unarmed. "Who do you have with you there?"

"This is my friend Scott Paulk," Joe said, hooking his finger toward his buddy as they climbed aboard.

"How close of a friend?" Backwater Barry asked, a frown creeping across his face.

"Not in the carnal sense," Scott said.

"Funny guy, huh?" Backwater Barry said. "Seriously, Joe, how well do you know this guy? I know you're cool and all, but I don't let just anybody up here on this boat to rap with me."

"Oh, yeah, this looks like a real exclusive cruise ship," Scott said. "If I'd known, I could have worn my black tuxedo, white gloves, and monocle."

"Scott, please," Joe said. He was trying to head off trouble. Too late, it seemed. Backwater Barry took a step toward Scott, scowling and clenching his fists.

"Monocle, huh?" Backwater Barry said. "Well, it would be easier to hold a monocle in place if I popped you one in the eye."

Scott had never been one to back down from a brawl. He moved toward Backwater Barry, his hands open but his arms tensed for action. Scott and Backwater Barry stood about three feet apart now.

"Popped me one in the eye?" Scott said. "That's a clever comeback for a homeless guy. Speaking of which, homeless guys are usually the ones who end up on the wrong end of a beat-down, just so you know."

Joe stood by, fidgeting. If Scott wanted to fight a bum, he would fight a bum. There would be no talking him out of it. At the appropriate moment, Joe would just have to step in and try to pull them apart before either Scott or the bum got too badly hurt. Hopefully, Backwater Barry wasn't carrying a knife.

"Well, Mr. Scott Paulk, in case you hadn't noticed, I live on this boat," Backwater Barry said. He and Scott were almost nose to nose now. "So, technically, I'm not homeless, now, am I? And as far as beat-downs go, we'll see who winds up on which end of what."

Scott started to reply, then stopped short. A look of surprise passed across his face as he studied Backwater Barry's features up close.

"Wait a minute," Scott said. "You look really familiar. I think I know you."

"Doubt it," Backwater Barry said. "I try to steer clear of the queer bars in Midtown."

"No, man, ease up for a second," Scott said. "I've got it now. You're Barry Brett, aren't you?"

Now, it was Backwater Barry's turn to be surprised. "You must be thinking of somebody else," he said unconvincingly after a pause.

"Don't think so," Scott said. "I didn't recognize you at first because of that street look you're cultivating."

Backwater Barry finally broke the tension with a laugh. "You know, for a guy who looks like a Beale Street bum himself, you seem to know a bit about our fair city," he said.

"And for somebody who used to be such a big wheel, you sure do a good job impersonating a river rat," Scott replied.

Joe sidled up to Scott, looking confused. "Who's Barry Brett?"

"Come inside and have a beer with me and I'll tell you," Barry Brett said.

And so Joe and Scott did.

Barry Brett was the descendant of one of the half-dozen families that founded Memphis. His family started out as traders, moving animal pelts, dried meat, and other items up and down the Mississippi River on flatboats. As generations passed and technology advanced, the Brett family remained in the distribution business—by train, truck, and eventually airplane. Memphis was perfect for a distribution business, positioned at the confluence of the continent's longest river, two interstate highways, and the nation's busiest cargo airport. BrettCo Inc. grew into a multi-billion-dollar enterprise.

But even though his family had plenty of money, Barry was determined to make his own way in the world. He graduated with honors from White Station High School and Rhodes College, then decided to invest some of his inheritance in a new business called DUI Busters. It was a chain of liquor stores with a twist—like most pizza places, it offered delivery service. The concept caught fire, leading to franchises across the country.

As DUI Busters branched into sketchy neighborhoods, security concerns arose. But Barry Brett was an innovator. He came up with the idea of a "hat cam"—a tiny video recorder that fit into the top of his delivery drivers' caps. The recorders transmitted video wirelessly back to the drivers' vehicles. Which meant that, more often than not, robberies of DUI Busters delivery people led to convictions, thanks to the hat cams.

The innovation helped DUI Busters hire and keep delivery drivers. And Barry patented it and sold to other delivery businesses, adding to his fortune.

But Barry was never a good fit for the Memphis social scene. He was lousy at small talk and hated the country-club gossip rich folks seemed to adore even more than their money. When he was in his early thirties, Barry dropped off the grid. He simply stopped showing up at society functions. His business interests were run by capable managers, so his presence wasn't required.

Where he went, nobody knew.

And for the most part, nobody cared. He was just one less billionaire for people to envy.

While Barry loved living in Memphis, he was tired of the pressure that came with being a pillar of society. He moved to the houseboat, hiding in plain sight, as it were.

Barry, Scott, and Joe had gone through a case and a half of Miller Lite by the time Barry finished telling his story, with occasional contributions from Scott. Barry's willingness to go his own way caught Scott's fancy. Scott was obviously a fan. And as cynical as he was, Scott wasn't a fan of many things or many people. Especially not billionaire bigwigs.

"Wow," Joe said when Barry finished.

"Yeah, wow, I guess," Barry said. "I never thought anybody would recognize me. Nobody looks at homeless people, you know? And I figured this old houseboat just a few miles from where I grew up would be a perfect place to hide. Everybody would expect me to get far away from Memphis. So this was a perfect spot."

"Good plan," Scott said.

"It was, until you came along," Barry said.

"Barry, er, Mr. Brett, your secret is safe with us," Joe said. "Right, Scott?"

"Oh, absolutely," Scott said. "I'm good at keeping secrets."

"So, you still haven't told me what brought you out here to-day," Barry said.

"Well, Scott didn't believe your story about seeing those city surveyors checking out the land on the east shore," Joe said.

"I do now," Scott said. "I thought you were just some bum."

Barry laughed. "I guess I am a bum now. And by the way, I wish you'd keep calling me Backwater Barry. I like the sound of it. And yeah, I'm sure they were city surveyors. In my previous life as a captain of industry, I had dealings with city government from time to time. So I recognize the logo. And when you live out here, you tend to pay attention to strange people wandering around in places where nobody normally goes. So I crept up the bank one day and got a close look at one of those city trucks."

"Why would Mayor Pigg have surveyors out here?" Joe said.

"I have no idea," Barry said. "But it shouldn't be hard for you guys to find out."

"How would we do that?" Joe said.

"Well, you might learn a lot by checking the property records," Barry said. "If you know who owns that land, you might get a better idea of what the mayor's up to."

"That's right," Scott said. "And that's what we're going to do. Right, Joe?"

"Right," Joe said.

"That's the spirit," Barry said. "Of course, I'd be happy to let you search the records from here, but computers are one of the things I gave up when I downsized my lifestyle. But unless you're in a hurry, there's no harm in you guys sticking around for a couple more beers."

So they did.

Chapter 13

"Waldo, have you lost your ever-lovin' mind?"

Mayor Pigg was talking to Waldo Jefferson, president of the Memphis City Council. And in a reversal of their last conversation, this time the mayor was doing the shouting.

"Whatever do you mean, Mr. Mayor?" Jefferson replied, feigning deference he clearly didn't feel toward Pigg.

"You know egg-zactly what I mean," Pigg said. "You hardly left my office after we worked out our little arrangement before the phone started ringin' with all your sleazy buddies. Seems like everybody needs some kind of special incentive before they'll vote for the Barbecue Hall of Fame."

"Well, you know how that goes, Mr. Mayor," Jefferson said. "Word travels fast when politicians sniff out a project with real 'revenue-enhancing' potential. Something like this is practically like printing money."

"Ya think, Waldo?"

"I know so. And I know what you're tryin' to do, Mr. Mayor."

"What's that, Waldo? What do you think I'm tryin' to do?"

"You're tryin' to keep as much of it for yourself as possible. You don't want to share the wealth."

"Share the wealth?" Pigg said. "Share the wealth? Why on earth would I need to share the wealth? This was all my idea. I don't remember us hatchin' this scheme over beers. I remember you musclin' in and demandin' a cut. And then tellin' every crooked jackleg on the city council and the plannin' commission so I get to spend my spare time playin' *Let's Make a Deal.*"

"'That's the one with Bob Barker, right?" Jefferson said. "I used to love watchin' that cracker."

"Waldo, I don't think you realize what a big mistake you're makin'.'"

"Oh, am I?" Jefferson clearly felt full of himself. "Seems like you really want this to happen, Mr. Mayor. And if it's gonna happen, you need me. And you apparently need some of my crooked jackleg friends to make it happen, too. So you don't exactly have a lot of leverage, if you feel me on that."

"I'll tell you what I'm feelin', Waldo," Pigg said. "I'm feelin' that maybe you're not as smart a politician as you think you are."

"Oh? How do you figure?"

"It's how you don't figure that's the problem."

"How I don't figure?"

"Yeah, you think you got a bead on where the money is to be made on this project," Pigg said. "But you haven't even scratched the surface. What I've got goin' could make what your brother-in-law and you'll get on that PR contract seem like couch change."

"Do tell, Mr. Mayor."

"Well, I'm not goin' to tell you any more right now," Pigg said. "But I can cut you in on sumpin later. Sumpin big. But I'm not gonna have enough money to go around if you keep tryin' to cut in everybody who ever carried a campaign sign for you."

"Oh, so you're sayin' I need to be discreet?"

"Only if you like money," Pigg said. "Do you feel me now?"

"Oh, I feel you, all right, Mr. Mayor. I feel you."

"So if anybody starts askin' how to vote on the World Barbecue Hall of Fame, what are you gonna say?"

"Well, I'm gonna tell 'em to vote their conscience, of course," Jefferson said with a chuckle. "I'll see ya around, Mayor Pigg."

Pigg exhaled deeply as his office door closed behind Waldo Jefferson. He wasn't anxious to share his expected fortune with that blabbermouth. But of course, he hadn't told Waldo everything. Waldo didn't know about Chicago. That would be a disaster. Chicago was a crooked politician's 401(k) plan. Anyway, maybe today's talk would keep Waldo at bay for a while.

Mayor Pigg's relief turned out to be short-lived. Before he had time to rummage his desk drawers for one of his bottles of whiskey, his police chief, Zack Bruno, entered. From the anxious look on Bruno's face, Pigg could tell the news was not good.

"Let me guess," Pigg said. "We've got rioting in the Pinch District."

His underling didn't react to the joke. "Sir, I need you to come with me," Bruno said. "We've got a situation that requires your, ah, personal attention."

"So tell me, Chief Bruno."

"I'm afraid this isn't something I can tell you, sir. I need to show you."

"So show me."

"I will, sir," Bruno said. "But we need to take a ride down to Whitehaven for this."

Ten minutes later, Bruno and Pigg were headed south on the Interstate 240 loop. Pigg gave up trying to get any information on the way there—"Seeing is believing" was all the police chief would say.

Bruno steered his black unmarked Dodge Charger onto Interstate 55 southbound, then took the Elvis Presley Boulevard exit.

At one point, Whitehaven had been among the most exclusive neighborhoods of Memphis—a suburb, really, before the city's growth had swallowed it whole. Then white flight began. Many former Whitehaven residents had moved a few miles south across the state line to a Mississippi suburb known as Southaven.

Not all of them, though. So Whitehaven became something of a puzzle, a mishmash of stately homes with upper-middle-class owners and run-down bungalows owned by the less well-to-do, who flooded into the neighborhood to fill the void left by the Southaven refugees.

Whitehaven's poor side was in evidence on Elvis Presley Boulevard. The road was an unbroken string of pawnshops, liquor stores, and fast-food restaurants. It was quite an anomaly that Graceland, the city's biggest tourist attraction, happened to be on this street.

"Oh, good Lord, no," Pigg groaned as Bruno pulled into the Graceland parking lot. An unwritten rule had been observed by Memphis politicians for generations: leave Graceland the hell alone.

Elvis Presley's home drew millions of visitors to the city, even though the singer had been in the ground for more than thirty years. The executives at Elvis Presley Enterprises were marketing wizards, always finding ways to keep their product fresh and appealing. They promoted a cult of personality around Elvis—one that appealed even to a generation of fans born after the singer's death.

Which meant Elvis Presley Enterprises pumped plenty of money into the local economy while asking for little from local government. That's why Pigg knew any trouble on the Graceland grounds was big trouble.

"We need to go around back," Bruno said, leading Pigg toward one of the mansion's outbuildings not open to tourists.

Outside the door stood several of Bruno's men and a gaggle of nervous-looking Elvis Presley Enterprises executives. It was early evening, after Graceland had closed to visitors but before the summer sun had set.

"Good Lord," Pigg muttered again as he and Bruno pushed past the crowd and into a small room in what Pigg figured was the mansion's servant quarters.

"Good Lord!" he shouted after taking in the scene before him.

The room was filled with more cops, who were guarding the most unusual set of prisoners Pigg had ever seen.

The two who caught his attention first were a pair of extremely well-endowed young women—one blond, one brunette, and both stark raving naked. Two naked young men were there, too, also well endowed in their own way. A couple of the prisoners were dumpy-looking older men. Mercifully, they were fully clothed in jeans and sweaty T-shirts. Also present was a tall, trim fifty-ish man with bright blue eyes, carefully coiffed gray hair, and a mauve Armani suit.

"Why, Mayor Pigg, we meet at last," the guy in the suit said, not at all rattled at being detained by the Memphis Police Department.

"Yeah, yeah, we meet at last," Pigg said. "Just who the hell are you? And who are your friends? If you're in town for an American Nudist Society convention, I bet the folks here at Graceland would have given you a group rate, if you only asked."

"Mr. Mayor, I'm not a tourist," the man said. "I'm Augustine Eldridge. I moved to Memphis relatively recently. I'm trying to put Memphis on the map in the filmmaking industry."

Even Pigg had to chuckle at that. "On the map, huh? You figure you're doin' us a favor by makin' your dirty movies here? So what happened? You and your crew get done shootin' for the day and decide to head over here for a look-see?"

"Worse than that, Mr. Mayor," Bruno said. "They were trying to film a porno movie right outside the gates of Graceland. They waited until the mansion closed for the day, then watched until the security guards were out of sight. That's when those two guys and those two gals over there stripped down and started going at it while the rest of these pervs filmed it. The Graceland guys saw the whole thing on their security cameras and reacted quickly, but even so, things, uh, were pretty far along before they got down there and restrained them. We couldn't find the clothes for those four. We think passersby might have grabbed them off the sidewalk while the security guards were taking those four kids down. Everybody is looking for some kind of souvenir from Graceland, you know."

"Izzat so?" Pigg said, turning his focus back to Eldridge. The naked girls giggled in the background. "So what were you thinkin', that you could make a nookie movie and trade off the Elvis name? Maybe call it *All the King's Women* or sumpin like that?"

"No, but I must admit *All the King's Women* is a pretty good concept," Eldridge said. "You thought of that right off the top of your head? Maybe you and I should go into business together."

Eldridge's cast and crew laughed at that.

"You're feelin' your oats pretty good for a guy who's about to get booked into first-class accommodations at 201 Poplar," Pigg said, referring to the address of the Shelby County Jail. "So I'll ask you again, and for the last time, what are you doin' here?"

"Well, Mr. Mayor, if you must know, I've been working on this film project around Memphis for several weeks. I've shot scenes at all the city's major landmarks—Sun Studio, The Pyramid, the Interstate 40 bridge over the Mississippi, the Mud Island River Museum. You name it, we've hit them all. Of course, the work here at Graceland was going to be our climactic scene, in a manner of speaking, before those guards so rudely interrupted us. The film is called *Memphis in Lay*, and it's sure to get the city noticed. It'll get more press for Memphis than that Tom Cruise movie *The Firm* ever did. Which, come to think of it, wouldn't be a bad subtitle for our movie."

"You say that like you think it's still gonna happen," Pigg said. "Chief Bruno, did your men confiscate their camera equipment?"

"Sure did. It's right over there," Bruno said, gesturing to a small hand-held video camera and a battery-operated hand-held spotlight.

"Well, Mr. Augustine Eldridge, I hate to tell you this, but your hard work is about to get destroyed," Pigg said, although he thought to himself that it might be worth a quick screening first. "And you and the *Memphis in Lay* cast and crew will be laid up in the county jail for quite a while."

"I don't think so," Eldridge said. "Could I have a word with you in private, Mr. Mayor?"

Pigg turned to Bruno, who simply shrugged. Pigg nodded

toward a small bathroom adjacent to the room they were in. Eldridge followed him there.

"Mr. Mayor, I'm disappointed we got off on the wrong foot here," Eldridge said after Pigg closed the door. They were practically nose to nose in the half bath. Or as close to that as they could be, given Eldridge's height advantage. "But I don't think you want to press charges here."

"Oh, I don't?" Pigg said.

"No," Eldridge said. "You see, there's not a lot you can charge us with. We were on a public sidewalk, so that's not trespassing. And my crew members and I haven't done anything except watch four very attractive people letting nature take its course. Which, even in Tennessee, is not a crime."

"Well, what about those four 'very attractive people'?" Pigg asked. "We'll charge them with public indecency or sumpin along those lines. I think the lawyers call it lewd and lascivious conduct."

"Well, under different circumstances, you might make that case stick, and a judge might even sentence them to a little jail time," Eldridge said. "But here's what makes this situation different. For one thing, I don't think you want the negative publicity this case would bring. We're talking about a trial that would get coverage from everybody from the tabloids to the major television networks. That's publicity I'm guessing the good folks at Elvis Presley Enterprises would prefer to avoid. For another thing, you wouldn't win. Your officers treated those young people inhumanely by detaining them without offering them any clothing or blankets to cover themselves. After Abu Ghraib and Guantanamo Bay, the general public won't put up with that kind of humiliating treatment."

"Humiliatin'?" Pigg shot back. "Those guys and girls look like they spend more time naked than they do wearin' clothes."

"I wonder if a jury would see it that way," Eldridge said. "And you should know that as soon as we were approached by the Graceland security guards, I hit a distress signal on my cell phone that paged my associate, Pedro Suarez, whom I believe you recently met. As we speak, Mr. Suarez is making arrangements with our lawyers, who are not only excellent in criminal defense cases but will no doubt prepare civil suits against you, your city's police department, and Graceland. Do you think Graceland's executives will want this case to go forward? Have you talked to them yet?"

"Um, no, I haven't," Pigg mumbled.

"No, of course not," Eldridge said. "Otherwise, you and I wouldn't be in this cramped, stinky bathroom. My crew and I would be on our way home, and you'd be headed back to your office to draft a letter of apology, with hopes I wouldn't sue you for enough to foreclose on that Pigg Pen of yours. Fortunately for you, I'm not interested in getting into the restaurant business. I employ a much prettier class of people in my line of work. But you and I also have some other business, which is yet another reason why you're about to let me and my employees go."

"What business would that be?" Pigg said, dreading what he knew Eldridge would say next.

"I understand you have some interest in purchasing my studio headquarters at the intersection of Front and Auction."

"Studio headquarters?" Pigg sputtered. "That dump?"

"I like to think of it as a fixer-upper," Eldridge replied. "But there's no way it's going to be that—and certainly no way it's going to become the World Barbecue Hall of Fame—if I'm sitting in a jail cell. So what do you say, Mr. Mayor?"

Mayor Pigg hesitated, considering his options. Of which only one made sense. He opened the door to the bathroom.

"Bruno!" Pigg bellowed in the direction of his police chief. "Let'em go!"

"Thank you, Mr. Mayor," Augustine Eldridge said as he squeezed past Pigg and headed toward the outbuilding's exit. Then he paused to look back. "And by the way, the asking price for my property just went up to twelve million."

Chapter 14

Joe had never been in the register of deeds' office before.

The register was the keeper of all deeds and property transaction records in Shelby County. However, as a lifelong renter, Joe never had a reason to look through property records. He had tried looking up the records on the register's website but encountered a cryptic message: "File not found." So he had decided to visit the office in person.

It wasn't where Joe expected it to be. Joe had assumed it would be downtown, as most government offices were. And for many years, it had been. However, because so much of the county's population base had shifted away from Memphis and into Shelby's eastern suburbs, many of the county government offices had relocated to a complex of buildings in East Memphis, near a forty-five-hundred-acre park called Shelby Farms.

After driving around the nondescript buildings along the park's western border, Joe found the one he was looking for. He parked and went inside, trying to act as casual as possible as he strolled to the counter.

"Help you?" a dowdy-looking middle-aged woman asked.

"Yes, ma'am, I hope you can," Joe said, offering his most charming smile. "I need to look at some property records."

"That's why most people come here," the woman said.

"Right, I suppose it is," Joe said. "Don't guess you get a lot of people coming in to order a Starbucks Frappuccino, do you?"

The woman just stared back.

"Okay, so anyway, here's what I need," Joe said. "I need to look up the ownership deeds for these pieces of property."

Joe slid a piece of paper across the counter. He and Scott had managed to look up the legal definitions for every property along the Wolf River Harbor's eastern shore. The Internet was a wonderful thing.

"What do you want them for?" the woman asked.

"I don't need to answer that, do I?" Joe said. "I mean, the records are supposed to be available for public inspection, are they not?"

"Are you a reporter?" the woman asked.

"No, I'm a paralegal." Joe didn't like to lie, but he was getting the idea that, public records law or no public records law, this woman wasn't going to cooperate until her curiosity was satisfied. "My law firm represents a client who has some interest in these properties. And what that interest is, I'm not at liberty to disclose."

"Oh, you're not?"

"No, I'm not," Joe said.

"Well, I'm not sure I'm at liberty to let you see those records."

"I see," Joe said. It was time to play his bluff. "Well, the partners at my firm are convinced I'm legally entitled to examine those records. You know they're right, and I know it, too. So I suggest you get them, or you may find yourself in the middle of a legal action against the register's office. Do you think your bosses would like that?"

The woman glared at Joe for a long minute. "Wait here," she finally said as she picked up the paper with the property information and headed toward the back of the office.

Joe waited—five minutes, ten, fifteen. He saw the woman talking earnestly with two men. Finally, she returned to the counter.

"Sorry, but those records are not available," the woman said, a trace of a smile crossing her lips.

"Not available? But they're public records," Joe said.

"Yes, I think you mentioned that before. But those records are not here."

"Not here?" Joe said. "Then where are they?"

"You would have to ask the mayor about that. He requested those records be sent to his office."

"The mayor?"

"The Memphis mayor. Pete Pigg. Maybe you've heard of him. But if your firm's client has an interest in these properties, surely you must also know of Mayor Pigg's interest. Which law firm did you say you work for?"

"I didn't," Joe said, turning on his heel to make a hasty exit.

On the drive back downtown, Joe's mind raced. It appeared Barry's information was on the money. Mayor Pigg was definitely up to something. But what?

Joe knew one thing: he couldn't waltz into Pigg's office and demand to see the records, as he'd tried to do at the register's office. After all, Joe was working for the mayor, more or less. Asking for those property records would surely attract suspicion.

It was late in the afternoon. Scott wouldn't need to be at his Elvis impersonator gig for a few hours, when the nighttime crowds started to pick up on Beale. So Joe decided to stop by Scott's place for some strategizing and perhaps a beer or four.

Joe was lucky enough to find a parking place on the block of Beale just east of where the entertainment district began. He walked two blocks to Scott's apartment, which was up a dark flight of stairs wedged between two brick storefronts. Joe was always careful to watch where he stepped. Late at night, vagrants and drunken revelers sometimes used the steps as a toilet. Or as a bed. Or, sadly enough, sometimes both.

"Scott, you up there?" Joe called from the steps, which thankfully were clear for a change. "I'm heading up."

Technically, no one was supposed to live on Beale Street because none of its property was zoned for residential use. But Scott didn't live according to society's conventions. He had convinced the private firm that managed Beale Street's operations that it could make a little extra money by renting him the storage space above an old juke joint. Which was money off the books for the firm's CEO, of course. And as a bonus, Scott was an extra set of eyes around the property to watch out for burglars and other mischief-makers. At least in theory.

After several loud knocks, Scott finally answered.

"Yeah?" he said from behind the door in a voice that sounded as if he'd been smoking cigarettes in his sleep.

"Scott, it's me, Joe. Let me in, man."

The door cracked open just enough for Joe to slip in.

As usual, a trip inside Scott's apartment was an all-out assault on the senses. It was a loft apartment, more or less—one big room with small partitioned sections for the sleeping area and bathroom. An assortment of photos and movie and concert posters covered the walls. Scott's kitchen furniture was a metal fold-up card table with four metal folding chairs. In one corner of the room was a lime-green cloth-covered couch that looked like it had been stolen from a dorm room twenty years ago. Which it might well have been. A ratty end table and a couple of nondescript garage-sale chairs completed the furnishings. The floor was covered with clothing, CDs, tools, pizza boxes, and other takeout containers. Scott and a few of his friends had managed to hook up a sink, a fridge, and an old stove.

The pulsating sounds of Jimi Hendrix's "All Along the Watchtower" blared from behind the sleeping-area partition. Scott worked as an Elvis impersonator, but his musical tastes were eclectic.

And although he and his buddies had installed some overhead lighting, the apartment was illuminated by kerosene lamps on the card table and the end table. The sharp smell smacked Joe in the face as soon as he stepped inside.

"Dang, man," Joe said. "That kerosene's a little much, don't you think?"

"Oh, sorry about that," Scott said. "You know what I found? I can save some bucks by burning kerosene instead of using the electric lights."

"Really?"

"Sure, man. It all adds up."

"Well, can you at least open a window?" Joe asked.

"Sure," Scott said, yanking one of the ancient windows open about halfway. The smells and sounds of Beale Street immediately began to intrude. A restaurant somewhere nearby was cooking fried bologna sandwiches with grilled onions. And "Soul Man" was playing over the street's outdoor sound system. "So, to what do I owe the honor of this visit?"

"Just got back from the register's office," Joe said.

"Well?" Scott said, poking his head into the fridge to retrieve a couple of beers. "What did you find out?"

"Nada," Joe said. "The lady behind the counter said the mayor's got all the property records."

"Interesting," Scott said. "So it sounds like maybe Barry is on to something."

After initially dismissing Backwater Barry's theory about Pigg's involvement in a shady land deal as the ramblings of a booze-addled bum, Scott had totally changed his tune when he learned who Barry used to be in a former life. Apparently, Barry Brett had a cult following among counterculture types like Scott.

"So it would seem," Joe said. "But if the mayor's got all the records, how do we prove it?"

"Don't you work for the guy? Why don't you sneak in and copy the records?"

"Come on, Scott. I'm in PR, not espionage. Besides, I don't technically work for the city, except as a subcontractor. I can't get access to his office after hours when the mayor's not there."

"Okay, let's think about this," Scott said. "We go in there together and get the mayor to drink with us. Then, after he gets plastered, we rummage through his files until we find what we're looking for."

"Are you nuts?" Joe said. "First of all, what makes you think he'd want to drink with us in his office? You and he may have been drinking buddies at his place, but he's mayor of Memphis now. And he's not exactly a big fan of mine."

"Hmm," Scott said. "Are you sure you aren't making excuses 'cause you're chicken?"

"I'm not chicken, but I'm not looking for a career suicide mission either. There's got to be another way."

Scott and Joe sat in silence a few moments, taking long pulls off their beers.

"I have an idea, but you're not gonna like it," Scott finally said.

"Probably not, given your track record. What's the idea?"

"Well, if you don't like the get-the-mayor-drunk-and-rifle-his-files scenario or the break-into-the-mayor's-office-while-he's-not-there-and-rifle-his-files scenario, then we have to find a way for him to tell us willingly."

"And why would he do that?"

"For us, he wouldn't," Scott admitted. "We're just a couple of schmoes. If we asked the mayor about his business, he'd get suspicious."

"Yeah, and ... ?"

"That means we need help from somebody. Somebody the mayor trusts but who would also relay information to us."

"Well, I suppose I could ask Calvin Cameron to find some things out for us, but I'm guessing he might be suspicious, too."

"Joe, you're not thinking this through. We can't trust that little weasel from the tourist information bureau. He's part of the establishment. Hell, he might be in on whatever the mayor's up to."

"So we need someone who's not part of the establishment."

"Right. But someone who's accepted by the establishment. You know, a celebrity. Like your new girlfriend, Dawn."

"Scott, have you lost your ever-lovin' mind? First of all, Dawn is a big-time actress. I barely know her—"

"But second of all, you're just dying to get to know her better, because you start to drool every time you think about her. So what better way to get to know her than to ask her for help?

Didn't you say she's not as much of a true believer about this Barbecue Hall of Fame as Mayor Pigg thinks she is?"

"Well, she did seem hesitant, but that was just a vibe I picked up, more than anything she said."

"So find out if your instincts are correct," Scott said. "Joe, I know you pretty well. If you don't take advantage of this opportunity to get to know her, you'll still regret it twenty years from now. Check that, sixty years from now. We'll be sitting on the front porch at some nursing home, and I'll turn off my hearing aid so I won't have to listen to you moping about your missed opportunity for the ten millionth time."

Maybe it was the beer, but Scott was starting to make sense.

"Okay, so how do I get her to help?" Joe asked.

"Well, tell her you want to do a good job publicizing this project, and you need to gather some information about how it will fit into the surrounding neighborhood. Get her to ask the mayor about property ownership. He might tell her things he wouldn't tell you or me. After all, she's the great Dawn. She goes by only one name, so you know she's big."

"You know, I've never dated a woman who went by one name."

"Does that mean you'll do it?"

"Are you going to dog me until I do?"

"Yes."

"Well, in that case, why not? It's worth a shot."

"That's the spirit," Scott said. "Let's have a couple more beers so we can discuss strategy."

Chapter 15

William "Billy Boy" Bradwell was not having a good time.
He was in his skybox in Arrowhead Stadium for the
Kansas City Chiefs' first preseason game. And it wasn't much of
a game.

The coach had decided to give extended playing time to the
fourth-string quarterback, who was only slightly more likely than
the late Johnny Cash to take a snap during a regular-season game.
The Tampa Bay Buccaneers were playing most of their starters,
especially on defense, and had already picked off three passes in
the first half.

On top of that, it was hot. Which was a switch. Bradwell was
fond of saying there was no colder place than Arrowhead Stadium for the final game of a 4–12 season. But Kansas City was
as brutally hot in August as it was cold in late December. And
of course, the air conditioning in Bradwell's suite wasn't working
properly.

Bradwell figured he deserved better. He was, after all, one of the team's owners. However, his shares were worth only about 5 percent of the team. The majority owners had been trying to buy Bradwell out for years, but he refused to sell. Which meant that Bradwell and the majority owners didn't exactly get along. So maybe it was more than coincidence that the AC in his skybox wasn't working.

"Old-money snobs," Bradwell muttered as a drop of sweat rolled down his nose.

Bradwell, by contrast, considered himself a self-made man. His father had owned a small cattle ranch near Topeka, which Bradwell had inherited. Bradwell had gradually expanded his landholdings and livestock as neighboring property owners agreed to sell out to him under suspicious circumstances. The rumor was that Bradwell's method of persuasion involved some level of criminality, though no one ever came forward to press charges.

The Triple B Ranch became one of the most successful beef-producing operations in the state. Then Bradwell began branching out. First, he got into the processing end of the meat business by developing a beef jerky called "Rip-A-Chunk," which was sold at convenience stores throughout the lower forty-eight. Then he opened a chain of Billy Boy's barbecue restaurants, first in Kansas City, then Wichita, then Oklahoma City, then Tulsa, and eventually all the major cities in Texas. Next came retail sales of Billy Boy's Cow Sauce, a peppery, tomato-based barbecue sauce served in his restaurants.

All of this had made Bradwell a wealthy man. Wealthy enough that he didn't suffer indignities like a skybox with malfunctioning air conditioning well. In fact, his reputation was that of a man not to be trifled with, period. He was a ruthless businessman not afraid to squash anyone who happened to get in his way.

"They don't know who they're dealing with," Bradwell muttered, thinking how he might even the score with the team's majority owners. They were rich and powerful like him, of course, but nowhere near as ruthless. Few were.

Bradwell wasn't going to stick around for the whole game. Why should he? He could be back in his penthouse condo sipping fine bourbon whiskey in sixty-eight-degree comfort instead of enduring this torture. On top of everything else, the skybox wasn't even clean. A newspaper from a couple of days ago lay on the floor, probably left by someone on the cleaning crew.

Bradwell bent to pick it up. He was about to fling it into the trash can when an article caught his eye. It was a brief item on the back of the front section about the mayor of Memphis storming out of a press conference after being hounded by reporters. The story mentioned that a serial arsonist was on the loose in Memphis and that the mayor was catching criticism for the inability of his police force to bring the criminal to justice. Bradwell skimmed that part, though. What caught his attention was the reason why the press conference had been called in the first place. This yokel mayor wanted to build a Barbecue Hall of Fame. In Memphis. Not in Kansas City.

That's not gonna fly, Bradwell thought. *If there's gonna be a Barbecue Hall of Fame, it needs to be here in K.C.*

Clearly, this was an idea Bradwell needed to steal. Well, he didn't really consider it stealing. He organized his life around the principle of survival of the fittest. He was a schoolyard bully who had never grown up, because he never needed to. In fact, being a bully had served him rather well.

When he wanted to expand his ranch, he simply went to the adjoining property owners and told them to sell or he'd have their legs broken. Or worse, if they complained to anyone. Only one owner had called his bluff. He still walked with a cane, Bradwell recalled with some satisfaction.

When he got into the beef jerky business, a couple of the convenience store chains were reluctant to carry his untested product. But then Bradwell pointed out that many of the franchise operators were illegal immigrants. He threatened to organize a boycott against the chains that wouldn't carry Rip-A-Chunk. Most decided it was easier to accommodate Bradwell than to deal with a boycott.

Bradwell borrowed the concept, the menu, and even the recipes for his chain of restaurants from a gentle old couple running a small barbecue place in Amarillo, Texas. As with the property owners around the Triple B Ranch, he employed threats of physical violence. While there may have been doubts that he'd actually send hit men after property owners early in his career, he clearly had the wherewithal and a ruthless heart by the time he crossed paths with the Pattersons. They meekly submitted to his will.

The Cow Sauce recipe was theirs, too, of course. If Bradwell was going to play the game, he went all in.

So now he had a new angle. He'd do whatever was necessary to take this rube Memphis mayor's idea and make it his own. The meek existed to be exploited by the strong. And William "Billy Boy" Bradwell was strong.

Those fools in Memphis would find that out soon enough.

Chapter 16

In hindsight, Joe realized that maybe his choice of location was a little off.

He, Dawn, and a film crew were trying to shoot a TV spot encouraging Memphians to get behind Mayor Pigg's plans for the World Barbecue Hall of Fame. Joe had written the script and picked the location. And on paper, The Pyramid seemed like a logical choice. After all, it was one of the city's most recognizable landmarks, and it happened to be across the street from the site Mayor Pigg had picked for his pet project.

The Pyramid was impressive. As the name suggested, it looked like one of the ancient pyramids of Egypt, except that its exterior skin was not stone but shiny metal. Which meant the glare could be blinding, particularly in the midday sun.

Rather than reschedule the shoot, the crew had decided to wait until there was enough cloud cover that Dawn wouldn't appear to be speaking from inside a sunburst. Joe had already apologized profusely to the crew and Dawn, but they seemed to take it in stride. The crew members were quick to point out that they were paid by the hour. And since Memphis taxpayers would be picking up the tab, they could wait all afternoon. They took shelter in two large vans, running the air conditioning and drinking some type of undisclosed beverage out of Styrofoam cups.

Dawn had retreated to the shade under one of the building's entry concourses, so Joe decided to take advantage of the opportunity to speak to her alone.

"Hey, Dawn," he said. "It's okay to just call you Dawn, isn't it? I mean, I can call you Miss Dawn if that's more polite. Or even Ms. Dawn."

Dawn's appealing little laugh sent Joe's heart racing. "Just Dawn is fine. By the way, I haven't had a chance to tell you yet, but I really like this script."

"You do?" Joe said, blurting his words louder than he intended. "I mean, thanks. I haven't done a lot of writing for TV. I mostly do print work."

"Well, you've got talent," Dawn said. "Maybe I could introduce you to a few people I've met from Hollywood after this is over."

Joe blushed deeply. He couldn't tell whether Dawn was kidding or not. "Um, that would be great. I mean, if you're serious."

"Sure," Dawn said. "It would be nice to help somebody else from Memphis get into the business. Assuming you want to make a change from what you're doing now."

"Well, considering that a few days ago I was banging out press releases about pawnshops, I think it's safe to say I'd be willing to look at other career opportunities."

They both laughed at that, which helped Joe relax. Her easy-going demeanor gave him confidence. He figured it was now or never.

"Dawn, can I ask you something?" Joe said.

"Uh-oh, here it comes," Dawn said. "You want me to make an appearance at your younger brother's next birthday party?"

"Oh, no, nothing like that. It's just that I need to talk to you about this Barbecue Hall of Fame project."

"What about it? Do you want to make revisions to today's script?"

"No. I mean, not unless you do. I think the TV spot is fine. But I guess I'm having some, um, concerns about this project. Why it's happening, I mean."

"Why it's happening?"

"Well, I mean, why is the mayor so gung-ho about this?"

"You don't think it's because he's got the best interests of Memphis taxpayers at heart?" Joe couldn't tell for sure, but Dawn's tone gave him the idea that maybe she questioned the mayor's motives as well.

"Well, I don't know that he doesn't," Joe said. "It's just that the way this is all happening is kind of . . . weird."

"How so?"

"Well, for one thing, at the first meeting I had with the mayor, he said he needed this project to distract attention from the city's river cruise boats being sold to a casino. But that's hardly gotten any attention at all. It was a headline that day, but it's been ignored since then. Lately, the newspapers and TV have said a lot more about that arsonist than they have about any cruise boats. I don't think most locals care whether we've got the cruise boats or not."

"So? Couldn't that just mean his plan worked? He came up

with a good news story to distract the media's attention from a bad news story. Isn't that what politicians do?"

"Yeah, I guess so. But something doesn't feel quite right. I mean, the mayor is so fixated on that site right over there. Out of all the places in downtown Memphis, why there?"

Dawn stepped into the sun long enough to peer across Auction Avenue at the mayor's proposed site. It wasn't much to look at. The property was surrounded by a brick-and-stucco wall so close to the street that it was frequently hit by cars driven by late-night revelers. The building inside the wall was hard to see from the street, but what was visible didn't look good.

"Well, I have to agree with you about the site," Dawn admitted. "Then again, I don't know much about real estate."

"Well, neither do I. But a friend of mine saw some city employees surveying property north of here—several miles, all along the Wolf River Harbor. He thinks the mayor may be planning something with that property, too. Maybe something big."

"So what do you want to do?"

"Well, I'd like to find out what the mayor's up to. That's all. Maybe there's nothing to this at all. I guess I just want to find out for myself."

"You mean you don't want to be involved if something shady's going on?"

"No. I mean, well, yeah. I don't know that anything shady is going on. But I want to make sure. You know what I mean?"

"You know, Joe, now that I think about it, I kind of do, too. I know this sounds sappy, but I really do love Memphis. I picked up a vibe the first time the mayor talked to me about this. And I don't want to find out later that . . . Well, I don't want to find out anything I'll be embarrassed about."

"So you'll help me, then?"

"Sure. What did you have in mind?"

"Well, I tried to get a look at the property records for all that land along the harbor. But the mayor's got those files in his office."

"You want me to sneak in there and steal the files?"

"Oh, no, nothing like that. I was just hoping maybe you could talk to him, see if he'll tell you anything about what he's doing."

"I think I could do that," Dawn said with a chuckle. "I could be wrong, but I believe Mayor Pigg may have a crush on me."

"Yeah, him and about ninety million other men."

Now, it was Dawn's turn to blush. Or was the Memphis midafternoon heat just getting to her? Joe couldn't be sure.

"So, are you one of those ninety million?"

"Let's put it this way: I've never missed one of your movies on its opening weekend. And if one of your older movies comes on at midnight, I stay up to see it through to the end."

The words were out of Joe's mouth before he thought what he was saying. Could he really be having this conversation with a movie starlet? And one who was the pride of Memphis, no less?

"You're really sweet, Joe," Dawn said. "I think I'm going to enjoy working with you."

Joe suddenly felt warmer on the inside than he did on the outside. He didn't want to say anything to ruin a perfect moment. That was okay anyway, because several of the crew members were starting to disengage themselves from the vans, looking a bit wobbly as they did. The sky above had turned overcast enough for shooting to begin.

"Guess we'd better get back to work," Dawn said. "But there is one thing I need to tell you, Joe." Her words carried that serious tone a woman uses when she's about to tell a man she already has a boyfriend.

Joe drew a deep breath and braced himself. "Yeah?"

"I want to change one part of your script, if you don't mind."

"Oh? What's that?"

"Well, the part where you have me saying, 'This is the dawn of a new era in Memphis tourism.'"

"Oh, yeah. Right. You think that's too cheesy?"

"Just a little bit," she said, wrinkling her nose and holding her thumb and forefinger about an inch apart.

When he was younger, Joe hadn't been good about accepting criticism of his writing. He would let some minor gripe bother him for days. Not this time, though. More than likely, he would dwell on how Dawn had said she looked forward to working with him.

"Consider it changed," Joe said.

Although he couldn't help thinking he was seeing the dawn of a great new friendship.

Chapter 17

Mayor Pigg glanced at the article in *The Avalanche* again, then tossed the paper across his desk in disgust.

"What do you think about that, Chief Bruno?" the mayor said.

Zack Bruno read the headline and began the story under Alvin Allen's byline. The story was an update on one of the first properties burned down by the arsonist Allen and the rest of those snarky reporters insisted on calling "the Ghetto Blazer."

The house had been located on a corner lot in New Chicago, a North Memphis neighborhood that had fallen on hard times. At one point in its history, New Chicago had been a thriving African-American community with its own grocery stores, barbershops, laundries—a self-contained neighborhood with almost everything residents needed in their daily lives, all within reasonable walking distance.

However, as with so many other neighborhoods in inner-city Memphis, the years had not been kind. The businesses had all moved out. The people who could afford to move did. The rest found themselves trapped in a place where property values were declining almost as fast as the crime rate was rising.

The house the Ghetto Blazer struck had been owned by an absentee landlord for many years. At first, the landlord was able to find renters for the place—enough to make his modest investment in the property worthwhile. Especially since he didn't make any repairs to the place unless threatened by a court order.

Tenants came and went. The landlord had to charge progressively lower rents as the years went by. Eventually, as the house became more and more of a dump, the landlord was unable to charge enough to cover the cost of his property tax payments. So he didn't pay his taxes. By that point, he had made back his investment in the place several times over.

After a lengthy legal process, the city had seized the property for nonpayment of taxes. The house couldn't be resold unless someone was willing to settle the unpaid tax bill, which at that point totaled more than twenty thousand dollars. It would have cost at least three times that much to repair the place to bring it into compliance with the city's codes—another requirement before the property could be sold. Homes in that neighborhood weren't selling for anywhere close to eighty thousand dollars, the minimum investment a prospective buyer would have to make.

No one at city hall had the political will to fix up the property. It was, after all, just one of thousands of parcels the city had seized through the years. Demolishing them all would cost a lot of money. And the people who lived in the neighborhoods weren't the kind to demand political change. Most had enough problems without trying to fight city hall. So in New Chicago and other neighborhoods throughout North Memphis, South Memphis,

Orange Mound, and later Hickory Hill and Whitehaven, city-owned properties sat like rotting cavities in a mouth that hadn't seen proper dental hygiene in years.

But then the Ghetto Blazer struck. He torched the place, for no reason the fire department's investigators had been able to determine. It wasn't just another case of homeless people building a fire that eventually got out of control, although that happened, too. No, the Ghetto Blazer had definitely known what he was doing. The arson investigators found the charred remains of the metal gas cans he'd left behind.

Whoever he was, the Ghetto Blazer wanted people to know the fire was arson, not an accident. But he hadn't left any clues at that fire or at any of the others he started. After a while, he stopped leaving behind the metal cans. By then, everyone knew when the Ghetto Blazer had struck anyway.

No one in the police or fire departments could figure out who this guy was or what made him tick. One theory was that he was a firefighter who reveled in the glory of putting out the very fires he caused. But a check of duty logs revealed there wasn't enough overlap among the firefighters who worked the arson cases to make that theory stick. Almost everyone on the fire department had fought at least one of the Ghetto Blazer's fires, and usually several. But no one was at every one. Or even most of them.

Could the Ghetto Blazer be someone higher up in the fire or police departments who enjoyed the media attention? Doubtful. The media had turned on both departments, calling them inept for their inability to find whoever was responsible.

There was talk that the firefighters' union was behind the blazes, in an effort to bolster its pitch for pay increases and better benefits. But that didn't make sense either. The union had just agreed to a three-year contract a few weeks before the fires began.

Chief Bruno scowled as he read a brief recap of the Ghetto Blazer's exploits. He couldn't tell the mayor this, but he and his investigators were nowhere near finding the guy.

But the main point of Alvin Allen's article was to document what had happened to the New Chicago property since the fire. The city, as the property's owner, had been required to clear away the remnants of the house, leaving behind a piece of vacant property. Since renovation costs were no longer an issue, that property had been purchased with the help of a federal community block grant by New Chicago Now, a nonprofit neighborhood organization. New Chicago Now had helped a developer find financing, some private and some government-backed, to build a small grocery store. It would be New Chicago's first since 1964. In New Chicago, the return of commercial development—any commercial development—was big news. A grocery store in New Chicago was as big a deal as a Saks Fifth Avenue would have been in the ritzy suburbs of Germantown and Collierville. The mayor and New Chicago's city council representatives were scheduled to appear at a groundbreaking for the store next week.

"Touchin' story, huh?" Mayor Pigg said as Bruno finished reading and looked up.

"I guess," the chief said. "Is that a problem?"

"Course it's a problem. And you know why it's a problem?" Pigg said. "Because this Ghetto Blazer's been on the loose so long that New Chicago had time to buy the property and find some sucker willin' to invest money there. Even if a lot of it's taxpayer money, do you know how difficult that is, chief? And here's what bothers me: that means this arsonist has been doin' his thing, uncaught by your guys, for a long time. A very long time."

"Mr. Mayor, I understand your frustration—"

"I'm not sure you do, chief. You see, the press has been beatin' up on us—well, more on me than you—ever since I've been in office. You know how much of a distraction that is?"

As if on cue, the mayor's cell phone began chirping the first few bars of "Proud Mary." He had switched the ring tone. He could listen to "Walking in Memphis" only so many times in any given day.

"'Lo?" the mayor said. Bruno started to get up until Pigg motioned for him to stay.

"Mr. Mayor, we need to talk," the voice on the other end of the line said. It was Red Maloney, president of the Union of Trade Unions Local 317.

"What can I do for you, Red?"

"Well, I understand you had a meeting with Little Bobby Shotwell that didn't go so well."

"Oh? How do you figure?"

"I don't know what you said to him, but Little Bobby was not too happy with you, Mr. Mayor."

"Well, that's because Little Bobby was tryin' to shake me down. Did he tell you that? Or was it the other way around? Did you tell him to do that to me?"

"Mr. Mayor, we go back a ways. You know me better than that."

"I thought I did, Red, I thought I did. But you know how things go in business. Sometimes, people get greedy. Is that what's goin' on here, Red? You're gettin' greedy?"

"I don't believe what I'm hearing here, Mr. Mayor."

"Well, I thought you and me had a pretty good business deal here. We get the World Barbecue Hall of Fame, paid for mostly with taxpayer money. Then the value of the property around it goes up. Suddenly, what used to be crappy industrial property is a good spot to put luxury waterfront condominiums. Lots and lots of waterfront condominiums. And guess what? You and me just happen to own that land. So we'll make a buck or two on that. Plus, you'll make some nice kickbacks because your guys will get most of the construction work for the Barbecue Hall of Fame and all those condos. Which means I'm gonna make some nice kickbacks, too. And here's the best part: while I'm gettin' rich, I'm also gonna become a folk hero with local voters, 'cause I'll be the mayor who finally revitalized the Wolf River Harbor. They'll rename it Piggtown or sumpin like that. Does all that sound okay to you, Red? Is that or is that not what we've been talkin' about for the last coupla months?"

"It is, Mr. Mayor, it is."

"So why'd you send that Shotwell punk down here to bother me?"

"Mr. Mayor, I didn't. I swear to you, I didn't know he'd come asking for money. You know how that kid is. He's always trying to work the angles."

"Well, I'm not doin' any side deals with him. I'm already havin' to do more horse tradin' with city council members and plannin' commissioners than I'd like. And that kind of thing has a way of—cover your ears, chief—cuttin' into my profits. So you tell young Mr. Shotwell to keep his mouth shut and not make any trouble on this project, or I'll see to it that the city of Memphis never uses another unionized shop the rest of my time as mayor. If you want to pay that little squirt out of your end of the take, that's your business. But keep him away from me, understand? I've got enough problems to worry 'bout."

"Yes, sir, Mr. Mayor. I certainly see your point," Red Maloney said, although he was grinding his teeth on the other end of the phone. Threaten to cut the unions out of city contracts? On Red Maloney's watch? But Red knew now was not the time to pick a fight, not with so much money at stake. "Look, don't you worry about Mr. Shotwell. I'll have a talk with that boy."

"You do that," Pigg said before abruptly flipping his phone closed. He turned his attention back to Chief Bruno. "Now, chief, you understand that whatever you hear in this office is like that attorney-client privilege thing. Or maybe we'll just call it mayor-slash-guy-who-wants-to-keep-his-six-figure-job privilege. Understood?"

"Absolutely, Mr. Mayor."

"Good. Now, back to business. I want you to arrest this Ghetto Blazer prick, and I want you to arrest him soon. I'm not worried about pullin' patrolmen out of other parts of the city, I'm not worried about blowin' budgets on overtime, none of that stuff. I want you to use whatever it takes to catch this guy."

"I'll do my best, Mr. Mayor," Bruno said tightly.

"Well, I'm guessin' you've been doin' your best, chief. So what I'm askin' is that you do better than your best, if keepin' that six-figure salary is sumpin you want. So get to it. Meetin's over."

Chief Bruno slowly stood, straightened his blue dress uniform, and headed for the elevator. He rode to the first floor, then headed out the front door and across Civic Plaza toward 201 Poplar.

It was only a two-block walk, so Bruno was still fuming when he reached the building that housed the Shelby County Jail. The stark concrete high-rise was also home to most of the local courts and the police headquarters.

"Bridgette, get all my lieutenants in the executive conference room for a meeting right away," he said as he passed his receptionist on the way into his office.

He pulled a bottle of water from the mini-fridge beside his desk and swigged half of it down, trying to calm his anger. *That stupid mayor. Just catch the arsonist? Sure, that never occurred to me. Now that I know what to do, I'll sure go out and do it.*

Bruno was surprised Mayor Pigg had appointed him police chief in the first place. At the time Pigg was elected, Bruno was roughly equal in seniority to two other deputy chiefs who could have been considered to be in line for the job. However, for reasons not completely clear to Bruno, one of the deputy chiefs didn't get along with Pigg. Something to do with a decades-old argument over a woman, Bruno had heard. The other deputy chief had health issues and a facial tic that tended to manifest itself during televised press conferences.

So, by default, Bruno had been Pigg's choice. It was an uneasy alliance right from the start. By state law, police chiefs had to be commissioned law enforcement officers. And most of Pigg's buddies he might have liked to appoint tended toward the other side of the legal spectrum, which was why Bruno still had a job. At least for now. Pigg would dump Bruno in a heartbeat. Bruno knew that. He was trying to build up his savings before taking retirement. As a fifty-five-year-old man in reasonably good health, Bruno knew he would likely live as a retiree for quite a while. So he wanted to hang on to his job as long as he could, no matter how much he hated Pigg.

After giving his lieutenants time to assemble, Bruno walked into the conference room. He made no attempt to conceal his anger.

"Ladies and gentlemen, this business with the serial arsonist has gone too far," Bruno said. "My marching orders are to make sure this guy gets taken down, no matter what. Overtime expenses are not an issue. Equipment costs are not an issue. Nothing is an issue except catching this guy. Understood? Now, does anybody have any ideas?"

"If overtime's not an issue . . . ," one of his lieutenants, Chuck Guy, said.

"It's not," Bruno snapped. "What's on your mind, Chuck?"

"The only way to get this guy is to go undercover," Lieutenant Guy said. "He's too smart to get picked up by a regular patrol. He's too good at recon for that. He watches these places for a long time before moving on them. Why, I have no idea, because the places he's hitting aren't worth the trouble of burning down. But he obviously watches them. So the only way we'll succeed is if we get people out in these neighborhoods long enough that they blend in with their surroundings. And the best way to blend into these neighborhoods is to pose as homeless people."

"Homeless people?" Chief Bruno said.

"Drug dealers or prostitutes would be too conspicuous," Lieutenant Guy said. "They might scare him away. But he's hit places in areas that have homeless people. He seems to think they're harmless, which for the most part they are. So if we get some officers posing as homeless people, and they stay under cover long enough for this guy to get comfortable having them around, then maybe we can get close enough to throw a net over him."

"I don't like it," one of the other lieutenants, Jeff Bane, said. "This guy's been hitting every dilapidated neighborhood in Memphis. And in case you haven't noticed, the city has a lot of those. Trying to get an undercover cop near the next building he hits would be a total crapshoot."

"Maybe it is a crapshoot," Lieutenant Guy said. "But at least we'd be at the table, rolling the dice. Our investigators haven't come up with any leads. At least this gives us something to work on, instead of just sitting around waiting for the next arson to come in."

"Do you realize how many man-hours it would take to do what you're suggesting?" Lieutenant Bane countered.

"You heard what the chief said," Lieutenant Guy said. "Overtime is not an issue. And I'm guessing it would be okay to pull officers off other cases to make this a priority, right, chief?"

"Absolutely," Chief Bruno said. "Nobody over at city hall is chewing my ass about how many prostitution busts we're making. In fact, if I know our mayor, he'd probably be pleased if we made less of those."

The room erupted in laughter. Even Chief Bruno had to crack a thin smile at his joke. He was glad to see his charges held the mayor in the same esteem he did.

"Okay, that's it," Chief Bruno said. "Lieutenant Guy, I want you to head this up. Get some roster sheets for undercover personnel and a map of the city and meet me in my office."

Chapter 18

D awn couldn't be sure she wasn't making a big mistake.
About getting involved with this stupid World Barbecue
Hall of Fame project. About trusting Joe Miller when he said he
thought something hinky was going on. About agreeing to meet
with that creepy Mayor Pigg again. Particularly about meeting
him at The Olive Pit, that bar where the mayor had first tried to
put the moves on her in his transparently crass manner.

As a celebrity, Dawn had learned to give her trust grudgingly.
Almost everyone she encountered was trying to work some kind
of angle. They wanted her for her fame. Her looks. Her money.
Or usually all three.

Why had she trusted Mayor Pigg enough to say yes to him
in the first place? Well, she loved her hometown. Always had, despite its flaws. She could have been living the good life in Southern California, sharing a twelve-bedroom mansion on Santa
Catalina Island with a show-biz friend, but Dawn had decided
on Memphis. For better or for worse.

So when Pete Pigg had approached her, it was hard to say no. Although the man made her skin crawl, he was the city's duly elected mayor. And that counted for something, right?

But the deal had never felt right. Dawn had learned a thing or two about business. And she could tell Mayor Pigg had an agenda beyond what he'd told her.

So when Joe Miller started raising questions, well, it had reinforced the doubts she already had. Of course, it didn't hurt that she thought Joe was kind of cute. Not in the flashy movie-star way of so many guys who tried to hit on her. Dawn didn't know Joe well enough to trust him either. But he presented himself as the kind of guy Dawn maybe could like: sweet, kind of shy, goofy, maybe, but with a good heart and without all that Hollywood phoniness or rich-guy snobbery she'd seen too much of in her life. Not that she thought of him as boyfriend material or anything. Well, maybe he was and maybe he wasn't. He was probably too shy to make a move anyhow. And given the nature of their work relationship, that was probably a good thing.

Anyway, she'd decided to go out on a limb and trust Joe, which meant setting up another meeting with Mayor Pigg. So here she was, looking around The Olive Pit, half-hoping that important city business had called Hizzoner away. No such luck. She saw him near the back of the bar, waving at her with one hand while his martini sloshed out of the glass he held in the other. She forced a small smile as she moved toward the mayor's table.

"Well, well, hello, Miss Dawn," the mayor said, rising to give her an awkward one-handed hug and a peck on the cheek. In doing so, he managed to spill his drink on her back while holding it precariously. Dawn flinched, both from the unwelcome embrace and the chilled vodka mixture, but Pigg didn't seem to notice.

"Hello, Mr. Mayor," Dawn said, trying to sound friendly but not seductive.

"Please have a seat," Pigg said. "What would you like to drink?"

Dawn looked at her watch. Quarter 'til noon. The mayor apparently made a habit of drinking in the morning. "I think I'll pass," she said.

"Oh, come on," Pigg said, sounding like a teenage boy begging his parents for the car keys. This obviously wasn't his first martini of the day. "The last time, you didn't drink either. But we're partners on this Barbecue Hall of Fame now, dear, and partners drink together."

"I'd really rather not," Dawn said. The mayor wasn't doing anything to put her suspicions at ease. Was he completely unconcerned about how it might look to his constituents for him to drink in public? Or were the rules different for elected officials than for celebrities? If she were drunk in public, the video of her exploits would be posted on the TMZ website within hours.

"Oh, just one li'l one," Pigg said. "This place has the best selection of vodka in the city."

Dawn saw no easy way out. She needed to start off on the right foot with the mayor if she had any hope of getting information out of him. And obviously, he wasn't going to relax until she ordered something.

"Oh, all right," Dawn said. "Let me look at one of their drink menus."

"Naw, never mind that," Pigg said, signaling a waiter with a flip of his chubby hand. "Let me order sumpin for you. You know Stoli vodka, right? Well, have a Stoli Vanil. It's sweet—just like you, sweetheart."

Before Dawn could object, Pigg placed an order for a Stoli Vanil on the rocks.

"I tell you what, I bet those Russians don't know a thing about barbecue, but they got vodka down right," Pigg said. "Hey, come to think of it, maybe that's sumpin the Barbecue Hall of Fame needs—international exhibits. I bet they barbecue some crazy things over in Czechoslovakia or wherever."

"Well, that's what I want to talk to you about today," Dawn said, hoping to get the conversation onto a coherent track.

"Czechoslovakia?" Pigg asked, looking puzzled.

"No, the Barbecue Hall of Fame," Dawn said. "I have a few questions about it."

"Oh? Like what, sweetie pie?"

"Obviously, I think the Barbecue Hall of Fame is a great idea, and I'm glad you asked me to help out with the publicity." Dawn took a breath—hopefully not deep enough for the mayor to notice—before launching into the script Joe had suggested. "But I wonder about the location."

"What about it?" The mayor's tone turned serious. And serious conversation was definitely not what he wanted with Dawn.

"I don't mean to be critical, of course," Dawn said. "I'm in the entertainment business, not the real-estate business, so I don't know as much about this sort of thing as you do. But it seems to me that there won't be much stuff around there for tourists to do once they've visited the Barbecue Hall of Fame."

Dawn's drink arrived, and she took a sip as casually as she could. It tasted like the vanilla extract she had tried once as a kid while her mother was baking a cake, only the burn going down the back of her throat was pure vodka.

"See there? Now, isn't that good?" Pigg said, ignoring her

wince. "Not my thing, of course, but I know quite a few ladies who love Stoli Vanil. Anyway, what were we talkin' 'bout?"

"The location of the Barbecue Hall of Fame," Dawn said. "I wonder if there might be a better spot for it somewhere else. Like maybe in the south part of downtown, near Beale Street and the NBA arena? Lots more tourist traffic down there."

"Oh, li'l darlin', I've got my reasons for pickin' that spot," Pigg said. "As mayor, I talk to the people in our plannin' department. And they tell me that part of downtown is goin' to take off. You know the neighborhood around there? It's called Uptown. And they say Uptown is the next Harbor Town. It's where all the growth is headed in the next ten years."

"Really?" Dawn said. "That is so interesting. I had no idea Uptown was such a hot spot. Because it looks pretty quiet to me." Dawn tried to act impressed. If the mayor was going to be coy, she needed to turn on the charm to throw him off guard.

"Oh, yeah," Pigg said, pausing to take a big swig of his drink and signal for another. "You should see the plannin' maps in my office. All this computer-generated here's-what-Memphis-will-look-like-in-2025 kinda stuff. Would you like to see those plannin' maps?"

"Maybe someday," Dawn said with the prettiest smile she could muster. "So Uptown will be the next Harbor Town? Harbor Town is where I live."

"I think I heard that somewhere," Pigg said. "So, whereabouts in Harbor Town? I'm guessin' one of those big three-story mansions overlookin' the Mississippi River. Am I right?"

Dawn immediately regretted mentioning where she lived. She realized she needed to change the subject quickly. "It's got a water view," she conceded. That was pretty nonspecific, just in case Hizzoner had any inclination to stalk her. "Anyway, what do your planning experts say is likely to be built in Uptown?"

"Oh, this and that," Pigg said. "Probably a good mix of businesses and homes. Who knows? Maybe some condos? Developers are fallin' all over themselves to develop condos right now. So how come I've never seen your house, Miss Dawn?"

"Well, I don't throw parties or anything like that," Dawn said. "I like my privacy. That's why I'm living here instead of California."

"Yeah, yeah, I guess I can see that," Pigg said. He took a swig off his fresh drink, which had arrived just after he drained the one before it. "But don't you invite friends over? Southern hospitality and all, you know."

"I guess I'm not very social," Dawn said. "I have my closest friends over from time to time, but I'm not into the dinner-party scene. Dinner parties are usually about gossip, and I try to avoid gossip as much as possible in my line of work."

"Am I one of your close friends, Miss Dawn?" Pigg said, leaving his jaw half open as he finished the question. His eyes had a glazed look Dawn recognized all too well.

"Of course you are, Mr. Mayor," Dawn said.

"Well, when do you s'pose you'll invite me over to see this fantastic waterfront home of yours on . . . Well, I'll be damned!" The mayor's gaze shifted from a point roughly even with Dawn's collarbone to a handsome, stylishly dressed man striding across the room toward them.

"Mayor Pigg, what a pleasure it is to see you again," the man said, extending his hand. From the reluctant way the mayor shook it, Dawn could see this wasn't exactly one of his best friends. The man then turned to her, flashing a huge smile. "Would you mind introducing me to your lovely companion?"

"This is Augustine Eldridge," the mayor said through gritted teeth.

"Please, call me Gus," Eldridge said, firmly but gently taking Dawn's hand. "Would it be cliché for me to kiss the back of your hand?"

"Probably," Dawn said. The man didn't release his grip.

"Well, I'd like to do it anyway," Eldridge said, giving her hand a kiss that was uncomfortably long and wet. "There. I've always thought that was something gentlemen did to ladies in the South. And since I recently moved here, I'm trying hard to fit in."

"Well, you've got the hand-kissing part down," Dawn said, finally slipping her hand free. "My name's Dawn, by the way."

"Oh, I know who you are," Eldridge said. "I recognized you from your movies. Although I must say you're much more exquisite in person."

"Thank you very much, Mr. . . . . Gus," Dawn said. "And may I ask how you and the mayor know each other?"

"Well, we've been discussing a possible business transaction," Eldridge said, grinning in Pigg's direction. "Your friend the mayor is a tough negotiator, but I have a feeling we're going to work something out."

"And what line of work are you in?" Dawn said. She wasn't really curious, and she certainly wasn't interested in dealing with another leering man right now. But she had gotten nothing out of the mayor. Maybe this guy could tell her something she and Joe could use.

"Well, like you, I'm in the filmmaking business, Dawn," Eldridge said.

"Really?" Dawn said. "What have you worked on? Anything I would recognize?"

"Oh, I should hope so," Eldridge said. "Most of my movies are big sellers."

At that moment, Dawn's phone chirped. She breathed a sigh of relief as she looked at the number on her caller ID. It was Joe. She and Joe had worked out a deal where he would call midway through the meeting so she would have an excuse to bail, if necessary.

"Excuse me, gentlemen. I have to take this," Dawn said, smiling slightly as she stood and headed toward The Olive Pit's foyer.

Eldridge's eyes remained fixed on her butt as she made her retreat. So did Pigg's. Actually, so did the eyes of most men in the place.

"Wow," Eldridge said. "I really like her. Mayor Pigg, I must say you have excellent taste in drinking companions."

"Um, thanks," the mayor said. "She's a partner of mine in the Barbecue Hall of Fame."

"She is, is she? That's quite a partner to have."

"You know it. So, are you gonna help us out?"

"Well, now, Mr. Mayor, that depends. I've already given you my price for that property."

"I think you know as well as I do that your price is ridiculous."

"I thought you might feel that way," Eldridge said. "So maybe I can give you a break."

"You can?" The mayor's mood brightened.

"I could, if you're able to do something for me."

"And what would that be?"

"Well, you know the line of work I'm in. And you obviously know what line of work your friend Dawn is in. If I could get her to act in one of my movies—"

"You can't be serious! Gus, you know that's not gonna happen. Dawn's a real honest-to-God movie actress. She makes real honest-to-God movies that people can see in theaters without sticky floors. She's not gonna do one of your naughty movies."

"How do you know that? Seems to me you ought to ask and see what she says. If she's your business partner, you ought to be able to make her understand how helping me could save millions on your land acquisition. And you know what, Mr. Mayor? You're good at persuading people to do things that put money in your pocket. Besides, you never know. She just might like working in my genre. It could be one of the more exciting challenges of her acting career."

"Listen up, Gus. I don't know if you realize this, but I'm in fact the mayor of this town you're livin' in. I'm not some glorified pimp."

"Well, not to put too fine a point on it, but you seem like a barbecue-hawking shyster who's only in city hall because it's a way to make money on the side. But I'll tell you what. You get Dawn to do one of my movies and I'll knock 25 percent off my asking price. And if you don't, my asking price goes up 25 percent."

Dawn was on her way back to the table. "Gentlemen, I'm sorry about this, but I have to run," she said.

"As do I," Eldridge said. "Dawn, it was a pleasure to meet you. And Mr. Mayor, it was good to see you again. I sure hope you'll think about my offer. I'd love doing business with you. I'd really love it, actually."

Chapter 19

William "Billy Boy" Bradwell hadn't felt this good in a long time.

It was a hot day, sure, but the wind whipping off the water made the temperature feel just right. But it wasn't just the weather. Bradwell felt good about what he was going to do.

He gripped the steering wheel of his custom-made pontoon boat, savoring the moment. Then he turned to look back into the faces of the men in the flotilla of pontoon boats behind him in the swift-flowing waters of the Missouri River.

"Are you ready, boys?" Bradwell shouted over the steady purr of the engines.

A series of grunts came back in reply. Bradwell sighed. It was so hard to get good help these days.

"*That's weak!*" Bradwell roared. "I said, '*Are you ready, boys?*'"

"*Yeah!*" they roared back. They knew where their corn was shucked. If they couldn't muster enough enthusiasm, Bradwell would see to it that they were shoveling cow nuggets out of his stockyards before sundown.

"*That's better!*" Bradwell hollered. Those shots of Jack he'd drunk before hitting the water were having the desired effect. He felt warm and tingly inside, with just a trace of a buzz running through his skull. "*Now, let's mooooooooove on out!*"

The exaggerated *mooooooooove* was from his TV commercials. Bradwell used it all the time. "Let's mooooooooove on out!" was his personal catch phrase, one of the few ideas he hadn't stolen from someone else. Moo. Cows. He was in the beef business. It was perfect. All his hired help told him so. And Bradwell told himself that anyone who didn't get the joke just didn't know what funny was.

Bradwell pulled the throttle, sending his boat forward at a steady pace, considering the weight it was carrying. A lot of weight. Delicious, money-making weight.

Behind the steering platform where Bradwell stood, the rest of the boat had been converted into a cattle enclosure. Bradwell was shuttling four bovine passengers down the river, as was each of the four boats behind him.

"Everybody doin' okay back there?" Bradwell called over his shoulder.

The question met with some lowing from one of the more vocal cows. Chances were that this experience would spook her enough to make her moo good and loud. Which would get the other cows mooing, too. That was okay by Bradwell. In fact, for what he had in mind, it was perfect.

In a matter of minutes, the flotilla reached downtown Kansas City. Crowds of curious onlookers gathered on both the Kansas and Missouri sides of the river. Cattle drives weren't uncommon in this part of the world, although they usually took place out in the vast plains. People didn't see cattle drives in Kansas City proper. And certainly not on the water.

Billy Boy smiled and waved at the crowds. By the time the pontoon boats reached the confluence of the Missouri and Kansas rivers, he spotted a TV station traffic helicopter overhead. Then another. Then a third. Billy Boy was loving this.

After reaching the designated spot on the east bank just south of the big downtown arena, Bradwell guided his craft toward shore, where some of his hired help tied up the boat and helped him ashore. He strode to a podium decorated with the Rip-A-Chunk and Billy Boy's Cow Sauce logos. The reporters were already waiting. He counted at least fifteen or twenty of them, which was pretty good.

The Kansas City newspaper and all the local TV stations had representatives there, as did several trade publications and one of the Topeka TV stations. Billy Boy didn't see anyone who looked like they were from the national press, but that was fine. The local reports would be picked up by the network affiliates, and the article from the Kansas City paper would be picked up by wire services around the country.

"Hey, how y'all doin'?" Bradwell said with a grin as he reached the podium. "I thank y'all for comin' out today. So, what do you think of Billy Boy's armada? Pretty impressive, huh?"

The other boats were doing their best to hold their positions in the current. As Bradwell had hoped, a whole lot of mooing was in the air now.

"As you can see, I brought a few friends with me," Bradwell said. "We're here at this beautiful site, almost within spittin' distance of the Kansas City Stockyards, to announce an exciting new project. One that involves some of my friends back there on the boats. They're going to be working close with me on this project—real close. You see, ladies and gentlemen, I'm planning to build the greatest tourist attraction Kansas City has ever seen. I'm talkin' about Billy Boy Bradwell's World-Famous Barbecue Hall of Fame. And you know that it has to be here, because Kansas City barbecue is the only kind in this world that really counts. Now, I'll take a few questions."

Four hundred miles away, Mayor Pete Pigg watched Billy Boy Bradwell's performance on the TV in his office.

The reporters were tossing Bradwell softball questions. Why weren't they raking him over the coals the way the Memphis reporters always did Mayor Pigg? And Billy Boy's stunt with the cows and boats? The reporters apparently thought it was cute. If Pigg had tried something like that, someone would have called the Society for the Prevention of Cruelty to Animals on him. Or they would have wanted to know if taxpayer money was used to rent the boats. And what was the deal with the cows anyway? Didn't those rubes in Kansas City know real barbecue was made with pork, not beef?

Mayor Pigg didn't think his mood could get any worse. Then his cell phone rang. Waldo Jefferson was on the line.

"Yes, Waldo?" the mayor growled.

"Are you seeing this, Mr. Mayor?"

"That clown in Kansas City? Yeah, I'm watchin' it."

"Any ideas?"

"Ideas? You mean besides gettin' a barge to run him over on his trip back upriver?"

"This isn't a good time to make jokes, Mr. Mayor. I don't know if this has occurred to you yet, but the world isn't big enough for two World Barbecue Halls of Fame. And in case you've forgotten, you've got a problem with your site here in Memphis. The property your whole plan depends on is owned by a smut lord who won't sell."

"Actually, *we've* got a problem," Pigg said. "Because neither one of us is gonna make any money off this deal unless we get our Barbecue Hall of Fame up and runnin' first."

"So, like I said, any ideas?"

"Yeah, I got one," Pigg said. "I've learned sumpin important about our friend Gus Eldridge. He's got a weakness for a certain world-famous actress who happens to be from Memphis."

"You talking about Dawn?"

"You bet I am."

"And what does the smut lord want with her?"

"Well, he's hopin' she'll be in one of his movies."

"Mr. Mayor, have you flipped out? You know she's not gonna do that."

"Well, Waldo, you and me have to think of a way to make her do it. Because we've got millions of dollars at stake."

"What are you gonna offer her, money?" Jefferson said. "You can't pay someone like that. She's got plenty of money. She's already famous. You don't have any leverage on her."

"We'll get some, Waldo, we'll get some. I just haven't figured out how yet."

Chapter 20

The warehouse was as dark as a cave. It was built in the 1950s, or maybe even before. Modern warehouses weren't much to look at, but those from the middle of the twentieth century had a particularly Spartan air to them.

The only windows were tiny ones in rows up high where the walls met the ceiling. They should have let in more moonlight, but the panes were coated with decades of dust.

The Ghetto Blazer knew there was little to see inside anyway. All the fixtures—copper pipes, anything of value—had been stripped out long ago. The floor was littered with debris—mostly fast-food wrappers, beer cans, wine bottles, and other alcoholic beverage containers.

Obviously, this had been a popular spot with winos at one time. But for some reason, they had all moved on. The Ghetto

Blazer knew this because he had been keeping an eye on the place.

He got to work quickly. This was one of the bigger buildings he had targeted. It was in a part of North Memphis that had once been a thriving industrial district. But all the factories and warehouses had been shuttered long ago, leaving a vast urban dead zone—nothing but blight for several square miles.

The Ghetto Blazer finished sloshing accelerant along the walls and floor. The warehouse windows were too high to throw a Molotov cocktail through. He would have to throw from inside, then get out quickly—a bit different from his usual MO, but not a problem. It would take a couple of minutes for the trails of accelerant to connect with each other. He would have plenty of time to get out.

With a deep breath, the Ghetto Blazer lit the Molotov cocktail and tossed it into the far corner, near the spot where the foreman's office was located. *Whoosh!* The fireball quickly lit the room. And what the Ghetto Blazer saw in that light made his heart sink. In the corner beside the office door was a figure lying on the floor.

A wino was in here, after all! How could he have missed the guy? Would the wino have the presence of mind to get out before fire engulfed the whole warehouse? No, the Ghetto Blazer couldn't take that chance. The wino might be sick, injured, or too drunk to move. The Ghetto Blazer had to help him.

The man stirred slowly as the Ghetto Blazer reached him.

"Hey, buddy, get up!" the Ghetto Blazer said. "We gotta get out of here!"

The only response was a groan. The Ghetto Blazer reached down with both hands, preparing to hoist the wino over his shoulder and carry him out if necessary. He couldn't afford to spend any more time trying to coax the man to his feet. Fingers of fire were already crawling across the warehouse.

Suddenly, the wino reached up and grabbed the Ghetto Blazer by both wrists with surprising strength.

"What are you doing?" the Ghetto Blazer shouted. He wrenched his right arm free, stripping off the surgical glove on that hand in the process. But the wino held fast to his left arm. Was this guy crazy?

In an instant, the wino was on his feet, twisting the Ghetto Blazer's left arm behind his back. The Ghetto Blazer couldn't believe it. Someone was mugging him in the middle of an arson. Only in Memphis.

"Dude, I'm not carrying any money," the Ghetto Blazer said. "And in case you haven't noticed, this building is burning. We need to get outta here!"

"I know it's burning, you piece of crap!" his attacker said as he expertly kicked the back of the Ghetto Blazer's left knee, sending him tumbling face-first into a pile of debris on the floor. "You're the Ghetto Blazer. And you're busted. The next time you strike a match, it's gonna be to light a smoke in the hoosegow, boy!"

So it wasn't a wino at all. It was a cop. *It's true that no good deed goes unpunished*, the Ghetto Blazer thought.

He felt the sharp bite of metal on his left wrist as the cop snapped on a handcuff. The cop's knee was planted firmly in the middle of the Ghetto Blazer's back.

"All units, all units, move in!" the cop shouted into the radio attached to his collar. "I'm in the warehouse at 318 Ewart Drive, and I've got the Ghetto Blazer in custody! I repeat, the Ghetto Blazer is in custody! And I need immediate assistance from the fire department!"

The radio message gave the Ghetto Blazer time to think as the cop pressed him into the rotting trash. But what could he do? With the cop's weight on his back, he was immobilized.

If he was caught, he was caught. But he wasn't going down without a fight. He reached out with his right hand for any kind of weapon. After a second or two of searching, his fingers closed around the neck of an empty whiskey bottle.

"All right, put your other hand behind your back right now, jerk-off!" the cop said. "If you make me do it, you're not gonna like the way it feels."

Suddenly, the trail of kerosene on the wall nearest the two men erupted in flames, causing the cop to flinch and reflexively jump to his feet.

"Holy crap!" the cop said.

The momentary distraction was just what the Ghetto Blazer needed. With the knee lifted off his back, he rolled toward the cop and swung the bottle with all his strength. It was a backhanded shot with much less force than the Ghetto Blazer would have liked, but it caught the cop, who was still stooped over, flush in the nose. The bottle didn't shatter the way they always did in the movies, but it made an effective club all the same. The cop fell backward on his butt, surprised and groaning in pain. A blood trickle quickly formed in his right nostril.

Both men scrambled to their feet, but the Ghetto Blazer got there first. He swung the bottle again, this time with a more powerful sidearm motion, striking the cop in the left ear. The force of the blow was so strong that the bottle slipped out of the Ghetto Blazer's hand and went skittering across the floor. The cop went down a second time, blood gushing from the left side of his face. He wouldn't get up so quickly after a blow like that.

The Ghetto Blazer knew he had little time before police and firefighters started arriving. So he ran, half expecting the cop to scramble to his feet and tackle him from behind.

The Ghetto Blazer ran out the door and down an alley. As he so often did, he disappeared into the night. The fire was now big enough to be seen from outside the building. And the wail of sirens was getting closer.

Inside, Detective Chuck Sykes was shaking off the cobwebs and talking on his radio again. The fire crackled and popped on the walls around him as he tried to collect his thoughts.

"Folks, the situation has changed. The Ghetto Blazer is not in custody. I repeat, he's not in custody. And I'm going to need some medical attention when those fire trucks get here."

Despite the growing fire, he remained in the building, frantically scanning the floor. Blood trickled down the side of his head. The temperature was rising to an uncomfortable level. And the heat and smoke made his eyes water. The blows to his head had made his vision blurry.

But after what he'd just been through, he wasn't leaving without it. No way. He wasn't going to lose a potentially case-breaking piece of evidence under a firefighter's boot.

There it was! He whipped off his wino shirt, a dirty plaid button-down, and used it to pick up the whiskey bottle at his feet, careful not to touch the bottle's neck.

"I'm outbound from the building right now," Sykes said into the radio. "Any units in the area, hold your fire. It's me, Detective Chuck Sykes, not the perpetrator. And I'm coming out in a big hurry."

Fortunately for Detective Sykes, the Ghetto Blazer knew what he was doing when he set the fire. Although it was spreading quickly, the path through the door was unblocked by flames. The arsonist knew to leave himself an escape route.

As he reached the door and exited the building, Sykes barked one more order into his radio. "Tell those crime scene investigators at the lab to get ready. They've got some fingerprints to analyze tonight."

Chapter 21

"**H**ave you completely lost your mind, Mayor Pigg?"

It wasn't the first time Mayor Pigg had heard that question. In fact, he'd been hearing it a lot lately. Still, it hurt when it came from such a pretty young lady.

"Now, Miss Dawn, I wish you'd hear me out," the mayor said into the telephone.

"Hear you out? Hear you out? How do you think you can explain this so it doesn't sound completely crazy?" Dawn knew she was losing her cool, but she couldn't help herself. So much for putting on a friendly front with Hizzoner.

"Augustine Eldridge is actually a nice guy," Mayor Pigg said. "I know what he's suggestin' sounds a little unorthodox, but if you could just talk to him."

"Talk to him? There's nothing to discuss. You say he wants me to star in a porno movie!"

"Well, he didn't actually say anythin' about a starrin' role, but I imagine you're right about that," Mayor Pigg said. "I mean, given how well known you are and everythin'."

"Yeah, I'm well known. I'm well known because I've worked hard to build a career in real movies! Real movies that require real acting! Not movies where you spread your legs and wail like a banshee!"

Despite Dawn's hostile tone, the mayor had to admit he was getting turned on. But he needed to stay focused. Millions of dollars in land acquisition costs were at stake here. Plus a lot more money later.

"Listen, Miss Dawn, no one is sayin' you have to do the movie," the mayor said, back-pedaling as quickly as he could. "I just told Mr. Eldridge I might be able to set up a face-to-face between you and him. If you don't like what you hear, walk away."

"Why would I even entertain the idea?" Dawn asked.

"It's, uh, related to the World Barbecue Hall of Fame," Pigg said. He wasn't sure he was choosing the right words, but it was too late to gracefully back out now. "You want to help the project, right?"

"I said I did, but—"

"If you wanna help, you need to do this," Pigg said. "Mr. Eldridge owns the property where we need to build the Barbecue Hall of Fame. And he's prepared to, uh, give us a substantial discount on the price if you'll just talk to him about this."

"That's the stupidest thing I've ever heard," Dawn shot back.

"Okay, it's stupid. He's stupid. But it's the only way we can move this project forward."

"There are other ways."

"Like what?"

"You could meet his price."

"Dawn, I'd love to do that, I really would. But the city will be purchasin' this property. And I have to be a good steward of taxpayer dollars. Besides, the city council would never go for his askin' price. It's well above the appraised value. And usin' eminent domain on a project like this is a real nonstarter. Thanks to the state legislature, the laws are real strict about limitin' the reasons government can take private property if the owners don't want to sell. It has to be for roads, bridges, stuff like that. And as great as this project is goin' to be, I don't think we could sell that to the state supreme court, sweetie."

"Okay, so? You can't get Mr. Porn King's property. Find another site and build the Barbecue Hall of Fame where the land is cheaper and the owner will sell."

"No can do, babe," the mayor said. "It's gotta be that site. I can't tell you why, but it's gotta be that site."

"Well, if you can't tell me why, then I can't meet with your good friend Mr. Eldridge," Dawn said. "You tell me why it has to be that site, and I'll meet with him."

"Dawn, I . . ."

"You obviously need time to think about this," Dawn said.

With that, Mayor Pigg found himself listening to a dial tone. As he stared at the ceiling tiles in his city hall office, he felt his scalp reddening with anger.

Mayor Pigg didn't need this kind of aggravation. It seemed like everything was going wrong in his world. The FBI's latest stats had Memphis ranked as the nation's number-two most crime-infested city. On top of that, the latest issue of *Crunches!* men's health and fitness magazine had an article that named Memphis the number-two most unhealthy city in America. Pigg had only the gang-bangers in Detroit and the gluttons in New Orleans to thank for keeping his city from being the absolute worst in those two categories.

That wasn't all. Cedric had called earlier in the day to tell him about the latest promotion at Carnivore Charlie's. That jerk Nick Nelson had come up with a new specialty drink called the Ghetto Blazer, a mocking reference to the mayor's inability to catch the arsonist. According to Cedric, it was selling quite well. And why not? Even tourists who knew nothing about the city's politics would go nuts over the potent mixture of rum, sangria, and Kahlúa, topped with a flaming hit of Everclear.

Plus, some redneck in Kansas City was threatening to ruin all his hard work on the Barbecue Hall of Fame. If the Kansas City project got off the ground first, it might dry up political support for his own project. And that in turn would make it impossible to flip that crappy land he'd bought on the east side of the Wolf River Harbor. How would he ever sell it? Not even he could get away with putting a park or a community center in the middle of an industrial wasteland. Reporters might be dumb, but they weren't that dumb.

And now Dawn was giving him lip. What kind of Southern lady hung up on a gentleman? A gentleman who was the duly elected chief executive of the city of Memphis, no less. So what if she was a hotshot actress? This was his town, and she was living in it!

He'd have to teach her a lesson. If Pete Pigg had a talent for anything besides barbecue and promoting himself, it was for settling scores.

Still, that would have to wait. He needed this dumb skirt to make his project go. Should he tell her? That would mean cutting one more person in on his little secret. And unlike the city council members, planning commissioners, union officials, bond attorneys, and assorted construction vendors he knew would work with him, he couldn't say the same about Dawn. She was just too, well, honest. Especially for a famous person. And she was rich enough that Mayor Pigg wasn't sure he could bribe her.

She was too stuck up for her own good. Why the hell couldn't she just talk to the pornmeister? Was she too good for that? Hell, a woman that good looking should use her God-given attributes to her advantage every chance she got, the way Pigg saw it.

No two ways about it, bringing her into the inner circle on this project would be a gamble. She might blow the whistle on the whole thing. Maybe even get some law enforcement outside the Memphis Police Department involved. Unless Mayor Pigg could come up with some lie about why the site had to be at the northwest corner of Front and Auction.

He needed to think. He was reaching for the whiskey bottle in his drawer when the intercom buzzed.

"Yeah?" he said.

"Chief Bruno is here to see you, sir," the voice on the intercom said.

"Send him in," Pigg said. "Better to see a cop in here than on the side of the highway on a Saturday night, I guess."

Chief Bruno entered and sat across from the mayor. The grizzled policeman's face rarely changed expression, but he wore a slight smirk today.

"Well, chief, you look like you're about to burst into song," Pigg said.

"You may, too, when you hear what I've got to say," Bruno replied.

"Oh, yeah? It hasn't 'zactly been the best mornin' I've ever had, so makin' me sing might be a tall order. Whaddaya got?"

"It's about the Ghetto Blazer case."

"You got sumpin on it?"

"Yes, Mr. Mayor, we have something," Bruno said. "In fact, I'd say we've got a major break that should lead to an arrest."

Chapter 22

"Where were you last night?" Joe asked. He and Scott were sitting in the parking lot of Heck's, drinking beer and waiting for their Wiffle ball game to start.

"I was busy," Scott said.

"I thought you were going to meet me here after you finished Elvising," Joe said. "I stayed until Heck closed the place down."

"I had stuff to do and people to see. What are you, my mother? I haven't had a curfew since the fifth grade."

"What's with you, man?" Joe said. "You've been acting weird all night."

It was true. More than anyone Joe knew, Scott was a happy-go-lucky sort. Nothing ever bothered him. He never stressed about his job, or money, or women, or any of the other things that brought most normal people down. He was always upbeat, always the life of the party, the ultimate happy drunk.

Not now, though. He had been quiet and out of sorts all night.

Part of it might have had to do with the fact that their game was delayed. The Sunday-night Wiffle ball league had twelve teams, which meant six games every week. The first game was scheduled to begin at five. Games were supposed to last only about an hour, thanks to rules like one strike per batter and any ball hit in the infield being an out. So the second game was scheduled for six, the third for seven, and so on.

Except the schedule never played out that way. A game would run a few minutes long. Or the next group of teams would waste too much time taking batting practice and warming up their pitchers. Delays led to more delays farther down the schedule, so the game slated for eleven often didn't get cranked up until well after midnight.

Joe and Scott's team was stuck with the eleven o'clock game this particular night. And when the allotted time rolled around, the teams from the nine o'clock game were still plodding along in the seventh inning.

Several times during the night, Scott had grumbled, "Can't these pitchers get anybody out?" But most of the time, he sat in silence, staring at his cup of beer as if all the secrets of life might be contained inside.

Joe was tired, too. Tired of waiting to play, but also tired of his friend's moping.

"Sorry, man. I didn't realize it was such a chore for you to come over here and drink a few," Joe said. "So what did you have to do last night that was so important? Find a new woman?"

"Something like that," Scott said, still staring at his beer.

They sat for a few moments until the pop of a bat against a Wiffle ball interrupted the quiet. One of the teams, a bunch of brawny construction workers from Southaven, had just hit another home run. The hitter loped around the bases, a beer in one hand and a cigarette dangling from his mouth as his teammates hooted in appreciation. The outfielders on the other team swore while their pitcher stalked around the mound in frustration. Joe had stopped trying to keep up with the score, but the team in the field was way behind.

The home run had landed near the van of the Detroit Tokers. The Tokers were scheduled to play against Joe and Scott's team again. But the delay in the start of the game didn't faze them. They were drinking shots of whiskey out of a bottle they had smuggled from the bar into the parking lot. Occasionally, one or two of the Tokers would disappear into the van, a beat-up VW, to do God knew what. Well, maybe only God knew for sure, but everybody else in the parking lot at Heck's had a pretty good idea.

Joe decided to take a different tack to break the ice. "That pitcher could use a little more break on his curveball. Those guys from Southaven couldn't hit much better if they were using a tee."

Scott said nothing.

"Look, Scott, I know something's bothering you," Joe said.

"Nothing's bothering me, except this stupid game is gonna take all night," Scott said.

"That's never bothered you before," Joe said. "You love hanging out here all night, pounding brewskis and Wiffle balls. You have somewhere else you need to be tonight?"

"Naw," Scott said. "Nowhere I need to be."

"Then what is it?" Joe said. "I've known you a long time. And if anybody can tell something's not right with you, it's me."

"So you're a psychic now?"

"No, man, I'm not a psychic. But you've been moping all night. And you never mope. You're always the one to get after me if I'm down about my job or women or whatever."

"Look, it's not something I wanna talk about."

"Oh, Scott, but I think you do," Joe said. "I think you want to tell me what's bothering you. Otherwise, you wouldn't be acting this way. You'd be trying to cover up and act like everything was normal. You know it and I know it. So tell me, what's up?"

Scott sighed and held up his beer cup, studying it carefully before draining the last swallow. "You're right, I have known you a long time. I like to think we can talk about anything. Anything but this."

"Okay, now you really have to tell me," Joe said.

"I'm going inside to grab another beer," Scott said, heading toward the bar's back entrance. "You want one?"

"Scott, don't change the sub—"

Out of nowhere, a swarm of black-clad men were converging on the parking lot from all sides.

"*Five-oh! Five-oh!*" screamed one of the Detroit Tokers, who had emerged from the van just in time to take in the scene. He and a teammate darted for a dark, abandoned alley behind Heck's. They didn't get far before they were met head on by two more of the black-clad men emerging from the shadows. The men quickly wrestled the two squirming Wiffle ball players to the ground.

"*All right, nobody move!*" one of the men shouted.

Play on the Wiffle ball field stopped. And after seeing the fate of the two Detroit Tokers, the other spectators seemed inclined to stay put.

Scott, who had just started on his beer run when the men appeared, was a few feet from Joe. Four of the men approached him, two from the front and two from the back. It took a second to register in Joe's mind, but all four had guns drawn. At that point, the whole scene seemed to slow down, like Joe was watching it happen in slow motion in a movie.

"*Down! Down on your knees!*" the men shouted at Scott.

He obeyed, and as soon as he did, one of the men behind Scott kicked him hard enough to knock him on his stomach.

Another of the men was standing in front of Joe now, gesturing at him with a nightstick. "Don't you move," the man growled. "Don't you move, or you'll be down on the ground with your buddy."

Joe couldn't budge, even to nod in understanding. He just gawked helplessly.

"Scott Paulk, you're under arrest," one of the men said, roughly snapping on a pair of handcuffs. "You're charged with twenty-six counts of arson, twenty-six counts of destruction of property, one count of resisting arrest, one count of especially aggravated assault against a police officer, and probably some other charges to be named later."

As he lay face down, Scott turned his head to glance back at Joe. The expression was hard for Joe to read. Was it anger? Resignation? Bemusement? Joe couldn't tell. All he could do was stand rooted in place, watching as the cops roughly hauled his best friend to his feet and dragged him away.

Chapter 23

M ayor Pigg was having a good night for the first time in a while.

Business at the Pigg Pen was better than it had been in weeks. Maybe it had something to do with the fact that one of the city's health inspectors had found rat droppings in Carnivore Charlie's pulled pork. And the fact that one of the Beefeaters—Carnivore Charlie's scantily clad waitresses—had been arrested by an undercover officer for selling weed in the parking lot.

Not coincidentally, both of those incidents were strategically leaked to WDUS-TV ace reporter Zip Smithers, who played them up on consecutive nights during sweeps week.

Of course, Carnivore Charlie's owner, Nick Nelson, denied the whole thing. The rat crap was planted in the food tray. The drugs were planted in the girl's car. Which of course was completely true. But by the time Smithers finished editing excerpts from the interview, Nelson came across like a paranoid nut who couldn't handle the pressure of running a Beale Street restaurant.

For Smithers, the stories were huge scoops. Which of course furthered his legend as "the Scrapper" of local TV news. "That Zip Smithers, nothing gets by him," his loyal viewers said.

What his loyal viewers didn't know was that Zip Smithers and Mayor Pigg had been partners for years in a small bar and restaurant in Destin, Florida. Although the business was only marginally profitable, Pigg had sensed that being partners with one of the city's most popular TV personalities would serve his long-term interests. Which turned out to be true, especially after Pigg was elected mayor and needed to discreetly leak information to the press corps without having it traced back to him. In fact, Pigg could kick himself for not checking Smithers's vacation schedule before calling that first news conference about the World Barbecue Hall of Fame. At roughly the same time Pigg was getting grilled by the unfriendly pack of reporters, Smithers was blowing his meager share of the Destin bar's profits on hash and hookers in Las Vegas.

The city health inspector and the cop were in Pigg's ample back pocket, too.

The health inspector had been drinking on the job for years, the result—or perhaps the cause—of an unhappy marriage. His supervisor had built a paper trail against him, and the inspector was about to get fired right around the time Pigg took office. Pigg, knowing the restaurant business and sensing an opportunity, saved the old drunk's job—for future considerations, such as his dirty little contribution to Carnivore Charlie's inspection report.

The cop who busted the waitress was the son of one of the Pigg Pen's best customers, a regular who spent many a night drinking with the proprietor. The customer's kid wanted to go to the police academy. But in view of his juvenile court record for assault and destruction of property, he never would have been considered by the police department. With a few phone calls, Pigg had managed to get the juvenile court records redacted. Other cops knew what Pigg had done. Chief Bruno probably knew. But they also knew when to pick their battles. It would be hard for people with their skill sets to get jobs anywhere else that paid nearly as well as the Memphis Police Department. Sure, cops in those piss-ant suburbs like Bartlett and Germantown ran a lesser risk of getting their heads blown off during traffic stops. But the pay in Memphis was hard to beat.

As much as Pigg enjoyed Carnivore Charlie's troubles, he realized they were only temporary. And as much as he hated Nick Nelson, Pigg had to give him his due. Nelson's customers would quickly forget about rat droppings and drug arrests and return to Carnivore Charlie's. It was hard to beat the combination of pretty ladies and barbecued meat on a stick.

The mayor had an even bigger reason to be happy this night, though. For weeks, the media had killed him over that stupid yahoo who was burning down some of the city's crappiest ghetto properties. Truth was, if not for the negative press, Pigg would have liked to give the guy a medal. After all, most middle- to upper-class Memphians couldn't be bothered about what happened in the inner city. But this stupid guy the press had taken to calling the Ghetto Blazer cared enough to set a good portion of it on fire. Why? Mayor Pigg didn't know, and he honestly didn't care. Every time the Ghetto Blazer struck, that was one less blighted property. In all honesty, the mayor would have loved to let the Ghetto Blazer keep going until he burned out the city's core.

But the press coverage was relentless. The mayor was ineffective in his efforts to stop this "domestic terrorist," the reporters said. They actually called the guy a terrorist. They made him out to be Osama bin Laden with a gas can. And if the mayor couldn't stop one arsonist, they said, how could he control crime in the city? Did the mayor not care about the inner city, because its residents didn't help get him elected?

Frankly, the mayor would have loved for his bouncers at the Pigg Pen to take every reporter in the city out to one of the alleys behind Beale Street and beat them to death. But he was a first-term mayor who wanted a second term, so he had to care about what those reporters said. Or at least pretend to care.

The police couldn't catch that arsonist until the mayor had laid down the law with Chief Bruno. And the chief had finally gotten serious enough about the problem to put some manpower on the streets. And one of those cops, God bless his soul, had gotten close enough to the Ghetto Blazer to retrieve the evidence needed for an arrest. From what the mayor was told, the evidence against their suspect was airtight. The police were going to take down some clown who worked part-time on Beale Street—a drifter, practically—who had been a patron of the Pigg Pen for years. It could be happening even now, as the mayor was thinking about it. Pretty soon, the cops would have this kid in custody, and one of his biggest problems would be solved.

And what would be wrong with that? Yes, Mayor Pigg knew the kid. He had even cultivated a friendship with him because the kid drank like a fish and rarely ran out on his tab. But Mayor Pigg had a hundred "friends" like that—people he pretended to like because it was good for his business. Actually, since he'd become mayor, he had probably a thousand friends like that. So now this kid would be spending the night at 201 Poplar. Good riddance. And tomorrow morning, Mayor Pete Pigg would call a press conference and denounce the kid—what was his name, Scott Faulk?—as the biggest scourge to hit Memphis since the yellow fever epidemic.

That was the real reason for the mayor's celebration. And he was doing it up right. He was at his favorite East Memphis bar, the Grapes of Wrath, a little place just off Poplar Avenue, one of the city's main thoroughfares, near the mayor's home in the upscale Chickasaw Gardens neighborhood. Pigg loved the place for its selection of wines and its proximity to his house. Not that he had to worry about DUIs. Chief Bruno knew where his bread was buttered. No cop was going to stop the mayor. At least not if he valued his job. Still, Pigg liked the convenience of having a bar so close. He couldn't count the number of times he'd made it home without remembering any part of the drive.

So Pigg was celebrating with a fine Cabernet from South Africa sprinkled with flecks of black pepper. Pigg couldn't explain why black pepper made red wine taste better to him. It just did. He was alone at a corner table. It wasn't easy to find alone time since he'd become mayor. But the Grapes of Wrath staff knew his moods well enough to understand when to keep people away.

"Here's to you, Scottie boy," the mayor muttered, chuckling as he raised his glass to take a sip of wine. He almost choked on that sip. From where he was seated, Mayor Pigg could see the TV above the bar. The ten o'clock news was starting, and the footage from the lead story made him sit up with a start.

"Hey! Turn that louder!" the mayor shouted at the bartender.

The anchor threw the story to a reporter in the field as the sound came up.

"Thanks, Deke. I'm here at a spirited meeting at the Mount

Olive Church of the Holy Gospel. Hundreds of people have turned out for this meeting organized by the church's pastor. He's with me right now. Reverend Smoot, can you tell us about the purpose of tonight's gathering?"

The camera cut to a good-looking forty-ish black man with close-cropped hair and a pencil-thin mustache. Watching from his seat, the mayor groaned. The Reverend Smoot was a charismatic preacher who had a huge following. And he wasn't afraid to bang heads with the powers that be at city hall. In fact, he was nicknamed "Reverend Smooth" for his ability to whip crowds into frenzies when it served his purposes.

"Why, I surely can, I surely can," the Reverend Smoot told the TV reporter. "As you well know, our mayor, Mr. Pigg, has been talking a lot lately about this World Barbecue Hall of Fame that he wants to build downtown. Of course, it has to be downtown. The white business community has to have everything downtown. They say that Memphis is only as strong as its heart and soul. Well, let me tell you and your viewers a little something that you may or may not know. The hearrrrrt and the soooul of Memphis are not in downtown! They're in the neighborhoods where good folks are just trying to get by! North Memphis, South Memphis, Orange Mound. What's Mayor Pigg's plan for helping those places?"

The camera panned the church, where a big crowd was whooping and nodding with the Reverend Smoot's words.

"Do you think the people in those neighborhoods will be getting any of that barbecue?" the Reverend Smoot continued. "You know the answer to that! Not one morsel of that fiiiiine barbecue pork will make it to the mouths of the good people in North Memphis, South Memphis, and Orange Mound! Nor will any of the money from this Barbecue Hall of Fame project! It'll all go into the pockets of Mayor Pigg's rich, white, fat-cat friends! And that, ladies and gentlemen, is unacceptable!"

The crowd was growing more agitated. As the camera panned wide, Mayor Pigg saw something that brought a dull ache to the pit of his stomach. Standing along the back row of the church was one of the few white faces in the crowd. It was Little Bobby Shotwell.

Mayor Pigg's cell phone rang. This time, it was the first few bars of "Honky Tonk Women" by the Rolling Stones.

"Yeah?" the mayor spat into the phone.

"Mr. Mayor? It's Waldo," Waldo Jefferson said, his tone just as sharp as Pigg's. "Are you seeing this? On the TV news?"

"Yeah, Waldo, I'm seein' it," the mayor said.

"Well, what are you gonna do about it?"

"What am I gonna do about it?" Pigg said. "Have you looked at those faces? Those are your people in that church. You're supposed to be the silver-tongued politician who keeps a lid on the black neighborhoods while we push this deal through, or did you forget that? I mean, there must be some reason I let you be my partner on this project."

"That was before Reverend Smoot rolled onto the set," the city council chairman said. "Having him come out negative complicates things."

"Complicates them how?" Pigg said. "You've just gotta go back out there into your neighborhoods and tell 'em Waldo Jefferson says this is a good deal for everybody."

"Mr. Mayor, you don't know politics on my side of town," Jefferson said. "Rule number one is that you don't piss off the preachers. You do that, you might as well hang it up. Now, normally, I would expect Reverend Smoot to talk to me about all this before he went public."

"Well, I've got a pretty good idea why he didn't keep you in the loop, Mr. Council Chairman. Did you happen to see Little Bobby Shotwell smirkin' in the back of the church? You know he had a hand in stirrin' all this up."

"And now that it's stirred up, it's going to be next to impossible to get it unstirred. Here's the problem I see, Mr. Mayor: This project that's supposed to make the two of us rich men still needs approval by both the planning commission and the city council. Now, those planning commissioners, they're in love with the smell of cement. They'll rubber-stamp just about any project that's put in front of them. But the council is another story. Because out of the other twelve people on the council, seven of 'em share my skin color. And as much as I might twist their arms, not one of them is gonna take on Reverend Smoot."

"Are you tellin' me you can't flip a few votes even with the Memphis Tourist Information Bureau runnin' a propaganda campaign that's gonna make this sound like the greatest thing since screw caps on beer bottles?"

"Well, maybe I could if we were close to putting this project up to a vote. But the longer the good reverend gets people riled up, the harder it's going to be to get the other council members to piss into the political winds. And in case you've forgotten, we don't even have the land to do this project yet. Your man who's a cross between Hugh Hefner and Oliver Stone doesn't want to let it go, at least not for a price we can pay. When are you going to fix that, Mr. Mayor?"

Pete Pigg was silent for a few seconds. He drained his wineglass in one gulp, then smiled slightly at his sudden flash of inspiration. "Waldo, just try to keep the outrage of the black community down to a dull roar for a few days. I think I've got an idea how we might get this project back on the fast track."

Chapter 24

S cott Paulk knew something wasn't right.

He had been arrested before—a couple of times, actually—so he didn't expect a pleasant experience after the cops swarmed him at Heck's.

The first time he had been arrested was during his senior year in high school. He and some other kids were smoking weed in the parking lot behind school one Friday night. Scott never was much of a pothead. While he had fallen in love with drinking around age twelve or fourteen, he'd never seen what the big deal was about marijuana. Some of his friends claimed to get high off the stuff, but it never did much for Scott but leave him with a headache the next morning. Still, he did it with his friends to be cool. And on that particular night, they happened to get caught. Unfortunately for Scott, he had turned eighteen a few weeks earlier, so he was arrested and booked as an adult. The rest of his friends were still underage, so they got away with probation and juvenile rap sheets that disappeared when they came of age.

Scott had spent a night in the holding tank at the Criminal Justice Center, known more colloquially by its street address, 201 Poplar. The cast of characters at 201 Poplar was scary. Drunks. Gang-bangers. Whacked-out crack addicts. Armed robbers who wouldn't think twice about shooting somebody over a ten-dollar bill. It was the longest night of Scott's life. He couldn't sleep because of the voices arguing, hustling, screaming, and jabbering incoherently, all echoing off the walls. He was glad when his court appearance rolled around the next morning.

The judge went easy on Scott. He got into a diversion program, which meant he, too, was essentially on probation for twenty-four months. He didn't have to go back to jail after his parents bonded him out following his arraignment hearing.

Scott swore he'd never go through that again. He was determined to stay out of jail, even though the experience had elevated his street cred with his buddies.

Then he got into a bar fight his sophomore year at Middle Tennessee State. Some guy made rude comments to a girl Scott was drinking with. Not a girl he was hitting on, even. Just a classmate Scott studied with sometimes. Scott and the girl had hit one of the bars on the city square to unwind after a night of college algebra. Some jerk who had about three too many pitchers of nickel beer bumped into the girl, spilling Busch Light on her new sweater. Which might have been forgivable, if he hadn't offered to lick it off.

One thing led to another, and pretty soon Scott and the drunk dude were trading blows. Then the guy pulled a knife, so Scott brained him with a beer bottle. When the cops sorted everything out, they decided to charge Scott with aggravated assault with a deadly weapon. That meant a trip to the Rutherford County Jail—which was no garden spot but still nicer than 201 Poplar—and then an uncomfortable session in which Scott had to explain to a judge why he was in trouble again while still on diversion.

The aggravated assault charge didn't stick. After interviewing witnesses at the bar, prosecutors decided they didn't want to try to make that case to a jury. They told Scott he could avoid jail time by pleading to simple assault, with an agreement that he would pay a five-hundred-dollar fine and extend his probation by twelve months. He took the deal.

Scott had been careful since those two run-ins. He didn't stay out of trouble exactly, but at least he avoiding getting caught. Until this particular night.

Something about this arrest was different. The cops didn't take him to the central booking area to be fingerprinted. They didn't interrogate him. And they didn't put him in a cell with the general population.

In addition to housing the Shelby County Jail, the high-rise Criminal Justice Center was home to the police headquarters and most of the local courts. The cops took Scott to a holding cell adjacent to one of the courtrooms, a room used primarily when people became unruly during court proceedings and had to be physically restrained until they calmed down.

Scott sat in that cell—small, windowless, maybe eight feet square—for what seemed like hours. Sometimes, he heard voices—cops, he assumed—talking outside the door. Sometimes, nothing. What were they planning to do? Hold a press conference and parade him in front of TV cameras? Beat the crap out of him? They certainly weren't going to read him his rights and let him call an attorney. That much seemed clear.

He tried to run through his options in his head. The problem was, he really didn't have any. Since the cops had arrested him, chances were they had enough evidence to make the charges stick. Scott couldn't afford a fancy lawyer. And the way the criminal justice system worked, that was pretty much the end of the story. With his record, Scott was looking at some serious prison time. Depending on how things went, he might die inside. It happened to people younger than he was. Scott felt like his life had slipped totally beyond his control. Not that he had ever felt he was in control. He had always drifted through life, taking whatever opportunities presented themselves but mostly just hanging around, waiting for lightning to strike. And this was in a sense that proverbial bolt of lightning. But the kind of lightning that killed, not the kind that magically transformed him into a superhero.

Scott was slipping into despair when a commotion started outside his cell door. He heard some voices he recognized as those of the police officers assigned to stand guard. Then another voice, even more familiar, although Scott couldn't quite make it out. Finally, after several minutes of discussion, the voices faded and the door swung open.

In strode Pete Pigg, the honorable mayor of Memphis, the proprietor of the Pigg Pen, and Scott's occasional drinking buddy. The expression on Pigg's face was the most sober Scott had ever seen.

Having no place to sit in the tiny cell, Mayor Pigg stood for several uncomfortable seconds staring Scott up and down. Scott would have said something, would have reacted in some way, except he couldn't figure out what type of reaction would make the most sense in a situation like this.

Then the mayor spoke. "Well, well, Scottie, my boy, it looks like you've got yourself into quite a mess here."

Scott blinked but said nothing.

Realizing he wouldn't get a response, Pigg continued. "You know, Scott, bein' the mayor of this city ain't the gig everybody thinks it is. Oh, sure, it's great to have people treatin' you nice wherever you go. People wantin' to do you favors and give you money. Women wantin' to . . . well, you name it. But the truth is, the job is a pain in the butt. Problems, so many problems, most of which the Lord Almighty himself would be hard pressed to solve. And no matter how you decide to fix them, somebody's gonna be unhappy. Crazy, whacked-out neighborhood activists who don't have the sense God gave little green apples. Business people who think government's primary job should be to help them get richer. Other politicians who think everythin' you do is a move calculated to screw over their grand ambitions for runnin' for whatever seat they've got their eyes on."

The mayor paused again. Scott shrugged.

"But you know the worst of all of it, Scottie boy?" Pigg asked. "The worst is dealin' with the media. Those people are vultures. They dig and dig and dig until they find a flaw—doesn't matter if it's a big one or a small one—and then they use that to define you. 'Oh, the mayor can't stop crime. He can't improve our schools. He can't keep the riverboats from leavin' town. He can't keep the Grizzlies from losin'. And worst of all, he can't stop some loser who decides he wants to burn down the city's ghetto property, one buildin' at a time.' See where you fit into this story, Scott?"

"Maybe," Scott said sullenly.

"That's good, Scott, because until you said that, I wasn't sure you still have a brain in your head." Pigg seemed to be enjoying himself, which unnerved Scott. "So here's the deal. Night before last, one of my undercover officers had a run-in with this serial arsonist, the guy they call the Ghetto Blazer. My guy gets into a scuffle with him, nearly puts him down for an arrest, but the little weasel hits him with a bottle and gets away. Sound familiar?"

Normally, Scott was a master of the comeback quip, able to turn the words of anyone who taunted him upside down. Now, though, he was at a loss.

"But you know what, Scott? We happen to have sumpin called crime scene investigators here in Memphis. Maybe you've seen sumpin like 'em on the TV. And guess what they did? They dusted that doggone bottle. And you know what? They found fingerprints matchin' this guy named Scott Paulk, who just happened to have his fingerprints on file, on account of his criminal record. And you know what else? When our undercover guy looked through our files and saw your photo, he said, 'That's the guy. That's the punk who brained me with that bottle and got away. He's the one who set that buildin' on fire the exact same way dozens of others in the 'hood have been torched the last few months.' You know what that means, Scottie?"

"I guess you're gonna tell me," Scott said.

"I'll tell you exactly how this is gonna go," Pigg said. "Our district attorney is gonna take all this evidence before a judge. The judge is gonna agree not to grant bail, based on the DA's claim that you're a flight risk. You're gonna sit in jail a few months until the case comes to trial. Meanwhile, the media—I told you they're jerks, Scott—they're gonna convict you in the court of public opinion. Your face will end up on TV a million times as 'the Ghetto Blazer.' When you finally go to trial, you won't stand a chance. The evidence against you is pretty overwhelmin', buddy boy. And with your record of priors and the circumstantial evidence linkin' you to the other arsons, well, you might need to live as long as Methuselah before you see the light of day again. Do you follow me so far?"

"I think so," Scott said. "So, you got any good news for me tonight?"

At that, the mayor laughed. "As a matter of fact, Scott, I think I do. All that stuff I just told you about, it doesn't have to happen. At the moment, there's no record of you being arrested. None at all. Some dope smokers at Heck's may have seen it, but they'll keep it to themselves unless they want to have cops kickin' down their doors to find out what they've got under the glow lamps."

"So I haven't been arrested yet?" Scott said. "It sure feels like I have."

"Nope, not yet," Pigg said. "Not yet, and maybe not ever. That depends on you, Scott."

"Depends on me how?" Scott was genuinely puzzled.

"Well, Scott, I'd like to ask you a little favor," the mayor said, trying to suppress the smile creeping into the corners of his mouth. "And if you do that favor, maybe all of this will go away. You'll be back drinkin' with your buddies on Beale tomorrow night, just like this never happened."

"What's the favor?"

"Well, I need you to burn sumpin for me, Scott. You like burnin' things, don't you?"

Scott said nothing.

"You don't have to answer that," Pigg said. "I don't know why you burned all those buildings. And you know what? I don't even care. I really don't. You could burn 90 percent of North Memphis, South Memphis, and Orange Mound and it would probably increase the city's tax rolls. What I'm here to ask you to do is burn one more buildin'. One particular buildin'. At the intersection of Auction Avenue and Front Street."

"That old rattletrap?" Scott said. "It looks like it could fall down any day on its own. Why do you need me—or anyone—to burn it?"

"Oh, I've got my reasons," Pigg said. "And the less you know about those, the better. But I'll tell you what. If I let you loose and that buildin' happens to go up in flames—say, within seventy-two hours—then those charges might just go away in a hurry."

"And if I decide I don't want to do that?" Scott asked, already knowing the answer.

"Well, Scottie, things could get bad," Pigg said. "I might not see you at the Pigg Pen for quite a while. Shoot, I might be retired and livin' down in Destin by then. Am I bein' clear enough?"

"Pretty clear," Scott said.

"I'll tell you what," the mayor said, finally unable to suppress his smile. "I'm gonna give you a day or two to think about it. I'm gonna have the cops take you down to the holdin' tank, just so you can see what your life would be like for the next twenty or thirty years if you turn down my offer. Give it some thought. Good night, Scott. I'll drink an extra brewski down on Beale in your honor."

With that, Mayor Pete Pigg turned, rapped on the door, and exited after the guards opened it. The door slammed shut, leaving Scott to ponder his options, which seemed every bit as hopeless as before.

Chapter 25

Joe Miller was not having a good morning.

He'd spent the night at 201 Poplar, although he was in police custody only part of the time. After the raid at Heck's, he'd been stuffed into a police car and taken downtown, but he hadn't actually been booked into the Shelby County Jail. Instead, he was taken to an interrogation room, where different groups of police officers took turns yelling at him. They wanted to know all about Scott Paulk—how long Joe had known him, what type of person he was, if he had an unusual interest in fire, what had inspired him to become the person the media was calling "the Ghetto Blazer."

Joe couldn't help them much, even if he had wanted to. He honestly answered how long he and Scott had been friends. But as for the more personal questions, it was hard to know what to say. Joe had always thought he knew Scott, that Scott was a what-you-see-is-what-you-get kind of guy. But if what the cops were saying was true, Joe thought maybe he didn't know his friend well at all.

Scott had never been an angel, Joe understood that. Scott liked to drink, party, and chase women. And if some guy wanted to start a fight, Scott wouldn't back down. Scott could be cocky and a little too direct in some of his comments. That made him like 95 percent of the guys Joe had hung around with ever since college.

But an arsonist? Burning down vacant buildings for no reason at all? That didn't make sense. Joe didn't have any idea Scott had that in him. And yet, as Joe thought back, he should have seen the signs. Like the time he caught Scott with that black smudge on his face at Heck's. Scott had said it was eyeliner, part of his Elvis makeup. But the smudge actually looked more like that black goo football players put under their eyes to reflect the glare of stadium lights. Or the kind commandos used to make themselves harder to see when they were sneaking around at night.

And that kerosene at Scott's apartment? What a dumb cover story Scott had cooked up for that—saving money on electricity by burning kerosene lamps. Yet Scott had always been a bit eccentric. No, make that a lot eccentric. After years of dealing with Scott's weirdness, Joe had learned to overlook things that seemed off or out of place. It made their friendship go a lot easier when Joe didn't question every little thing Scott said or did. Scott was just Scott.

But now Joe wondered just who Scott was.

Joe didn't know the person the cops were talking about. He could tell they were trying to lock him into a story, to get him to acknowledge that he was an accessory to Scott's crimes. Joe wasn't worried about his answers to their questions, though. One of his uncles had been fond of saying, "If you tell the truth, you never have to remember what you said."

And in this case, Joe knew he had no information that would incriminate Scott. Other than the bit about the kerosene. But the cops surely had searched Scott's apartment and found that already. Joe could honestly say he knew nothing about what was going on. Scott had kept him completely out of the loop.

In a way, that hurt. Weren't they supposed to be best friends? How could Scott have been involved with this for months and Joe never had a clue?

Finally, the cops had turned Joe loose. They warned him not to leave town, that he could be picked up again and arrested at any time.

Joe spent the next few hours trying to bail Scott out of jail. The trouble was, there was no record of Scott's ever being booked. The receptionist in the jail's booking area told him that in a flat monotone. Maybe the police would bring the paperwork downstairs in a little while.

So Joe waited, watching bail bondsmen come and go, sometimes accompanied by unhappy-looking family members. Nothing—and no one—in the jail looked clean. Joe didn't even want to lean against the counter in the booking area, much less sit in one of the flimsy-looking plastic chairs in the waiting room.

A little while turned into a long while. Joe asked the receptionist again if the paperwork had come back on Scott Paulk. The answer was no. Maybe it would in a little while longer. So Joe waited. But the answer was still no. And each time Joe asked, the receptionist grew more impatient, as if clicking on her computer screen and answering a simple question were the most difficult tasks in the world.

Finally, Joe asked if there was anyone else he could talk to about his friend's status. The receptionist suggested the jail's watch commander, relieved to be able to point this relentless pest in a different direction. But the watch commander wasn't available, so Joe waited and waited. He asked the receptionist when the watch commander might arrive. It was the middle of a shift change, she said, so it could be awhile. It was nearly six in the morning before Joe finally saw the watch commander, who was every bit as unfriendly and unhelpful as the receptionist. "Check back later in the morning," the watch commander suggested.

Joe finally had enough. On the drive home, he allowed himself to think maybe it was all a terrible mistake and the cops had let Scott go. Maybe Scott's voice would be on his answering machine, making some joke about how the Detroit Tokers had engineered the whole police raid just to get out of playing Wiffle ball against them.

But Scott had left no message on Joe's machine. Joe didn't know what else he could do but wait. Although he had been up all night, he knew sleep was impossible. It was around the time he normally went to the office, and even though he felt like calling in sick, he decided work might take his mind off this mess.

Joe arrived at his office about a half-hour earlier than usual. At least it would be quiet. Or so he thought. Within five minutes of the time he sat at his desk, the phone rang. The nervous voice of Calvin Cameron was on the other end of the line.

"Joe, Joe, where have you been?" Cameron fairly shouted.

"Actually, I'm here early," Joe said. "I thought I'd get caught up on—"

"There's no time for that," Cameron said. "You need to get over to the mayor's office right now. He said he wants to see you the minute you get in."

"Did he say why?" Joe wasn't in the mood to work on the mayor's pet project right now.

"No, he didn't. He just said you need to get moving."

After hanging up, Joe took the short trolley ride to city hall. The mayor kept him waiting, as usual, in his outer office while he made several phone calls.

Yeah, real urgent, Joe thought, listening to the muffled sounds of the mayor's voice through the office door. He couldn't tell for sure, but the mayor sounded in a cheerful mood, which irritated Joe even more. Finally, the receptionist's intercom buzzed, and she told Joe the mayor was ready to see him.

The mayor remained seated, his fat hands resting far apart on his desktop. He leaned back in his chair, appraising Joe as he entered. His eyes were red from drink, lack of sleep, or probably both, but he had a strange grin on his face.

"Good mornin', Joe," the mayor said. "I think you might want to sit down."

Joe did.

The grin grew into a smirk. "Heard you had a rough night," the mayor said.

"I've had better," Joe replied. So the mayor knew about what had happened at Heck's.

"Sounds like you and your friend Scott got yourselves into a little trouble."

Joe didn't appreciate the way the mayor was toying with him. "Listen, Mayor Pigg, I have no idea what's going on here."

"Oh, you don't?" the mayor said. "Well, allow me to fill you in. Your buddy has been arrested for burnin' down buildings all over town. We've got enough evidence to put him away for a long time. And you know what else? I think you're involved, too."

"I'm not involved," Joe said. He didn't want to hang Scott out to dry, but he couldn't think of anything else to say to the mayor's accusation.

"So you say, Joe, so you say," the mayor continued. "But you know what? I bet if my chief's men spend enough time workin' on it, they can get a confession out of you and a corroboratin' statement from your buddy. And then you'll be goin' inside, too."

"Bull," Joe said.

"Think so? Just whose office do you think you're sittin' in? I'm the mayor of this city, son, and if I want it to happen, then by God it's goin' to happen. I could have you arrested right now and type up confession statements for you and Scott that would say whatever I want them to say."

"This isn't some banana republic," Joe said.

"No, son, this is Memphis," the mayor said. "And this is how things get done around here."

"We've still got a court system in this country, and the rules aren't made in Memphis," Joe said. "They're dictated by the Constitution and the Bill of Rights."

The mayor laughed out loud. "You mean your right to a fair trial?" he said, making air quotes with his fingers. "Boy, you can have a trial if you want one. But you know what? I've got the full resources of city government behind my legal team. You guys, unless I miss my guess, might scrape enough money together for pizza on Saturday night. And what's your story? 'Oh, I didn't do it. I wasn't involved.' Who do you think a jury's gonna believe, a coupla young scumbags barely gettin' by or the lawyers who represent the people of this great city?"

"This isn't fair," Joe said.

"Fair's got nothin' to do with it, boy," the mayor said. "Fair went out the window for most of us around the time we started kindygarten. But there is a way out, Joe. For you and your friend."

"What's that?"

"It's real simple. I just need you to talk to your buddy. He's over at 201 Poplar now."

"He is?" Joe said. "I was there all night, trying to get in to see him. They said they didn't have any record of him being there."

"That's because they don't have a record of him bein' there," the mayor said. "And they won't. As far as he, you, and the court system are concerned, it'll be like none of this ever happened—if you can get him to do one little favor for me."

"What favor is that?"

"He'll tell you about that if he needs to. In fact, if you guys are workin' together, as I 'spect you are, then he's probably gonna need your help."

"What kind of help?"

"You guys can work that out. Just go down to the jail and make him see things the right way."

"But if they don't have a record of him there, how am I going to find him?"

"That's real simple. Just go up to the bookin' desk and hand them this."

Mayor Pigg reached across the desk and handed Joe a business card. The card bore the name of Police Chief Zack Bruno.

Chapter 26

The police chief's card worked like magic.

All the uncooperativeness and indifference Joe had encountered the night before melted away. Within fifteen minutes of entering the booking area, he was seated face to face with Scott in one of the small, drab rooms at 201 Poplar in which inmates were allowed to confer with their attorneys.

It was little consolation, but Scott looked every bit as haggard as Joe felt. Of course, they'd been that way together many times, usually while nursing hangovers. But the mood was different now. And Joe was pretty sure the guards weren't going to serve up screwdrivers and Bloody Marys.

The two friends stared at each other, neither knowing exactly what to say.

Finally, Joe took a stab. "Well, we probably had to forfeit the Wiffle ball game last night."

"Guess so," Scott said. "It's a shame, too. I felt like it was going to be a good night for me at the plate."

"Well, maybe our game will get rescheduled," Joe said.

"Yeah, if anybody ought to understand trouble with the law, it would be the Detroit Tokers."

That was all the idle banter Joe could stand. "So, you mind telling me what's going on, Scott?"

"Well, Joe, I can't really say. It's hard to keep up on current events while I'm locked up in here."

"Very funny."

"I guess it's what they call gallows humor."

"Scott, could you please drop the jokes for once and tell me what's going on?"

"Don't worry about it."

"Don't worry about it? You're not the only one who's in trouble here."

"I'm not?" Scott seemed surprised.

"No, of course not. I'm in the middle of this, too."

"No you aren't," Scott said. "They can't do anything to you because you haven't done anything wrong."

"I know I haven't, but that doesn't seem to matter to Mayor Pigg."

"What did he say to you?"

"He said the cops have the goods on you, Scott. And unless I can convince you to do some favor for him, we're both going to prison for a long time."

An expression passed across Scott's face that Joe had never seen before. It looked like a wince of anguish.

"But you're not involved," Scott said, his voice cracking. "He knows it."

"That doesn't matter much to the mayor," Joe said. "And he seems confident about his ability to carry out his threats. So, Scott, my question again is, what's this all about?"

"I'm afraid the more I tell you, the worse things will get for you."

"How can they get worse?" Joe said, his voice rising. "Would you please just start talking?"

"What did the mayor say I've done?"

"He said you're the Ghetto Blazer."

A long pause.

"And what if I am, Joe? What would you think of me then?"

"What would I think of you? Well, it would depend on why you did what they say you did. I've known you a long time. And I know you've done randomly stupid things."

Scott fidgeted.

"But you know what, Scott?" Joe continued. "I know you're not stupid. You act like you don't care about much except drinking and chasing skirts, but I know you better than that. If you did this, I believe you had a reason. I'd just like to know what that reason is."

"Pride," Scott said.

"Pride? Pride in what? Your ability to barbecue a building?"

"No, man. Pride in my town."

"That doesn't make sense, Scott. If you have so much pride in Memphis, then why would you want to burn half of it down?"

"You're not seeing the big picture here."

"So what's the big picture, Scott?"

"Do you know why people like New Orleans?"

"What's that got to do with anything?"

"Think about it, Joe. New Orleans is a nationally known—no,

make that internationally known—tourist town. People go there for the food, the music, the nightlife. They go to ride the trolleys. They go to be near the Mississippi River, the Big Muddy. They go because of the town's history and all the great architecture and all those cool homes in the Garden District."

"So? What's that got to do—"

"It's got everything to do with this," Scott said. "Put it together. What does New Orleans have that Memphis doesn't? We've got great barbecue, great catfish, great Southern cooking. We're the birthplace of blues and rock-and-roll, which are infinitely better musical genres than jazz, which is what New Orleans is known for. We've got Beale Street and the rest of the downtown entertainment district. We've got trolleys. We've got the Mississippi, too. We've got tons of history—not all of it good, but neither is the history of New Orleans. And we've got beautiful Southern Gothic homes, particularly in parts of Midtown and East Memphis."

"Scott, I'm still not following you. I know you've got all day to sit here and reflect on civic virtues, but . . ."

"Man, Joe, you're thick. People love New Orleans. It's the Big Easy, the Crescent City. But Memphis? We're the punch line to national jokes. And I think it's because all the good stuff we've got here is overshadowed by the problems—the crime, the crappy schools, and the blight. Especially the blight. It's like a cancer choking this town. After Katrina, the world saw New Orleans has a lot of those problems, too, but they're confined to places tourists never visit. But there's so much blight in Memphis that you can't miss it. You stray a couple of blocks outside the entertainment district and you're in a bad neighborhood. You take a wrong turn in Midtown, you're in a bad neighborhood. You go to

Graceland—which of course is the first thing tourists do when they get here—and you have to go through a bad neighborhood. You visit the National Civil Rights Museum—the second place people want to visit—and you have to go through a part of downtown nobody's gotten around to fixing up. You see what I mean, Joe? Visitors come here and get so freaked out about all the bad parts of Memphis that they forget all the great things we've got going for us."

"So your plan was what? To burn down all the parts you don't like?"

"Well, somebody has to start somewhere. Listen, a lot of that blighted property is controlled by out-of-town owners who aren't willing to spend what it would take to fix it up. They'd rather just keep the property on their books as a tax write-off. And a lot of it has been acquired by the city and county government through tax sales. So who in our local government do you trust to keep that property up? Mayor Pigg? His buddies on the city council? Unless some developer comes along and stuffs money in their pockets, they'll just let that property sit forever. And for the most part, developers won't mess with inner-city land. It's cheaper and easier to keep building on vacant land in the suburbs, which then need to have government services extended out to them. That's urban sprawl, and taxpayers end up paying for it. More cookie-cutter developments out in the sticks, which lose their appeal as soon as the newness wears off. And taxpayers end up subsidizing that, while the urban core—the part of Memphis that made the city cool in the first place—slowly rots away."

Joe was silent. "Okay," he finally said. "So you had your reasons. Maybe you had the best intentions. We could argue all day about whether it was smart to do what you did. But that doesn't change the fact that you're in a lot of trouble now. We're both in trouble. Unless you do what the mayor wants you to do."

"I can't," Scott said quietly.

"Okay, so you can't. Can you at least tell me what it is you can't do?"

"Maybe sometime. But I need to think this through first. I'm afraid if I tell you, I'll just get you deeper into a pile of horse crap where you don't belong in the first place."

Joe sighed. His head was throbbing, as it often did when he felt overwhelmed with stress. "In that case, I guess I'd better get going," he said. "Do you think you can hold out in here for a while?"

"Sure," Scott said. "Not my first time behind bars, if you'll remember."

"I'll come back to visit as soon as they'll let me. Watch out for yourself, all right?"

"I'll do my best," Scott said, not entirely convincingly.

The guards escorted Joe out of the Shelby County Jail. As he headed back toward his office, he felt a knot in his throat. Joe and Scott had always been there for each other, had always been able to help each other out of whatever jams they got into.

But Joe knew he couldn't get the two of them out of this all by himself. So he flipped open his cell phone and called the one person he knew who might actually have the clout to take on Mayor Pigg and all the resources of city hall.

Chapter 27

Waldo Jefferson didn't have much of an appetite, and that was rare.

He glanced down at his lunch—a huge porkchop covered with onions and mushrooms, alongside collard greens, stewed tomatoes, and sweet cornbread—without enthusiasm. Across the table from him was the Reverend Smoot, who was preaching a mini-sermon between bites of his fried catfish and hush puppies. They were seated in a back corner of It's a Wing Thing, a soul-food restaurant near South Parkway in Orange Mound. The room was dimly lit and the décor Spartan, the red-and-white checkerboard tablecloths adding a splash of color to the otherwise drab surroundings. The walls were covered with photos, framed newspaper clippings, and autographed jerseys highlighting the exploits of the Melrose High School football team, a regular participant in the state playoffs. The owner, a former Melrose player from the early 1970s, kept a close watch on the city council president and the reverend. If any other patrons appeared to be headed in that direction to interrupt their conversation, the owner shooed them away.

"See, the thing is, Waldo, we come from different worlds," the Reverend Smoot said. "You're a politician. You're worried about the world we're living in here and now. But I'm a man of God. I'm worried about the next world. And because I'm worried about getting to the next world, I've got to do everything I can to bring social justice to this one. And that means not letting Mayor Pete Pigg and his rich friends get even richer, while folks in this part of town starve to death."

"Well, Reverend Smoot, with all due respect, it doesn't look like you're starving," Waldo Jefferson replied. "From where I sit, it looks like you're doing pretty well for yourself. You've got yourself a nice big congregation. And they may not be the richest folks in the world, but after one of your silver-tongued sermons, they're pretty generous when the collection plates get passed around."

"Waldo, that money goes for our church's many ministries."

"Oh, I know that, reverend. Just like the mayor and I are pushing this project because it'll be good for the whole city. It'll create jobs and bring in tourists. Which means more money for everybody."

"That sounds great for the reporters, Waldo, but you and I know it doesn't work that way. All the jobs this project creates will go to businesses owned by the mayor's buddies. You think the average small business owner here in Orange Mound's got a chance of winning a bid for that work? Not unless he's contributed at least five figures to the mayor's political campaign. Or can offer 'other considerations' to Hizzoner."

"Reverend Smoot, you sound like a cynical man."

"Cynical? Let me tell you about cynical. You talk about tourism. When's the last time we saw a tourist here in Orange Mound? Or North or South Memphis? Not unless they're lost. So when you say some barbecue museum is going to help the whole community, you and I both know that's a bunch of bull."

"And that's what you tell the reporters, reverend. You did a great job of that the other night. So you got your story, and I got mine. No telling who's going to end up winning."

"I'm confident I'm going to win, Waldo."

"I know, I know. You've got the Lord on your side. But you know what? I'm not so sure I see the hand of God at work in all that many zoning cases. More often than not, I see the hand that's carrying the best political chits winning those cases."

"This town still has more churches than it does gas stations or discount drugstores."

"For now, anyway," Jefferson said. "But that's changing, reverend. And you know what? If the good people of Orange Mound, North Memphis, and South Memphis ever get a taste of the good life you're always talking about, that might not exactly be in your best interest."

"I'm not sure I follow you, Mr. Council Chairman."

"Well, if all these poor folk get a little money in their pockets, they might decide to move to better neighborhoods out east. And if they do, chances are they won't drive back for church on Sunday. That means your collection plates might get a little lighter. And that would mean you won't be able to pursue your 'many ministries' as you'd like, Reverend Smooth."

The Reverend Smoot smiled slightly at the use of his nickname, even though it seemed an insult in this context. "Waldo,

Waldo, Waldo. Now who's being cynical? You and I really do come at this from different directions. But I am a man of God, which means I believe in making peace, not war. So I think there's a way I can make my congregation happy and you can make your constituents happy. A way everybody can win."

"You know my favorite three words in politics, reverend? *Win-win situation.* So if you know how to make this one, I'm all ears."

"Glad to hear it, Waldo. Here's my idea. I'll get behind this project and tell my congregants just what you said—that it's good for the whole city. You and I can do a news conference together. We can even bring the mayor along, if he'd like to win a few votes in the black community when he runs for reelection. How does that sound?"

"Wonderful," Jefferson replied. "What do you need in return?"

"It's simple, really. I understand the mayor's planning a development project on the east bank of the Wolf River Harbor."

"I don't know where you get your information, reverend, but—"

"Now, Waldo, you ought to know better than to lie to a man of the cloth. You and I both know that's what this is really about. My sources on this are rock solid." In fact, they were. One of the city surveyors doing measurements for the mayor's project happened to be a member of the Reverend Smoot's congregation.

"Okay, let's suppose the mayor is planning something for the east bank of the harbor. And if he is, it'll be good for the whole community, by the way. But why's that of interest to you?"

"You know, the parsonage at my church isn't very fancy, Waldo. It's no good at all when I'm entertaining visitors from out of town—deacons, bishops, people coming in for church conferences, and the like. So I'd like to have one of those fancy houses built for me. And my church, of course."

Waldo Jefferson smiled. That was one thing he loved about Memphis. Preachers and politicians really did speak the same language. "A new house? Yeah, I can see where a man like you might need a new house for entertaining visitors. Like maybe a certain young woman in the choir with big boobs and a big butt. Good-looking thing, although I hear she can't sing a lick."

"Waldo—"

"Don't bother to deny it, reverend. I've got my sources, too." Not that the Reverend Smoot's affair with LaShay Jackson was any big secret. That kind of gossip spread quickly in Memphis. "Besides, I can see some other benefits to you having a house over there."

"Like what, Waldo?"

"That house would give you a place of residence in District 7. You know, in case you might want to run for office someday. With the endorsement of the city council president."

"That's true, I could. But isn't that Desmond Roland's district?"

"It is."

"Now, if memory serves, didn't Desmond Roland make a bid to be council president last year?"

"He did."

"And didn't most of your colleagues on the council vote you into the job because you had more seniority than Desmond?"

"More seniority, and I got out and worked their districts in the last election."

"So I'd be helping you out by running for council against old Desmond, then."

"You would. But I'm not sure Desmond's got the heart to

make a tough run for reelection. You know how it is around here. Most incumbents get reelected without much of a fight. But if Desmond knew he was going to have to run against someone like you—particularly someone like you who had my backing and the backing of several of my friends on the council—well, he might decide to go for one of the open seats on the Shelby County Commission instead."

"He just might. And you know, I have prayed about whether I might be able to serve God better from an elected position of authority."

"Oh, I'm sure God agrees you could," Jefferson said. "And after a few years on the council, I'm sure God might even see fit to guide your way right into the mayor's office, reverend."

The Reverend Smoot paused for as long as it took to stuff a hush puppy into his mouth, chew it thoroughly, and swallow it. He allowed a thin smile to cross his lips. "You know what, Waldo? I think you're right. That term *win-win situation* sounds pretty good to me."

Waldo smiled, too, then finally turned his attention to his food. His appetite had suddenly returned.

Chapter 28

When the guard told Scott he had a visitor, he expected maybe another talk with Joe or, much worse, a follow-up chat with Pete Pigg, his erstwhile drinking buddy and now the dishonorable mayor of Memphis.

Instead, there sat a strikingly beautiful black woman in her late twenties or early thirties. She was thin but not overly so, and clad in a cream-colored dress suit. She had light brown skin, pale green eyes, and blond dreadlocks tied in a loose ponytail that traveled halfway down her back. She sat with a perfectly upright posture that accentuated her well-proportioned body.

Scott took a few seconds to drink it all in before he finally spoke. "Well, if you're here for a conjugal visit, I'm definitely up for it. I mean, it's been awhile since I spent any time here at 201 Poplar, but you're a definite service upgrade."

"Very funny, Mr. Paulk," the woman said, not the least bit fazed.

"Hey, I'm only half joking," Scott said. "If you're working for the mayor and he brought you in to get my cooperation, he definitely knows my weakness."

"I don't work for the mayor, Mr. Paulk," the woman said calmly.

"Then who do you work for, lady?"

The woman said nothing, instead staring into Scott's eyes long enough to make him uncomfortable. And it was hard to make Scott uncomfortable. There was nothing romantic about her gaze. Scott could tell she was sizing him up. For what purpose, he couldn't tell.

"That depends," she said finally. "If you behave yourself, I might end up working for you."

"I'm not hiring right now," Scott said. "But if I ever get out of here, well . . ."

"I was told you have an interesting sense of humor," the woman said. "In fact, I was told you're pretty much of a wise-ass. But if you're interested in getting out of here, I can help."

"Well, you obviously haven't smuggled a hacksaw in here under your dress," Scott said. "Because, believe me, I would have noticed."

"You'll need more than a hacksaw to get out of this one, Mr. Paulk," the woman said. "You're facing some serious charges. And in case you've forgotten, the mayor of Memphis is committed to keeping you here. So much so that he encouraged his police officers to ignore the rules of due process."

Scott was taken aback. The woman obviously knew about his situation. And Scott had been under the impression Mayor Pigg was keeping a tight lid on the situation, at least until he got the answer he was looking for from Scott.

"So you're a lawyer," Scott said.

"I am," the woman said, extending a delicate, long-nailed

hand across the table. "Raina Johnson, Mr. Paulk. I think I can help you, if you're willing to drop the *Rebel Without a Cause* act so we can talk this through."

"What's to talk through? No offense, Counselor Johnson, but as you said, the mayor has it in for me, and he's willing to break the rules to keep me cooped up here. In fact, I don't even know how you found out about me."

"I found out about you because your friend Joe called my friend Dawn," Raina Johnson said. "Joe explained your situation to her, and she explained it to me. And I have to admit, getting you out of here is going to be a challenge, but not necessarily an insurmountable one."

"Really? How'd you even get this meeting? The cops have kept me under wraps since my arrest."

"I have sources within the police department. They helped me ask the right questions. Once the police knew that I knew you were here, cooperation wasn't as much of a problem as you might expect."

"So you got in the door, and I'm glad for that," Scott said. "But do you know anything about the evidence they've got on me?"

"In fact, I do, Mr. Paulk. By the way, is it okay if I call you Scott? Since we've already discussed conjugal visits, I feel like we ought to be on a first-name basis."

"Sure, Scott is fine. Can I call you Raina?"

"Sure. And to your other question, I have quite a bit of information about the evidence the police have collected against you."

"Look, unless you're Johnnie Cochran, Perry Mason, and that lawyer dude on the billboards all rolled into one, I'm not sure you can do anything for me. Assuming I could afford to pay you. Which I can't."

"What, being an Elvis impersonator on Beale Street isn't bringing in the big bucks?" Raina said. "But don't worry about money. I'm taking the case as a favor to Dawn."

"A favor to Dawn?" Like so many things that had happened to him recently, Scott had a hard time processing this. A starlet was sticking up for him? Even through Joe, it was hard to believe. Especially through Joe, come to think of it. Joe seemed about as far from having a relationship with a Hollywood actress as anyone Scott could imagine.

"Yes, Dawn and I were friends growing up in Collierville. And I still owe her one for giving me advice when we were both cheerleaders during our junior year at Collierville High. She was right about dating skill-position players. You just can't trust them. Worst prom experience ever, but it taught me a life lesson."

"This is clearly a story I'd like to hear more about sometime," Scott said. "But even if you're willing to help me for free, there still isn't much to work with here. Raina, they've got the goods on me. They've got a fingerprint on a whiskey bottle used to brain an undercover cop in a vacant industrial building in the middle of an arson."

"A partial fingerprint," Raina said. "I'm not surprised Mayor Pigg neglected to tell you that. But you know what, Scott? A lot of fingerprints are on that bottle. You have no idea how many people handle a bottle of whiskey from the time it rolls off the assembly line until it ends up in a landfill somewhere. Or as powdered glass on the streets of Memphis, as the case may be. At least five distinct sets of prints were lifted from that bottle. Now, in two of those cases, the prints don't match any in the police files, probably because the people who own them haven't gotten into trouble with the law. At least not yet. However, you and two other people with identifiable prints on the bottle do have criminal records. One is a guy who works in the distillery's distribution plant. Apparently, his hobby is growing weed on his farm on the outskirts of Lynchburg. He's done time for that. The other guy is a drifter who presently lives in Memphis. He's got a long rap sheet for drunk and disorderly conduct, burglary, aggressive panhandling, public drunkenness, and a whole range of other petty crimes."

"Okay, so what does all that mean?"

"Well, Scott, it means that proof you handled the whiskey bottle at some point in your life isn't the same as proof you're the guy who clobbered that cop in the head. And given your track record of partying, the fact that you touched a whiskey bottle somewhere in town is hardly compelling evidence, in my mind."

"What about the ID? Mayor Pigg said the cop made me at the scene."

"A cop says he can positively identify you after seeing you in a darkened industrial building—which, by the way, was burning to the ground at the time. And he was woozy from getting knocked around with a whiskey bottle. Scott, I don't claim to be as good as your billboard hero, but if I can't establish reasonable doubt out of that, then I'm not much of a lawyer."

"But Mayor Pigg is gonna sit on this," Scott said. "He told me so. Until . . . well, until I do something for him that I really don't want to do."

"Mayor Pigg can't sit on this anymore," Raina said. "If the police don't book you through the usual process, I'll take my case to the media. And the usual process requires a bail hearing, which I think would result in a judge releasing you on your own recognizance. The district attorney doesn't work for the city—he's a duly elected officer of state government. And once I make him aware of—how shall I say this?—the negative publicity that might result from pursuing a case with such weak circumstantial evidence, I think he'll see things my way. Plus, our DA is a law-and-order guy who's big on morality, at least in public. Our current mayor runs a bar on Beale Street. The DA might have statewide political ambitions, which wouldn't be helped by covering for a sleazy mayor—slash—saloon operator on a case that should never see the light of day."

Scott sat in astonished silence. "Do you really think you can work all those angles and get me sprung from here?" he finally asked.

"I can. And I will."

"Then, Raina, I misjudged you," Scott said. "And I apologize for that. I could use your help, obviously."

"Apology accepted," Raina said, rising gracefully and again offering Scott her delicate hand. "And you'll get my help. Don't plan on spending another night here."

"I appreciate that," Scott said, holding her handshake for as long as he thought he could get away with it. "I really do. And even if I misjudged you, I have to say this: I wasn't entirely joking about the conjugal visit. If that's still an option, I'd like for us to pursue it."

Raina Johnson hesitated a moment, then threw back her gorgeous mane of hair and laughed. "I think we're a ways from that. But if we can get you out of here and back on the road to being a solid citizen, then maybe that's something we can discuss. Okay, Scott?"

Scott nodded. It was definitely okay with him.

Chapter 29

Billy Boy Bradwell was drinking his second double whiskey on the rocks in the Kansas City airport bar when his visitor arrived.

"Thank you for agreeing to meet with me," Pedro Suarez said as he slid into a seat across from Bradwell.

The bar was crowded, the tables packed too close together. It didn't matter, though. Most of the people there were wrapped up in their own little worlds—watching the NASCAR race on TV, catching up on e-mails, reading or chatting with their traveling companions. Nobody paid any attention to the big redneck cowboy and the flashily dressed young Mexican.

"Well, I had my doubts," Bradwell said. "I don't understand why you couldn't tell me whatever it is you have to tell me over the phone."

"My boss, Mr. Eldridge, has a business proposition for you.

And he prefers to discuss business face to face."

"But I'm not face to face with him. I'm face to face with you, Mr. . . . I forget your name."

"Suarez. Pedro Suarez. And I assure you Mr. Eldridge confides in me and trusts that I will accurately represent his views during this meeting."

"You will, huh? Let's get to it, then. I'm a busy man, and I've got better things to do than sit around in airport bars jawboning with foreigners."

"For the record, Mr. Bradwell, I hold dual citizenship in Mexico and the United States. But I appreciate your concern about the time. So I'll get right to business. We're aware of your plans to build a Barbecue Hall of Fame here in Kansas City."

"Yeah, good news travels fast," Bradwell said with a chuckle. "Did you see my cattle on those pontoon boats? That little stunt was covered on two of the major networks and most of the cable news channels. And of course the clip ended up on YouTube. Seems like it doesn't matter what you have to say, as long as you've got good video. Everybody across the country knows what Billy Boy Bradwell is planning to do for his hometown."

"Yes, very impressive. And perhaps you've heard how the mayor of our town plans to build a Barbecue Hall of Fame in Memphis."

"I might have heard a thing or two about that," Bradwell said, his eyes narrowing to thin slits. "But let me tell you something. There's not gonna be any comparison between my project and what that ignoramus is planning down there. We're gonna get our project done first, and we're gonna get it done better. And people aren't gonna want to visit two Barbecue Halls of Fame. They're gonna visit the best one. Shoot, I bet your mayor doesn't even have the financing to get his project off the ground. But even if he does, it's gonna look like the hall of shame compared to what I'm planning."

"I appreciate your passion for your project, Mr. Bradwell," Suarez said, declining to order a drink when the waitress finally made it to the table. "And Mr. Eldridge thinks he can help you see it through."

"Now, why would he want to do that?" Bradwell said, leaning forward to place his face only a few inches from Suarez's. "How do I know you're not working for the mayor? Because if I find out you are, I promise that you and I are gonna have some problems down the road. And a lot of people say I'm a bad person to have problems with."

"So we've heard," Suarez said calmly. He didn't flinch or even blink as Bradwell loomed near him. After years in the bar business, he couldn't be intimidated by some big blowhard violating his personal space. "Mr. Eldridge has thoroughly investigated your business practices and your . . . reputation for getting things done. And I can assure you that Mr. Eldridge isn't in league with the mayor. In fact, you might say Mr. Eldridge and Mayor Pigg have a serious business disagreement."

"A serious business disagreement, huh? Well, I've had a few of those with folks over the years. But I usually find ways to solve them."

"And that's exactly why I'm here—to offer you a solution."

"I'm listening." Bradwell leaned back in his chair and folded his arms across his chest.

"As you may know, Mayor Pigg has taken a particular interest in building his Barbecue Hall of Fame on a piece of property Mr. Eldridge owns."

"Is that so?"

"It is," Suarez said. "And I'm fairly certain you knew that already. One of the things we've learned about you is that you do your homework."

"Maybe," Bradwell replied. "So why are you here talking to me? Are you planning to sell that property to the mayor? Because that would be a real bad business decision on your part. Or Mr. Eldridge's. Or for that matter, even the mayor's. Whoever the hell I'm actually talking to here."

"As I said, I am authorized to represent Mr. Eldridge. And we would very much like to negotiate a deal with you that we believe would be mutually beneficial."

"So, let's hear it."

"Well, as you may know from your research, Mayor Pigg has so far been unwilling to meet our price on the land."

"So, this is about money?" Bradwell said, chuckling again.

"Isn't it usually?" Suarez said.

"Not for me, not with this Barbecue Hall of Fame," Bradwell said. "I've got plenty of money. I'm close to selling my Cow Sauce from coast to coast. And my restaurants are gonna be there soon, too. I got me a huge ranch outside the city, a penthouse in downtown K.C., seventeen of the finest cars and trucks you'll ever see, and the best luxury box a fella could ever hope to have at Arrowhead Stadium. No, this project is about something more important to me."

"What's that, Mr. Bradwell?"

"Respect. I'm gonna put Kansas City on the map as a major tourist destination. People go to St. Louis to see that stupid arch. But you tell me, would people rather look at a big hunk of metal or eat barbecue? This project is gonna bring thousands of visitors to Kansas City—millions, even. Those people are gonna spend money while they're in town. That's gonna make the local business owners happy. Some of them still call me a redneck rube behind my back. But by the time this thing plays out, they'll put a statue of me downtown."

"Mr. Eldridge thought your motivations might be more than financial. You have a dream you want to turn into a reality. And so does Mr. Eldridge."

"Oh, yeah? What's his dream?"

"His dream is to become the king of the adult film industry east of the Mississippi. And coincidentally enough, he plans to build his production studio on the same spot Mr. Pigg wants for his project."

"Yeah, that sounds like a problem," Bradwell said, his eyes now open wide and glimmering with understanding. "So what's this business proposal you're hinting about?"

"Even though you say your Barbecue Hall of Fame isn't about money—and I believe you—I'm sure you wouldn't mind making some. And we plan to make some—actually, quite a lot—from our filmmaking. So what we're proposing is this. If you're willing to pay the amount of money we told the mayor we would accept as a buyout offer, you could help finance the demolition and construction work we'll need to do on our property to make the studio viable."

"And what would I get in exchange for my investment?"

"An ownership position in Mr. Eldridge's filmmaking business. Not a majority position, you understand. Mr. Eldridge wants to maintain control over the business model he has created. However, your ownership would entitle you to a proportional share of our profits, which we expect to be quite substantial. Other than the studio construction project, we expect our overhead costs to be low. And the appetite for our product is strong. I can fax you some business projections, if that might help you make up your mind."

"Interesting," Bradwell said. "Never thought I'd be considering going into the nudie business. But I have to admit what you're saying about the moneymaking potential is true. Porn is one of the few things in this world that's recession-proof."

"And you can see the other advantage as well," Suarez said. "If you help us get our studio built, Mayor Pigg won't be able to use that spot for his Barbecue Hall of Fame."

"You're making sense now, Pedro. But what's to stop your mayor from picking another site?"

"He might do that," Suarez acknowledged. "But that would throw his project off schedule for months, even years. Land acquisition takes time, particularly when multiple property owners are involved, some of whom might not be willing sellers. You know how slowly government works. Which should buy you time to get your project done before his. And then he might realize he's at such a competitive disadvantage that he'll just let the whole matter drop."

"So how much are you asking for your property?"

"Fifteen million."

Bradwell choked on the sip of the drink he'd just taken. He recovered and motioned to the waitress to bring him another. "Fifteen million? That's pretty steep."

"That's a matter of opinion. The fact is, Mr. Eldridge owns property at one of the most strategic locations in Memphis. And you understand the earning potential of our filmmaking operation. You would make your money back several times over in a few years. Plus, you would neutralize your adversary, which would make it easier for you to accomplish your goal. Which is a moneymaking proposition in its own right. For a relatively small up-front investment, you would open two new cash flows in your business portfolio, both of which should be quite substantial."

"I don't consider fifteen million 'a relatively small up-front investment,'" Bradwell said.

"No? Perhaps our research into your background has a few gaps, then. Anyway, the operative word is *relatively*. It may seem like a lot of money on the front end, but clearly someone with your business sense can understand the earning potential we're talking about here."

"I can and I do. I tell you what, Mr. Pedro Suarez. Send me your business plan and profit projections for this film studio when you get back to Memphis."

"I can certainly do that," Suarez said as he stood to leave. "We're confident that once you study this, you'll see what we're saying is true. The earning potential is enormous. For both projects. And you'll get that statue downtown, too."

"I'll be in touch," Bradwell said, reaching to shake Suarez's extended hand without rising from his chair.

"With good news, I hope," Suarez said.

He turned toward the airport gate where he had arrived only a short while earlier. Suarez had no time for sightseeing. He needed to catch the next flight home to let Augustine Eldridge know Bradwell's reaction to his pitch.

Chapter 30

"Chief Bruno, you're makin' me very unhappy."

Mayor Pigg hovered over his police chief, who was seated in his usual chair across from the mayor's desk.

"Mr. Mayor, I understand," Chief Bruno said. "But this came as a complete surprise."

"You know, I would like to believe that," Pigg said. "But there was an individual put into your jail by your men. And now he's out, and you say that's a surprise. How can sumpin like that be a surprise?"

"Well, Mr. Mayor, as you know, I'm the city police chief—"

"That can be changed."

"Yes, yes, I know, Mr. Mayor. You remind me of that often. But it's the Shelby County Jail. It's controlled by the Shelby County Sheriff's Department, which is run by a completely different guy. He's got his own hat and badge and everything. And he's not me."

"What about professional courtesy?"

"Well, as a matter of fact, the sheriff did give me a call when he found out this was going down. But by that time, it was too late. The whole thing was already in motion."

"So what happened?"

"The kid has a lawyer."

"The kid? The one who lives in a storage attic above Beale Street? He's got a lawyer?"

"Apparently. And a pretty forceful one, too. She got a Shelby County Circuit Court judge to come to court after hours to hear a writ of habeas corpus."

"A what? That sounds like some kind of Scandinavian sex toy."

"No, Mr. Mayor, a writ of habeas corpus is a legal request to give a suspect an opportunity to appear in court."

"And the judge granted it?"

"Why wouldn't he? It's a reasonable request."

"I thought no one knew our boy was in the hoosegow."

"That lady lawyer sure did."

"A *lady* lawyer? Well, who is she?"

"Defense lawyer. She's handled some big cases."

"Like what?"

"Remember the 'Git Some' Bandit?"

"The guy who robbed all those convenience stores?"

"Got the nickname because he always yelled, 'Git some!' while he was shooting up the canned peaches and marshmallows."

"She defended that scumbag?"

"Not exactly. She defended the first guy we picked up. We got a bad description from one of the witnesses. We thought it was a guy some of our patrolmen had seen around the neighborhood. Turned out to be a case of mistaken identity. And the lady lawyer made that real clear. Shot our case full of holes in a hurry, to be honest. She's a looker, but she's also a bulldog in court."

"Can she be bought?"

"I'll pretend I didn't hear that. You know I'm the chief of police."

"Yeah, yeah, we were discussin' how temporary that could be," Pigg said. "So I'll repeat: can she be bought?"

"Well, Mr. Mayor, as you may know, buying people off isn't part of my job description. But if you want my opinion, looking at it objectively, my guess would be no."

"Oh? Why not?"

"Well, from what I hear, she may be part of that rare breed of lawyers not motivated primarily by money."

"There's lawyers out there that aren't in it for the money?"

"That's the word on the street. Apparently, this girl was a whiz kid in school. Could have been just about anything—scientist, financial trader, whatever. But she went into law because she's one of those true believers who want to keep people from being screwed over by the justice system."

"There's money in that?"

"Some, if you're good enough at it. But this kid is from a family that's got money already. And she has rich friends, too."

"Like who?"

"Well, like your friend Dawn," Bruno said. "Apparently, they're old chums from school."

"How do you know that?"

"Well, Mr. Mayor, we keep coming back to this, but I am the chief of police. I have a few resources at my disposal."

"Resources I'm payin' for."

"With taxpayer money."

"Which becomes my money, in a sense."

"I'll pretend I didn't hear that either."

"Chief, you may need to go on disability if this deafness continues to be a problem. So anyway, this hotshot lady lawyer went into court with this writ of habeas whatsis. Then what happened?"

"Well, the assistant DA arguing the other side of the case basically agreed with her about the writ. In fact, the writ was issued jointly by both lawyers. Which made it tough for the judge to say no."

"Now, why on earth would an assistant DA help a defense lawyer spring somebody?"

"Maybe he was looking at the big picture, Mr. Mayor. As in, if the kid doesn't get a chance to appear in court and get a bond hearing, the whole case is procedurally screwed. Then the kid walks."

"So the assistant DA basically took the kid's side, is what you're tellin' me."

"Well, the DA was apparently surprised—and not pleasantly so—to learn a prisoner was sitting in jail that we hadn't told anyone in his office about. And we kept it that way per your instructions, Mr. Mayor."

Mayor Pigg was still standing over Chief Bruno, who didn't look the least bit intimidated. If anything, he was fighting to suppress his irritation. And not really succeeding.

"So, I'll circle back again: how did this lady lawyer know we had the Ghetto Blazer in the clink? You didn't book him. I sure didn't call no press conference. So what happened?"

"Let's do a little detective work, Mr. Mayor," Bruno said, finally rising from his chair. As he did, the mayor recoiled. He wasn't used to people who worked for him showing any kind of backbone. And the chief looked like he could whip just about any of the bouncers at the Pigg Pen. Maybe all of them at the same time. "Let's think about this. Who did you tell after we picked the kid up?"

"Nobody."

"Wrong, Mr. Mayor. You told that kid's friend, Joe Miller, the one working for you on the World Barbecue Hall of Fame project."

"Okay, that's right, I did. But I needed him to lean on the Paulk kid. Get him to see things our way."

"Right. So maybe he told somebody."

"Who does he know?"

"Well, let's think about who else is working for you on the Barbecue Hall of Fame."

"Cal Cameron?"

"No, Mr. Mayor. Think shorter but better looking. Much better looking."

"Dawn?"

"Makes sense. She knows the lady lawyer. She knows Joe. In police work, this is what we call connecting the dots."

"You know, Chief Bruno, I can't say I care too much for the tone you're takin' with me tonight."

"Well, Mr. Mayor, I think you should accept it at face value when I tell you I'm better at police work than you are."

"Chief, you know I don't like you. In fact, I'm lookin' for the right reason to fire you. So what about the legal arguments involved? The facts of the case, maybe?"

"It wasn't the time to get into legal arguments. After the judge granted the writ of habeas corpus, they brought the kid in. His lawyer then petitioned for the kid's release."

"And where was the assistant DA while this was goin' on?"

"Agreeing, mostly. Agreeing that no charges had been brought against the kid—again, per your instructions, Mr. Mayor. Agreeing there was no evidence to hold him, since there were no charges. But the state reserved the right to file charges at a later date, if compelling evidence becomes available."

"So the kid walked?"

"Right out the front door."

Mayor Pigg groaned. "I feel like that fat guy from *Deliverance*."

"I'll let that pass without comment, Mr. Mayor."

"Very funny, chief. So what's your plan for gettin' this back on track?"

"Beg your pardon?"

"More hearin' problems. Clean out your ears when you get back to your office, will you, chief? What I asked was, what do we have to get that kid back where I need him, which is in the clink?"

"Well, at this point, somebody needs to talk to the DA. Unruffle his feathers, so to speak."

"Why would I do that? He's not 'zactly my favorite person right now."

"Nor are you his, I suspect. Here's the thing, Mr. Mayor. Whether you appreciate it or not, I've been a cop for a while. And during that time, I've learned a thing or two about working with district attorneys. They don't like being surprised. And nothing surprises them more than hearing about people being arrested and detained in their jurisdiction from someone other than the cops who work in that jurisdiction."

Mayor Pigg sighed. Running drunks out of the Pigg Pen at closing time was so much easier than dealing with all this mayoral crap. "So what do we do? To make this right with the DA, I mean."

"Well, an apology would be a good start."

"I'll delegate that to you, chief. Since you're so good at working with district attorneys, you seem like the best man for the job. Heck, buy him a Whitman's Sampler if you want. Sounds to me like you're pretty close buddies, the way you're stickin' up for him."

"Well, Mr. Mayor, there is such a thing as professional respect. So, sure, I'll handle the apology."

"What else?"

"If you plan to rearrest that kid, the DA's going to want some evidence. District attorneys really like evidence. Makes winning cases so much easier."

The mayor paused and studied the chief, who was still standing over him. "So, do we have it? I mean, enough to keep the kid locked up?"

"You're asking my opinion as a professional law enforcement officer? Wow, that must hurt."

"Yes, I'm going to need some Prep H after you leave. So, what's your expert opinion, Chief Bruno?"

"We've got enough to make a good case. Maybe even enough to persuade the DA to ask for the kid to be held without bail. Because of the nature of the crimes and all that. Serial criminals tend to get a judge's attention."

"But it's not a sure thing that he'll be denied bail?"

"Elvis used to say the only sure things in life were hookers and Coupe de Villes. Or so I've heard."

"Could the kid post bail if the judge decided to set one?"

"Well, I'd have to say so. He's a friend of a friend of one of this city's wealthiest residents."

"In that case, Chief Bruno, you better turn on the charm with your boyfriend in the DA's office. Not only do we need him to get on board and charge this kid, we gotta convince him to fight for holdin' the kid with no bail. If you can't do that, maybe you better get used to the sound of 'Lieutenant Bruno.' Or maybe even 'Security Officer Bruno.' Now, did you hear that clearly enough?"

Chief Bruno stared down at the smaller man, clenching his jaw and fists. His police training had taught him not to let people provoke him. But that was a long time ago. And none of the instructors at the police academy had ever dealt with a piece of work like the Honorable Pete Pigg.

"I hear you, Mr. Mayor," the chief finally said, doing his best to keep his voice under control.

Yeah, I hear you, all right, Chief Bruno thought as he turned to leave. *Unlike that pig in the cartoons, you don't stutter.*

Chapter 31

The mood at Heck's was festive—particularly after the second bucket of Blue Moon beer arrived.

After getting sprung from jail, Scott had managed to talk Joe, Dawn, and Raina into joining him for what he called a "post-incarceration celebration."

It hadn't been easy. He first asked Raina, who expressed reservations about complicating the lawyer-client relationship. She relented only after Scott said it would be a good opportunity to discuss legal strategy.

When Joe heard Raina was going, he started to beg off, saying he didn't want to be the third wheel. So Scott suggested he invite Dawn. Which made sense to Joe, since having Dawn there might make her old friend Raina more comfortable. Joe probably had other reasons, too. Rationalizing was easy for Joe.

Heck's was a good spot for such a gathering, since anyone

who failed to follow Dawn's privacy rules would get a stern warning from the bouncers. Heck was willing to cut a few favors for Joe and Scott, two of his most reliable customers.

The quartet made small talk over cheeseburgers and fried pickles. Then Dawn and Joe decided to walk over to the jukebox to pick out some tunes.

"Cute couple, don't you think?" Scott said to Raina, gesturing toward their friends with a half-eaten pickle.

"Do they know they're a couple?" Raina replied.

"Maybe not yet," Scott said, pausing to crunch down another bite. "But I bet they will be."

"So, are you a fortune teller as well as an Elvis impersonator?"

"Well, the two professions do tend to attract a similar clientele on Beale Street."

"How does one become an Elvis impersonator anyway, Scott?"

"Same way performers get to Carnegie Hall: years of practice."

"Did you just wake up one day and decide that's what you wanted to do with your life?"

"Maybe not my whole life. But yeah, it seemed like a good idea at the time. Still does."

"Ever think about doing something else?"

"Like what? Become a lawyer?"

"I'll bet you could if you put your mind to it, Scott." That piercing stare was back. But Scott had enough beer in him by that point that the stare didn't faze him as it had at the jail.

"It could have an appeal, if I could go into practice with a certain lady lawyer. We could spend the afternoons checking out each other's briefs."

"I can't tell you how many times I've heard some variation of that joke. Do you ever have serious moments, Scott?"

"According to the cops, I'm a serious arsonist."

"So they say."

"Do you believe them?"

"It's my job to represent you, no matter what I might believe or how I might feel."

"And how might you feel if you believed I was an arsonist?"

Raina sighed and took a swig of her second Blue Moon. She glanced at Dawn and Joe, who were still talking at the jukebox. Then Raina studied the frothy orange slice wedged into the beer bottle's neck before finally returning her eyes to Scott.

"I can tell you this much," Raina said, her voice deepening. "I've known that woman over there a long time. I knew her before she was famous. She was always the prettiest girl in school."

"I bet that was a debatable point," Scott said. "You had to be in the discussion."

"She was one of the smartest kids, too," Raina said, brushing aside the compliment. "And extremely popular, of course. And rich. But she never let that go to her head. And after she got famous, her personality never changed. She never stopped being the girl I could call on a Wednesday evening and talk to about boy troubles."

"Were there a lot of boy troubles?"

"I'm trying to make a point here, Scott. The point being that with Dawn, what you see is what you get. She's the most down-to-earth person I know. And she believes your friend Joe has a good heart. So she wants to help him by helping you."

"So, by extension . . ."

"By extension, I have to assume that under your thinly veiled sexism and juvenile humor, a pretty good guy must be lurking somewhere."

"My sexism is thinly veiled? Maybe I'm being too subtle."

"And you're making it difficult to pay you a compliment.

What I'm trying to say is that if you did what the cops say you did, then I assume you must have a good reason. At least you think it's a good reason."

At last, Scott's face turned serious. "Raina, do you want me to tell you—"

"No, Scott, I don't. Not right now. Because I'm still your lawyer. And I could be wrong about you. You might try to explain yourself, and I might not like your reasoning. Then it would be tougher for me to represent you."

"I really would like to explain—"

"Someday. Not now. Not until this is over."

"I'm out of jail."

"But Scott, you must know this is nowhere near over. They're going to rearrest you. Not involving the DA's office was a big mistake on their part. But once the cops and the prosecutors get on the same page, I expect you'll be picked up again."

"I thought you said their evidence was crap."

"That's not quite what I said. I said it has some holes. Or at least issues that we might be able to convince a jury are holes. But I don't want it to get that far. Juries are unpredictable. And as you know, jail is not a fun place. And prison would be worse."

"So, how did you find those holes or issues or whatever they are?"

"I have sources."

"In the police department?"

"As a matter of fact, yes. I know someone who shared the evidence they have against you."

"Isn't that illegal?"

"Holding you without charging you or bringing you before a judge was illegal. In fact, my source made a legal wrong right by tipping me off about the case they were building against you. As your lawyer, I should have been given that information anyway."

"Your source sounds like a crusader for truth and justice."

"He owes me."

"Now, this is getting interesting. What does he owe you for?"

Raina sighed again and took a longer pull off her beer. "Mainly, he owes me for being a crappy boyfriend."

Scott hiked his eyebrows in mock surprise. "Oh, another one of those. Like the football player in high school."

"Pretty much. Another guy who slept around on me. And now he feels guilty, so he's trying to get back on my good side."

"And is that working out for him?"

"No, it isn't. I've seen his kind too many times."

"Oh, really?"

"Yes, really. I've dated way too many players in my life."

"I wonder why that is."

"It could be because I'm attracted to confident, happy-go-lucky types. Guys who think they've got the world in their back pockets."

It was Scott's turn to pause and stare. "You know, maybe you need someone who's more romantic. The kind of guy who would carve your initials into a tree or something."

With that, Scott turned to the dry erase board on the wall next to the booth. He picked up a Sharpie and scribbled, "SP + RJ = ???"

"Let's not get crazy, Mr. Paulk," Raina said, grabbing an eraser.

"Too late for that, Ms. Johnson," Scott replied, grasping her delicate hand that held the eraser. They struggled as Raina tried to erase the graffiti and Scott tried to stop her. Raina brought up her free hand to fend Scott's away, but Scott reached up and grabbed that hand with his free one.

Scott's grip loosened as their eyes locked and their playful glances abruptly changed into something else. Scott continued his hold, using his thumbs to lightly caress the tendons and blood vessels on the backs of Raina's hands.

"Why don't they teach you about these situations in law school?" Raina asked. "This whole attorney-client thing can get really complicated."

"It's complicated only if you overthink it, instead of following your instincts," Scott said.

"Yeah, instincts," Raina said, her voice growing distant. "Instincts can either keep you safe or drive you down the road to ruin."

"Been on that road before," Scott said. "It's easy to find an on-ramp, but off-ramps are hard to spot."

"Indeed they are."

After that, neither said anything, choosing instead to keep their gazes locked on each other.

As they did so, they were oblivious to the scene playing out across the bar.

"How is it possible that one jukebox can carry so many Journey songs?" Joe said as he and Dawn flipped through the selections.

"Hey, I hear 'Don't Stop Believin' ' is making a comeback," Dawn said.

"What about this one?" Joe pointed to a top-forty song by a hot new female artist whose looks made her a popular target for tabloid gossip.

"God, no. Nothing from her," Dawn said. "She was in a movie with me once. I can't stand her. A total prima donna."

"Really?" Joe said. "So she's the type who insists on having the biggest trailer on the set?"

"Something like that. She has to be the center of attention. Even if it means screwing the director and half the crew."

"You don't like being the center of attention, Dawn? Because it seems to me you usually are."

"That's not something I've ever particularly needed or wanted."

"Maybe you made a bad career choice, then."

Dawn chuckled, casting a sideways glance back toward Scott and Raina. "Maybe I did. But there are definitely perks to having the whole world know your name."

"Not the whole world. I'm guessing you're a virtual unknown in parts of Afghanistan."

"Maybe, maybe not," Dawn said. "I did a USO tour with the troops over there, you know."

"Makes me want to enlist," Joe muttered.

Dawn laughed again, a confident, self-assured laugh that melted Joe's insides. Then, after glancing back toward Scott and Raina once more, she spoke in a low and more serious tone. "You know, Joe, I'm worried about your friend."

"I'm worried, too," Joe said. "I've got a nagging feeling that Scott's troubles are just beginning."

"Me, too. I wish we could do something to get him out of this situation."

"I was thinking the same thing. Hey, they've got some Adam Ant tunes in here. I keep forgetting, is he alive or dead?"

"Who's Adam Ant?"

"You're killing me. You can't be that much younger than I am."

"Oh, I think I read something about him in *People*. Didn't he end up in a nut house?"

"Dawn, for such a nice lady, you sure can be cruel."

"Oh, I'm just teasing. I'm the subject of enough tabloid gossip that I like to turn the tables every once in a while."

"Got it. But back to Scott, yeah, I'm worried, but what can we do?"

"I don't know. What are you thinking?"

"I'm thinking that finding out what Mayor Pigg is up to is the key to this whole thing."

"Why do you say that?"

"I mean, Mayor Pigg has always been a little weird, but he's been riding nonstop on the crazy train since he went public about the Barbecue Hall of Fame. From what a friend of mine tells me, he's got a special interest in the site where he wants to put it. My friend has seen city trucks surveying not only that property but the surrounding property."

"Yeah, we talked about that already, remember? I tried to help you find out what Mayor Pigg is planning. If I close my eyes, I can still smell the martini breath. But what's that got to do with Scott's situation?"

"I'm not sure. When Scott was in jail, he almost told me why he was being held like that, in secret, with no charges filed against him. But he didn't."

"And you think the mayor somehow set Scott up?"

"Well, it makes sense. Holding somebody in jail without arresting him requires the cooperation of a lot of people in law enforcement. Cops. And as mayor, Pigg effectively has control of the Memphis Police Department. He's the boss of the chief of police."

"Are you saying the whole police department is corrupt?"

"No, not necessarily. But if he had a few corrupt cronies and maybe a few others who were willing to look the other way, maybe he could get Scott busted and still keep the whole thing under wraps."

"Until Raina got involved."

"Right, until Raina got involved. Did I ever thank you for that, by the way?"

"Yes, about thirty-seven times, I think. Although I lost count after we started on the Blue Moon."

"Well, thanks again. So, anyway, I don't know. But I feel Mayor Pigg has it in for Scott for some reason. And it's not over an unpaid bar tab at the Pigg Pen."

"Do you want me to talk to the mayor again?"

"I'm not sure how much good that would do, Dawn. After all, you already tried. And he didn't really tell you anything about what he's planning, did he?"

"No, he didn't," Dawn admitted. "But if I were to meet with that porno director like he wants me to, then maybe he would open up and give me some information in return."

"I don't think that's a good idea."

"Maybe not, but what other options do we have at this point? This isn't about just you and Scott, you know. If the mayor's up to something, I need to protect my reputation. Remember, I was right there beside him when he announced this project."

"Dawn, you know that any porno director is by definition a sleaze ball. You know why he's interested in talking with you. He wants you to be in one of his movies."

"I'm not talking about making a movie for him. I can't believe you think I would even entertain that idea."

"Well, I . . . I hope you wouldn't," Joe sputtered. "But if you meet with the guy, that's what he's going to try to do. And guys like that are pretty ruthless."

"I appreciate your concern, Joe, but I'm a big girl."

"I know you are. And I know you can take care of yourself.

It's just . . . I have a bad feeling about this. I don't trust the mayor. I don't trust that porn king. There has to be a better way to find out what's going on."

"You really do care, don't you, Joe?" Dawn smiled another one of those smiles that brought the color to Joe's cheeks. And he was pretty sure it wasn't the beer talking.

"Um, yeah. I didn't think there was any real question about that."

They looked at each other a few seconds before Dawn turned back to the jukebox.

"Here, let's shake things up. Let's go with Def Leppard's 'Photograph,' then Barry Manilow's 'Can't Smile Without You,' and we'll finish the set off with Dolly Parton's 'Coat of Many Colors.'"

Before Joe could protest, Dawn punched in the selections and looked at him with an impish grin.

"Well, that should set some kind of tone for the night," Joe said. "I'm not sure what kind, but it'll be interesting to see how the rest of the patrons react."

"Hey, 'Photograph' is a great dance tune."

"It would be if you were a guy's dance partner, Dawn."

"Aw, Joe. You're so sweet." Dawn took another sip of beer, then shook her head and laughed again. "You know, Joe, this is the strangest double date I've been on. My best friend from high school, a guy I barely know, and a serial arsonist."

"Alleged serial arsonist," Joe said. "But we do make quite a quartet, don't we?"

"Indeed we do, indeed we do."

The opening bars of "Photograph" started. Joe wondered if it was too late to circle back to what Dawn had just said. He decided it wasn't.

"Um, Dawn, is this a double date?"

"Wow, I knew I said a bunch when I let that slip." Dawn suddenly took more than a passing interest in the bottom of her beer bottle.

"A bunch . . . or too much?"

"Hmm. Let's just say 'a bunch' for now, okay? Let's not put labels on things."

"Sounds good to me."

They listened to the building sound for a few seconds more.

"Maybe we should head back to the table," Dawn said, starting to turn.

"Hey, Dawn." She turned back toward Joe. "I don't want to be a guy you barely know. So if you ever want to know anything about me, please ask, okay?"

"Okay. As a matter of fact, I do have a question."

"Name it."

"Have you ever tried to dance to Def Leppard?"

Chapter 32

William "Billy Boy" Bradwell chose to meet with Red Maloney last. He knew the old union boss would be tougher than the others.

Waldo Jefferson, the esteemed city council president, had been easy. He was willing to do what he was told for five thousand dollars up front plus 1 percent of the gross from Augustine Eldridge's first film in the new studio.

The Reverend Smoot—the "pimp-daddy preacher," as Bradwell later referred to him—had driven a harder bargain. He was a long-term thinker, as one might expect a man of the cloth to be. But rather than being overly focused on the hereafter, the Reverend Smoot's long-term vision involved 1 percent of the gross for the first five movies, plus an all-access pass to visit the sets during filming. And "introductions" to any of the actresses who struck his fancy. *Just in case they need him for spiritual counseling,* Bradwell thought wryly.

Neither man would publicly support construction of a movie

studio to be used for creating adult movies, of course. But they would keep a lid on opposition from a huge chunk of the city's population. And that was worth cutting them in on a share of the wealth. Or at least promising to cut them in.

Red Maloney wouldn't be so easy. Maloney had played the game too long to settle for a quick score.

The meeting took place in Bradwell's hotel room at The Perfect Union, a new place at the intersection of Union Avenue and Front Street in downtown Memphis. Actually, The Perfect Union dated to the late 1920s. It had started as an office building, then was converted into apartments in the mid-1980s, then into a condominium complex for a couple of years before hotel developers, plied with generous incentives from the city, converted it to its current state.

The Perfect Union was in many respects a typical downtown Memphis building. The façade was painstakingly faithful to the original construction, with its brick skin, concrete Corinthian trim at the corners, and red-and-white awnings at ground level to complete the retro look. The interior was all about appealing to the yuppies. Hardwood floors. Granite tabletops in the kitchenettes. Track lighting. Vaulted ceilings. Showers with platforms where bathers could sit. Or do whatever.

Billy Boy Bradwell took his meeting with Red Maloney in the office of his suite overlooking the Mud Island Harbor, the southern tip of Mud Island itself, and beyond that the mighty Mississippi flowing endlessly toward New Orleans and the Gulf of Mexico. And from there, who knew? It was easy to get lost in thought watching that water.

"Thank you for meeting with me, Mr. Maloney," Bradwell said absent-mindedly as he sat in an overstuffed chair twirling one of his ranch's branding irons with the three interlocked Bs.

"You're welcome, but I'm still not quite sure why I'm here," Maloney said.

"I need your help, Mr. Maloney, simple as that." Bradwell spun the branding iron in a tight circle on the hardwood. It would probably leave scuff marks. But what did he care? He could afford it.

"Help with what?" Maloney said. At six-foot-four and 250 pounds, he cut an intimidating figure. Much more so as he stood near Bradwell's chair, proudly defiant in the face of this newcomer. Red Maloney had been in the unions since he was seventeen and had been a boss since age twenty. So this Yankee puke from Kansas City wanted to meet with him? Big deal. Was Kansas City part of the North or the South, anyway? Then again, what did it matter?

"I want your help making a terrific project become a reality," Bradwell said. "Along with some local partners, I want to turn Memphis into the mecca of the adult film industry, Mr. Maloney."

Red Maloney stroked his red beard before letting out a snort. He really was red, on top and on his chin whiskers. Some of his friends said he looked like Mel Gibson's friend in *Braveheart*. It wasn't an image he tried to discourage.

"I'm listening," Red said.

"That's great, Mr. Maloney. So here's the deal. I and some friends of mine would like to convert a building—okay, let's call it what it is, a run-down, dilapidated dump in downtown Memphis—into a world-class movie studio. A studio capable of bringing millions of dollars to this community. And we'll need construction people to make it happen."

"I'm still listening," Red said. And he was.

"But here's the thing, Red, and this is critical. I need you to publicly support this project—and not the World Barbecue Hall of Fame the mayor has proposed for the same site."

"And why would I do that, Mr. Bradwell? Or can I call you 'Billy Boy'?"

"You can call me what you like," Bradwell said. "But I think you need to get behind this project, and sooner rather than later."

"What's wrong with later, Mr. Bradwell? You may not know it to look at me, but I'm a thinking man. And that means I like to think things over."

"You know, Mr. Maloney, in my experience, guys who spend too much of their time thinking always miss out on the big deal. And I'm prepared to offer you a great deal."

"How great, Billy Boy?"

"Well, let's start with the basics. We agree to hire only union laborers on this project. We're not the government or any public agency, so nobody will pay attention if the budget includes a couple of positions for no-show guys. Positions with paychecks that could go straight into your pocket, Mr. Maloney."

"Two positions? I was thinking more like ten," Maloney said, stroking his red beard for effect. "Plus, I would need to be the project manager. Which is a six-figure salary in and of itself. For at least a couple of years. Which assumes the construction would stay on schedule. Which it wouldn't. If it's a two-year project, I'd project at least another year of delays. Do you understand where I'm coming from, Mr. Bradwell?"

"Mr. Maloney, I totally respect you," Bradwell said, spinning the branding iron faster and faster along the floor. "But as a businessman, you know that five positions would be too many. I'm an executive, and I have to keep an eye on the bottom line."

"The fact that I'm standing here in your hotel room tells me you understand how helpful a guy like me can be for a project like yours. Or unhelpful, if you know what I mean."

"Yes, that's what I've heard. I know Mayor Pigg has contacted you and some other key people in town to get your support for his project."

"You've got good sources, Billy Boy, I'll say that. Lots of Yankees move to Memphis and it takes them years to figure out how this town works. But if you've done your homework, you know it's not smart to go against the mayor. You know the expression, 'You can't fight city hall.'"

"Well, Red—you don't mind if I call you Red, do you?—I believe I can fight city hall and win. If you knew anything about me, you'd know that not many like to go up against me."

"Billy Boy, let me tell you something. If you weren't born in Memphis, some people will always think of you as an outsider. And those 'some people' control what happens around here. So while you may have a lot of clout in Kansas City, that doesn't count for jack crap in Memphis. So saying you'll go up against city hall and win, well, it just sounds crazy."

Bradwell stared at his spinning branding iron, not even bothering to make eye contact with Maloney. "Red, I've told you what I'm going to do. And I've told you how what I'm going to do can profit you. I'm a man of my word. So I'll give you my word on one more thing: you'll be better off taking my offer than trying to jack up your take."

Maloney laughed. "You know, Billy Boy, that sounds an awful lot like a threat. And I'm usually the one who makes the threats. You might say I've got a vested interest in this Barbecue Hall of Fame project. And my interest is substantial enough that, quite frankly, your little offer comes across as insulting."

"Well, let me add injury to insult then," Bradwell said, bringing the branding iron up quickly to strike Maloney directly in the crotch.

The old union boss doubled over, releasing a groan that sounded to Bradwell like a cow mooing. Bradwell then windmilled the branding iron, striking Maloney across the right cheek and ear. Maloney crumpled to the floor, not quite unconscious but close.

"Now, I don't know what kind of deal you cut on the mayor's project, Red. And frankly, I don't care. What I need is to get your support—and by extension, the Union of Trade Unions Local 317's support—behind my project. I know all about you union types, and you don't intimidate me. You or any of your goons try to muscle anybody working on my project, anybody associated with my project, or anybody even coming within twenty miles of my project, and you'll have big trouble. The thing about muscle is that it's cheap to buy, Red, and I've got plenty of money."

Maloney tried to rise to a crawling position, which prompted Bradwell to kick him in the crotch with a heavy cowboy boot. Maloney returned to a prone position on the floor, emitting a low gurgling sound.

"Now, here's the most important thing to remember about this little chat we're having," Bradwell said, leaning over Maloney's damaged ear, which was bright red with splotches of purple. "If things get ugly and people have to get hurt, I'll make sure you get hurt worse than anybody else. Does that make sense to you, Red?"

Maloney grunted in the affirmative.

Also, I don't need you talking to your mayor friend or anybody else about what happened here. If anybody asks, you got injured on a job site. Understand?"

Another grunt.

"Okay, now that we've got that part straight, let me tell you something else. My offer to cut you in on this deal just expired. You're going to support me because you know I'll come back and put this branding iron in a very uncomfortable place in your body if you don't. Got it?"

Still one more grunt in the affirmative.

"Good deal. Now, walk or crawl out of here. I've got some other business to take care of."

Chapter 33

Mayor Pigg's phone was ringing again. This time, the ring tone was Alannah Miles's "Black Velvet."

Pigg struggled with his chubby fingers to flip the phone open. "'Lo?" he said into the receiver.

"Mr. Mayor, Alvin Allen from *The Avalanche* here." It was not a voice Mayor Pigg particularly wanted to hear. Today or ever.

"Well, hello, Mr. Allen! And what can I do for you this fine day?" Whatever his failings, Pigg could do false friendliness with the best of politicians.

"I'd like a comment for a story I'm working on, Mr. Mayor."

Uh-oh, Pigg thought. *That's two "Mr. Mayors" in the first thirty seconds.* In Pigg's experience, excessive formality from a reporter meant trouble.

"I kinda figured you weren't callin' to re-up my subscription, Alvin. Because I think I just sent you folks a check about a week ago."

"No, that's not it, Mr. Mayor." No laughter, and still all that formality. Pigg braced for the impact. "Actually, I'm working on a story involving some property owned by Augustine Eldridge. Are you familiar with Mr. Eldridge, sir?"

"I know him by reputation, mostly. I can't say I approve of his line of work."

"Right. Do you know William Bradwell as well?"

A knot began to tighten in Pigg's ample stomach. "I believe I've heard the name. Meat packer somewhere out in Montana, right?"

"Not quite. Mr. Bradwell is a cattle rancher, food product distributor, and restaurateur of some prominence in Kansas City."

"Oh, yeah. It's comin' back to me now. Although I wasn't aware Mr. Bradwell is a food distributor. I've been usin' his Rip-A-Chunk strips for flypaper. I had no idea they were for human consumption."

"So you do know him. Well, Mr. Mayor, it seems Mr. Bradwell is branching out."

"Do tell."

"Mr. Bradwell confirmed to me that he and Mr. Eldridge have entered into a partnership to renovate a building Mr. Eldridge owns at the intersection of Front Street and Auction Avenue. They plan to convert the building into a movie production studio—the biggest east of Death Valley, they say."

"Uh-huh." Pigg didn't know what else to say. He was still trying to process this new information. Which wasn't easy. In addition to the knot in his stomach, he felt the blood pounding through the suddenly bulging veins on his forehead.

"And unless I'm mistaken, Mr. Mayor, that is the same property you recently expressed interest in using for the World Barbecue Hall of Fame."

"Uh-huh." Alvin Allen's voice seemed faint as the sound of rushing blood filled the mayor's ears.

"And since you're familiar with Mr. Bradwell's business dealings, maybe you're also aware that he recently announced plans to build a Barbecue Hall of Fame—much like the project you propose—in Kansas City."

"I'm sorry, Alvin. Is there a question in here somewhere?"

"I guess my main question is how these developments might affect your plans for the World Barbecue Hall of Fame."

"I don't know that they do, Alvin."

"You don't?"

"No, Alvin. This is all news to me. I don't know anything about the project those gentlemen are proposin'."

"So you don't have any comment about the merits of it?"

"The merits of what, Alvin? A nudie movie studio?"

"Is that what you think it will be?"

"Isn't it, Alvin? I mean, you tell me. You've obviously talked to them about their plans. Did they tell you what kind of movies they plan to make there?"

"They said it would be an art house studio."

"Art? Damn, Alvin. I'm surprised at you, if you really believe that."

"It's not about what I believe, Mr. Mayor. It's about what my sources tell me."

"Sources? You know, seems I remember a story you wrote right after I was inaugurated in which you described me as the 'portly pol' in a sentence that wasn't attributed to anybody. I'm guessin' you just thought it sounded good."

"Mr. Mayor, we're getting off the subject here."

"Well, I don't like this subject, Alvin, and I don't want to comment on it. Besides, I've got some mayorin' still to do today, so I'm just gonna wish you a blessed day and hang up now, okay?"

And he did, not waiting for Alvin Allen's response.

Mayor Pigg stared at the clock on his desk, whose face was

set inside the belly of what appeared to be a miniature stuffed boar. Half past four. Plenty of time for Alvin Allen to finish his story so it could be splashed across the front page of tomorrow's newspaper.

Mayor Pigg snatched up his phone before it could ring again and started pushing buttons.

"This is Gus Eldridge," the voice on the other end of the line said.

"Gus, you really messed up this time," Mayor Pigg said.

"Why, Mr. Mayor, I'm not sure why you think that."

"Because I just got off the phone with Alvin Allen, that's why."

"Oh, yes. Mr. Allen was over here a little while ago. He wanted to talk about some plans I have to redevelop what should be—what will be—one the premier locations in downtown Memphis."

"Cut the crap, Gus. Alvin told me all about you snugglin' up to Billy Boy Bradwell!"

"Yes, Mr. Bradwell recently approached me with a business proposition. After careful consideration, his proposal seemed to be mutually beneficial. So we have entered into an agreement in principle to act as co-developers of this wonderful project. And of course, we'd like to have your support, too, Mr. Mayor, since you speak so often of your love for the city of Memphis."

"Gus, that weaselly reporter ain't there no more. And I doubt he'll be headed back unless you two set up a date for after he files his story. So you can cut this I'm-in-it-for-the-civic-good crap. I know you're doin' this to jack up the price for that land of yours."

"I happen to think a movie production studio would be great for this town. And I think most of your constituents will agree with me on that. You'd better get out there and do some poll testing, Mr. Mayor."

"You've lost your mind if you think the city of Memphis

wants to be known as the new capital of the porn industry!" Pigg said. "Take a look around. Notice that all the strip clubs are gone? I won't have to do nothin' to stop you. The church folk will rise up and give you a lashin' with the buckle of the Bible Belt!"

"Oh, I don't know about that, Mr. Mayor. People will tolerate a lot in the name of economic development. Memphians want their town to be thought of as a highly moral place, but they don't seem to do much to stop the crime ravaging the inner-city neighborhoods. And they don't seem upset about all those casinos thirty minutes away in Tunica, Mississippi. And they don't seem upset about that dog track right across the river in West Memphis, Arkansas. No, they're looking around at what other communities have and wishing they had something like it. They call Las Vegas 'Sin City.' Well, don't you think Memphis would love to have the worldwide reputation of Las Vegas, even if it cost the city some of its precious moral purity? And as for the strip clubs, prosecutors love to make headlines. But then they get distracted by other issues that can grab even bigger headlines for them. And once that happens, I'll bet you the deed to your restaurant that strip clubs will start sprouting up like weeds. Because there's a market for their product. Just like there's a market for mine."

"I'd hardly call what you're sellin' a product, Gus."

"Get off your high horse, Mr. Mayor. For some reason, you don't strike me as a guy who's lived his whole life without ever sampling the pleasures of adult entertainment."

"Be that as it may, it doesn't 'zactly hurt my political image to go up against you on this."

"Mr. Mayor, you can fight me if you want, but you ought to take stock of where we are. I've got the land I want. My partner and I both have deep pockets, which means we've got the resources to help people understand the benefits of this project.

This is all about jobs—construction jobs, production jobs, and eventually tourism jobs. I think my studio will draw more tourists than your World Barbecue Hall of Fame. People have to eat to live, but there's something they love doing even more."

"Gus, are you so blinded by your ego that you can't see what's goin' on here? You know Billy Boy wants to build a Barbecue Hall of Fame in Kansas City. You know his project will stand a better chance if he beats me to the punch. But the kind of studio you're talkin' about would take awhile to get off the ground. That crappy buildin' you've got on that land is a total knockdown job. And if he gets his Barbecue Hall of Fame finished before your studio—and you know he's gonna keep his investment in your project small until it is—chances are he'll walk out and leave you holdin' the bag."

"What makes you think that, Mr. Mayor?"

"Gus, if you don't know the answer to that question, then you haven't done your homework on Billy Boy Bradwell. You think he's gonna treat you any different from the other business partners he's had through the years? You, the fancy California boy who dresses funny and couldn't stand the smell of a cattle ranch? Oh, yeah. You and Bradwell make quite a pair."

The line was silent except for Pigg's breathing, which was still loud and ragged.

"Why do you need my property for your barbecue project, Mr. Mayor?" Eldridge finally said. "Surely, there are lots of places you could put it. The city of Memphis must own scores of inner-city properties with tax delinquency problems."

"There's no shortage of those, that's true. But I need your land, Gus. Why do you need it?"

"Well, you know the saying about real estate: God's not making any more of it. It's a prime downtown location. I know it. And you must know it, too, if you want it so bad."

"But you'll need a ton of money up front to make your project happen. And unless I'm wrong about this, Gus, you're not set up to absorb heavy costs on the front end. You know your business, but I've always heard the goal is to make 'em cheap and sit back and rake in the bucks. Plus, can you shut down production for the year or two or three it'll take to finish that project? You don't think you'll keep makin' movies outside the gates of Graceland, do you? This may not be Minnesota, but it does get chilly in January and February for actors who work in the state of undress you require. The women might put up with it if you pay 'em enough. But what'll happen to the guys outside in that weather? Certain parts of the male anatomy don't do so well in the cold."

"I gave you a fair asking price for my property. And you rejected it. So now I've got a better offer."

"No, you've got another offer. Not a better one. Not unless Billy Boy Bradwell wakes up one mornin' and decides to stop bein' Billy Boy Bradwell."

More silence on the line.

"Are you prepared to make a counter-offer, Mr. Mayor?"

"How about this? You back down on your askin' price, down to sumpin reasonable I can sell to the taxpayers. Then we find some nice land for you from that list of tax-delinquent properties. We'll make sure you get some kind of federal anti-blight grant to cover the demolition costs. Then we'll give you a tax freeze and a cartload of other government incentives. For a project that creates jobs, we can build roads and other infrastructure. And those big infrastructure projects carry big budgets. So maybe some of the money in the construction reserve fund might accidentally make its way into your pocket as reimbursement for unspecified 'owner property enhancements,' if you know what I mean."

"That's an interesting offer, Mr. Mayor. But for reasons you've already outlined, I suspect I'd lose my investment partner if the studio relocated to a different site."

"And for reasons I've already outlined, you're gonna lose your investment partner anyway. And I think you underestimate the benefits of government backin'. Those construction reserve funds can run into the millions, all set aside for no specific purpose other than to be available in case unforeseen circumstances drive up costs. Once a budget is set for a taxpayer-funded project, nobody squawks unless there are cost overruns. But nobody's gonna notice if there are just enough 'unforeseen circumstances' that the construction reserve fund sits at zero when the project's done."

"Mr. Mayor, you sound like a man who's given this quite a bit of thought."

"Have you heard the expression *win-win situation?* This can be one of those, Gus. Or if you keep goin' down the path you're on, it can be lose-lose for both of us. So what do you say?"

"Well, I'm willing to discuss it further. But I can't publicly pull back on Billy Boy yet. That's going to be on the streets tomorrow when Mr. Allen's story hits the newspaper. And the diversion could actually benefit us, if we decide to do business together."

"Speakin' of what we can and can't do in public, one thing I couldn't do if we relocate your project is come out and say what it really is. We'd have to use that 'art house' crap you fed Allen. Now, after the thing's built and all the media attention moves to sumpin else, you can do what you want there. As mayor, I'll have to put my hands up and say I can't interfere with free speech and artistic expression and all that."

"Since we're negotiating, Mr. Mayor, I have to ask for one other incentive. You're right about this project needing substantial money on the front end. And even though you've indicated you're willing to facilitate a generous government contribution, I'll still need an infusion of cash."

"You got sumpin specific in mind?"

"I'm interested in making the kind of movie that would cement my reputation as the greatest producer in this industry. I can do that with one adult film with an honest-to-God celebrity in it. People fall all over themselves logging on to the Internet to see a few minutes of grainy sex video with Paris Hilton or Rob Lowe or whoever. If I could get someone like that in a film—a film with real production value—after that person has already made a name as a legitimate star, well, I could sell as many copies as I could produce. People have a celebrity fetish. If they'll pay two dollars for supermarket magazines with stars wearing swimsuits, imagine how much they'll pay to see a high-quality video production of what they really fantasize about!"

"I hope we're not back to this again, Gus."

"If you mean convincing your friend Dawn to be in one of my movies, then we are."

"She already told me no."

"So get her to change her mind. You were very persuasive with me just then. Be that way with her."

"Gus, I can't offer her the same incentives I offered you. And she was firm in her answer. Firm as in, she basically told me to go to hell. She's gone too high in the business to show up and strip down at your studio one day."

"Well, at least convince her to meet with me. Maybe I can persuade her."

"You're in a dream world if you think you can. That girl lives in a different universe from ours, Gus."

"Maybe so, but why don't you set up a meeting and let me give it a shot?"

"Gus, if that's what it takes to turn this into a win-win situation for us, consider it done."

Chapter 34

J oe Miller felt pretty good about life, all things considered.

Yes, his best friend was in a mess—a mess somehow tied to the mayor's pet project. A project Joe was involved in, too.

And based on the mayor's comments, Joe figured it was just a matter of time before he was caught up in Scott's mess, too. Really, he already was. That's what friends were for.

Then again, Scott seemed to spend his life moving from one mess to another. If Scott could take it, so could Joe. And Scott and Joe had a helpful new ally in Raina Johnson, courtesy of Joe's new friend, Dawn.

And Dawn was the main reason Joe felt so good these days. It defied explanation. Joe hadn't tried to put any moves on Dawn. He wouldn't have known where to begin with someone like that. Dawn was a movie star—one of the city's biggest celebrities. One of its biggest living celebrities, anyway. And Joe was, well, just an ordinary Joe.

But for whatever reason, Joe and Dawn seemed to click whenever they were together. Joe found her easy to talk to, easy to be with. Sure, she was incredibly good looking, which was distracting. But Joe wasn't as mush-mouthed and scatter-brained as he thought he would be in her presence. Most of the time, anyway.

Joe felt so good that he drove to Overton Park, a few miles east of his downtown apartment, and took a long walk. Overton Park was one of the city's greatest assets—a three-hundred-acre oasis of trees and lush grass in the heart of Midtown. The Brooks Museum of Art and the Memphis Zoo occupied part of the park, as did a nine-hole golf course. The rest was a pleasing mix of rolling fields, walking and jogging paths, and old-growth forest.

Joe spent an hour there, watching people walking dogs, playing Frisbee, and necking on picnic blankets. Maybe someday he would even work up the nerve to bring Dawn to the park on a date. Now, that would be fun.

That daydream kept Joe's mind occupied on the drive home. But the reverie ended as he pulled up in front of his apartment. Two uniformed police officers stood outside his door, along with two men who weren't wearing uniforms but were obviously cops as well.

"Are you Joe Miller?" said one of the men in street clothes, a young, heavyset guy with a blond crew cut.

"I'm guessing you know I am," Joe said. "Otherwise, you wouldn't be here."

"That's right, we do," the blond guy said as the two uniformed officers circled behind Joe.

"What's going on?" Joe asked.

"We need you to come with us, Mr. Miller."

"Am I under arrest?"

"Do you want to be?" Blondie was doing all the talking. The uniformed officers didn't say anything, nor did the other plain-clothes guy.

"If I'm not under arrest, I don't want to go anywhere with you. One of my friends got taken away by the cops a couple of days ago, and he tells me it wasn't a pleasant experience."

"Don't get smart with me, boy. The law allows us to take you into custody and detain you for up to forty-eight hours without making an arrest. And believe me, if you put up a fight, we can have some fun during the take-you-into-custody part."

"Yeah, you guys are brave when it's four to one." Joe didn't know why, but he felt sassy at the moment. Just a defense mechanism, he supposed.

"You think it would be an even fight if it was one on one, tough guy? Just get in the car, Joe."

So Joe did. He didn't know what angle the cops were working, so he didn't want to press his luck. And with Dawn's friend Raina on the case, Joe felt it was better not to rock the boat.

The ride to 201 Poplar was quiet. The uniformed cops left, and the two plain-clothes detectives took Joe to an interrogation room. It looked pretty much the way the interrogation rooms did in the movies. The detectives motioned for Joe to sit in a metal folding chair, while they pulled up chairs across the table from him.

"Do you know why you're here, Joe?" This was the other cop, thin and athletic, with a black pompadour and a thick mustache.

"No idea. You guys are trying to set a world record for the number of times you can harass me and my friends in a week?"

"Joe, you're in trouble, so I think it would be in your best interest to start cooperating with us."

The blond guy remained silent as his partner spoke. Maybe they talked in shifts.

"That's what you guys told my friend when he was in here," Joe said. "And you know what? You were bluffing. You had no evidence. Which is why he's out singing on Beale Street right now in a ridiculous Elvis costume instead of being locked up in here."

"A technicality. Your friend Scott Paulk remains the prime suspect in a string of arsons that have plagued North Memphis, South Memphis, and Orange Mound over the last few months. The charges against him will be refiled soon. And you'll be charged as an accessory to his crimes."

Even though Joe tried his best to act tough and defiant, the words stung. "You're crazy," he managed to sputter.

"Some would say it's crazy to go around burning up vacant buildings in the ghetto. Unless you did it for the publicity. Which wouldn't surprise me any. Two young punks laughing it up, getting themselves on TV."

"That's not what happened."

"What did happen, then?"

"I have no idea what you're talking about. I haven't burned any buildings. And I haven't helped Scott or anybody else burn any buildings either."

"The evidence suggests otherwise."

"What evidence? There can't be any evidence. Because I haven't done anything wrong."

"What about those cans of kerosene we found in your apartment? The ones with your buddy's fingerprints all over them? That's strong evidence, son. And I think most juries would see it that way."

"I don't have any kerosene in my apartment!" Joe felt whatever color he had left in his face draining away. "And how could you get into my apartment anyway? Don't we have laws in this country against illegal search and seizure? I've got a good lawyer. She'll have a field day with this."

"Joe, the search was legit," the cop said, sounding bored. "We got an anonymous call from someone who reported seeing a man carrying containers of kerosene into your place."

"What man? That wasn't me!"

"Can you prove it, Joe?"

Joe was starting to get lightheaded. "This isn't right," he managed to say.

"Since you're a known associate of someone under surveillance for suspicion of arson, it was easy to get a judge to give us a warrant," the mustached cop said. "We followed the proper procedures. And the district attorney's office has been advised of the events I just described. Based on the evidence we found during our search, the DA is prepared to accept our recommendation that we arrest you. But first, you have a visitor."

"Is it my lawyer?" Joe said. "Because I'd really like to talk to her right now."

"I bet you would. But you're not so lucky. Your visitor will see you in a few minutes."

With that, the cops stood and walked out, closing the door behind them. Joe heard the lock snap into place and felt thoroughly trapped.

He wasn't sure how long he waited. It could have been ten minutes, or it could have been an hour. His thoughts were racing so fast that he couldn't keep track of time. This whole chain of events was unbelievable. Just a few days ago, he and Scott had been drinking beer and joking around on the Wiffle ball field. Now, those carefree days were long gone.

Even if he managed to stay out of jail, Joe was pretty sure he'd lose his job. And while he didn't love the work, it was a paycheck. Joe had never developed a Plan B in case PR didn't work out as a career.

And what about Dawn? Would she want anything to do with

him? She had stuck by him through Scott's troubles and helped make them better, at least temporarily. But her reputation could be at stake if the media found out she was palling around with a jailbird. Make that two jailbirds. And Joe definitely didn't want to do anything to make her life more difficult.

Joe's head spun as he contemplated how this would all turn out. For the life of him, he couldn't see the end game. Would he go to prison and get killed by an inmate? Would he be ruined financially? Subjected to international ridicule if the press found out about his relationship with Dawn—whatever that relationship was?

The future was impossible to see through the fog filling Joe's brain. But the immediate past was clear enough. Joe knew he had been set up. So it was no surprise when the next person who walked through the interrogation room door was none other than the Honorable Pete Pigg, mayor of Memphis.

"Joe, my boy, we gotta stop meetin' like this," Pigg said.

Chapter 35

Just a few hours ago, Joe had been daydreaming about his next meeting with Dawn. Now, she was standing right in front of him, and Joe couldn't have been sadder. From the look on her face, she felt the same way, too.

Mayor Pigg had laid it all out for Joe. He was going to be prosecuted alongside Scott for a series of crimes that had plagued the city and dominated the news for months. The mayor assured Joe that this time, no one would walk out of jail on technicalities. The legal i's and t's would be dotted and crossed. And the evidence against them was rock solid. Against Scott, there were fingerprints on the bottle used to assault a police officer and the police officer's identification of him as the assailant. Against Joe, there were the cans of kerosene found in his apartment, covered with Scott's fingerprints. Forensic evidence showed kerosene was the accelerant used in all the fires. And kerosene had been found in Scott's apartment as well.

Mayor Pigg assured Joe that no fancy lawyering would save

him or his friend. And that long before the case went to trial, Joe and Scott would be judged guilty in the media. And for good measure, Mayor Pigg planned to tell the tabloids about Joe's relationship with Dawn, embellishing the facts where necessary to wreck her career.

Unless. Unless Dawn met with local businessman Augustine Eldridge, who hoped to open a new art house movie studio. It would be a creative meeting between two people in show business. A chance to exchange ideas and proposals. If Dawn was willing to take that meeting, Joe and Scott's legal troubles would go away.

Why that meeting was so important to Mayor Pigg, Joe had no idea. But he imagined the worst. Just like putting the World Barbecue Hall of Fame at that dumpy site across from The Pyramid, there had to be more to the mayor's request than he was letting on.

And now Dawn was here, standing across the table from Joe in the interrogation room. From the look on her face, Joe could tell she had endured a similar conversation with Mayor Pigg.

"Oh, Joe," she said as she sat down. Her eyes were red and watery.

Joe tried to turn away before his watered up, too. It didn't work. "Dawn, I'm so sorry I got you into this mess." The words felt like they were choking him.

"Joe, I don't know what's going on here, but I know it isn't your fault."

"Actually, I think it is."

"No, Joe. You know better than that. The mayor's up to something. That's why he's coming after you and Scott."

"Yeah, something weird is going on, that's for sure. But I've lived the kind of life where it was just a matter of time before I ended up in a situation like this."

"What on earth are you talking about?"

"Ever since college—before college, even—I've lived my life like I didn't give a crap. Because I didn't. If school or work was too hard, I didn't mess with it. To me, it wasn't cool to care too much about anything. Particularly anything I wasn't sure I could do. Fear of failure, you know? So I just went for whatever was easy. Easy major in school. Easy job. Easy women, when I could find them."

Dawn looked at him with surprise.

"Oh, I'm not really a horn dog, Dawn," Joe said. "I just got into the partying life. Not quite as much as Scott, but I was right there with him for a lot of it. And I liked meeting girls from that scene. They'd be drunk, I'd be drunk, so whatever happened happened. If I got lucky—which didn't happen nearly as often as I would have liked—then great. But if I got rejected, it was no big deal. It wasn't like I was investing any time or emotional energy in a girl, so I didn't feel the same rejection as when you strike out with somebody who means something to you."

"Sounds like a defense mechanism," Dawn said.

"It was. It totally was. I went out and got drunk to avoid being serious about my life. Partying became my substitute for getting involved with anything or anyone I cared about. And then you came along, Dawn."

"Me?"

"Yep. And guess what? I finally found something—someone—I care about. And because of the life I've been living, I got myself into trouble. And it looks like I'm dragging you down with me."

"Joe, you're wrong. You're not in here because you haven't lived a perfect life. You're in here because Mayor Pigg is, well, a filthy pig. He doesn't mind using people, hurting people if he has to, to get what he wants. Nothing you could have done differently in your life would have kept you out of this."

"I'm not so sure about that."

"I am. Joe, you're not the only person who's missed some opportunities and made bad choices. We've all done that. Even me." Tears were flowing freely down Dawn's cheeks now.

"You?" Now it was Joe's turn to look startled.

"Even me. Especially me. Joe, you've known me for only a short time. And when you live the kind of life I've lived, where fame and fortune come fast, you're bound to make mistakes."

"I can't imagine that."

"Imagine it. For a long time, I lived that partying lifestyle you described. Hollywood chews up a lot of people."

"But you're the city's sweetheart. The real-life Memphis Belle."

"Image management. People know my name, but they don't know me. I've made the same mistakes you've made."

"Did any of your mistakes land you in jail, facing the wrath of a vengeful mayor?"

At that, Dawn managed to choke out a laugh, although it sounded more like a cough through her tears. "Maybe not. But I'm going to make sure you're not in this situation much longer."

Joe's dominant emotion instantly flipped from sorrow to fear as he caught the meaning of what Dawn was saying. "You can't possibly be considering the mayor's offer," he said.

"It's a good deal. I meet with his sleazebag producer friend, and he lets you go and stops bothering Scott. And let me tell you, I've had to meet a lot of sleazebag producers in my time."

"Dawn, this is dangerous."

"I know, I know. But I wouldn't agree to meet Eldridge at his house, as he suggested. We're meeting at a public place, the Pigg Pen. That should be safe. Plus, we've got to find out what's really going on with Mayor Pigg. He and Eldridge are working together. So maybe I'll learn something about this Barbecue Hall of Fame project that will help us."

"Dawn, you can't. You know what the guy is after. He's a porno producer. He wants to get you in one of his movies."

"I've said no to a lot of sleazebags."

"But what if the mayor doesn't keep his word?"

"That's a chance we'll have to take."

"No!" Joe jumped to his feet. "You can't do this, Dawn."

Chapter 36

Dawn hoped she was doing the right thing. She paused in front of the Pigg Pen and took a few deep breaths.

She hoped Joe was worth it. She certainly thought he was. Of course, she wasn't doing this just for Joe. She had been at the press conference when the mayor introduced his project. If something shady was going on, she needed to know before the tabloids did. James Bond wasn't likely to share the big screen with a love interest who had a real-life criminal record.

So meeting with the smut king was important on both a personal and a professional level.

Dawn summoned her strength for what she expected to be an awkward and unpleasant meeting. "Might as well get this over with," she finally muttered. As she approached, two massive bouncers stepped away from the door and motioned for her to join the bedlam inside.

The Pigg Pen's interior was about as understated as one might expect from its owner. Interspersed on the walls with the usual fluorescent beer signs were watercolor paintings by a local artist of pigs doing various human activities—pigs riding motorcycles, pigs skydiving, pigs relaxing by the pool, and, of course, pigs playing poker.

Overhead, giant inflatable pigs with wings hung from the ceiling. On occasion, some enterprising or dexterous drunk tried to get a pig down and take it home as a souvenir, which invariably led to an unpleasant encounter with one or more of the bouncers. Pigg liked to brag that his establishment was an Alcatraz for flying pigs.

The Pigg Pen's famed bone buckets were only about half full at this time of night, although a scattering of bones on the floor suggested some patrons were having trouble hitting even an oversized target with their throws.

The servers, the Pigglettes, were in their usual attire—short white halter tops and hot pink running shorts with curly pig tails attached. Not even the bouncers could prevent a pig tail or two from being snatched during the crush of happy hour.

As Dawn entered the Pigg Pen, someone dressed in a pig costume ran by with someone in a chef's outfit brandishing a spatula in hot pursuit. Apparently, Mayor Pigg hadn't waited for the opening of the World Barbecue Hall of Fame to put that idea to the test.

As usual, the crowd was raucous. A society of accountants was in town for a convention, and many of its members had headed straight to the Pigg Pen after their last breakout session of the day ended at four-thirty—meaning they already had a couple of hours of drinking under their belts by the time Dawn showed up. They were loud and boisterous, flirting with the Pigglettes and members of a bachelorette party. The bachelorettes were camped out on the patio at the side of the restaurant, but they made frequent trips inside the main section of the Pigg Pen to visit the bathroom or get refills at the bar. They drew hoots whenever they passed near the accountants' tables, which didn't seem to discourage them in the least.

As Dawn scanned the main room, she saw Mayor Pigg, Augustine Eldridge, and another man at a table in the back. The three rose from their seats as she approached.

"Good evening, Dawn," Eldridge said. He introduced the third member of his party, Pedro Suarez. Eldridge was dressed in loafers, tan slacks, and a green silk shirt that was far too unbuttoned for Dawn's taste. "You look as lovely as I remember from our first meeting. Please join us."

Dawn did, even allowing Pedro Suarez to pull out a chair for her.

"Thank you for coming," Eldridge said.

"You're welcome," Dawn said. "So long as you understand I'm doing this only because Mayor Pigg agreed to release my friends from jail."

"Whatever the reason, I'm glad you're here," Eldridge said.

"Before we get into this, let's have some drinks," Mayor Pigg suggested. "Pedro, would you please have the bartender make us four Russian Matadors?"

Pedro nodded and headed to the bar, where a tall, lanky kid who didn't look old enough to serve alcohol was trying to manage the frenzy of patrons surrounding him.

"Oh, no, I'm not drinking tonight," Dawn said. "This is strictly business."

"Aw, Dawn, we've had this conversation before," Mayor Pigg protested. "In Memphis, havin' a drink with friends is part of doin' business. And in case you haven't noticed, we're in a bar. And not just any bar, but the best bar on Beale Street, which is to say the best bar in the whole wide world."

"Be that as it may . . . ," Dawn said.

"Come on, Dawn," the mayor said. "Since you're here, I'd like your opinion on this new drink I'm thinkin' about puttin' on the menu. Always trying to come up with sumpin new to stay ahead of the competition, you know."

"What's in a Russian Matador?" Dawn asked.

"Vodka and sangria!" Mayor Pigg announced proudly. "Get it? Russian, vodka. Matador, sangria."

"Um, frankly, that sounds hideous," Dawn said.

"Why?" Mayor Pigg said. "People mix vodka with fruit drinks all the time. Sangria's a fruity drink, just with a little extra kick. After all, who says a mixer has to be nonalcoholic?"

Pedro returned with four drinks, placing one in front of Dawn and handing one to Eldridge and Pigg. He kept one for himself.

"Let's do a toast," Eldridge suggested. "If Dawn doesn't like the drink, I'm sure Mayor Pigg will take it in stride."

With that, all four raised their glasses and drank. Dawn took only a sip, figuring it would make the evening go by faster if she humored these men. No way would they get her drunk. She'd learned a little during her time in Hollywood, after all. And while her drink was funny tasting, it wasn't nearly as strong as she expected.

Much as she hoped Eldridge would get to business right away, he didn't. He began by heaping praise on Dawn, recounting her career from her first big break to her recent projects. He was frequently interrupted by members of the accountants' convention, who staggered over to the table to ask first for autographs, then for Dawn's phone number. The bouncers shooed them away and Pigg apologized repeatedly, noting that his clientele tonight was primarily tourists who didn't know the rules about respecting Dawn's privacy.

Dawn took a few more sips of her drink to alleviate her boredom and discomfort, while her three companions quickly finished theirs and ordered themselves another round. At that rate, she'd probably end up calling taxis to take them home, she thought dreamily.

Suddenly, the noise level increased as the night's entertainment, the No Talent Clowns, prepared to take the stage. The band members, shirtless but covered in clown makeup and wigs, drew cheers from the crowd as they launched into a ridiculously overwrought rendition of "Stray Cat Strut."

Dawn had trouble hearing Eldridge over the din. And trying to do so made her suddenly very tired.

"Gus, it's getting too loud in here," Mayor Pigg said. "I've got an office in my storeroom where we can continue this conversation."

Eldridge said something in response, but Dawn couldn't make it out. Then they were standing—very suddenly, she thought—and lifting her to her feet.

They helped her toward a set of double doors that led to the Pigg Pen's storeroom. As she entered the room cluttered with boxes and assorted trash, she saw through blurred vision a camera set up on a tripod in the far corner. And that was the last thing she remembered before she passed out.

Chapter 37

The metal door opened with a loud buzz and a click. Joe stepped into the parking lot behind 201 Poplar. He was glad to see the outside world again. Even though he had been detained only a few hours, nothing was pleasant about being arrested.

Even Scott, who was cavalier about most things in life, had been clear with Joe about that. Scott knew having an arrest record enhanced his coolness factor and his street cred. And depending on how much he had to drink and whose company he was keeping, Scott occasionally shared his jailhouse stories.

But with Joe in their occasional serious moments together, Scott always said that jail was no place he ever wanted to return to. And now Joe knew what he meant.

Joe took a deep breath of air that smelled of car exhaust, used wine, and a hint of rotten garbage. Still an improvement over the inside of 201 Poplar.

Scott was waiting in the parking lot with his new friend and legal adviser, Raina Johnson. They were a welcome sight. But not as welcome as if Dawn had been standing there with them.

"Hey, bud, looks like you got your cherry popped," Scott said.

"I assume you mean that in the metaphorical sense," Joe replied. "Because, for the record, I didn't engage in any carnal activity in there."

"So, for you, it was pretty much like being on the outside," Scott said.

"Scott, take it easy," Raina said. "Your friend just got out of jail."

"Thank you, Ms. Johnson," Joe said.

"You need to start calling me Raina. Lord knows, your friend isn't so formal with me."

"Okay, thank you, Raina," Joe said. "Thank you for getting me out. I assume this was your doing, right?"

"Well, partly," Raina said. "But our mutual friend Dawn had something to say about it, too."

Joe's heart, already in a low place, sank further. "I was afraid you'd say that. Please don't tell me she took Mayor Pigg's deal and agreed to meet with that scumbag."

"I'm afraid so, Joe," Raina said.

"Why did you let her do that?" Joe said.

"Joe, you haven't known Dawn as long as I have," Raina said. "But I think you know her well enough to understand you can't talk her out of something she's put her mind to."

"So what did she tell you? What did she agree to do?" Joe said.

"She agreed to meet with the mayor and the mayor's friend Augustine Eldridge at the Pigg Pen," Raina said. "For a few minutes, to hear them out."

"Oh, no," Joe said.

Scott was silent, which was rare.

"Did you tell her that's a really bad idea?" Joe asked.

"She didn't seem to think so," Raina said evenly. "She believes it's the best way to get you and Scott out of this mess."

"Hey, I don't like it either," Scott said finally. "This is a crappy setup from the get-go."

"So why is he here?" Joe said, still looking at Raina but pointing to his best friend.

"Because the way things have been going between you two and the cops, I was afraid they'd pick him up again as soon as they released you," Raina said. "I wanted to be here when you got out, with Scott beside me. To make sure you both were okay before I gave Dawn the go-ahead for her meeting."

"When did you last talk to her?" Joe asked.

"About ten minutes ago," Raina replied. "She wasn't going to leave for her meeting until I told her everything was okay."

"So she hasn't left yet?"

Raina stared at the pavement for a long few seconds, then gave a sigh. "Joe, as soon as they started processing the paperwork to get you out, I told her to go to the meeting."

"Why would you do that?" Joe asked, his stomach churning. "Aren't you worried that Eldridge is up to no good?"

"Hey, Joe, we got this," Scott said. "That's why I went along with this thing up until now. Raina cut a deal to get you out, and made sure they didn't pick me up in the meantime. So now you and I get to go all Eliot Ness on a bar and rescue your lady!"

"Scott, I don't—" Raina began.

"Well, I do, pretty lady," Scott said. "I sat here and played it cool, because that's what you told me we needed to do to get Joe sprung from the big house. But now he's out. His lady's in trouble. We know where she is. Now, it's time to go get her."

"Do you think she's already at the Pigg Pen?" Joe asked.

"Probably," Raina said. "When I spoke with her, she was at her house on Mud Island, so she was only five minutes away by car."

"So we don't have any time to waste," Joe said.

"Do you really think Mayor Pigg and Augustine Eldridge would try something stupid? In a public place like the Pigg Pen?" Raina said. "Dawn thinks the mayor's bark is worse than his bite."

"Raina, the Pigg Pen is the beast's lair," Scott said. "Once Dawn's on his turf, there's no telling what might happen. Plus, we don't know anything about this Eldridge guy. But I think it's safe to assume the worst."

"Scott's right," Joe said. "I don't know what might happen, but I've got a bad feeling about this. We need to get over there."

"So what are we waitin' fer?" Scott said, doing his best imitation of Mickey the manager from the *Rocky* movies.

"I don't believe this," Raina said. "Did you go completely crazy in just a few hours in jail, Joe? I expected Scott to want to run off and act like a fool, but you're supposed to be the voice of reason in your buddy act. You could get into even more trouble if you go barging into the Pigg Pen to break up that meeting."

"I know that," Joe said. "But sometimes you have to put reason aside and go with your instincts."

"Tell her, Joe!" Scott said, reverting to Elvis mode, swinging his hips and pumping his fists.

"Cool it, King!" Joe shouted at his friend before turning back to Raina. "Look, we don't have time to argue. If the mayor is so desperate to set up this meeting that he was willing to spring me to make it happen, there's got to be more to it than meets the eye. Scott and I have to go over and see what's what. If everything looks okay, we'll hang back. But I'm not going to just sit around and hope Dawn will come out of this okay. And as her friend, you shouldn't either."

Raina paused and bit her lower lip. "What if things get rough? The Pigg Pen's bouncers are built like refrigerators. And the mayor may have warned them to look out for you."

"That's why we'll bring reinforcements," Joe said.

"Who do you have in mind?" Scott asked.

"What about your buddies down on Beale Street?" Joe asked. "They would be close."

"Yeah, a little too close to the mayor," Scott said. "No street performers, servers, bouncers, chefs, or anyone else on Beale Street wants to make trouble for the mayor."

"What about the guys from the Wiffle ball league?" Joe said.

"Did you lose track of time in jail?" Scott said. "It's Wednesday. The teams won't show up until the weekend."

"Barry Brett." The name popped out of Joe's mouth almost before it popped into his head.

"Good call," Scott said. "He may be Super Bum now, but he's probably got about a zillion dollars stashed in a Swiss bank account. He'll help us out with bail money if this goes bad."

"You'll need more help than that," Raina said.

"No time to round up anybody else," Joe said. "But before we get Barry, let's swing by my place. I need to pick up something out of my canoe."

"I'm going with you," Raina said.

"Oh, hell, no," Scott said. "I can't go for that."

"You'll have to, Scott," Raina said.

"Raina, now is not the time to play," Scott said.

"I'm not playing," Raina said firmly. "I've known Dawn a lot longer than you two have. I don't want to see my oldest friend get hurt. And she's more likely to get hurt if the two of you go charging in there without a plan."

"Joe, help me out here," Scott said, turning to his friend.

"Sorry, Scott. I hate to go against you, but I'm taking Raina's side on this. If we're going into the Pigg Pen badly outnumbered, we can use her help."

"So what's the plan?" Scott said.

"I'm working on that," Joe said.

Chapter 38

"We don't have a minute to waste," Augustine Eldridge said. "Mayor Pigg, please tell your young friend behind the bar it's time for his debut performance in the adult film industry. Pedro, take Dawn's clothes off. I'll get the camera ready."

The mayor nodded and headed into the bar.

Dawn, arguably the city's biggest celebrity, lay unconscious on a stack of beer crates in the Pigg Pen's storeroom. It wasn't the Russian Matador that got to her. It was the Mexican sedative Pedro Suarez had slipped into the drink before handing it to her. Too powerful to be approved by the Food and Drug Administration for over-the-counter use in America, the sleeping pills were readily available in Suarez's native land. Pedro used them to sleep when he was trying to come down off a high. And on occasion, he passed a few along to his boss, no questions asked.

"That kid at the bar? This is his scene?" Suarez said, surprise and disappointment on his face.

"Yeah, why not?" Eldridge said. "Mayor Pigg says he's seen the kid in the restroom, and he's definitely got the goods."

"Well, boss, you promised I could be in one of your movies someday," Suarez said, glancing longingly at Dawn's motionless body. "And I was thinking that maybe, particularly since we need to keep as few people involved in this project as possible, that—"

"Pedro, we don't have time to argue about this," Eldridge said. "We've got one of America's hottest movie stars laid out on those crates. We've got exactly one take to make the movie we've always wanted—one with a big-name star *while* she actually is a star. Can you imagine how much we'll make with this movie?"

"I know, Mr. Eldridge, but—"

"No offense, Pedro, but this would be like putting the third-string quarterback in with the Super Bowl tied in the fourth quarter," Eldridge said. Then he took note of Suarez's quizzical look. "Okay, it's like putting in the third-string goalie in a tie game in the World Cup finals. The point is, you've never performed on camera before."

"Boss, I could handle it. I mean, look at her."

"It's not as easy as you think with other people watching and the cameraman shooting over your shoulders and between your legs and every other place he can get. A lot of men have performance anxiety in that kind of situation."

"I wouldn't."

"Listen, Pedro, this isn't about being macho. You'll get your opportunity. I promise you that. But tonight, we can't take chances. She's going to look right for one take only."

"And what makes you think that bartender can pull this off but I can't?"

Eldridge sighed. He wasn't used to Pedro putting up so much

resistance. Normally, Pedro did what he was told. It was so hard to find good help these days.

"Like I said, we've got an honest-to-God celebrity sprawled out on those crates. I've got to put the guy who gives me the best chance to make a great movie out there. And Mayor Pigg vouches for this kid. If I'm going to keep the mayor on my side, we need to let this happen the way he wants it to happen."

"And what's the mayor going to be doing during the filming?"

"Same thing I suspect you'll be doing, Pedro. He'll be trying his best not to drool all over himself."

"So Mayor Pigg gets half the kid's pay for setting this up?"

"Half, 60 percent, 80 percent—what do we care?" Eldridge said. "We pay them a little money and they split it however they want. When this movie comes out, we'll be rich."

No, you'll be rich, Suarez thought, *while I get a few more crumbs*.

"Do you even think this will work, boss? I mean, she's sleeping."

"Well, it's not going to look like she's sleeping the way we shoot it, Pedro. It's going to look like her eyes are closed because she's in ecstasy. On the shots that hide her face, we'll mix in sound effects. Who could tell the difference? When you've heard one woman moaning, you've heard them all."

Pedro Suarez hesitated long enough to mull his options. He had the promise—even though it had been repeated many times without being fulfilled—that he would someday star in one of these movies. It would be the day that launched the career of his dreams. It just wouldn't be this day.

A familiar story. Too familiar.

"Pedro!" Eldridge said sharply. "She's not going to undress herself!"

Chapter 39

As Raina walked toward the entrance to the Pigg Pen, she began fishing around for her cell phone. In doing so, she managed to spill the contents of her purse, sending her wallet, tubes of lipstick, an eyeliner pencil, a pack of gum, and other assorted items skittering across the cobblestones of Beale Street.

"That was clumsy!" she exclaimed. She knelt to scoop up the purse's contents before they were trampled by tourists, doused with beer, or worse.

"Would you big, strong men mind helping me?" she asked the two massive bouncers standing near the doorway, who replied by wordlessly moving toward her. They bent to help, trying not to be too obvious about peering down her blouse.

All too easy, Raina thought. She saw Joe and Scott shoot past the bouncers on either side, nearly colliding as they reached the doorway at the same time.

Once inside, Joe and Scott took stock of their surroundings. The bar, currently unattended, was to their right. A small stage where some guys in clown makeup were performing was to the left. The entrance to the patio was also to the left, just beyond the stage. Against the back wall were two sets of doors, one leading to the Pigg Pen's storeroom and kitchen area and the other to the bathrooms.

"Scott, I don't see her," Joe said loudly enough to be heard over the band and the obnoxious accountants.

"Storeroom," Scott replied. "I've been here enough to know that whenever Pete Pigg wants to meet in private, that's where he goes."

"Okay, but those two goons at the door aren't the only bouncers in this place. So where's our distraction?"

As if on cue, they heard screams from the patio area.

The two bouncers at the bar's patio entrance had been watching the homeless man with the beat-up baseball cap and the scraggly beard making his way up the side street. It was a well-known fact that the homeless viewed patio patrons as the low-hanging fruit of their profession—less mobile and thus easier prey. This particular homeless man had his hand in an oversized grocery bag, which wasn't particularly unusual. Although open containers of alcohol were legal in the Beale Street entertainment district, the homeless were used to concealing their vices.

The bouncers' suspicions turned to outright alarm when the man ripped away the bag to reveal a loaded pistol crossbow.

"*Your papers, please!*" Barry Brett shouted as he approached the bouncers, who retreated quickly onto the patio. The patrons who were not too shocked to move began to scatter.

"*Don't ever buy a pig in a poke!*" Barry shouted as he took aim at one of the inflatable balloons overhead. His shot punctured it with a loud pop.

The bouncers reversed course and charged the strange-looking assailant. No doubt, the boss would give them extra cash or free alcohol for pounding this lunatic into the concrete.

But Barry was faster on the reload than they expected. Unlike their full-sized counterparts, pistol crossbows in the right hands can be reloaded in seconds. And Barry had the right hands.

The bouncers came to such an abrupt stop that their legs flew out from under them. One landed across the laps of the bride and two of her bridesmaids, pulling the vinyl tablecloth covered with food and drinks on top of them as he fell. One of the bridesmaids, already the worse for wear, promptly vomited on the bouncer.

The other bouncer didn't fare much better. He fell against one of the giant bone buckets, causing it to flip over and bury him in a cascade of gnawed-up pig products. He rose to his hands and knees, trying to get the bucket off his head.

"*Your papers are not in order!*" Barry bellowed as he stepped forward and kicked the bucket hard. The bouncer fell back to his stomach and lay still.

Hearing the commotion the band was competing against, one of the No Talent Clowns peered through the doorway from the main room.

Barry waved the still-loaded crossbow in the air. "Hey, '*Tears of a Clown.*' Haven't you heard? There's no one around!"

The No Talent Clown didn't bother to answer. He dropped his bass guitar and sprinted for the front entrance, yelling a warning to his band mates as he went. Most of the people in the front room followed the musician's lead, creating a stampede of drunk accountants and screaming Pigglettes. Four bouncers from the main room, including the two who had blown their assignment at the front door, didn't have much luck swimming against the stream of humanity headed away from the patio.

Barry glanced at the members of the bachelorette party as they made their escape, leaving the guest of honor and two of her best friends trapped beneath the stunned bouncer. That prompted Barry to launch into the opening lyrics of Elton John's "Kiss the Bride."

Meanwhile, Joe and Scott moved quickly inside the storeroom. As they burst through the doors just as the chaos on the patio began, they saw Mayor Pigg and Augustine Eldridge fiddling with a camera on a tripod. A young bartender was shirtless and halfway out of his pants nearby. And Pedro Suarez was standing over Dawn, fiddling with the buttons on her blouse without as much enthusiasm as one might expect.

Joe charged forward and hit Suarez's face full blast with his can of mace. Pedro clutched his eyes and fell to the floor screaming.

Scott gave the bartender who was tangled in his pants a hard enough shove to topple him. He stepped over the bartender and lifted his foot. "Dude, you've got parts exposed that you totally don't want me to stomp." The bartender took his meaning and lay still.

Glancing at Dawn's motionless body, Joe was filled with rage. "What have you done to her?" he demanded of Pigg and Eldridge.

"Why, nothing, young man," Eldridge said. "It appears your friend had a bit too much to drink and—"

"That's bull!" Joe shouted. "If you hurt her, I promise both of you will leave here tonight on stretchers!"

"What's goin' on out there in my bar?" Pigg demanded as the din outside grew louder.

"That's the Memphis cavalry arriving," Joe said. "I wouldn't count on your security to help you out of this one, Mr. Mayor. I expect they're kind of busy."

"You got some people bustin' up my bar, boys?" Pigg said.

"Because I think you already got enough trouble as it is."

"You don't know from trouble, Mr. Mayor," Joe said. "You have the city's most famous person unconscious in your storeroom, with a pornmeister, a couple of his buddies, and a camera set up to do everybody knows exactly what. This won't look good for your political career."

"Yeah, yeah, yeah. And after the dust settles, the cops will sort everythin' out," Pigg said. "And in case you forgot, I run the cops around here, boy. Also in case you forgot, you and your buddy happen to be the prime suspects in a series of arsons."

"You don't think the national press, the tabloids in particular, will be in your business when they find out Dawn is involved?" Joe shot back.

Eldridge stood by calmly while Scott paced around the bartender, hoping for an opportunity to stomp some junk.

The mayor paused to consider the situation. "You know, you're right. This is a Messican standoff." Then Pigg glanced at Pedro, who was still writhing on the floor. "Okay, maybe that was a poor choice of words."

"May I make a suggestion, Mr. Mayor?" Eldridge finally offered.

"By all means."

"It seems like this night has taken a turn for the worse for all of us," Eldridge said. "I think it would be in everyone's best interest if we all just walked away, preferably before the police get involved."

"Not a bad idea, Gus," Pigg said. "In fact, you can take the back way out. There's a door that'll bring you into the kitchen. It leads out to the loadin' dock in the alley."

"That will work," Eldridge said. "Just let me grab my camera and tripod."

"What about him?" Pigg asked, gesturing to Suarez.

"I don't think he can make it out on his own," Eldridge said. "And I can't carry him and the camera equipment. Could you help me out, Mr. Mayor?"

"Sure can," Pigg said. "I'll tell the cops he got maced while he was harassin' some woman in the bar. Happens all the time around here. And I don't think Pedro will say any different, since he's part of this here, too. Right, Pedro?"

Pedro screamed something unintelligible from the floor as his boss headed out the back door.

"Well, Joe, you and your buddy are free to take Dawn and go, too," Pigg said. "Obviously, the less that's said about tonight, the better for everyone."

Joe and Scott quietly approached Dawn. They lifted her, each draping one of her arms around their shoulders. They started toward the storeroom door and the din inside the bar.

Joe turned back toward the mayor. "You know this isn't over."

"Not by a long stretch," Pigg said.

Together, Joe and Scott half-carried, half-dragged Dawn through the bar and outside, where they blended into the bedlam of Beale Street.

By that point, Barry Brett had advanced to the door leading from the patio to the main room. The patio bouncers and the remaining bachelorette party members had fled onto the side street as he moved toward the interior of the bar. Now, he was singing Prince's "When Doves Cry," only with slightly modified lyrics.

"*When pigs fly!*" he belted out as he took aim at a sprinkler head with his crossbow. The shot once again hit the mark, causing not only that sprinkler but all the others in the bar to simultaneously erupt.

As water flooded the Pigg Pen, Backwater Barry fled through

the patio entrance and into the neighborhood south of Beale. It was called a "transitional neighborhood," which meant law-abiding people mostly avoided it. He met the getaway car, driven by Raina, at the designated rendezvous point a few blocks away. Joe, Scott, and Dawn were already inside.

Chapter 40

"*Shh! Shh! Shh!* I love this part!" Scott shouted.

They were watching the "hat cam" video Barry Brett had made during his visit to the Pigg Pen. The camera jerked as Barry danced to his off-key rendition of "Kiss the Bride." His arms, one of them holding the crossbow, were the only parts of him visible. But the camera concealed in Barry's baseball cap had picked up some great footage of the bewildered bridesmaids and hapless bouncers.

Joe, Scott, and Barry were watching the video for the seventh time on the TV in Raina's condominium in suburban Collierville. They had spent the night there—Dawn sleeping the drugs off in the master bedroom, Raina in the guest room, Joe on the couch, Scott on the recliner, and Barry on the floor. The condominium was a quaint loft-style design on the second floor above an antique shop on Collierville's town square. With the Memphis police paying so much attention to Scott and Joe, everyone agreed it was safer to stay outside their jurisdiction for the time being.

"Man, the hat cam rocks!" Scott said. "How did you ever think of that?"

"It's just a new use for something somebody else invented," Barry said. "Like DUI Busters. I didn't invent the concept of delivery service. But nobody had done it for liquor stores before. So I did, and people liked the idea. I suspect most drunks don't want to drive. I gave them a way to keep their buzz going without getting behind the wheel. Same deal with the hat cams. Lots of businesses use hidden cameras and microphones for security. TV reporters use them all the time, too. But it never occurred to anybody to put hidden cameras on delivery drivers. At least nobody who went out and got a patent like I did."

"You know, as your lawyer, I'm not entirely comfortable that you made that video," Raina said, shaking her head at the men's choice of entertainment. She had returned to the living room after checking on Dawn, who was still sleeping. "It shows you committing a number of criminal acts."

"Oh, I plan to get rid of it," Barry said. "It's just that, living as a homeless guy, I haven't had that much fun in a long time. I don't go out in public much anymore. I wanted Scott and Joe to see what I did to keep everyone busy while they were in the back helping Dawn."

"I'm grateful for that," Raina said. "Thank you for helping save my friend. But weren't you worried somebody might recognize you, Barry?"

"Not really. I'm a lot scruffier and dirtier than I was when everybody considered me a pillar of society. Plus, it's hard to recognize people out of context. If you see your mailman out on the town after hours in street clothes, you may not recognize him. On top of that, most people on Beale Street are tourists anyway. They don't know Barry Brett from George Brett."

"Who?" Raina asked.

"We'll talk baseball later, pretty lady," Scott said. "Just watch this. This is classic!" The video had reached the part where Barry took out the sprinkler head.

"Where did you learn to shoot like that, Barry?" Joe asked.

"I live on an abandoned houseboat at the quiet end of the Wolf River Harbor. What else do I have to do with my time?"

After they watched the video again, Barry popped the DVD out and rose to leave.

"Where are you going?" Scott asked.

"Back to the boat, man," Barry said.

"Are you sure that's a good idea?" Joe said. "After last night, you may be on the mayor's hit list the same way Scott and I are."

"I appreciate the concern, Joe, but nobody will come looking for me. I'm just some crazy homeless guy in a city with a lot of homeless people. And the homeless are invisible."

"Unless they have a loaded crossbow," Scott said.

"Can we give you a ride? We're about thirty miles from down-town," Raina said.

"Not necessary. I'll find my way back. Besides, if I'm seen riding with you, that probably would put me on the police's radar. Thanks for thinking of me last night, though. It was fun to get out for a while. Almost made me miss being part of the so-called real world."

After saying their farewells to Barry, Scott, Raina, and Joe talked until Dawn woke up around noon. The four of them walked to a coffee shop a few doors down from the antique place. By that time, the lunch crowd had mostly cleared out, which allowed them to grab a booth in an isolated corner.

"Thank you again for what you did last night," Dawn said for about the twentieth time. "I can't believe I was so stupid to let Eldridge get the better of me like that."

"You weren't stupid," Joe said. "You were trying to help me. And I thank you for that."

"What kind of mess have we gotten ourselves into?" Dawn said, rubbing her still-aching forehead.

"I'm not sure," Joe said. "But I still think this is all tied to the World Barbecue Hall of Fame, one way or another."

"So what's our next move?" Scott asked. "I want to do something besides just waiting for the police to pick us up again."

"We've got to find out why that property the mayor's interested in is so important," Raina said. "I'll get a look at those records today."

"I already tried that, remember?" Joe said. "Mayor Pigg has confiscated them."

"True, but the people who work at the register's office are used to dealing with lawyers. I'll go down there and use some lawyer-speak on them. Maybe I can scare them enough to get them to reclaim the records from Mayor Pigg. After all, they don't work for the city, they work for the county."

"Worth a try, I guess," Joe said.

"What do we do in the meantime?" Scott asked.

"Stay here," Raina said. "Pigg's cops don't play by the rules, so there's no guarantee they won't try to snatch you. But that's a lot less likely here than in Memphis. The Collierville police don't like having their turf trampled on any more than other cops do.

In fact, after we get done here, I suggest the three of you go back to my condominium."

"No way," Scott said. "If you're going downtown, I'm coming with you."

"Scott . . . ," Raina said wearily.

"No, Raina, Scott's right," Joe said. "You're mixed up in this now, too. And as we saw last night, things could get rough. And believe me, Scott's a good guy to have around for the rough stuff."

"Hey, thanks, buddy," Scott said, nodding.

"So why don't we all just go down there together?" Dawn asked.

"I don't think so," Joe said. "We're more likely to attract attention as a group. And Dawn, you and I need to spend the afternoon working on a strategy anyway."

"A strategy for what?" Dawn asked.

"A public relations strategy," Joe said. "We have to figure out a way to get people asking questions about what Mayor Pigg is doing. Maybe then we can force him into making a mistake."

"I like it," Scott said.

"I do, too," Dawn said. "But you're the PR expert, Joe. What do you need me for?"

"First of all, I don't really qualify as an expert," Joe said. "In fact, I'm not sure public relations is a field that lends itself to having experts. But I do have some experience that might be helpful. And Dawn, you're a celebrity. You don't have any trouble getting media attention when you want it. So we need to figure out how to get your media contacts interested in this story."

"You two should stay out of sight," Raina said. "Dawn, you attract attention wherever you go. And attention is not what we need right now."

"We can do what we need at the condo," Joe said. "No worries there."

So Joe and Dawn and Scott and Raina went their separate ways. Joe and Dawn spent the afternoon trying to figure out how to expose what Mayor Pigg was doing. Which was problematic, since they didn't know what Mayor Pigg was doing. And then there was the risk that calling Mayor Pigg out in the media could result in a mud-slinging contest. And Dawn had a lot more to lose reputation-wise than the mayor did.

So they tossed around some ideas but didn't decide on anything. By the time Scott and Raina returned around five o'clock, Joe and Dawn's conversation had devolved into small talk about their personal likes and dislikes. While he had hoped to come up with an airtight plan, Joe couldn't consider an afternoon that helped him get to know Dawn as anything but time well spent.

Raina and Scott's report about the visit to the register's office darkened the mood, though.

"Well, Joe, let me start off by saying I didn't do any better than you," Raina said.

"No?" Joe said, more than a little surprised. After watching Raina in action, Joe had expected her to come back with armfuls of property records.

"I'm afraid not," Raina said.

"I thought they might react differently if a lawyer asked for the documents," Dawn said.

"I thought so, too," Raina said. "But the clerks weren't intimidated in the least. Or if they were, they're a lot more intimidated by the thought of getting the mayor angry."

"That's the truth," Scott said. "Raina hit them with some heavy legalese. She was all 'open records law' this and 'illegal concealment of assets' that. But those ladies behind the counter didn't buy it."

"Did they know who you were?" Joe asked.

"I think a couple of them recognized me," Raina said. "I've gone in there to look for records a time or two before. But it's never been a problem. Whatever Mayor Pigg is holding onto, they're not trying to make him give it up. That much was clear."

"So where does that leave us?" Dawn asked.

"I could go for a good B and E," Scott suggested. "Breaking into city hall would be a killer adrenalin rush."

"Scott, I'm already trying to keep you out of jail on charges you committed just about every unsolved arson in the city's history," Raina said. "As your lawyer, I have to tell you that now is not the best time for you to break into any more buildings."

"You should have just said 'any buildings,' counselor," Scott said.

"Duly noted," Raina replied. "But I think you get my meaning."

"I agree," Joe said. "I'm not sure what our next move should be, but a commando raid isn't what we need right now."

"Totally different story from what you said last night," Scott noted.

"That," Joe said, shooting a glance in Dawn's direction, "was a totally different situation."

"So what do we do?" Scott said.

"I think we stirred the pot when we busted in on Eldridge last night and ruined his plans," Joe said. "And it sounds like Raina and Scott stirred it more with their visit to the register's office."

"I neglected to mention that we got escorted out by a couple of Shelby County deputy sheriffs after Scott referred to one of the male clerks as a 'babified bureaucrat,'" Raina said.

"Scott's subtle that way," Joe said. "Anyway, we've stirred up a whole lot of mess. So maybe it's time for us to lay low and see what happens next."

Chapter 41

The meeting took place on a paddle-wheel riverboat called the *Big Muddy Express.*

Augustine Eldridge had insisted on a public place. Mayor Pigg had insisted on a place where he wasn't likely to be recognized.

The *Big Muddy Express* fit both men's needs. Dinnertime cruises on the Mississippi were a big hit during summer, so the boat was packed with passengers. However, most of them were tourists, for whom Mayor Pigg was just another fat, sunburned drunk living it up in downtown Memphis.

Pigg knew the boat's owner but wasn't on friendly terms with him. In fact, in his pre-mayoral days, Pigg had raised the ire of the city's riverboat operators by suggesting the boats shouldn't be allowed to have liquor licenses, since the river fell outside the jurisdiction of the Memphis police. That was only partly true, since the river was divided equally between Tennessee and Arkansas at the point where it passed through Memphis. But as a business-man who wanted to keep as many tourists on Beale Street as possible, Pigg had unsuccessfully tried to make that argument.

Although the riverboat operators hadn't forgotten, Pigg had little chance of running into his rival this particular night. Pigg knew for a fact that the owner of the *Big Muddy Express* spent most of his time downriver in the Garden District of New Orleans getting drunk in stately restaurants. And Pigg knew the college kids the owner hired to run the boat tours weren't likely to rat him out.

Pigg found Eldridge near the back of the boat watching a spectacular sunset over the tree-lined Arkansas shoreline. The tranquil scene sharply contrasted with the noise generated by the river water churning through the big paddle wheel. Since the dinner hour was starting, most of the passengers had headed below decks to feast on barbecued catfish, baked beans, and cornbread with raw onions. The rest kept their distance from the paddle wheel. Pigg and Eldridge were as alone as they could be on a ship this size.

"Heck of a spot you picked out," Pigg said over the din. "Has all that porno soundtrack music made you deaf or sumpin?"

"Hardly," Eldridge said. "But if you're wearing a wire, the sound quality won't be great."

"That what you think?" Pigg said. "That I'm wearin' a wire? I've got more to lose than some skin flick maestro. I'm the mayor of the eighteenth-largest city in America."

"Be that as it may, I'm taking no chances tonight," Eldridge said.

"Oh, come on," Pigg said, unbuttoning the loud Hawaiian shirt he was wearing. "Are you satisfied? Now, can we get away from this noise?"

"You could be hiding a wire in your pants," Eldridge pointed out.

"Oh, you can't be serious."

"Oh, I am, I am," Eldridge said. "So unless you like shouting over this wheel, drop your pants."

Pigg reluctantly lowered his Bermuda shorts and red bikini underwear to his ankles, which caught the attention of a couple necking ten yards away. They quickly moved toward the front of the boat. This would make an interesting story for their friends back in Poplar Bluff, Missouri.

"All right, Mayor Pigg, put your clothes back on. You've convinced me," Eldridge said after a few agonizing seconds of giving the mayor's fleshy body the once-over. Eldridge nodded in the direction of the spot where the couple had been standing. "Let's continue our discussion over there."

"Don't usually get naked in front of men," Pigg said as he reassembled his wardrobe and followed Eldridge. "But I guess you've seen about as many naked folks in your line of work as doctors do."

"None with bodies like yours, Mr. Mayor," Eldridge said.

"Why, thank you," Pigg said. "So, why are we here tonight? What's goin' on that you couldn't tell me over the phone?"

"It's what isn't going on that's the problem," Eldridge said. "Last night, as you may remember, our meeting with Dawn was interrupted by that group of young thugs."

"Yeah," Pigg said. "That's too bad."

"Yes, it is too bad," Eldridge said. "That was almost surely our only opportunity."

"Gee, really? You don't think Dawn will reshoot?"

"Go ahead and make jokes, but that means a film project I estimated to be worth millions isn't going to happen."

"Well, that's the way the cookie crumbles," Pigg said. "Find yourself some more strippers, and you're right back to the editin' room, I imagine."

"You reneged on your part of the deal, Mayor Pigg."

"Reneged?" Pigg said. "Does that mean what I think it means?"

"Probably not," Eldridge admitted. "It means you didn't hold up your end of the bargain."

"What do you mean, I didn't hold up my end of the bargain? You wanted a meetin' with Dawn, and you got one. It's not my fault it went down that way."

"Actually, it is your fault," Eldridge said. "Where was your security?"

"They were a little busy," Pigg said. "Not long after we got Dawn in the back room, some crazy homeless guy started shootin' up the place with a crossbow, of all things. Did a ton of water damage to the Pigg Pen."

"All the same, you didn't hold up your end," Eldridge said. "I'm not able to make the movie I wanted. And I haven't seen my associate, Mr. Suarez, since we parted ways last night. Since he checks in regularly with me, I can only assume he's gone missing."

"I don't think he was thrilled about you takin' off without him. Said sumpin about you valuin' your camera equipment more than him."

"Still, that wouldn't have happened had you controlled the situation in your own bar. Why don't your security men carry mace or pepper spray?"

"Used to. Then one night, a fight got out of hand, and one of my bouncers shot his pepper spray. Took out the idiots fightin' but also the guy and his date at the next table over. The guy happened to run one of the city's biggest car dealerships. And his date wasn't his wife."

"Sounds tragic."

"Haven't gotten a good deal on a car since that happened. So now my bouncers fend for themselves. Usually, they can. It's not every night we get some whacked-out freak who thinks he's William Tell."

"Yes, it was an unusual night."

"Well, I guess we each have a sad story, Eldridge. But we had a deal," Pigg said.

"Good choice of words, Mr. Mayor," Eldridge said. "We *had* a deal. We don't have one anymore."

"You backin' out on me?"

"I'm afraid so," Eldridge said. "We have no contract. I thought you were offering a deal that would be more lucrative than Mr. Bradwell's. But now it appears his deal is much more advantageous for my long-term needs."

"You think he's not goin' to weasel out on you, Gus?"

"I don't know that he will, and I don't know that he won't," Eldridge said. "What I know is that you failed to deliver what you promised. So I'm glad I have a backup plan."

"Eldridge, I've got half a mind to throw you over this railin'," Pigg sputtered.

"Mayor Pigg, it would be a bad idea for you to try that," Eldridge replied, his voice sounding almost weary.

"Why's that? I get the feelin' nobody would ever miss you. And not everybody who falls into this river gets found."

It was true. Because of the Mississippi's powerful and treacherous currents, drowning victims were sometimes found miles downstream from where they entered the water. And sometimes not at all. Who knew how many human skeletons, picked clean by catfish, crawfish, and other bottom feeders, were tangled in the rocks and roots along the mighty waterway's route?

"I'm not going into the water," Eldridge said quietly.

"Oh, yeah?" Mayor Pigg said. Although he wasn't exactly in prime shape, Pigg felt he could take this sissified California boy anytime he wanted. "You sure 'bout that?"

"Yes, I am," Eldridge said, pulling out a small revolver.

Pigg flinched at the sight of the weapon. He hadn't expected the porn king to be prepared for violence. "Well, aren't you full of surprises tonight, Gus?" Pigg said, forcing a nervous laugh. "To look at you, I wouldn't think you'd be the type to be carryin'. Thought you had people to do that for you."

"This may come as a surprise, Mr. Mayor, but people besides rednecks in pickup trucks carry firearms," Eldridge said. Although in truth, the mayor was right: Eldridge hadn't drawn his own weapon in years. "My only regret is that I didn't have this with me last night at your place."

"So, you gonna shoot me, Gus?"

"Only if I have to."

"That might look bad for you," Pigg said. "I can see the headline in tomorrow's *Avalanche*: 'Porn King Guns Down Beloved Mayor.'"

"*Befuddled* seems like a better word choice than *beloved*," Eldridge said. "But if it comes to that, it would clearly be a case of self-defense. And Tennessee juries are notoriously sympathetic to law-abiding citizens who take matters into their own hands and exercise their Second Amendment rights."

"Law abidin'? I hate to tell you, Gus, but you're not gonna win Citizen of the Year honors around here. A jury might not show a lot of love for a guy who guns down an unarmed man. The mayor, no less."

"Mr. Mayor, from what I've observed about your popularity,

I might get a commendation in addition to an acquittal. I might save the taxpayers the cost of a recall election with just one bullet. And as far as you being unarmed, I could say your weapon fell overboard. I imagine quite a few guns are thrown into this river."

"You willin' to take your chances with that kinda story, Gus?"

"Let me put it this way. If you attack me and I'm forced to shoot, I like my chances a lot better than yours. It's easy to win an argument when you're the only person alive to give your version of events."

Pigg was at a loss for words. He just stared at Eldridge, breathing raggedly.

"But I don't want to kill you, Mr. Mayor, I really don't," Eldridge said. "You mock me, but I'm a businessman. And what I would like to do is get back to the business of doing business."

"Meanin' what?"

"Meaning I want to fulfill my partnership obligations with Mr. Bradwell without any interference from you. I own the property you want, but I'm not going to sell it to you. I'm going to develop it—with Mr. Bradwell's help—into a world-class studio. Then Mr. Bradwell and I will make our money. And I'm guessing Memphis is like California in at least one respect: money talks. Money buys power and influence. Money shortens memories. In five or ten years, after a few high-profile civic endeavors, I'll be accepted as one of the city's leading citizens. And if you're willing to put this bad blood between us aside—as I am—I might even throw a campaign contribution or two your way. So what do you say to that?"

Pigg wasn't happy, but he managed to force a laugh that sounded more like a smoker's cough. "Doesn't look like you're leavin' me much of a choice."

"I would think that, as an elected official, you're faced with tough choices every day. Or what should be tough choices, for a man of conscience. So perhaps you should be grateful that I'm making your best option—your only option, really—so clear in this case."

"You've got an interestin' way of lookin' at things, Gus," Pigg said. "You're right about cuttin' down my options. But if I were you, I wouldn't wait by the mailbox for a thank-you card."

And with that, Mayor Pigg headed below decks to see how much catfish he could scarf before the ship's crew stopped serving dinner.

Chapter 42

When Chief Bruno arrived at The Olive Pit, Mayor Pigg was seated in his usual booth in the back corner. Other than the bartender, they were alone. Which wasn't a huge surprise, since it was eight o'clock in the morning.

Chief Bruno would have preferred to meet at city hall, but the mayor said he needed some "hair of the dog" to combat his hangover from the night before. The bar usually didn't open until noon, but Pigg had called the owner and suggested it might be a good idea to open early. Either that, the unspoken threat went, or face a suspension of his liquor license for a week or so.

Mayor Pigg was drinking a dirty martini with about ten olives packed into a highball glass.

"You wanted to see me, Mr. Mayor?" the chief said.

"We've got business to discuss," Pigg said. Then he called to the bartender for two more martinis. "Have yourself a drink, chief."

"I like to wait until after breakfast for that," Bruno replied. "Particularly when I'm on duty."

"Oh, just go with it," Pigg said. "You should be glad you've got a boss that doesn't mind if you have a snort or two."

"So, why did you want to see me?" Bruno said.

"I need you to arrest Augustine Eldridge."

"On what charge?"

"That's for you to figure out, chief. As you like to remind me, you're the law enforcement officer."

"I guess we're going to have another discussion about evidence and probable cause, aren't we, Mr. Mayor?"

"Not necessary. I'll leave you to figure that out."

"Any particular reason why I need to arrest Mr. Eldridge?"

"Yeah. Because I told you to."

"It's nice to be kept in the loop sometimes."

"And sometimes it isn't. Just do what I said."

"Is it safe to assume this has something to do with your plan to build the World Barbecue Hall of Fame on Mr. Eldridge's property?"

"You can assume anythin' you want. Just make sure you put him in jail and keep him there."

"That's always easier to do if I have a valid reason. Judges go for that sort of thing, you know."

"You're not gettin' squeamish, are you, chief?" Pigg asked. "You didn't seem to mind puttin' those two pukes in jail for the Ghetto Blazer case. Could that be because they were embarrassin' you with the press?"

"No, I did that because you told me to. I didn't like it, even though at least one of those boys is probably guilty. But you threatened my job, if you remember."

"Oh, I remember," Pigg said. "And if you need me to threaten your job again so you can go to sleep with your holier-than-thou conscience clear, I'll do it. You can type up an arrest warrant, or you can type up a resignation letter. Makes no difference to me."

"You'd like it if I quit," Bruno said. "But who would you get to replace me?"

"I don't know, maybe somebody who would contribute a few thousand to my campaign account and get the cops to knock on doors for me in the next election. Shouldn't be hard to find somebody willin' to take a six-figure salary to do that. If you had any sense, you wouldn't mind doin' those things."

The two fell silent as the bartender approached with the drinks. After putting one in front of each man, he quickly retreated out of earshot. *Smart kid*, Mayor Pigg thought.

"And here I believed my job was to do police work," Bruno said.

That brought a barking laugh from the mayor, who then finished the martini he had been working on and chewed a couple of olives with his mouth open. "God, Bruno, how long have you lived in Memphis? In government, nothin' is what it should be. And while you think you're Joe Friday from *Dragnet*, the reality is you gotta be more than that. Job one, always, is makin' the boss look good. And to make me look good, I need you to arrest Gus Eldridge. I don't wanna give you reasons. I don't wanna have a strategic meetin'. I just want you to do it."

Chief Bruno's face reddened, but he kept his tone easy and level. "So my input means nothing?"

"Not really," Pigg said. "And if you think I'm scared to fire you, you really are as dumb as you're actin'. Fire a library director or a public works director, people might wonder why. The press might ask questions. But a police chief? With the crime in this city, everybody'll assume it was because you couldn't get the job done. Which, by the way, is pretty much the truth."

"You think I'm doing a bad job as chief?"

"The stats say you are," Pigg said. "Crime hasn't gone down a lick since you've been in the big chair."

"You don't think that could be because of all the poverty, all the poorly educated kids growing into dead-end adults, all the blight—all those things that are out of my control but a halfway effective mayor might be able to improve?"

"I've got better things to do."

"Like this World Barbecue Hall of Fame? That'll really make a difference."

"It'll make a difference for me and all the people in this city who count, Chief Bruno."

"I see. So there it is."

"Yep. There it is."

"Well, since you have such low regard for my ability to do police work, I don't know why I'm telling you this. But your barbecue project may have more trouble ahead."

"What do you mean?"

"I understand that the Ghetto Blazer and Dawn's lawyer friend were at the register's office yesterday afternoon asking for records about the property around the project site."

"What?" Pigg said, interrupting his drinking in mid-guzzle. "Why didn't you tell me sooner?"

"Mr. Mayor, I don't think you've noticed, but when we talk, you do most of the talking and I do most of the listening. I didn't have a chance before now."

"How do you know they were there?"

"Mr. Mayor, in spite of what you think, I happen to be a pretty good police officer. And that means I've got sources in a few places where it's good to have sources."

"Well, la-ti-da for you, Chief Bruno! Don't break your arm pattin' yourself on the back."

"I'll try not to."

"You know what this means, don't you?" Pigg stopped to take a big hit off his martini. Chief Bruno hadn't touched his.

"I have no idea what this means."

"It means you gotta arrest Dawn and her lawyer friend, too."

"What?" Bruno said, recoiling in his chair as if he had been hit. "You can't be serious."

"Serious as a heart attack. And you gotta do this one right. Get an undercover lady cop to say they tried to hire her for a lesbian three-way. Or better yet, get one of the real prostitutes you pick up to say that. Hookers will say anythin' to get out of an arrest. That's much better than bringin' another cop into the circle."

"Why would we arrest them? They haven't done anything illegal."

"Bruno, have you got some kind of short-term memory problem? We've been over this. It's not about law and order and the scales of justice and all that crap. It's about advancin' my agenda. And if they're gonna poke around those property records, I need to take them out of circulation. As soon as you pick 'em up, I'll let my reporter friend Zip know we've got a movie star and her gal pal locked in jail. Once that hits the tabloids, they won't have time to worry about the World Barbecue Hall of Fame."

"Maybe we should talk about this after you sober up, Mr. Mayor."

"What do you mean?"

"Let's think this through. You're talking about arresting a

movie star and her best friend, then framing them for some sex scandal. You're right, that's the kind of story that will attract coast-to-coast media attention. From real news reporters. Not just hacks who'll write or broadcast anything you tell them. Reporters who'll find out if the case against Dawn is solid. Which of course it wouldn't be. So we'll end up looking like yokels in the eyes of America. Is that what you want for Memphis?"

"It wouldn't have to be that way, if you did your job right. Just think up some good charges, cook up some evidence, and get those girls in jail. I can't wait to go through the grocery line and see those gals in prison jumpsuits starin' at me from the front pages of the tabloids."

"You think it's that easy, Mr. Mayor?"

"It should be, if you're half the cop you claim to be."

"And if I can't make it happen the way you want it to happen?"

"Clean out your desk and type up a resignation letter. Simple as that."

"Simple as that?"

"Yep."

With that, Chief Bruno stood and walked out of The Olive Pit, mulling his options. He could give up his job, or he could give up the last shred of ethics he had by arresting a couple of innocent people and intentionally destroying their lives.

Or maybe he had another choice.

Chapter 43

Augustine Eldridge felt like a cowboy.

He was certainly dressed for the part—flannel shirt, blue jeans, chaps, boots, even an Old West–style six-shooter. Billy Boy Bradwell had noticed Eldridge's revolver when they were changing in the dressing room next to the stables at Bradwell's ranch.

The morning after his conversation with Mayor Pigg, Eldridge had called Bradwell to make sure they were still on track with their plans. Alienating the mayor was one thing, but Eldridge didn't want to get Bradwell mad, particularly since Bradwell had the financing to make his movie studio on the Mississippi a reality.

Bradwell was anything but mad. He surprised Eldridge by inviting him for a visit to the Triple B Ranch outside Kansas City. In fact, Bradwell had paid to charter a plane and fly Eldridge out that very day.

They made small talk after Eldridge arrived. Then Bradwell suggested they take a horseback ride before dinner. Eldridge wasn't an outdoor type, but he figured he could put up with a little discomfort to keep someone who could bankroll a multimillion-dollar project happy. And when they were changing into their riding clothes, Bradwell insisted they carry six-shooters for the full cowboy experience. The old Western guns were more accurate for shooting varmints than Eldridge's revolver anyway, Bradwell said.

Riding wasn't an altogether unpleasant experience, although Eldridge couldn't figure out a way to sit in the saddle that prevented his private parts from getting banged up whenever the horses moved at more than a walk. And Bradwell wasn't having any of that. For him, riding meant going at a fast gallop.

So they galloped, through huge, rolling pastures and scrubland. Eldridge was so intent on hanging on for dear life that he lost track of time. Had they been gone ten minutes? An hour? He couldn't say. His hands ached from holding the reins, and his leg and butt muscles were sore from digging his heels so tightly against his horse's sides. Eldridge was about to suggest they return to the Triple B for margaritas and Tex-Mex, as Bradwell had promised, when Bradwell pulled his horse to a stop and signaled for Eldridge to do the same.

"Quite a ride, huh, city boy?" Bradwell said.

"Yes, exhilarating," Eldridge said, only half-lying. *Terrifying* was probably a better word.

"Well, you're not the worst rider I've ever seen," Bradwell said. "With a little practice, you might be pretty decent at it."

"Maybe," Eldridge said. Once this ride was over, he wasn't likely to set foot near a horse again, unless it was to place a bet at a track.

Bradwell hopped off his horse with surprising grace and tied its reins to a bush. "Why don't you dismount and tie up for a few minutes?" he said. "I've got something to show you."

Eldridge did as Bradwell suggested, although it took considerable effort. He stumbled and nearly fell but recovered and tied off the reins just as Bradwell had done. It felt good to finally have his feet on the ground, even though he was a little unsteady.

"What do you want to show me?" Eldridge asked. As far as he could tell, they were in the middle of nowhere. Eldridge didn't even have a clue how to get back to the ranch.

"Well, I'll be honest with you, Gus. I didn't plan this to be entirely a social visit," Bradwell said, reaching into a saddlebag to produce a pen and some documents. "I need you to sign this paperwork for me."

"Strange place you picked for that," Eldridge said. "What are those documents?"

"They're the paperwork to quitclaim your property in Memphis over to me," Bradwell said.

"Quitclaim? You expect me to deed you my property for free?"

"Well, not free. I think ten dollars would be a customary charge for this kind of thing. It would look good on the paperwork."

"And why would I do that?" Eldridge said. "That isn't what we discussed in regard to our partnership agreement."

"Yeah, I know. But our partnership agreement was out the window when you went behind my back and tried to cut a separate deal with that fat toad, Mayor Pigg."

Eldridge was surprised. Bradwell wasn't supposed to know about that. "What makes you think I would do a thing like that, Mr. Bradwell?"

"Your man Suarez told me," Bradwell said. "He was out here yesterday."

"What did he say?"

"He told me about your plan to work with the mayor and cut me out of the action." Bradwell's voice, which had been low and level, started to rise a bit.

"Mr. Suarez doesn't work for me anymore," Eldridge said. "And so whatever he told you—"

"He told me he quit," Bradwell said. "Guess you did something to make him unhappy, which isn't too hard to imagine. He came out here and told me because he wanted to get on my good side. Because, unlike you, he realized my bad side is a pretty bad place to be."

"What did you promise him?" Eldridge said, confused, frustrated, and scared all at the same time.

"I promised him that if I ever hear he's back in this country, I'll have him killed," Bradwell said, reaching into the saddlebag again with his free hand. When he pulled out his massive paw, it held a whip. "Of course, before I told him that, I roughed him up, took his ID, and loaded him on a cattle truck headed for Mexico. My driver's instructions are to drop him in the most remote spot he knows between the border and Mexico City. And my driver ships a lot of meat down there, so he knows plenty of deserted roads."

"So that's what you plan to do to me?" Eldridge sputtered.

"Naw." Bradwell laughed. "Even though I don't much like wetbacks, he did me a favor by telling me what you were up to. So I went easy on him."

"Leaving him for dead in the middle of some desert is going easy on him?"

"Sure, I figure he's got a fighting chance. Plus, he's back in his own country where he belongs. Now, with you, if you don't sign these papers, I'm going to whip you to death right here and now."

Eldridge suddenly remembered the six-shooter and pulled it from his holster.

The move prompted a guffaw from Bradwell, who was standing six feet away. "You think I'm that dumb, boy?" Bradwell shook the handle of the whip to unfurl the strap. "That gun doesn't have any bullets. But I'm guessing your revolver back in my dressing room does. Or maybe not. From the way you're holding that thing, you may not know enough about guns to load one."

With a flick of his wrist, Bradwell cracked the whip. Eldridge felt a sharp pain as the strap wrapped around his gun-holding hand. With a quick jerk, Bradwell tore the whip away. The pain forced Eldridge to drop the gun, and the tug of the whip pulled him to his knees.

"Now, I hope I don't have to whip you too much before you decide to sign," Bradwell said. "I want to keep the blood off that paperwork."

"You think you can kill me right outside your ranch and get away with it?" Eldridge asked, cowering on the ground.

"Sure do," Bradwell said. "All I've got to say is that we went for a ride, something spooked your horse, and I couldn't catch you. Out here, people get lost and die like that sometimes."

"You don't think it'll be suspicious if somebody finds me all torn up by your whip?"

"First of all, it's not likely anybody is going to find you out here ever. And if they do, it will be after the critters pick your bones clean. Besides, my guess is nobody will come looking. The only people who know you're here work for me. If I go riding with somebody and come back alone, they know better than to ask questions. And I bet you didn't tell anybody you were heading here."

"What makes you think that?" Eldridge said.

"Somebody like you doesn't trust a whole lot of people," Bradwell said. "In fact, Mr. Suarez was probably the only person you trusted. And you see where that got you."

"So you think documents signed under duress in the middle of nowhere will stand up in court?"

"Absolutely. See, Gus, I've already taken the liberty of signing them and having them notarized. All we've got to do is fill in your signature and we're done."

"And then what happens to me?"

"Gus, the way I see it, you're going to sign one way or the other. But if I have to work up a sweat whipping you, I'll be inclined to go ahead and finish what I started. However, if you're a good boy and sign right now, then I'll let you off easy. I'll get my charter jet to fly you to California. As long as you keep your mouth shut about what happened here, you'll be fine. But if we go that route, I need you to know that if I ever hear of you being back east of the Rockies, I'll do the same thing I promised to do to your wetback friend if he comes in the States again."

Without another word, Eldridge held up his hand to take the documents.

"See there? I knew you were a smart businessman," Bradwell said. "Next, I'm going to find out how smart a businessman the mayor of Memphis is."

Chapter 44

Joe, Scott, Raina, and Dawn were still spending most of their time at Raina's condo, venturing out only for food or a drink or two. They always traveled together, figuring there was safety in numbers, provided they stayed in the suburbs.

Barry Brett stopped by the condo a couple of times to share some beers and keep them company. He came and went by night. No one in the foursome staying at Raina's bothered to ask how someone who looked like a hobo managed to get from his house-boat in downtown Memphis out to Collierville.

Raina managed her legal caseload as well as she could from home, dealing with clients by phone and rescheduling most of her appointments. Dawn, as an entertainer, had a flexible schedule. Her agent wasn't thrilled about her going to ground when she could have been making money off public appearances. But the agent was in Hollywood and she was in the Memphis area, so that was that. Of course, Scott's schedule was even more flexible. Beale Street could survive a few nights without an Elvis impersonator. It meant the juggling unicyclist would make more tips, but that was okay by Scott. Scott had been there the time the juggler hit a pothole, causing him to pitch face-first onto Beale Street's cobblestones while the unicycle spun backwards into a beer stand. Scott figured the guy deserved a financial windfall.

As for Joe, the only one with a straight desk job, he just wrote it off. He didn't bother to call his boss, knowing how the conversation would go. Joe had never been fired before—at least not since college—but no way was he going back to work for that PR firm and, by extension, that mayor. Not after all that had happened. Joe wasn't sure what kind of career arc he could expect after all this played out. Maybe he could get a costume and join Scott in becoming the world's first Elvis impersonator duo. Was the plural of Elvis *Elvi*? He would have to look into that. Maybe Joe could work on the sets of Dawn's movies as a best boy grip, whatever that was.

Since a couple of days had passed since their night at the Pigg Pen, Joe and his friends began to relax—until they heard a loud knock on the door one morning. Raina nearly fell over when she looked through the peephole. Joe, Scott, and Dawn immediately grew silent.

"Who is it?" Dawn whispered.

"Chief Bruno," Raina answered, her voice also low.

"Zack Bruno?" Joe mumbled. His mind raced as he tried to figure out an escape plan. The Memphis police chief had found them.

"Let's go out the back window," Scott said, his voice softer than usual but still not really quiet.

"Shh!" Raina hissed. "Let's think this through. We don't even know who he's here for."

"Gotta be me or Joe, right?" Scott said. "So we go out the back and keep you ladies out of any rough stuff."

Another knock, this one louder.

"First of all, Scott, it's a second-story window," Raina said. "If you guys jump, you might break your legs or worse. Plus, police could be back there."

"Well, how many are up front?" Joe asked.

"I could only see one—Chief Bruno," Raina said.

"You're sure it's Chief Bruno?" Joe asked.

"Positive, even though he's not in uniform," Raina said. "It helps to be able to recognize people like him in my line of work."

A third knock, followed by a shout muffled by the door: "Open up, please!"

"Okay, let's think about this," Joe said. "Why would the chief be at the front door instead of some of his officers? Does he have TV cameras out there and wants to look good for the bust? Are the rest of his guys hiding? Something's wrong here."

A fourth knock, with a louder shout: "Ms. Johnson, please open the door. I know you're in there. I can hear you and your friends whispering."

Raina went to the door and shouted back, "Do you have a warrant, chief? Because I've already had a couple of clients falsely arrested the last few days. It's getting sort of old."

A brief silence.

"No, I don't have a warrant, but I have some other paperwork you might be interested in," Chief Bruno said.

"What might that be?" Raina asked.

"It might be the kind of paperwork I don't want to tell you

about while I'm shouting at a door," Bruno said. "Now, please, young lady. I've been doing desk work the last few years. It's been awhile since I kicked in a door. But I can assure you I was good at it then, and I'm still good at it now. And you don't want to lose a door for what I have to show you."

Raina turned to her friends. Scott and Dawn shrugged, while Joe nodded. Slowly, Raina opened the door.

"Thank you," Chief Bruno said, peering into the condo from the doorway. He was casually dressed in tan slacks, a golf shirt, and a Memphis Redbirds baseball cap. He carried a briefcase. "Scott, Joe, Miss Dawn . . . Glad to see you're all here, too."

Raina stepped to one side and motioned the chief in. She kept the door open in case . . . well, in case a door needed to be open during an encounter like this. Too bad the next-door neighbors were practically deaf. Raina wanted some witnesses in case this went badly.

"Chief, if you're here to arrest Mr. Miller or Mr. Paulk, I first of all want to advise you that you're out of your jurisdiction," Raina began.

"Honey, please." Bruno cut her off with a wave of his free hand. "Arresting people in Collierville isn't much more difficult for Memphis cops than arresting people in Memphis, if that's what they want to do. Just more paperwork to fill out. We have interlocal agreements between the two cities, you know. Anyway, cops tend to look out for each other and do each other favors. Especially cops from neighboring jurisdictions who know getting cooperation from the guys across the line could be a matter of life or death someday. Is that why you're all hiding out here? Because you think you're safe from the Memphis Police Department in the suburbs?"

"Okay, so why are you here?" Joe asked. "And how did you know we'd be here?"

Bruno laughed. "To answer your second question first, contrary to what some people think, I'm actually pretty good at police work. So finding you holed up at your lawyer's condo was not difficult. This isn't exactly a safe house in Guam. To answer your first question, I believe what I have in this briefcase may be of interest to you."

Bruno opened the briefcase, removed two sets of expandable folders, and held them out. Joe and Dawn each stepped forward and took one.

"What's in here?" Joe asked.

"The records you and Ms. Johnson have been asking for," Bruno said. "All property along the east shore of the Wolf River Harbor, facing Mud Island. Also, I threw in the blueprints for the development Mayor Pigg plans to put on that property."

"So if the World Barbecue Hall of Fame is built, a run-down industrial area would be transformed into valuable real estate overnight," Joe said. "And whoever owns it would make millions."

"You got it," Bruno said. "And the mayor has quietly snapped up options to buy all that property through shell companies controlled by him and a few of his lackeys."

"Why are you telling us this?" Scott asked. "You're one of those lackeys."

"Well, I may be a lackey today, but who knows where I'll be tomorrow?" Bruno said. "A college buddy of mine runs a manufacturing company out in Arizona. Those solar cells for rooftops. I'm probably going to take my city pension early and see if he's still interested in hiring me part-time as a security consultant."

"But why?" Joe asked. "Why are you giving us this information?

And how did you get it in the first place?"

"Again, second question first. As I told you, I'm pretty good at police work, in spite of what my current boss thinks. As for the first question, before I ride off into the sunset, I'd like to know that somebody cares about what the mayor's up to before the bulldozers start plowing that place over. Better still, it would be great if somebody stops him from doing it. But I'll leave that part to you. I've given you the information you're after. Now, it's up to you to figure out what to do with it."

"And you're not worried about Mayor Pigg retaliating against you if he finds out you gave us this information?" Joe asked.

That brought a chuckle from Bruno. "You know, I wish he'd try. Now, if you kids don't mind, I'll be going. Since I'm about to retire, I need to get out to the golf course and work on my swing."

And with that, soon-to-be former Memphis police chief Zack Bruno turned and strolled out the door, humming what sounded like the theme song from *Law & Order* as he made his way down the steps.

Joe, Scott, Dawn, and Raina looked at each other for a few seconds.

"So, what now?" Scott said.

"Now, we research," Raina replied.

Chapter 45

Mayor Pigg's day got off to a great start.

When he arrived at his office at city hall that morning, he discovered a letter that had been slid under the door. But not just any letter—it was Chief Bruno's resignation!

Pigg had been trying to run Bruno off ever since it became apparent the chief didn't share his philosophy about law enforcement. That philosophy being heavy on the *enforcement* and light on the *law*. So while Pigg was relieved to have Bruno out of the picture, he was also curious. He made a few calls to the police department's administrative offices, but no one had seen Bruno that morning. And Bruno apparently hadn't given any indication he intended to resign.

A widower with no children, Bruno lived alone. No one in the department was able to reach him by telephone. One of the watch commanders sent a patrol car to the house, but Bruno's car was gone, and so was he.

It was possible Bruno was just out running errands or doing whatever the newly retired did with their time. But Pigg had a hunch Bruno was gone for good.

That was just fine by Mayor Pigg. Now, he could bring in a replacement better suited to running the kind of police department he wanted.

Ordinarily, the mayor's appointed replacement for police chief would have to be approved by the Memphis City Council. And council members tended to ask a lot of annoying questions about education, background, certification—that sort of thing. The good news was that the city charter did not require council approval for interim replacements, only permanent hires. Since Bruno had resigned less than a year into Pigg's term, Pigg could bring in someone to serve during his three-plus remaining years without worrying about the council's oversight.

He had someone in mind. In fact, he was waiting on his leading candidate to arrive when his cell phone chirped. His new ring tone was Chuck Berry's "Memphis, Tennessee."

"'Lo?" Pigg said.

"Mayor Pigg? William Bradwell here," the booming voice said.

"Yeah?"

"Just want to let you know how much I'm looking forward to doing business in your fine city." Mayor Pigg heard a lilt in Bradwell's voice that told him something was up. Something Pigg probably wouldn't like.

"Yeah, well, we'll see 'bout that, won't we?" Pigg said.

"Maybe sooner than you think, Mayor Pigg. Just wanted to let you know I've changed my plans."

"Oh? No movie studio with Gus Eldridge?"

"Nah, I like your idea better, Mr. Mayor."

"You do?"

"Absolutely. That's why I'm stealing it."

"How so?"

"I decided you have the right idea. That property down on the harbor is a perfect spot for a Barbecue Hall of Fame. So I'm going to build one there."

Pigg fumbled in his desk drawer for the bottle of Jack. He had to play it cool here. No sense tipping his hand. "I thought you were plannin' a Barbecue Hall of Fame in K.C.," Pigg said. "What happened to that?"

"I still am," Bradwell said. "But here's what I'm thinking. Kansas City barbecue is all about beef. Memphis barbecue is all about pork. So I'll build a Barbecue Hall of Fame for each."

"Interestin'. So that's what Gus wants to do with the property now? Because the last time I talked to him, he seemed set on puttin' a movie studio there."

"Actually, Gus and I have parted ways. But he made me a great deal on his land."

"He did? That's interestin', too, because I got the idea he was never gonna let go of that rathole. Least not for anythin' less than a lot more money than it's worth."

"Some people, you've just got to know how to negotiate with them, Mayor Pigg. You have to know what motivates them. How to work a deal."

"Izzat so? You drive a hard bargain? Sumpin like that?"

"Yeah, something like that. So I've got the title to the property, free and clear. I've got the money to make this happen. And I know how to work the people in your town—the same people who were lining up behind you for your little project. So there isn't a whole heck of a lot you can do to stop me."

"Is that a fact?" The more Mayor Pigg could learn about Bradwell's plans, the better.

"Yeah, that is a fact," Bradwell continued. "And I wanted you to know about it before you embarrassed yourself by trying to stop me. You know, if people in your town like the idea of a World Barbecue Hall of Fame, it's not going to matter to them who owns it. As long as it brings in jobs and tourists, they'll be happy as, well, hogs in mud. You like that one, hogs in mud?"

"Real funny. You like pig jokes, I guess. Well, here's one for you: you'll be openin' a Barbecue Hall of Fame in my town when pigs fly."

"Good one, Mr. Mayor, good one. Somebody told me you were the master of pig puns during your election campaign. But the fact remains, I'm going to do this. And I forgot to tell you the best part. I've already got a deal worked out with a vendor for the food concession at the Barbecue Hall of Fame. A local place, Carnivore Charlie's. You ought to like that, right? Using Memphis businesses keeps the money in the community. And I've heard you and the owner, Nick Nelson, go way back. Mr. Nelson told me some great stories about you. He and I are going to get along just fine."

"Now, you sure didn't need to tell me that."

"Yes, I did, Mr. Mayor. And let me tell you why. You need to know that I do exactly what I want. Nobody stops Billy Boy Bradwell. Not rough, tough cowpokes back where I come from, and not fat hick mayors. I didn't have to promise Carnivore Charlie's that vending contract. Fact of the matter is, I could have saved myself some money by getting all the barbecue joints in Memphis in a bidding war. Hell, you might have even bid on it."

Pigg heard ice rattling in a glass on the other end of the line. *I'd be taking a victory swig if I were you, too,* Pigg thought.

"But here's the thing," Bradwell continued. "I picked Carnivore Charlie's to teach you a lesson about what happens when people go up against me. Now, you've given me about all the trouble I want with this project, Mr. Mayor. So you should just step aside now and let it happen. I've got legal rights to the land. And I've got the money and the muscle to beat down any local opposition. So don't get any big ideas. If you go against me in public after I announce my plans, you'll come across as a mayor who's against creating jobs and getting rid of blight. And from what I know about Memphis and the problems there, that's not exactly a winning political platform."

Silence except for the mayor's ragged breathing. Pigg was trying hard to stay calm despite the taunts.

"Sounds like you've got it all figured out, Billy Boy," Pigg finally said.

"That I do," Bradwell said. "But don't feel bad about coming in second here, Mr. Mayor. You had a good idea. Hell, you had a great idea. I just got there first."

"Looks like you did."

"That's not the way it looks, Mr. Mayor. That's the way it is."

With that, Billy Boy Bradwell hung up. He had work to do to prepare for his moment of triumph.

After putting the phone down, Mayor Pigg chuckled to himself. So Billy Boy Bradwell thought he had all the bases covered. If only he knew about Mayor Pigg's ace in the hole. Of course, it was better that he didn't—and better still that he didn't know an ace in the hole existed.

Pigg poured a celebratory drink of his own. He, too, had

some details to finalize. The trip to Chicago was coming up soon.

He didn't have long to contemplate his conversation with Bradwell. Within a few minutes, he heard a booming knock on his office door. His new police chief had arrived.

Chapter 46

"Don't you like being rich, Barry?"

The question came from Scott. He, Joe, and Dawn were passing time in Raina's living room while Raina was in the kitchen studying the documents Chief Bruno had dropped off earlier that day.

"It has its ups and downs," Barry said, making a face that indicated this was an uncomfortable subject.

Scott pressed on. "More ups than downs, I guess."

"I can't lie. Never having to worry about money is great," Barry said. "But it can also be a hassle."

"How so?" Scott asked.

"Well, my father was always laying a trip on me about how it came with responsibility," Barry said. "He said the family had a duty to make the world—and this city in particular—a better place."

"That's a noble sentiment," Dawn said.

"It is," Barry said. "But in my family, it came with pressure.

I was always being measured against my ancestors. When your family helped build a town basically out of mud and sticks, it's hard to live up to that kind of legacy."

"Is that why you're living on an abandoned houseboat in the Wolf River Harbor?" This was Joe's turn.

Barry stared at the ceiling tiles and exhaled slowly before answering. "Yes."

"The pressure was that bad?" Joe said.

"Yes, it got to be that way."

"So your old man really did a number on you, sounds like," Scott said.

"No, he didn't," Barry replied.

"Then who?" Scott said. "When you're a gazillionaire, can't you pretty much tell people to kiss your butt if they don't like what you're doing?" Scott asked.

"The pressure came from me," Barry said. "Whatever I did, I felt like it was never enough. Dawn, I bet you can relate to that."

"Well, I'm not sure I can completely," Dawn said. "I know what it's like to feel you could do more. Do I sometimes feel I haven't given enough of my time or money? That I haven't given enough back in exchange for the perks of fame? Absolutely. I always think I could do more. All of us probably do, regardless of how much money we have in the bank. Even if you're not rich, you can always volunteer to clear underbrush or pick up litter along the riverbank. When you have money, people do expect more than that. But I'm not sure I follow the logic of checking out of society. Doesn't that just make it worse? Instead of feeling you're not doing enough, you're not doing anything at all."

Before Barry could answer, Raina let out a long, slow whistle from the kitchen.

"What's up?" Joe called out to her. "Did you find something?"

Indeed, she had found plenty. The police chief had provided her with copies of options to buy a sizable chunk of property surrounding Mayor Pigg's proposed World Barbecue Hall of Fame site. And copies of the articles of incorporation for the companies that held those options, all of which listed one Peter Pigg as the founder and registered agent.

Which made Mayor Pigg's motives quite clear. This wasn't about making Memphis a better place. It was about making money for him. He could rake in millions developing prime waterfront property around a major tourist attraction.

Or could he? Raina wasn't sure she believed her eyes.

"I found something, all right," Raina called back. "Barry, would you mind coming in here? I think you need to see this."

Barry sidled into the kitchen, beer in hand. "Yes, ma'am?" he said.

"Take a look at these documents, please," Raina said.

Barry did.

After a few minutes, he, too, let out a soft whistle.

"Yeah, that's what I thought," Raina said. "Did you know about this?"

"I had no idea," Barry said.

"How could you not know?" Raina said. "I mean, really."

Barry sighed. "There are probably a lot of things I should know but don't."

"Another big question: do you think Mayor Pigg knows about this?" Raina asked.

"If he does, he's probably trying real hard to keep it under wraps," Barry said.

Joe, Dawn, and Scott were at the kitchen door now.

"Don't keep us in suspense," Joe said. "What did you find?"

"Something that could stop the mayor's plans cold," Raina said.

"Maybe," Barry added.

Chapter 47

The meeting took place in a high-rise hotel suite overlooking Lake Michigan, a good distance from the sprawling head-quarters where Mayor Pigg's contact worked.

Pigg was in his usual pose—drink in hand, one foot on the room's handsome office desk. The man sitting in the chair across the desk also clutched a drink, but he looked far less relaxed.

"Glad we could finally get together and nail this down, Mr. Penderbrook," Pigg said. "You mind if I call you Terrence? If we're goin' in on a deal this big, we might as well be on a first-name basis."

"That's fine, Mr., uh, Pete." The man wore a neatly pressed blue suit, a conservative gray tie, and wire-rim glasses. He looked like an accountant, which wasn't entirely inappropriate, since one of his degrees was in accounting.

"First of all, Terrence, lemme see if I've got this sized up right.

You're the head of research and development for Amalgamated Foods, which happens to be one of the largest distributors of food and food additives in the world. One of those additives is sodium nitrate, a meat preservative used in lots of products sold in lots of places. Even in my restaurant back in Memphis. But medical studies have shown that sodium nitrate can cause liver or pancreas damage. Which in and of itself obviously ain't enough to stop people from usin' it. I mean, the stuff's in gunpowder and fertilizer, too, but that doesn't keep people from puttin' it in their mouths. How am I doin' so far?"

Terrence Penderbrook fidgeted but nodded for Mayor Pigg to continue.

"So the deal is that if your boys in the lab can come up with some kind of fake sodium nitrate that does all the good things meat preservatives are supposed to do without the crappy side effects, it would be worth billions, right?"

"I'm not sure where you get your information, Pete, but that's correct. At least, it could be. A synthetic version of sodium nitrate has the potential to be a breakthrough in food science."

"Yeah, well, we've got the Internets down south, too, Terrence," Pigg said, although the truth was a bit more complicated. "You'd be amazed what you can learn there. But in hindsight, maybe it wasn't such a good idea to put your theory into a memo to your bosses. Raised all kinds of expectations. And they agreed to make a substantial investment in your idea. An investment they don't want to lose. As we say where I live, maybe your mouth wrote a check your butt can't cash."

"I'm quite sure that information is not readily available on the Internet. Or available at all."

"Well, I've also got other sources," Pigg replied, taking another swig of his drink. *Yeah, like vacationing chemists who come into my bar,* he thought. Usually, Pigg didn't pay attention to what his customers said. But he was glad he listened that day when Penderbrook's employee had dropped his wife and kids at the Memphis Zoo, gotten his afternoon drunk on, and started spilling secrets.

"Anyway, your division, and you in particular, are under pressure to produce. You've got a lot ridin' on this super-duper substitute. But as I understand it, you're havin' problems with your testin' program. Seems I recall you guys had a new type of fake sugar not long ago. But somehow your wizards in the lab failed to detect that it had some side effects, too, like stomach crampin' and diarrhea. Probably rushed the stuff to market without really testin' it, would be my guess. Probably so you could skim some of the testin' budget for yourself. It's too bad you got that NAS-CAR driver to use your product in his tea before that big race in Charlotte. People in the South are still talkin' about what happened to him. I don't think that incident did much to help AmFo stock. That TV coverage of him developin' digestive problems in the winner's circle was graphic."

"Yes," Terrence said quietly, the memory none too faint in his mind. "It was a setback."

"Right, right, a setback. Like the *Titanic* hittin' that iceberg was a setback. I heard AmFo took a big hit in stock prices the Monday after that. So I guess you're on the hot seat. Another problem like that might not be the end of AmFo, but it would be the end of you."

"We've covered enough history," Terrence said. "Let's get this over with."

"Okay, okay. So here's where we are. I'm gonna open the

World Barbecue Hall of Fame in Memphis, where we're gonna sell a lot of barbecue. We're also gonna keep a register of guests, with information on how to get in touch with them. So when your fake meat preservative is ready to go to market, you put it in the food at our concession stands. Then we turn over our guest registers to you. We should be built in two years, which is about when you'll finish your lab work. So you test the product on our folks without any media scrutiny, then survey the guests to see if they have any problems rangin' from tummy aches to sudden death. How you handle the follow-up checks is up to you. When guests get contacted, they'll think they're bein' surveyed by our folks, not some food conglomerate with a PR problem. What's key for you is makin' sure there are no short-term side effects that would kill your product's marketability and get you killed in the press again. Now, that ain't gonna help in the long run. If your fake sodium nitrate turns out to be poison, the FDA is gonna find out eventually. But if the effects are all long-term, and they're not discovered for ten or twenty years, you could make billions until that time. You'd have the best product on the market for a good long run, all thanks to the World Barbecue Hall of Fame gener-ously offerin' up its visitors. And you could do the same for other products, too. If you need to test Red Food Dye Number 8, the World Barbecue Hall of Fame'll be the place where you can do it."

"For which you'll be handsomely compensated."

"What I'm lookin' for is a namin' rights deal—five million a year for twenty years, with two ten-year renewal options. It's an easy sell for AmFo. Judgin' from your annual reports, that's just a fraction of your marketing budget. And goin' forward, every piece of Memphis tourist literature will mention the Amalgamated Foods World Barbecue Hall of Fame. Has a real nice ring to it.

And from what I understand, you've got the contacts to make it happen."

"I do. Our marketing department is excited about this. Can I assume the money we pay for naming rights will go to the city of Memphis?"

"Well, sure. That's where AmFo can send the checks. What happens to the money after that is none of your business. Although my guess is it will be used to cover various and sundry operatin' expenses. Runnin' a hall of fame ain't cheap. At least as far as anybody back in Memphis knows."

"Fair enough. What else?"

"Well, obviously, none of this happens if I don't have a World Barbecue Hall of Fame to serve as AmFo's petri dish. And there's a man, William Bradwell, who stands in the way of that. If I'm not mistaken, Mr. Bradwell does a fair amount of business with AmFo."

"You could say that. We are his sole source provider of food additives."

"That must run way into the millions per year right there, with his restaurants, his sauce, and those processed food strips that taste like cardboard. So I guess if you told him that contract is in jeopardy, he might take a different view about his plans to open his own Barbecue Hall of Fame, right? Nobody besides AmFo can supply the volume he needs. And without your products, he'd have a serious problem with rottin' meat. Which translates to big bucks. I've seen news reports where he's said his Barbecue Hall of Fame isn't about the money. But when the money's way into the millions, maybe that's not quite true. If you hit a guy like that in the wallet, it hurts."

"I can talk to a few people who will convince him the Barbecue

Hall of Fame isn't in his best interest. Anything else, Pete?"

"Well, now that you mention it, Mr. Bradwell is technically the owner of the property I'd like to use. I'd appreciate it if you could convince him—or make someone from AmFo convince him—that he needs to deed that land back to the city."

Terrence Penderbrook sighed and stared at the ceiling of his company-rented suite. He'd spent years in school training as both a chemist and an accountant. He'd spent even more years working his way through the Byzantine ranks of AmFo management. And it would all end if he couldn't make his synthetic sodium nitrate work. A divorce would be inevitable, and his wife would almost certainly get custody of their kids. As an unemployed chemist, he'd have no way to pay either his mortgage or his gambling debts. It was no choice at all, really.

"Consider it done," he finally said.

Chapter 48

"No, no, no!" Pigg said. "This estimate is way too low, and you know it!"

It wasn't an unfamiliar argument for the insurance adjuster. He was used to owners of damaged property trying to inflate their repair estimates. And it was his job to resist those arguments.

After all, most owners thought their property was worth far more than it was. And insurance companies assumed their clients tried to scam them on claims. In this case, both scenarios happened to be true. But the adjuster also knew he wasn't talking to just any Memphis bar owner looking to make a financial windfall off an accident. This was the mayor of Memphis.

Sure, the adjuster could go strictly by the book and write an estimate that reflected the honest value of the work needed to repair the sprinkler damage at the Pigg Pen. But what would being honest get him in this situation? Probably business license trouble. Maybe even trouble with the cops, led by an imposing fellow seated a short distance from where Mayor Pigg and the adjuster were talking on the restaurant's patio. Mayor Pigg's interim police chief had been introduced to the public as Mervin Stonesmith. The adjuster had seen him on TV. Stonesmith had grown up in Memphis but earned his fame as a professional cage fighter under the nickname "Iron Justice." The adjuster wasn't aware of any law enforcement background Iron Justice might possess, and he certainly wasn't going to use this occasion to ask.

Police Chief Justice was seated at a table inside a tent raised in the street beside the Pigg Pen's patio. He watched as the bar employees moved other tables and chairs. Mayor Pigg had decided he would lose too much money if only the patio stayed open while the repairs to the Pigg Pen's water-damaged interior were under way. Coincidentally, the new police chief had decided the side street next to the patio needed to be temporarily closed due to unspecified public safety concerns.

So the tent had gone up to accommodate what Mayor Pigg was billing as "Beale Street's Biggest Barbecue Tent Revival." The special-use permits needed for an outdoor event on a public street would be forthcoming—whenever Mayor Pigg got around to signing them.

"Mayor Pigg, I'm not sure what you want me to do here," the adjuster said. He was already on his third estimate sheet, each with a higher bottom line than the one before.

"You're bein' too conservative, is all I'm sayin'," Pigg growled. "Why don't you just give me one of those sheets and I'll fill in the blanks for you?"

Before the adjuster could react to the ethical quandary that had been presented to him, his conversation with the mayor was interrupted by a large, intimidating man.

"Well, if it isn't Billy Boy Bradwell!" the mayor said. "Why, if I knew you were comin' to Memphis, I'd have cooked up some ribs!"

"You and I need to have a heart-to-heart, Mr. Mayor," Bradwell said. He glanced at the adjuster. "Alone."

"Okay," Pigg said. He held out his hand to take a claim form from the adjuster, then motioned for him to leave. "Somehow, I'm not surprised you're here," he said to Bradwell.

"Then maybe you won't be surprised when I tell you what a big mistake you're making," Bradwell said. "Leaning on AmFo to muscle me out of the picture? Surely, you don't think it's that easy!"

"It should be if you have any sense, Bradwell," Mayor Pigg said. "Unless I miss my guess, your supplier may have told you it's not such a great idea to pursue this Barbecue Hall of Fame project. Which is what I've been tellin' you for a while."

"I don't know how you got to AmFo, and I don't really care," Bradwell said. "But here's what you need to know. I understand a lot more about running a business than some piss-ant restaurant owner. You think I can't get other suppliers?"

"Not as big as AmFo," Pigg said. "You might split up your business among smaller companies, but they couldn't give you the same prices you get from AmFo. Over time, you'd lose more money on supply costs than you'd gain from a Barbecue Hall of Fame in Memphis. Particularly since I can guarantee you'd have some hidden costs here even if you manage to get the project approved by the city council. I mean, look at this place. See the water damage we've got here?"

"Yeah, and you could have fire damage to that tent if you're not careful."

Pigg laughed, then shouted in the direction of the tent. "Did you hear that, chief?"

"I believe I did," came the reply from behind the flap.

"Why don't you come over here to the patio and meet Mr. Bradwell? He's a barbecue tycoon. At least, what passes for one in Kansas City."

The tent flap slowly lifted and Iron Justice—all six feet ten inches and 325 pounds of him—joined them. For a change, Bradwell was forced to look up at someone.

"Now, Mr. Mayor, it sounded to me from where I was sitting that this gentleman threatened you," Iron Justice said. "Is that right?"

"Sounded that way to me," Mayor Pigg said. "But I bet he's sorry. You sorry, Bradwell?"

Bradwell shot poisonous glances at the two men but said nothing. He wasn't on his home turf anymore. And even if he could take the big man, who was carrying a gun and a billy club, there was a whole police force behind him that Bradwell would have to contend with if he wanted to make it out of Memphis.

"I mean, we can arrange for you to spend some time in the Shelby County Jail if you like," Mayor Pigg said.

"I'd get out," Bradwell said. "Then I'd make trouble."

"And I could do the same for you," Pigg replied. "You know, I've got a friend named Zip Smithers who's a TV reporter. He does a story that says there's E. coli bacteria in your Rip-A-Chunk beef strips, well, that'll be picked up by the national networks. And then people will just grab a bag of pretzels in the convenience store instead of chewin' on that salt-flavored cardboard you've been sellin.'"

"One crazy story from a reporter in Memphis wouldn't

amount to a hill of beans," Bradwell said. "Nobody would believe him."

"Really?" Pigg said. "Zip could interview another old drinkin' buddy of mine who happens to be an agriculture professor at the University of Northwest Arkansas. If I want him to, I'm sure the professor could say testin' is needed. Nobody would come out and claim E. coli has been discovered in Rip-A-Chunk. Just that it's possible. There have been enough outbreaks that people aren't gonna take chances. Just a *maybe* will send 'em runnin' to other products. You may have noticed there's no shortage of junk food in this country."

"So we can make each other's lives miserable," Bradwell said. "Where does that leave us?"

"Tell you what, Mr. Bradwell," Pigg said. "You've got the property rights to the land where I'd like to put my World Barbecue Hall of Fame. You deed 51 percent ownership to the city at no charge. And you keep 49 percent of the admission fees we charge. You probably didn't pay anythin' for the land when you took it from Eldridge, so that would be pure profit for you."

"You'd give up that much? Why?" Bradwell asked.

"I anticipate some other revenue streams from this project that you won't be privy to," Pigg said. "And the city would have full operational control of the Barbecue Hall of Fame. You'd be a silent partner. And I do mean silent."

"What else?" Bradwell said. "I could still build a Barbecue Hall of Fame in Kansas City and keep 100 percent of the profits."

"That's true," Pigg said. "I'm offerin' you free money. Plus, if you want it, I'd be willin' to throw in the concessions contract at the Memphis project."

"Why?" Bradwell said.

"Why not?" Pigg said. "I want to get this over and move on and make some money. You're big in the Midwest and West, but you don't have a foothold here in the South. This would be a high-profile opportunity to get your name out in this part of the country."

"It would indeed," Bradwell said.

"People would get to know your brand of Kansas City barbecue, for better or worse," Pigg said. "Could make or break your reputation around here. My bet's on Memphis barbecue."

Bradwell studied Pigg and Iron Justice for a long moment, then smiled. "No chance of that. Kansas City barbecue's the best. This will definitely make my reputation."

Maybe, maybe not, Pigg thought. *I guess that depends on how good AmFo's lab rats are at their jobs.*

"So, do we have a deal?" Pigg asked.

"We do."

And with that, the two former enemies shook hands.

Chapter 49

The five of them watched the news conference from the living room of Raina's condo.

"Terrific question, Zip," the mayor said with a grin as his friend pitched him another softball. "I'm obviously pleased with Mr. Bradwell's decision to acknowledge that a Barbecue Hall of Fame—the Amalgamated Foods World Barbecue Hall of Fame—belongs in Memphis. And we appreciate his donation of the property at the corner of Auction and Front, which will be an ideal location."

"Yeah, ideal for you," Scott said.

"So, Mr. Mayor," Zip Smithers continued, "where does this project stand? What's left to do?"

"Well, we'll need to go before the city council tomorrow night to get zonin' approval," Pigg said. "Our city fathers never anticipated anythin' like a Barbecue Hall of Fame on that site."

Joe clicked the remote off. "Well, that's it. The mayor has his pet project. He's got those votes on the council already lined up, no matter how many shady deals he had to cut to get them. He wouldn't put the rezoning request on the agenda if he didn't."

"It doesn't look good," Barry agreed.

"Unless . . . ," Joe said.

Joe, Scott, Dawn, and Raina looked expectantly at Barry.

"Yeah, unless," Barry said, stroking his homeless guy beard. "But that's a big unless."

No one said anything for a minute.

"Barry, you've got to do this," Joe finally said. "Based on what we've learned, you can stop the mayor's plan."

"That's easy to say from where you sit," Barry said. "But if I do, I'll have to reengage with society. And you know what? I worked pretty hard to get away from all that. It's fun living in the shadows."

"Is this the same guy who was shooting up sprinkler heads and terrorizing bridesmaids not too long ago?" Scott said. "How would this be different?"

"For the record, I don't think those bridesmaids were all that terrorized," Barry said. "They'll tell that story the rest of their lives. And going in there and acting crazy for a few minutes was fun. But this would be different. Maybe you can't understand, since you haven't been living off the grid like I have."

"This brings us back to that conversation we had earlier," Joe said.

"I wish it didn't," Barry said.

"But it does," Joe said. "Don't you see the opportunity you have to do something positive for the city? Would it kill you to suck it up and go to one meeting?"

"What you're asking me to do would require a lot more than that," Barry said. "You know how many times my family had to deal with city politicians over the years? It was never a pleasant experience. From what I've seen, politicians seldom do the right thing just because it's the right thing to do. They're always looking for something—contributions, endorsements, junkets on the corporate jet."

"So this is your chance to get payback," Scott said.

"Yeah, but let's think about what we're doing," Barry said. "Okay, so the mayor stands to make money off this deal. But what he says about a World Barbecue Hall of Fame isn't completely wrong. It would create jobs and bring in tourists. Which isn't exactly a bad thing for this city."

"But you of all people know how that would work," Joe said. "The primo construction jobs and lucrative contracts would go to a handful of the richest people in town—Mayor Pigg's cronies, the ones with the political connections. The regular folks, the ones who need the help the most, would see little, if any, benefit from his project."

"Unless Barry gets involved," Scott added.

"Let me tell you about getting involved," Barry said. "It's frustrating, especially in this town. You recruit a new business, you bring in a couple hundred jobs. Then you pick up the paper a couple weeks later and find out two other businesses are shutting down, cutting the same number of jobs or more. You spend money on charitable causes but find out it was a drop in the ocean in terms of taking care of the needs that are out there. It's like being on a treadmill."

"You think that's different from any other city?" Joe said. "Crime, poverty, and blight don't go away. What makes a good city great is that enough people try every day to keep it that way. Those cities have people who are willing to keep working to make sure the good news outweighs the bad. It's a never-ending fight in Memphis, like anywhere else."

"Yeah, but why does one of those people have to be me?" Barry said. "My family's been here since the beginning. Hasn't the Brett family done enough for Memphis?"

"Okay, if you believe that, why are you still here?" Joe said. "I mean, you weren't a hunted fugitive, at least until you turned Pete Pigg's restaurant into an honest-to-God watering hole. You could have left Memphis and gone anywhere in the world. You've probably got the net worth of a Central American country. And you have a thriving business. There's no reason you couldn't be living on your own private island in the South Pacific. Yet instead of doing that, you chose to go underground as a homeless person on a ratty old houseboat in the Mud River Harbor, right in the heart of downtown. While you're frustrated by the pace of progress and hate dealing with politicians, it seems to me you still must love Memphis. There's no other explanation for why you stayed. And by the way, your family must have realized the importance of fighting the good fight. Do you think your ancestors could have dreamed how Memphis would grow? Progress may be slow, but it happens."

Barry sighed. "It's one thing to keep tabs on a city you love, the way I've been doing. It's another to stick your neck out on something like this."

"It is," Joe agreed. "But take a look around this room. My man Scott, here, he loves this town so much he was willing to burn half of it down in the hope what got built back would be better. He may be psychotic, but his heart's in the right place."

" 'Preciate that," Scott said.

"And Dawn," Joe said. "She's a major movie star. She could be spending her time helping orphans in the Sudan or just sipping Margaritas back in Beverly Hills. But she's here in Memphis, trying to make a difference. Because it's her hometown. And she loves it."

"I do," Dawn said quietly.

"And Raina," Joe continued. "She's doing all she can to keep us out of jail, and she even risked her legal career to serve as our wheelman at the Pigg Pen. I don't think she'd do that if she didn't care about this town."

"I wouldn't," Raina said.

"And I'm all in, too," Joe said. "I don't have money, legal skills, or the instincts of a pyromaniac. But I'm here to the end. The question is, Barry, are you?"

"Yes," Barry said. "That is the question."

Chapter 50

Melissa and Kimmi made their way into the alley behind the Pigg Pen, struggling with the rolling food cart they had half-pushed and half-dragged from inside the bar.

The stench in the alleys that flanked Beale Street was always rank, but it was particularly overpowering during the warm-weather months, when the sun amped up the aroma of burned cooking grease, stale beer, and vomit to a nearly unbearable level.

Melissa and Kimmi were used to the smell. They had both been Pigglettes for several months. It took only a day or two for workers on Beale Street to realize the benefits of breathing through their mouths as they walked from the bars to their cars at the end of their shifts.

It was city council meeting night, and Melissa and Kimmi had been charged with the task of delivering the council members' dinner. Of course, they would have to endure leers and come-ons from their "customers" at city hall. Probably groping as well. But that was really no different from what they got every night at the Pigg Pen. And the council members tended to be good tippers—probably because they wrote their tips off at taxpayers' expense.

The Pigg Pen had won the contract to provide meals on council meeting nights through a competitive bidding process, of course. It was a prized contract not just because of the money but also for the bragging rights that came with it. Any restaurant in town would have loved to be able to advertise that it had the catering contract at city hall.

The Pigg Pen was the only prospective vendor to bid on the contract, though. It was amazing what a few well-placed calls from Mayor Pigg's friends could do to stifle the competition. No overt threats, just a few casual suggestions that restaurant inspections might go easier for businesses that decided to pass on bidding. Or that fewer undercover police operations would target underage drinking. Everybody understood how the game was played.

The Pigg Pen's contract called for two meals every other Tuesday for thirty people—the thirteen council members and their staffs. The first meal was lunch, since the council members spent those days in committee meetings before the regular meetings began at three-thirty. About half the time, the meetings ended early enough that council members could make it home in time for dinner. But two meals were part of the guaranteed contract, so that's what the council members got, regardless of how long the meetings ran. At fifty bucks per person per meal, the Pigg Pen sold pretty expensive barbecue. But again, the contract had been competitively bid, so who could complain?

"Help me get this cart into the car, Kimmi," Melissa said, not appreciating her coworker's decision to fix her hair during the most critical stage of the loading process.

"God, it stinks back here," Kimmi said, using her long brown locks to fan the stench away.

"No duh," Melissa said. "So the quicker you help me, the faster we can get into the car and crank up the AC."

Their conversation was interrupted by a familiar voice. "What's up, girls?" a blond woman said as she stepped from the shadows behind the bar.

"Oh . . . my . . . God! Is that really you, Dawn?" Melissa said, her hands flying to her mouth.

"You know it, girl!" Dawn replied.

"This is so . . . awesome!" Kimmi said, taking little hops while still tugging her hair.

"What are you doing here, Dawn?" Melissa asked.

"Well, can I tell you girls a secret?" Dawn said.

"Of course!" Kimmi said. "We'll never tell!"

"Okay, I was eating in the Pigg Pen with some friends," Dawn said.

"Where were you?" Melissa said. "I didn't see you."

"I was in another waitress's section," Dawn said. "But I noticed you. Both of you, in fact. And I told my friends you would be perfect for my next movie."

"No way!" Kimmi shrieked.

"Really?" Melissa said.

"I think so," Dawn said.

"Swear?" Melissa said.

"Well, we've got a lot to talk over," Dawn said. "Do you have a few minutes for me and my lawyer?" Dawn gestured toward Raina, whom the Pigglettes noticed for the first time.

"Of course!" Kimmi said. "We have as much time as you need! If you're the next Bond girl, could I be the bad girl he meets before he meets you?"

"Maybe," Dawn said. "Of course, I don't have a contract yet, but I certainly think you could carry a role like that."

"Wait a minute, Dawn," Melissa said. "We're supposed to make a delivery to the city council. Could we catch up with you later tonight?"

"Melissa, don't be dumb!" Kimmi cried. "If this is our big break, I'm not going to miss it to deliver overcooked ribs to a bunch of fat old people who don't need more food anyway."

"Listen, I completely understand," Dawn said. "Unfortunately, I can't wait around. I have to catch a plane to the coast later tonight. But my friends here could make your delivery while we talk."

Dawn gestured to Joe and Barry, both clean-shaven and dressed like they were headed to church. The Pigglettes noticed them for the first time also. Seeing Dawn—and a vision of their future careers in Hollywood—had given them a serious case of tunnel vision.

"Perfect!" Kimmi said. "Let's do it, Melissa!"

"Okay," Melissa said. "Do your friends know the way to city hall?"

"Oh, we know the way," Barry said.

Kimmi thought she recognized him from somewhere, but she couldn't say for sure. Was he somebody famous or just a customer from the bar? Oh, what did it matter? Dawn wanted to talk to them!

The two squealing Pigglettes surrendered the food cart to Joe and Barry, who quickly loaded it into Joe's car and headed north in the direction of city hall.

Meanwhile, at 125 North Main, Interim Police Chief Iron Justice was scanning the crowd in Civic Plaza. The plaza was one of the more scenic parts of downtown, decorated with paver stones and smooth marble. A set of trolley tracks bisected the plaza. A fountain across the tracks near the county and federal buildings anchored the other side.

Iron Justice had supplemented the usual complement of police officers who handled security at city hall. His new boss had given him one directive: keep the peace until the World Barbecue Hall of Fame zoning case was approved.

Iron Justice's flinty eyes scanned the crowd. His size made it easy to peer down at the faces streaming by. Some were headed to the meeting. Others were downtown office workers walking the Main Street Mall on either side of the trolley tracks.

He noticed a small crowd gathering in the middle of the plaza, where a man in an Elvis costume was preparing to sing. Iron Justice moved toward the impromptu concert. The guy in the Elvis costume looked like a photo Mayor Pigg had shown him—one of the two guys he was not to let into city hall under any circumstances.

"Hey, you!" he yelled.

Scott didn't wait for the big man to build up a head of steam. He took off running in the direction of the fountain, breaking off his rendition of "Jailhouse Rock" and drawing scattered laughter from the onlookers.

"Won't be worrying about jail if I catch you!" Iron Justice shouted.

For a big man, he was surprisingly fast, even though he had to shove aside bystanders as he gave chase. He quickly gained on Scott. At the last second, Scott cut quickly to his right. Iron Justice, intent on tackling and smashing his prey as he had so often in the ring, was unable to react and pitched face-first into the fountain. He was on his feet in an instant and about to resume his pursuit when he noticed that many in the plaza were using their cell phones to snap photos—some of him, some of Scott's rapidly disappearing rear end. In Memphis, Elvis being chased by the cops was great street theater. Iron Justice weighed his options. Pounding a civilian in broad daylight didn't seem like the right move for his first week on the job. Besides, he'd run the kid off.

While Iron Justice was distracted, Joe and Barry wheeled the food cart into city hall, past the bored cops at the security checkpoint, and into the break room behind the council chamber. As a former mover and shaker, Barry Brett knew exactly where to go. The break room was where all the wheeling and dealing got done during council meetings.

They left the cart and made their way to the back of the council chamber.

"One more stop," Barry told Joe, motioning to the media room overlooking the council chamber from the second floor.

"You mean my public relations career isn't over just yet?" Joe said as he and Barry headed for the stairs.

A few minutes later, the meeting was about to start. Mayor Pete Pigg was in fine spirits. He settled into his chair on the first row, right in front of the elevated dais where the council members and their staffs sat. Some of the council members were still in the break room behind the dais, stuffing their faces with barbecue, which was fine with Pigg. After all, it was his barbecue, and money was flowing into his pocket. Pigg sighed contentedly as he glanced around the chamber, the walls of which were decorated with photos of past council members. The seats were like something out of a 1970s movie theater—low, with squishy cushions that made it difficult for someone of Pigg's physique to climb in and out of them. Not that Mayor Pigg cared. No amount of personal discomfort was going to ruin this night for him.

Pushing the World Barbecue Hall of Fame through all the political barriers had been much tougher than he expected. But tonight, success was finally within reach.

Smut peddler Augustine Eldridge had ceased to be a problem. So had William "Billy Boy" Bradwell, who was now an uneasy ally. The title to the land was technically the city's but really Mayor Pigg's, for all intents and purposes. The demolition of the old wreck of a building that stood on the property was imminent.

Now, all that remained was zoning approval from a city council he had carefully cultivated with creative side deals and kickbacks. Sure, a couple of the council members were Boy Scouts who couldn't be persuaded by the usual means. But Waldo Jefferson had assured Pigg of at least ten and possibly eleven of the council's thirteen votes. And the zoning change needed only seven votes to pass.

Pigg rarely attended council meetings. Truth was, most of what the council did bored him to tears. All the proclamations, resolutions, and ordinances were pure window dressing. To Pigg, the council members were second-rate political hacks who didn't have the skills or gumption to grab the mayor's chair as he had. Occasionally, Pigg listened to the radio broadcasts of the council meetings over the intercom from his seventh-floor office, swilling whiskey and swearing whenever the members he disliked took their turns speaking. And since he disliked almost all of them, Pigg did a lot of swearing.

More often than not, though, Pigg was at the Grapes of Wrath while the council was in session. He could get through two or three bottles of wine while they debated licensing requirements for tamale stand operators. Why did he need to be there?

If the council did anything he didn't like, he could just veto it anyway.

But on this occasion, Pigg was in attendance to celebrate his victory. In any extremely unusual move, he had chosen to dress in a white linen suit with light blue pinstripes. His tie was wide and white. His black shoes had been polished that morning at the shoeshine stand in The Peabody. No overalls for the mayor today.

After gaveling the session, Waldo Jefferson briefly turned the floor over to a local preacher and a Scout troop for the invocation and the Pledge of Allegiance. Then he motioned for the sergeant at arms to pass him a handful of cards from citizens who had requested time to speak. Jefferson scanned the cards quickly until his eyes caught a name that caused him to recoil in surprise.

"Ladies and gentlemen, we have a special guest with us this afternoon," Jefferson announced after regaining his composure. "Mr. Barry Brett has requested time to speak. And without objection from the council, I'm going to go ahead and allow him to do so before we move forward with tonight's agenda."

This was not the way citizen comments were generally handled by the Memphis City Council. Typically, citizens weren't allowed to speak until the end of the meeting. The intent was obvious: it was a tactic designed to minimize the bellyaching council members had to hear from their constituents. Only the hardiest of gadflies were willing to sit through meetings that sometimes lasted six hours just for a chance to address the council for three minutes, which was the time limit set under the council's rules of procedure.

But the rules could be bent for people of influence, which Barry Brett certainly was. He had the personal wealth to write a hundred-thousand-dollar check to the campaign of any of the council members—or to any of their opponents. Sure, the money might have to be funneled through different people to meet campaign contribution limits, but it could be done. So if Waldo Jefferson wanted to put Barry Brett ahead of all the little people, that was fine with the rest of the council members.

Mayor Pigg, basking in his glow of contentment, hadn't seen Barry Brett slip into the back of the room. He did a double take as he watched the man who had formerly been one of the city's most powerful citizens rise from his seat next to Joe Miller. Barry Brett had disappeared from Memphis years ago. So why was he back? Seeing him seated with Joe couldn't mean anything good for Pigg. How had they gotten by his new police chief? It was so hard to get good help these days.

"Thank you, Council President Jefferson," Barry said upon reaching the microphone at the podium facing the dais. "And thank you to the rest of the council. I appreciate your indulgence in allowing me to speak. I'll be brief. On your agenda today is an item concerning a rezoning request for a parcel at the corner of Front Street and Auction Avenue. As you may know, my family once owned that property, along with various others around the city. After holding that property for many years, the family decided it was in the best interest of the city to sell the land to other owners."

Pigg coughed nervously, but otherwise the chamber was silent.

"However," Barry continued, "my family didn't sell the land without restrictions. You see, my ancestors helped found this city, and they wanted some input over how it would be developed in the future. So all the property was sold with restricted covenants. And those covenants require approval from the Brett family if land uses are going to be changed. My parents died young, and

I'm the last surviving member of the family. For a long time, I didn't share my ancestors' enthusiasm for this town. I didn't appreciate the importance of taking an active role in civic affairs. The way I saw it, Memphis didn't owe me anything, and I didn't owe Memphis anything. Memphis was just where I happened to grow up. I didn't realize what a special place Memphis held in my heart until some people I've recently gotten to know convinced me of that. Their enthusiasm for this town rubbed off on me, I guess you could say. So now, I am exercising the Brett family rights by withholding my approval for this proposed zoning change."

"Mr. Council President, this ain't right!" Pigg bellowed, suddenly on his feet as a murmur spread through the chamber. "Mr. Brett is raisin' an issue I'm not familiar with."

"Oh, I think you are, Mr. Mayor," Barry said. "You've seen the paperwork concerning the covenant restrictions. My associate, Mr. Miller, will provide copies to you and all the council members. Because these documents date all the way back to the founding days of Memphis and therefore have historical value, my family provided duplicates to the Tennessee Museum of State History in Nashville."

Joe stepped forward and handed a stack of documents to the sergeant at arms, who began passing them out to the council members.

"Mr. Jefferson, I would like a ten-minute recess!" Pigg yelled.

"No need to shout, Mr. Mayor," Jefferson said. "We'll stand in recess for ten minutes."

Pigg darted past Barry, who remained at the microphone, staring at the city's chief executive with a look of cool amusement.

Jefferson and Pigg disappeared into the break room behind the council podium, slamming the door behind them.

"You gotta do sumpin, Waldo," Pigg said. He and Jefferson were nose to nose in the small room. The catered barbecue laid out on a table nearby brought an overpowering smell to the confined space. But food was the last thing on Mayor Pigg's mind at the moment.

"Like what, Mr. Mayor?"

"You gotta put a stop to this thing," Pigg said. "Go back out there and tell Brett you're not familiar with this restricted covenant crap. Recommend provisional approval of the zonin' change until what he's sayin' can be researched further."

"But it's not crap, is it, Mr. Mayor?" Jefferson said. "I don't think a man like Barry Brett would stand in front of us unless he knew what he was talking about."

"Yeah, yeah, the covenants are legit," Pigg said. "I just didn't think anybody would find them. I've been keepin' the land records in my office so nobody would know about them."

"Looks like somebody did," Jefferson said.

"They went missin' the same day Zack Bruno resigned," Pigg said. "He must have given them to Brett or one of those kids."

"Why didn't you just destroy the records?"

"Wouldn't have done any good. As he said, duplicates are on file in Nashville. The best I could do was try to keep the copies here in Memphis under wraps until we got our zonin' straightened out."

"Which you didn't do. And now it looks like the game is up."

"What do you mean, the game is up, Waldo? You and I have too much ridin' on this to just let it go. I'm gonna make millions flippin' that land next to the Barbecue Hall of Fame. You're gonna have a fat public relations contract by way of your brother-in-law. We're also gonna get kickbacks on the construction contracts, plus a fat chunk of the reserve fund. Or does money no longer interest you?"

"It does, but I don't see how we can turn this to our favor. Brett can sue us if we try to violate the covenants. And he'll win. And getting successfully sued by one of the city's captains of industry wouldn't be good for your political career or mine. Not to mention that it's a bad idea to get billionaires mad at you. They have a way of buying trouble for people they don't like."

"Well, speakin' of billionaires, I think you should know I brought William Bradwell in on our deal," Pigg said.

"Why would you do that, Mr. Mayor?"

"He cut us a deal on the land in exchange for a no-bid contract on the concessions at the Barbecue Hall of Fame. Considerin' what else we've got workin' here, that's one of the least illegal things we're doin.'"

Waldo wasn't surprised. It was no big shock that the mayor had welcomed another player into the loop without telling him.

"So what do you suggest we do, Mr. Mayor?"

"What if we cut Barry Brett in on the action?" Pigg said.

"I think he's too rich to bribe, Mr. Mayor."

"Well, we'll never know until we try," Pigg said. "Just because he's got money doesn't mean he wouldn't mind makin' more."

"Okay, let me go back out and call the meeting to order," Jefferson said. "I'll move the rezoning to the end of the agenda. You can invite Brett to your office and see if he's willing to play *Let's Make a Deal.* Just don't cut me or any of the other council members out of anything when you cut him in."

They were interrupted by a knock on the door.

"Mr. Mayor? Mr. Jefferson?" It was the voice of Ted Smiley, the council's vice president.

"Yeah, what do you want, Smiley?" Jefferson said as he whipped the door open.

"Well, I just wanted to let you know that a couple of employees have called from their offices upstairs."

"So what?" Pigg said. "Can't you tell we're havin' a conversation here?"

"That's just it, Mr. Mayor," Smiley said.

"What's just it?" the mayor shot back.

"Every word you've said back here is being broadcast over the radio."

Chapter 51

J oe liked his new office on Front Street, with its sturdy oak desk, plush carpeting, and impressive view of the Mississippi River.

And the new job was great, too.

Barry Brett had decided to reconnect with the outside world and take an active role in helping shape the city's future. He had established the Brett Foundation, a nonprofit organization dedicated to providing grants for worthwhile projects around Memphis. Scott, Raina, and Dawn were the foundation's three-member board of directors, and Joe was executive director.

Plans for the World Barbecue Hall of Fame had fallen by the wayside—at least as a project spearheaded by Mayor Pigg.

Mayor Pigg, in fact, was now ex-mayor Pigg. He and Waldo Jefferson had been forced to resign after their conversation was caught on both audio and video. The hidden cameras used by

Brett's delivery drivers at DUI Busters were suitable for mounting on oversized toothpicks—the kind of toothpicks that might show up on a barbecue platter in a break room. It had been easy for Joe and Barry to sneak them in with the catered meal from the Pigg Pen. Thankfully, none of the council members had tried to actually use them as toothpicks, which would have made for some disturbing footage.

Putting the cameras in the break room was Barry's idea. He wasn't sure how the meeting would play out or what would be recorded in the break room, but he had dealt with Memphis politicians before. With the stakes so high on the Barbecue Hall of Fame, he had a hunch something incriminating would be said. He put it this way: "I trust them not to be trustworthy."

Barry had a wireless transmitter at the ready, too. After the mayor demanded the recess and raced into the break room with Jefferson, Barry sensed the time was right to patch the audio from Pigg and Jefferson's conversation to the radio station's microphone in the media room. It turned out that after years of watching the council members engage in underhanded deals, the radio operator in the media room wasn't above taking a bribe himself.

Joe had shared the video feed, also transmitted wirelessly, with one of the local TV stations, where it was broadcast endlessly over the next several days. The video also made its way to the Internet, where it quickly went viral.

Pigg had earned national derision as the "*Let's Make a Deal Mayor.*"

The local district attorney, still upset over how Pigg had cut him out of the loop on the Ghetto Blazer case, vowed to file public corruption charges against Pigg, Bradwell, Jefferson, and the other council members he could link to the Barbecue Hall of Fame project.

Meanwhile, the case against the Ghetto Blazer was dropped. Whatever evidence there was against Scott Paulk disappeared from the police files around the time Zack Bruno resigned as chief. The matter had become a less-pressing priority for law enforcement anyway, since the arsons had stopped. The Brett Foundation was focusing attention on projects aimed at reducing blight in North Memphis, South Memphis, and Orange Mound. Scott Paulk took a special interest in reviewing grant requests from those neighborhoods.

As for Scott and Raina and Joe and Dawn, they had come to an agreement on the terms of something called "double not-so-secret probation." If the guys could apply themselves to the foundation's work for a year—with no slacking, no drunken carousing, and especially no burning of buildings—then maybe, just maybe, the women might agree to give dating a shot.

The guys seemed up for the challenge.

And Joe was anything but bored.

Free Public Library of Monroe Township
713 Marsha Ave.
Williamstown, NJ 08094

Acknowledgments

Many thanks for reading this book, which wouldn't have been possible without:

My wife, Lynn, who gives my manuscripts a first read, and sometimes a second and third; I've learned that I ignore her advice at my own peril

Paul and Connie Brown, who never tire of listening to the tribulations of, and offering good advice about, their son-in-law's writing career

All the journalists I've worked with through the years, whose war stories supplemented what I knew about government corruption

The editors who've helped make my writing better

The teachers who inspired and encouraged me along the way

The authors whose work I admire

My friends who are practiced in the fine art of barbecue and were willing to share what they know

Other friends who gave me the moral support to keep going when things got tough

The staff at John F. Blair, Publisher, particularly Carolyn and Steve

The people of Memphis, whom I was privileged to live among for more than a decade

A NOTE ON THE TYPE

Adobe Jenson is an old style serif typeface
drawn for Adobe Systems by type designer
Robert Slimbach. Its Roman styles are based
on a Venetian oldstyle text face cut by Nico-
las Jenson in 1470, and its italics are based on
those by Ludovico Vicentino degli Arrighi.
The result is a highly readable typeface appropriate for large amounts of text.